THE 400-MILLION-YEAR ITCH

YEAR ITCH

SILURIAN TALES — VOLUME 1

THE 400-MILLION-YEAR ITCH

SILURIAN TALES — VOLUME 1

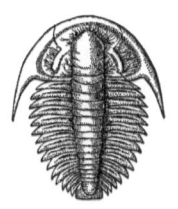

STEVEN UTLEY

T̰
p̰ Ticonderoga
publications

for

Lisa Tuttle

The 400-Million-Year Itch by Steven Utley

Published by Ticonderoga Publications

Cover by Charles Knight
  © The Field Museum #CK23BT

Designed and edited by Russell B. Farr
Typeset in Sabon and Castellar

A Cataloging-in-Publications entry for this title is available from The National Library of Australia.

ISBN   978-0-921857-16-4 (hardcover)
        978-0-921857-17-1 (trade paperback)
        978-0-921857-18-8 (ebook)

Ticonderoga Publications
PO Box 29 Greenwood
Western Australia 6924

www.ticonderogapublications.com

10 9 8 7 6 5 4 3 2 1

O ocean, far from thee we sit and spin our tale;
we turn toward thee our thoughts, our love, loud
and expressly we call on thee, that thou mayst be
present in the tale we spin as in secret thou
ever wast and shalt be!

Thomas Mann, The Magic Mountain

The salt of those ancient seas is in our blood, its
lime is in our bones. Every time we walk along
a beach some ancient urge disturbs us so that we
find ourselves shedding shoes and garments or
scavenging among seaweed and whitened timbers
like the homesick refugees of a long war.

Loren Eiseley, "The Hidden Teacher"

CONTENTS

INTRODUCTION

BY GARDNER DOZOIS

The collection you're holding in your hands, Silurian Tales, Volume 1: *The 400-Million-Year Itch*, contains some of Steven Utley's "Silurian Tales" (the rest will be published next year in Silurian Tales, Volume 2: *Invisible Kingdoms*), which at this point probably has a good claim to being one of the longest-running, continuously published series in modern science fiction. The first Silurian Tale was "There and Then," published in the November 1993 issue of *Asimov's Science Fiction* magazine. In the nineteen years since then, close to forty Silurian Tales have been published, across a wider variety of places than any other contemporary SF series I can think of: in traditional print magazines such as *Asimov's Science Fiction*, *The Magazine of Fantasy & Science Fiction*, and *Analog Science Fiction and Fact*, in anthologies such as *We Think, Therefore We Are*, and in online venues that didn't even exist when he started the series, such as *Sci Fiction, RevolutionSF,* and *Cosmos Online.* And new Silurian Tales are still being published, even as this book hits the bookshelves—perhaps someday relatively soon, there'll be enough of them for a third volume.

The Silurian Tales take us through an experimental space/time warp generated by only partially understood high-tech means and deep into the prehistoric past, where, millions and millions of years ago, a scientific research station is established, the scientists eventually bringing a U.S. Navy destroyer through the warp to act as a floating center of operations. A classic time-travel scenario. Almost any other SF writer who ever lived, almost any other SF writer working today, given this scenario as a starting point, would have taken their protagonists back to the age of the dinosaurs. The stories almost write themselves: a Tyrannosaurus Rex crashing through the jungle, roaring like thunder as it pursues fleeing scientists; Navy crewmen firing .50 caliber machineguns at the ravening Plesiosaurs who are trying to pluck them off the deck of the ship with their needle-toothed heads at the ends of their long, snake-like necks; a victim screaming and thrashing as a hungry Pterodactyl plucks them from the camp and carries them away to its nest.

Instead, almost perversely, Steven Utley takes us and his protagonists back to the Silurian Age, "The Age of Mud and Slime," in the title of one of his stories, one of the most boring of all prehistoric eras in terms of the possibilities for action-adventure stories it provides. No dinosaurs, which would not evolve until hundreds of millions of years later. No dinosaurs, in fact—no large land-dwelling creatures of any kind, not even trees or bushes, as only the most primitive sorts of plant and animal life, mosses and fungi, and insects such as spiders and centipedes, had as yet colonized the land, spreading a thin border strip of life along the shores of oceans and streams and lakes. Inland, all else is desolate and barren. Brackish swamps, desert, bare rock, devoid of life of any kind. Even the sea, where the first bony fishes are just starting to develop, provides no monster worse than giant 2.5 meter-long sea scorpions—which play no really significant role in the plots of any of the stories, although they're mentioned a couple of times.

Choosing such a landscape as the setting for time-travel stories is a move of breathtaking audacity, eliminating at a stroke most of the kind of materials from which such stories are usually fashioned. And having set his deliberately limited palette, Utley doesn't cheat by importing outside colors into the picture—his protagonists don't discover aliens, or find an ancient crashed spaceship, or encounter other time-travelers with whom they become embroiled in a time-war.

There's only the bleak landscape of the Silurian Age, and the peculiarities and paradoxes and intricate workings of time-travel itself, and, set against that plain, pure, desolate background, the characters, who are free to interact in the most subtle and movingly human of ways with little else to distract the reader from them.

Using only these limited means, like a boxer binding one arm behind his back before climbing into the ring, Utley has managed to produce some of the most complex, adult, and entertaining of modern science fiction stories, stories such as "There and Then," "The Wind Over the World," "The Real World" (one of my favorite stories of that whole decade), "The Despoblado," "The Age of Mud and Slime," "Invisible Kingdoms," "The 400-Million-Year Itch," and dozens of others.

If you haven't encountered the Silurian Tales before, I envy you the experience. If you have, you're probably already reading them, and not bothering with these words of mine at all.

GARDNER DOZOIS
SEPTEMBER 2012

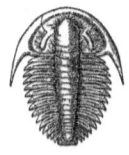

SILURIAN TALES — VOLUME 1

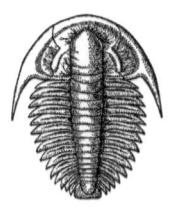

ALL OF CREATION

My mother's mission, late in life, has been to keep her children in touch with each other and with all our many relatives. She is compensating for the twenty years she lived as a military wife, following my father around the world at the Pentagon's whim, herding offspring the whole while.

The experience inculcated in her—and through her, in her children—an independent-mindedness which none of us probably would have acquired had we, too, grown up in her small hometown. Nevertheless, she always missed the company of her parents and other relations, and maintained lines of communication that sometimes stretched halfway around the world.

I too often yearned for the company of this large and varied lot of people. During our brief homecomings, with little time to make friends, I necessarily depended for playmates upon the family's considerable stock of first and second cousins.

By the time my father retired, I had gone out to make my own way in the world. My parents took a game stab at resettling in her hometown, an experience they afterward described as *claustrophobic*. "It was just like the old song says," my mother told me. "'How you gonna keep 'em down on the farm after they've seen Paree?'"

In any event, after three years they had uprooted themselves one last time to take their place in a community notable for its high percentage of retired military couples. And, almost before I realized it, fifteen years passed during which I saw virtually nothing of aunts, uncles, and cousins. My mother, who genuinely liked her siblings though she could not bear to live among them, kept me apprised of their children's comings and goings.

I always received the information in the spirit in which she tendered it, but never had a use for it until I decided to spend one of my supposedly significant birthdays, evenly divisible by five, by the nearest great expanse of salt water, the Gulf of Mexico.

I had led an entirely landlocked existence as an adult, but spent my impressionable years near those largish bodies of water, the English Channel and the East China Sea; recently, I'd become conscious of a profound and irresistible longing to reconnect mystically with that other mother, Ocean. Friends of a friend offered me their condominium by the beach on an island not far from Corpus Christi—in the off season, the discount was substantial.

When I informed my mother of my plan, she said, "Be sure to call your cousin Trey when you get there." I hadn't laid eyes on Trey, Walker S. Brown III, since shortly after the onset of puberty. "He and his wife," my mother told me, "live in Corpus Christi."

"What's he doing in Corpus Christi? What *is* there to *do* in Corpus Christi?"

"Now don't you be snide. I'm sure it's a very nice place. He's something with the marine museum there." I admitted that I was impressed with that. "Anyway," she went on, "be sure to call him. Corpus is practically next door." She had looked it up on a map. "If you don't call him, you'll hurt your Aunt Dixie's feelings."

"Perish forbid that I should hurt Aunt Dixie's feelings."

"You laugh now, but wait till she cuts you out of her will."

Despite that threat, I forgot all about calling Trey until I had actually installed myself in the condo. When I did call, he sounded surprised, but delighted, to hear from me and invited me to come stay in Corpus.

I had already paid for the weekend, though, and was determined to remain on the island, because I couldn't get my money back.

Trey then proposed that he come out the next day: "We can find you on the island easier than you can find us in Corpus anyway. But you *will* come into the city sometime. You have just *got* to see Lady Lex while you're here."

His wife Dianne had been listening in. She said, "He means the *Lexington*." I already liked her too much to point out that I knew about Lady Lex, a permanently moored twentieth-century aircraft carrier, in its day the biggest type of ship afloat. "That's the first thing Trey ever wants to show anybody from out of town."

"I *love* that old boat. I go there all the time"

"Eric, he makes going there sound like a big deal. It's moored right next to the museum."

"Sounds like fun," I said, rang off, then, familial obligations taken care of, collapsed into bed.

My cousin had put on some height and weight and lost most of his hair over the decades, and it took me a moment to see in his jowls and chins the boy I had once known. He introduced me to Dianne, petite, blonde, quite pretty, who greeted me warmly and revealed without prompting that Trey had been telling her all about me ever since I'd called. "He said when you were little kids you both wanted to grow up to be fossil-hunters or astronauts or something."

"Well, I am something."

I was in good spirits as we followed the path from the condo through the dunes to the beach. I asked about children; Dianne said they had a son, Walker IV, now in college. "We call him Quatro."

We walked for distance in the foam, till we came upon a boy of eleven or twelve, standing crouched by the water's edge, intent on what I first took to be only a large tangle of sea wrack. He looked up at us and grinned. "Come see the big ugly water bug I found."

The thing was about the size of my hand and lay on its back with its jointed limbs splayed brokenly.

"That's certainly a big ugly one," I told the kid.

Trey frowned as he peered down at the thing, nudged it cautiously with his foot, and flipped it onto its belly. He dropped suddenly to one knee and used a forefinger to scrape sand off the lozenge-shaped, segmented body. The seconds dragged out to a full minute.

Finally, I asked, "What is it?"

He didn't answer me immediately, but pointed to another, similar animal a few feet away, then to more just like it. "My *God*. They're all over the beach. There must be . . . Di, Eric, do you realize what these things *are*?"

"It seems familiar, but this is the first time I've been to the seashore since . . . "

"*Eric*."

"*You're* the marine biologist."

"These are trilobites, for crissake!"

"It's gotta be a mistake. Or . . . " I trained a suspicious eye on the boy. "Or somebody's trying to pull somebody else's leg."

Trey continued to poke and pry at the dead thing, but evidently he saw the look I was giving the boy.

"If it's a prank," he said, "it's a damn clever one. Too clever to have been cobbled up by a kid. You don't just doctor up a bunch of shrimp or crabs and pass 'em off as trilobites."

The boy swelled with triumph and defiance.

"Trey," I said, "have these things possibly been down there all this time, at the bottom of the bay?"

He shook his head helplessly. "No. Of course not. They have to have come from somewhere else."

"From way deep in the Gulf of Mexico, you think?"

"I don't know what to think right now."

"But isn't it possible . . . "

"*I don't know*. Until this very moment there's never been the slightest reason not to believe that trilobites died out completely in Paleozoic time. Their closest living relatives are horseshoe crabs, and there's no mistaking the one for the other. But there's no mistaking these, either. Di, did you bring your phone?"

"No. Sorry."

"Eric, I need to call the museum from the condo."

I handed over my keys.

"Stay right here," he said, "keep the birds away, don't let anybody move any of these things," and he jogged away heavily.

The boy positioned himself possessively between us and the greater part of the stranded arthropods. "I found them," he said, "they're mine."

"Looks like there are plenty here for everybody," Dianne said. "Surely, you can spare us a few."

He looked around as though computing just how many he might be able to spare us.

"My husband's a scientist. He wants to study them."

The boy did not seem too impressed. "Are they worth a lot?"

"No," I put in flatly. "Not in the way you're thinking. But if you help us keep the birds off so he can collect some for his museum, he might end up naming them after you."

Interest flickered in his face. "He can do that?"

"Yes. And once a scientist officially names something, nobody can name it anything else."

"First I wanna show my mum and dad." He nodded toward a couple who were approaching at a purposeful pace, then ran off toward them.

"Thanks for deflecting the money question," Dianne said.

"I deal with tougher questions from kids his age all the time."

Some distance away, the boy and his parents drew up in a knot, and there ensued much gesticulating on the boy's part and some sharp looks in our direction on theirs. I asked Dianne out of the corner of my mouth, "Can we actually not let anybody move any of these things? It's a public beach."

The kid and his parents drew near, and he looked around and said, "Where's the other man who's gonna name these things after me?"

Dianne essayed a smile that would have disarmed me in a hot second but somehow glanced right off the kid's parents. "He means my husband," she said, gesturing vaguely. "He's a marine biologist at the marine museum in Corpus."

The man ran his tongue around the corner of his mouth as he considered the dead arthropod. "What is this thing?"

The boy piped up precociously, "The man said it was a prehistoric trillobite!"

"It does appear," I said to his father, "to be a type of animal supposed to have become extinct hundreds of millions of years ago. Even before the dinosaurs."

The man regarded me with a mixture of incredulity and disdain, and looked as though he meant to challenge my remark, but then his wife, evidently a veteran observer of past encounters, made an abrupt show of consulting her watch and broke in chirpily with, "Dear, I just remembered, we have that thing to go to this afternoon."

The man exhaled harshly. "What thing is that, honey?" he asked, not taking his eyes off me.

She didn't explain what thing it was but instead said to me, "I'm sorry, I'm such a ditz for forgetting, but we've really got to get moving if we expect to be ready in time."

As they moved off, I asked Dianne, "Should I have handled that better—whatever it was?"

"I won't even venture to guess what it was."

Trey returned. "Carl and Bart are on the way. Bart knows this stuff better than I do." He grimaced at his wife. "He says I am, and I quote, nuts. Well, it is nuts. Trilobites."

"Maybe," I said, "they really are from someplace else. From some *time* else, I mean. As in time travel. The fabric of space-time tore open and let these things through."

"Eric, Eric, give me a break, Eric. Please."

"Well, right now, it's as likely as anything else."

"No, it's about as *un*likely as anything else." He glared at me in exasperation. "Even when we were kids, you always were into some weird damn thing or other."

"We both were."

"No. *I* was into science. Prosaic, down-to-earth science. *You* were into weird science—romantic science-fiction."

"Well, if this isn't a weird science-fiction thing . . . "

"Well, it *is* weird, but whatever it is, it's science, Eric. Some way or another, there is a logical, scientific explanation."

"I *know* from logical, scientific explanations," I told him, more heatedly than I probably intended. "After all, I am . . . "

"Guys," Dianne said evenly.

Trey and I looked at her and at each other, and both of us were abashed.

"Still," I said in a calmer tone, "the *obvious* logical, scientific explanation is there's a lost colony of trilobites at the bottom of the Gulf of Mexico. Why not? The coelacanth was swimming around off Madagascar all that time before anybody knew it was there."

"Yes, and stromatolites have survived in Australia, and *Lingula* is still around, too. And they're both a lot older than the coelacanth. But people have fished and shrimped in these waters for generations without hauling up even a single trilobite. Never mind a mess of the things."

"Which brings us right back to the only other logical scientific explanation I can think of. These trilobites were hurled out of their own time, into ours, and the shock killed them."

"Ah, God, Eric! I am *not* going to stand here arguing about time warps with somebody who used to pretend that Granddad's *cows* were dinosaurs."

"Hey! You pretended right along with me."

Dianne cocked an eyebrow, probably at both of us. Trey shrugged embarrassedly, and I said, "Until you come up with a better explanation, this is lost-world stuff or time-warp stuff." He turned his back on me. "Trilobites fresh enough to use as fish bait, Trey."

Looking out over the bay with his fists on his hips, Trey said, almost wistfully, "There's just not much room left anywhere on earth for macro survivors from prehistoric times. No lost worlds, no dinosaurs hanging on in Darkest Africa or the Amazon jungle. Darkest Africa's been fully illuminated."

Dianne nodded. "Fully and sometimes horrifyingly."

"Yeah. And the Amazon jungle's been turned into grazing land for cattle. And even the sea bottoms are no haven. They're home to some extraordinary life forms, but there's no part of the ocean floor that's older than one hundred million years. There's no stable marine environment where trilobites could have hung on since the Paleozoic."

He did not sound entirely convinced now.

Within the hour, Carl and Bart and two other people had arrived from the museum. Trey hustled them down to the beach, made cursory introductions, then pointed at the litter of dead arthropods. They oohed and aahed and whooped and wowed for a time, then fell to methodical work. Dianne and I helped the least-senior member of the team collect dead arthropods and seal them in refrigeration packs after they had been photographed and tagged.

We didn't get every one; a small crowd had gathered to watch, and now and then somebody further down the beach would step out and grab a trilobite and bear it away. I couldn't have said I blamed the souvenir hunters, and wondered what my own chances were of getting one. There were hundreds of the things.

And there was another puzzle: we found that the trilobites were restricted to a zone measuring just about two hundred yards in length; on either side of this definite boundary, we found no trilobites at all.

Inevitably, the local news team showed up and succeeded at collaring Trey long enough to wring from him the admission that he and his colleagues were from the marine museum and had come to the island to investigate "something unusual."

Trey was cool and collected in front of the camera. "In the days and weeks and, who knows, years to come," he said, "this discovery will be the focus of intense study. Science *is* about finding out things, constantly finding out. That's both good and bad from an individual's standpoint. You can never run out of things to learn, and you can never learn absolutely everything about anything. The universe is just too big and old and deep for us to fully comprehend. But we try because that's the kind of insatiably curious apes we are."

"Nice speech," I murmured to Dianne.

"He's an old hand at this," she said. "You should see him work a crowd at the museum."

"Doesn't look like I'll get the chance."

"Sorry about the Lady Lex."

"Don't apologize. This is worth a whole fleet of aircraft carriers."

The interview concluded, the news team withdrew, and we conferred with Trey. Dianne was hungry, but he and his team members were too excited to eat. I allowed that I was hungry, too, so she and I went down the beach, around the near end of the island, and lunched in "town"—the island didn't seem big enough for a town without quotation marks.

As we hovered over the wreckage of our seafood, she said, "Was that true about you two pretending cows were dinosaurs?"

"Yes," I admitted after a moment. "As boys we were irresistibly drawn to, fascinated by, crazy in love with dinosaurs. And with plate tectonics, the periodic table, the possibility of life on other planets, the possibilities of planets orbiting other Suns: not just for life, but intelligent life. But the first great weird thing of all was dinosaurs.

We discovered dinosaurs when we were six or seven years old, and immediately the dear dim departed beasts led us straight into the first philosophical quagmire of our lives. We set out to reconcile what we read in our first dinosaur books with what we read in a big, lavishly illustrated book of Bible stories for children that must have been handed down through the family for generations."

She grinned. "I'm sure you approached the problem with all the seriousness of medieval scholars trying to decide how many angels could dance on the head of a pin."

"I don't think either Trey or I could live in some cramped, impoverished, medieval cosmos. No more than my parents could live out their lives in a small town. Anyway, Trey and I came down firmly on the dinosaurs' side. We were convinced that God fashioned them for our personal delight. To a milder degree I still am. Well, naturally, various relatives reacted variously to our *prehysteria*, as one of them so cleverly dubbed it. Our great-grandmother couldn't look at a picture of dinosaurs without muttering about 'those tormented creatures.' Our grandfather, he was a lay preacher, he listened patiently to our questions and speculations that the geologic ages corresponded to the days of creation. Our parents, Eric's and my own, seemed to enjoy the impression we made on company, whether singly or in concert. My mother would tell people, 'Our son knows Greek and Latin words, don't you, Eric?' and I would happily roll *Triceratops*, *Ankylosaurus*, *Iguanodon* off my tongue. My male cousins 'n' Trey's tolerated our consuming passions as we tolerated theirs. Deals were struck, though sometimes only very grudgingly kept. If we played soldiers or cowboys this time, next time we had to go look for prehistoric monsters in the lost world of the cow pasture. Sometimes they reneged on the deals, but I believe Trey's and my childhood fantasies must have been mutually supporting. I could not and still cannot imagine any kid not wanting to go look for live dinosaurs, even in a cow pasture."

Around dusk, Trey wandered in from the beach, starving and dirty. Dianne had gone back into Corpus Christi to see to their cats. Trey and I took our dinner out onto the terrace.

I let him eat in peace for a time, then asked, "So what's the verdict?"

"Damned if they aren't trilobites. A distinct genus of mid-Paleozoic vintage called *Phacops*, according to Bart. Only they can't be. But they are. Even though they can't be. And we found some other things washed up, too. Little cephalopods of a type that's supposed to be extinct, and even a primitive kind of fish with an armored head and no jaws."

"Just like someone dipped a big net into a Paleozoic ocean."

"Yeah. Maybe you're right, Eric. Maybe it does mean . . . oh, I don't know what it means, except that some branch of science is about to be shaken up. Maybe several branches. I don't *know*."

"Bet you anything it's a time warp."

Trey rolled his eyes. "This thing does go beyond marine biology and palaeontology. Way beyond. I think I'd actually prefer a time warp to a colony of survivors from the Paleozoic. But let the physicists get ulcers worrying about the how of it."

While he continued eating, I tuned in the TV news, and we watched a local feature about the activity on the beach; virtually all that survived of Trey's interview was "something unusual." Although I squawked in protest, Trey only shrugged and muttered something about par for the course and went on eating.

Then, a tall, thin, hawk-nosed gentleman looked out of the screen at me and said, "I am only too familiar with the marine museum, and I have never agreed with the secular-humanist slant it puts on things. There are lots of eminent scientists who refuse to swallow the conservative-scientific-establishment line on evolution," and across the table from me Trey set his fork down with a sharp clack and said, "Not *good* scientists."

I looked at him quizzically.

"Jim Farlough," he said. "Corpus Christi's own creation quote scientist unquote."

"Whatever they've found," Farlough was saying, "it's certainly no more prehistoric than you or I. What this discovery proves—or, more accurately, disproves all over again—is the whole evolutionist view of the history of life on this planet. Every life-form in earth's history dates back to an act of creation that happened approximately 6,000 years ago."

I glanced at Trey again and saw and almost felt the warmth creep up his neck and spread across his cheeks and forehead.

"All the different water-dwelling creatures we know," Farlough went on, "and many we don't know, are alive now. Until the nineteen-thirties, scientists didn't know the coelacanth was 'down there.' They thought it was extinct because it was missing from the fossil record. Now we have proof there are trilobites down there as well, and who knows else is down there? Probably Leviathan itself is down there, living in the deepest part of the ocean and rarely if ever coming to the surface."

"Turn it off," Trey growled.

I turned it off. He pushed his plate away and leaned forward on his crossed forearms.

"How come a crackpot gets more facetime than you do?"

"That was Farlough's own show, especially for crackpots. But are they still crackpots if more of them listen to him than listen to me?"

"Yes. Back home, I teach, or try to teach, general science to middle-schoolers. Bad enough that I have to compete for their attention with entertainment media and what-have-you specifically designed as a distraction from learning. Worse that I sometimes find myself under fire from irate parents who don't want me teaching their kids that the Earth *isn't* only a few thousand years old, that . . . that the value of *pi* is either three or four but not something in between."

"And do you also tell them that the Earth orbits the Sun?"

"God gave us brains."

"He gave some people crappy ones. You know, Eric, I think sometimes, given the resources at their disposal, Americans must be the most shamefully, willfully ignorant people in the world."

After sundown we walked back out to the beach, and while Trey and his colleagues worked by lamplight I sat brooding at the base of the dune. Finally, I flipped open my phone and called my mother. She asked, "How's the mortality tour?"

"I haven't actually had a chance to dwell on birthdays since I got here."

"Well, happy birthday, son."

I had almost forgotten that it was my birthday.

She said, "Is that the sea I hear?"

"That or just static."

"You are calling from down on the beach, aren't you? How's the condo?"

"Kind of noisy around here right now."

"You can probably get your money back, you know."

"It's not that big a deal."

"Did you get to see Trey?"

"I'm looking at him right now. But he's too busy now for talk. Mum, don't worry, this is the most fun I've had since I discovered dinosaurs in Granddad's cow pasture."

After a long moment, she said, quite good-naturedly, "Eric, you are just about the strangest of my children. You always have been."

"I probably always will be, too."

After I had said goodbye to her, I sat listening to the surf, feeling the breeze on my face, inhaling Mother Ocean's own tangy breath, and gazing at the stars and the rising half-moon.

Something had been dancing around the edge of my consciousness for hours, possibly ever since I'd waded in the foam with Trey and Dianne that morning; now, finally, I figured I knew or almost knew what it was, and used the phone to run a quicksearch and make sure.

Quicksearch duly spat back a couple of lines from the first chapter of Thomas Hardy's *Return of the Native*: "Who can say of a particular sea that it is old? Distilled by the Sun, kneaded by the Moon, it is renewed in a year, in a day, or in an hour."

And not just the sea, I thought, but the world, the universe, space-time, all of creation was vast and magnificent and full of wonderful things. I said, quietly, gratefully, "Happy birthday to me."

THE WOMAN UNDER THE
WORLD

The pod splits open with a hiss, and the glowing being steps out, looks about itself in confusion, takes it cannot not say how long to understand what it is seeing, though it could not have said why what it sees is all so puzzling. It finds itself at one end of a chamber hewn from solid rock and braced with timbers. Behind it, the pod lies against the wall like a smashed tomato. Ahead, at the angle of a bend, it makes out the shapes of a large television screen and a battery of monitoring devices, including a television camera mounted on a tripod. Behind this array is a metal door. As vision continues to improve, a man's face appears on the television screen. His mouth moves, the glowing being knows the man is speaking, but nothing can be heard. It wants, and tries, to say, *What the hell's going on here? Where the hell am I?* but cannot be certain that it succeeds in uttering even the most inarticulate sounds. No, wait, the man on the screen flinches—response. So it has done something, not sure what, but something. The man looks offscreen and shakes his head. Then another face, a woman's, crowds into view and she, too, speaks soundlessly. The glowing being takes a step forward, and the expressions on both faces onscreen become alarmed. The man gestures unmistakably, *stop, move back, stay back*. The glowing being steps backward and notices a wide yellow and black stripe painted across the floor, just in front of its (are those *my?*) toes. The stripe's meaning is clear: This Far And No Farther. It looks at the television screen and nods, and now it realizes that the screen, the monitoring devices, and the metal door are reflected in a large mirror set in the angle of an L-shaped chamber. The real articles are at the far end of the other arm of the L, or perhaps even reflected through a series of mirrors set in the corners of a tremendous series of L-shaped chambers. The image of mirrors stretching toward infinity is dizzying. The glowing being staggers to the left, extends a hand to steady itself against the wall, sees or feels or in any event is aware of fingers burning into the rock like poking soft cheese. Draws back and astonishedly regards four smoking holes in the wall. Its gaze gradually travels up and across the wall, to dull gray metal housings mounted high, like wasps' nests. Pipes of the same metal extend from these housings along the juncture of wall and ceiling, around the bend of the L, through all the bends of the Ls, and disappear into sockets set above the metal door. More monitoring devices, it decides, shielded with lead, shielded cables. An abandoned mine or an unfinished section of some supersecret subterranean military complex buried deep inside some mountain. Yes. It's all starting to make sense, finally. Look at the screen, at the man and the woman. The man seems to pleading. For what? Logically, for calm and patience. Be calm, be patient. Whatever the hell this is all about, we're working on it. Yes. That's probably it. The man nods back, and then his face and the woman's collapse into a white dot at the center of the screen. The glowing being stands at its end of the chamber, on its own side of the yellow and black stripe And No Farther, and waits for it knows not how long.

Then the woman reappears onscreen and says, "Sorry about the accommodations," and the glowing being realizes without surprise, I can hear now. "We're preparing a facility for you. It'll be more comfortable. And safer. Safer for everybody. Meanwhile, this is the best we could do on short notice."

I know you, thinks the glowing woman (by now the glowing being has determined that much about itself, she is in fact a woman), and she says, "Micol" (for she has finally recognized Micol), "Micol," and, yes, unsurprisingly, that is her voice, "Micol, what—"

Micol flinches at the sound of her name, adjusts something at her end, announces, "That's better." She makes an elaborate business of examining the console at that end and avoiding eye contact at this end. She says, "You understand that it'll be best if you stay behind the yellow line there, don't you? We, uh, we don't want you frying the electronic equipment."

"Micol, what am I am doing here? Where *is* here? What happened?"

"We're trying to find out. Believe me." Micol's lips compress for a moment. "But this is so—you just have to be patient. Try and be patient. Please."

"Tell me what happened."

"There was an accident. No, I mean an incident."

"Well, one or the other, something's wrong with this picture. I'm supposed to be—the last thing I remember is the jump station, the tech counting down. What happened?"

"The chief'll tell you about it when he gets here."

"But where is *here?*"

But Micol doesn't answer the question, and the chief, when he comes onscreen, looks haggard and frightened, with eyes sunk in bruised-looking flesh. He says, "I'm going to make this as simple as I know how. I told you in the first briefing that the spacetime anomaly is essentially where Point A and Point B happen to come together. But, more exactly, they approach each other. They're separate points and always remain separate points no matter how closely they approach each other. There's always going to be an infinitesimal gap between them, possibly less than a Planck unit, right down at the level of quantum foam. But, still, a gap. Till now, objects, animals, people've all gone through without mishap. But we think Point A and Point B somehow got out of alignment on this particular occasion—when Phyllis Lewis tried to go through. Because of the misalignment, she didn't go through."

The glowing woman says, "Why are you referring to me in the third person?"

"Listen carefully. Phyllis Lewis didn't go through, she's safe, no need to worry about her, but something else *did* go through.

Whenever something goes through the spacetime anomaly, it produces a sort of echo, you might even call it a ghost. After-images, except that they aren't images, really, but electromagnetic shadows. Whatever goes through creates a sort of template, and for the briefest instant afterward there's something left. Sort of a free-standing, highly localized anomaly in its own right. In this case, it's been given definition by the *idea* of Phyllis Lewis. It thinks it *is* Phyllis Lewis."

"Well," says the glowing woman, in a flash of Phyllis Lewis' inimitable humor, "isn't that a kick in the teeth!"

By now the glowing woman has determined that she is myself, Phyllis Lewis, some approximation thereof. No: I am, I was, I am this person. I know everything she knew, remember everything she remembered.

I remember being shown one of the biological specimens the robot probe had brought back through the spacetime anomaly, remember looking at it blankly, asking, What is it? "Look at it," I was told. I *am* looking at it, I said, it looks like enough sushi for a family of six. "*Look* at it, Phyl!" I'm a tech, I protest, not a marine biologist. "Oh, come on, Phyl, think back to your books about prehistoric times. Here's a marine arthropod with a trifurcation running the length of the body, cephalon, thorax, pygidium—" The tone of voice compelled me to look at the creature more carefully. Then, of course, I realized what it was and even why I hadn't recognized it: it wasn't the kind of thing you expected to see in fresh condition. I said, incredulously, Jeez, it looks like a trilobite. "Yeah." But they all went extinct hundreds of millions of years ago. "Yeah." But—! "*Yeah.*"

I remember being asked to join an advance team that would go through the spacetime anomaly, to the world that lay at the other end or on the other side or wherever, whatever it was.

I remember going to Port Aransas on the coast for a weekend getaway with my husband—"our last chance," he called it, "for four hundred million years." We had rented a beach condo and arrived late in the afternoon, just as a storm broke; the ferry got us across the shipping channel a beat or two ahead of driving rain, howling wind, lightning and thunder. A thick smell of insecticide practically smacked us in the face when we opened the door. Our

choices were to endure it or go huddle in the car; we chose to
endure. The condo was furnished in Early Indifferent, everything
shading back and forth between beige and blah, upholstery,
carpet, walls, reproductions of two landscapes and one still life.
It barely qualified as décor at all. We turned the fans on high in
hopes of dissipating the smell and unpacked and made do while the
storm blew itself out. The rain had stopped by dawn the followed
morning, and the overcast was breaking up. Although the fans had
run all night long, the smell seemed undiminished in its potency;
we tried opening all the doors and windows, but the insecticide
smell finally drove us out of doors. Not that we really minded
being out of doors. I proposed a walk on the beach; we could make
our way around to the town when we got hungry. There were cacti
and little yellow blossoms among the dune grass, and small lizards
and a huge ant bed on the path itself. A bumblebee crossed in front
of us, then an orange butterfly. We marveled, and I said, You don't
expect to find *bugs* at the beach, and my husband said easily, "The
insecticide should've been enough of a clue." We emerged from the
dunes and held hands like teenagers as we walked along the beach.
Where vehicles hadn't packed it down the dark rain-dimpled sand
looked as fine and crumbly as brown sugar. Shells and pieces of
shells and tangles of orange-brown seaweed lay everywhere, gulls
wheeled overhead, sandpipers ran through the foam. A small
diving bird I couldn't identify repeatedly plunged headfirst into
the surf. Among the foraging wading birds was another I didn't
know, some kind of heron or crane, and I resolved privately to
brush up on my shore birds. I also saw a darting sand-colored crab
no bigger around than my thumbnail, the mouths of filter feeders'
dens, and a stranded Portuguese man-of-war. Nothing existed at
this end of the island that wasn't geared to the wants of tourists
and the needs of those who catered to tourists, but across the
channel on the mainland lay another world entirely, a landscape
littered with petro-industrial hardware. Visible from the island,
against a backdrop of cranes and oil storage tanks, an immense
rig for offshore drilling operations lay on its side like some child
Titan's discarded toy. Out to sea, a long low ship glided like a
phantom across the rim of the horizon, and I could just barely
see two upright rigs. Come on, I said, there's a little pagan ritual
we must perform here. We kicked off our sandals and waded into

the cool water up to our knees, stood feeling the wave action suck sand out from under our heels; he dipped his hand into the water, brushed his fingers across my face, and I ran my tongue over my lips and said, We've lived inland too long. I was excited, happy, and I felt I wanted, needed, to say more, perhaps something about the irresistible call of the sea, how the sea flavors our blood, but I felt too self-conscious. And then I noticed tears in his eyes. Darling, darling, I asked, what *is* it?

Curiously, though, as my sense of identity sharpens, my sense of being in a real place diminishes. In a dream strange things may happen in accordance with some strange or even indiscernible logic. You can accept a dream on its own terms up to a point beyond which an element of the dream becomes off-putting and you suddenly reject the dream. You remember that an important character in the dream is dead or that a certain activity or situation is simply impossible. And you awaken.

Then perhaps I am awakening. If I look away from the walls of my prison, they vanish, and the monitors, too, and everything else, and then when I look at them again they are there, but somehow less convincingly so.

I tell myself, Think this through now. Do you really believe that material things don't exist if you aren't looking directly at them? Or thinking about them? Perhaps the question needs to be inverted: Do you believe the things you are looking at and thinking about actually exist without reference to yourself? The chief speaks of a ghost. How do you confine a ghost? How do you transport a ghost to a place of confinement—especially if it is supposedly bleeding lethal radiation and can burn holes in solid rock with its touch? How can you even have substance or occupy space? You're supposed to be an electromagnetic pulse. Why even bother to construct a cage for a phenomenon as short-lived as an electromagnetic pulse? You'd fry electronic equipment. Is all of this, then, occurring only in my head, in my shadow of a head, that is, during an infinitesimal moment?

And now I recall a Durrell line read in college, "Are people continuously themselves, or simply over and over again so fast that they give the illusion of continuous features—the temporal flicker of old silent film?"

C'est fucking *moi.* You only think you were a person named Phyllis Lewis. You only think you have a body and organs. You only think you are, or at least were, human. But you are a ghost of a real human being, not even a real ghost at that. And there is no P.A. system here, no TV cameras or monitors, no prison deep inside the earth.

But part of me still wants to believe otherwise. It protests, How, then, do we communicate with—?

And then it catches itself up short. Of course: we don't communicate with anybody. There is no *them* with whom to communicate. It's just *you* and *I.* Talking to ourselves. Talking to myself. Existing for a timeless interval, but only as a side-effect or by-product of particle decay. And alone. Alone. Alone.

No. Not quite. My husband and I waded into the cool water up to our knees, and he dipped his hand into the water, brushed his fingers across my face, and I was happy, excited by the prospect of going through the anomaly but deeply satisfied to be standing knee-deep in water with my husband. And then I noticed tears in his eyes. Darling, darling, I asked, what is it? He almost sobbed. "Whoever says time travel won't have its martyrs, just as space travel did? This anomaly business is so new and different and—weird. Who knows what could happen?" Nothing is going to happen to me, I said, I'm going to slip through and help set up a jump station on the other side, and then I'm coming right back. To you. To all this. Promise.

I have, for as long as I do have it, for either a nanosecond or an eon, everything Phyllis Lewis has. I have my memories.

WALKING IN CIRCLES

"God *damn*," gasps a voice in my earphone, "that *hurt*."

Yes, it did, it hurt like hell, I agree completely, but I can't say so, it's all I can do to keep from retching from pain. I clutch the railing of the platform as if my life depended upon the strength of my grip; perhaps it does—I'm holding on to the only thing that can get me back, get me home, to the only world I've ever known till now. Very well, I admit it: I was scared. It's scary going through a spacetime anomaly, and it hurts like a son of a bitch.

Gradually, though, the nausea subsides, and the headache, and the muscle spasms. My eyes refocus. The air around the platform ripples gently, like heat shimmer in slow motion— this is the only visible manifestation of the anomaly, and it is a short-lived one. The world beyond looks starkly empty, half-finished, unused, a vast monochromic stony plain stretching away in every direction.

There's real heat shimmer out there: without soil, never mind plant cover, the land bakes. The shaded surfaces of rocks have a faint greenish tinge where lichens homestead, but the only vivid color is the blue of the sky.

Nervous laughter crackles in my earphones. One of my teammates, I'm not sure who, upholds the tradition of making memorable utterances on historic occasions; he says, "Whoa."

Well, it's not as if we're the first group of people to come here, or the second, so the occasion's not really all that historic. "Whoa" will have to suffice.

For all I can tell, the platform has materialized where and, when it was supposed to do so. The preceding team of visitors consisted exclusively of technicians who assembled the apparatus that maintains our synchronous link with Holocene time, "our proper matrix" or "the present," which is now "the future." The present present is really "the past."

Makes me glad that all I have to think about is collecting botanical specimens. Not, of course, that this is really all I have to think about.

Our own little party includes just one technician, brought along as insurance—in our hermetic clothing, with our headheld recorders, we all look like giant bugs, but he's distinguishable by his slouch and the tool belt strapped around his hips. As with some other forms of insurance, you hope you won't need this one because you aren't absolutely convinced that it'll be adequate if you do need it. At least, I'm not absolutely convinced. But there is a strong element of personal dislike, distrust, at work

He knows Merry Grenon, who now stands beside me on the platform. "Well, well," I distinctly heard him say when the team assembled for the first time, "it's the girl paleontologist, fancy meeting you here." She responded with a look that passed in a moment from surprise to contemptuous acknowledgement to a kind of amused tolerance. It was the last which smote me in the heart; I'd have preferred that she stop at contempt.

So, poised on the verge of the greatest adventure of my life, I found myself wracked by pure old human sexual jealousy.

Perhaps I read too much into her expression. Perhaps.

No, clearly, they know each other, they have some kind of history. This technician bears watching.

Well, anyway: "Whoa," and then the team leader wants to know if everyone is all right and though he could simply look around the platform and do a head count, he calls each of us by name, and we have to answer "Here" or "Yo." Articulate, that's us.

"Jesus effing Christ," someone says, "it's like goddamn Death Valley here, I'm burning up. Won't the A.C. in these suits crank up any higher?"

Nobody answers, everyone is surely thinking what I'm thinking, that maybe we should've listened to the physicists, but nobody wants to be the one to say it, everyone's too abashed.

I hear the team leader clear his throat, and then he says, "Check your respirators."

We have done so already, many times, but we do it again.

"Now," says Merry Grenon, "if we're through with all the mickeymouse—"

Unoffended, the team leader nods, signals to the technician to swing back the hinged portion of the railing, and at long last, we step off the platform, we half a dozen human beings, step through the shimmering air and set foot on Earth.

An Earth. Depending on what one chooses to believe, it is either our very own Earth during mid-Paleozoic time or else an alternate, virtually identical Earth—existing in an alternate, virtually identical universe—where conditions are virtually identical to those that prevailed on our very own Earth during mid-Paleozoic time. Adherents of the former idea generally are non-physicists, which is to say, my colleagues; I keep to myself the suspicion that probably only the chief adherents of the latter idea, the quantum physicists, know what they're talking about. The attitude among my colleagues is essentially, "But who the hell cares?" We're here, wherever it is, with no physicists among us. The technician doesn't count. The physicist who made it possible for us to "manipulate the spacetime anomaly" or "jump through the hole" is a notorious agoraphobe. The view here would send him into shock.

We fan out from the platform. A rivulet cuts across the barren and otherwise featureless landscape; its margins are marked by slimy mud and tangled patches of dull green plant tendrils. I would love to run to them; the best I can do is a sort of lurching waddle. Our bulky and uncomfortable clothing represents what we are now fast recognizing to have been a Pyrrhic victory over those smug physicist assholes. We had insisted throughout the planning phases that we didn't want to contaminate the pristine Paleozoic environment and possibly introduce a paradox.

I remember the physicist Cutsinger in particular because he had a habit of turning his eyes up in their sockets and shaking his head whenever we said such things.

"You people," he once told us, speaking as if to a classroom of slow children, "have watched too many bad sci-fi TV shows. You're going to leave tracks and collect stuff on this jaunt. Just like all the probes and all the people who went before you did. The allegedly pristine so-called Paleozoic environment is already contaminated. Now here comes the hard part, so listen carefully. A paradox is by definition an impossibility. You cannot travel directly backward into our own Earth's own prehistoric past. You can only move diagonally, into some parallel Earth's Paleozoic. Therefore, nothing you do in this parallel Earth's Paleozoic can make any difference here in our proper matrix, our twenty-first century of the Christian era, the present. You cannot overlook this absolute condition. Time travel in the sense you people use the term violates the laws of physics. Time travel is a gross contradiction of logic."

"Oh, yeah?" someone piped up in the back of the room. As I said: articulate, that's us.

Cutsinger got off then into his pet theory of infinite multiple universes. When he paused for breath. Merry Grenon popped up out of her seat and asked, "If it's true we're going to some universe not our own, how about the return trip? With all those universes floating around, how do we get home to the right one?"

Well, he talked about the apparatus and the synchronous link and still as if to a bunch of dunces.

Then Merry Grenon said, "This whole spacetime-anomaly thing, you know, hasn't done a whole helluva lot for your credibility."

Now he was nonplussed. (Always wanted to see somebody nonplussed.) "Whatever do you mean?"

"Isn't it true this spacetime anomaly just sort of fell into your lap in a manner of speaking? You weren't looking for it when you found it, right? And right up to the moment you found it you would've said it was impossible, right?"

"I'm certain—Doctor Grenon, is it? I'm certain that even in your own field, science is acknowledged to be a self-correcting system." (A sound like escaping steam arose from the people sitting around her, but Cutsinger pretended not to hear.) "Very well, grant me for the moment that the prehistoric world you're going to visit is one of a random selection of alternate worlds. We'll assume that we can't maintain a synchronous link. This, then, is the possible consequence of our not being able maintain continuity between, ah, one end of the anomaly and the other—the world to which you'll return will also be one of a random selection of alternate worlds, rather than this one—" he stamped his foot "—right here. How much difference will it make to you? None. Absolutely none. There is a virtually infinite selection of these alternate worlds. If you accept the most profound implications of quantum mechanics, and you earth-science types are goddamn well going to have to take my word for it, every either-or situation that arises in the universe demands a resolution. Whether it's a subatomic particle going this way or that, or whether you have coffee or tea for breakfast, each resolution causes the universe to split into replicas of itself. Given the frequency of resolutions at the submicro level alone, this splitting must occur billions of times per second. We don't feel the split because we ourselves split along with everything else. Each replicated universe continues to split, on and on and on."

"So," somebody demanded, after a moment, "which one's the real universe?"

Cutsinger rolled his eyes again. "The question's utterly meaningless."

I had to speak up then. "Which one's the real me, then? I don't think this question is meaningless at all."

Cutsinger grinned at me, entirely without mirth, and made an expansive gesture. "Why, all of you. Every single one of your billions and trillions of selves believes himself to be the unique, true, original self. But there is no such thing, not in any perceptible way. During the course of your life, some of your alternate selves may have diverged wildly from what you yourself regard as your norm. Some of them may even inhabit very strange alternate universes indeed. But every single one of you exists as completely as every other one of you."

He paused to gauge our reactions. I was making a sincere effort to get my mind wrapped around a difficult concept, but the general disbelief of my colleagues must have been palpable; Cutsinger heaved a sigh and said, "All right, if you don't want to hear about infinite multiple universes, how about a practical consideration? You're going to have ditch the suits if you ever expect to spend meaningful periods of time in the field. By meaningful periods I don't mean a collecting season, I mean from the time you eat or drink till the time you have to use the potty."

But we voted him down. And now here we are, suited from pate to peds, miserable, sweating buckets, plodding around as clumsily as though we were the first creatures in the world to try to invent bipedalism. And if we'd listened, we could have come in our old shirts, jeans, hiking boots.

Yet—I'm sure I can speak for every member of the team—we are happy.

We already knew a good deal about conditions here, of course. Before us, before anybody, robot probes came into this world and went out of it again loaded with specimens, samples, and recorded data about everything from insolation to, well, everything else. And all of the information matched what had already been inferred, bit by bit, from the geological record. Which is why we expect merely to confirm, for instance, that mean global temperature here is 20° C, about five degrees warmer than in Holocene time, that the atmosphere contains more carbon dioxide and less oxygen, though there is enough of the latter to produce ozone in sufficient quantities to screen out lethal ultraviolet radiation, with enough left over to encourage assorted invertebrates' expeditions onto land. Had we arrived, say, on the shores of the proto-Atlantic rather than somewhere (we believe) in the interior of the primordial North American continent, we would have expected merely to confirm that the salinity of that ocean is about the same as average oceanic salinity in the Holocene, but that oceanic oxygen content is low, barely a third of the Holocene level.

These and many other things are already known to us, and yet here we are, impelled by our hard-wired monkey instinct to see for ourselves. Nothing in my experience has ever given me the thrill I get from stroking, even with my fingers gloved, a fragile leafless Cooksonia stem.

Merry Grenon motions to me. I go over and squat next to her, and she gestures at the soft ground. "Someone's been here before us."

Before I think about what I'm saying, I say, "Who?"

"You mean, what? Diplichinites."

I've been too rapt in the tangible reality of Cooksonia to see past the plant cover. The patches of soft mud among the tendrils are covered with looping, crazily intersecting animal trackways, each consisting of a subcircular double row of small crescent-shaped indentations that come out of the water, describe a loop, and return to the water.

"Now why should they do that?" I wonder aloud.

"It's an arthropod's way of looking back over its shoulder. I think it's preadaptive behavior. Your more flexible marine invertebrates do the same kind of thing. It makes for efficient harvesting. Eat everything in your path and then everything inside your path. But it also helps you establish a sense of direction. Helps you find your way back to where you started. A useful skill if you're investigating a hostile new environment."

I watch her as she begins to measure. "Maybe they're just overwhelmed by their own daring. They come crawling out of the water and get a compound-eyeful of this landscape, and then it's, 'Omigod!' and back into the water."

"Can't really blame them for being a little hesitant, can you?"

A small scorpion emerges from cover near the water's edge and advances with seeming purpose directly toward my foot.

"Some," I say, taking a backward step to cover a shudder, "evidently are less hesitant than others," and she scoops the scorpion up in a specimen container.

"Out here," she says as she peers at it, "they have to cope with atmospheric pressure and gravity. And there's always the danger of desiccation. They could just stay home, where the living's easy."

"So could we," says the technician, behind us. "This is one inhospitable-looking place if you ask me." Not that anyone has.

She glances past me, nods to him, then clips the specimen container to her belt.

"Eventually," he says, "they do come out and keep on going. Always upward and outward. Up out of the sea, out onto the land. Out of the trees, out onto the veldt. Off the planet, out into space."

Christ. A poet. I was hoping he'd reveal himself to be an insensitive troglodyte.

She flicks on her recorder and draws a measuring tape from its hiding place on a glove finger. "Average trail's five centimeters wide and describes a loop—" she brushes at the sparse plant cover with consummate tenderness "—approximately one meter long. Six to ten footprints per centimeter comes out to—"

"About two thousand per meter," says the technician.

She nods again but doesn't look his way this time. "About."

It's time I get to work as well. I sort of nudge aside the technician, who gives me a look that's supposed to be superior, and set about collecting my plant samples in such a way that Merry Grenon and I stay abreast of each other as we advance, ducklike, at a squat, along the soft green margin of the rivulet.

It's exhausting activity, with the suits and all. We stop and listen to each other pant. Her face gleams behind her visor. "I hate," she says, "to have to admit those smarmy physicists were right," but she smiles at me, and my heart leaps.

Doctor Grenon, I want to say. Merry, when this is all over, I hope we'll continue to see something of each other. And I imagine her response: she looks at me seriously, searchingly, as she has never looked at me before. You mean, she says, with a catch in her voice, in a romantic kind of way? Surely she must have noticed how interested, how attentive, I've been ever since our introduction. Surely she knows that my interest is not merely professional. But perhaps she simply wasn't sure till this very instant. I wait for her expression to soften in token of the dawning of understanding. Then I smile and say. Of course I mean in a romantic way, and take her by the hand.

And surely the universe has split, replicated itself, and these things are occurring, these words are passing between two human beings identical in every particular to Merry Grenon and myself except that that other me is slightly braver and quicker. In my own universe I hesitate, the moment passes, a voice in my earphones says, "Time to head home, people, everybody back to the platform."

"So soon?" I say and look at my watch.

Merry Grenon shrugs and picks up her collecting case. "Time flies when you're having fun. Anyway, I'm about to drown in my own sweat inside this suit."

Everyone converges on the platform.

At the verge of the shimmering area, Merry Grenon pauses and points back the way we have come, and I look and see that the ground is now covered with intersecting human footprints that loop away from the platform and return. She laughs and says, "How perfect!" My hopes start to revive.

But when we have stowed our gear and arranged ourselves on the platform, though I've tried to find my way to her side again, she's somehow eluded me, she's standing beside my hated rival with the slouch and the tool belt as he kneels to make some minute adjustment on the apparatus. I hear her say to him, lightly, "Do try to get us home in one piece," and see him look up at her, see his infuriating grin through his visor. In some other universe, it is not so, it does not happen, but in this one I have to stand there and listen as he tells her insouciantly, "Baby, I'll take you where you wanna go," and it hurts it hurts it hurts like hell.

BEYOND THE SEA

How still the land is, and the air. The glowering sun, obscured by overcast as smothering as a blanket, seems fixed halfway up the sky. Walking along the beach, Zack sees a man, familiar yet unrecognizable, wading knee-deep in a tide pool. Out along the forereef, the sea moves and waves break in a monotonous pattern; in the rock-bound tide pool, the water is clear and still save whenever the man shifts position. His sweat-darkened tee-shirt clings like a second skin, and a ragged baseball cap is pushed far back on his glistening bald pate; he holds a net and carries an assortment of small receptacles and strange tools on a belt. The man makes a darting, scooping movement, and the net comes out of the water heavy with something dark and wiggling. He turns, sees Zack, grins in triumph as he holds up his prize.

Zack recognizes him now, even recognizes the tee-shirt adorned with Beethoven's faded but still formidable-looking visage, and says, Granddad.

The same, Granddad says. He detaches several items from his belt and hands them over. You'll probably be needing this.

Zack assembles the pieces into a clarinet. I could do this in my sleep, he says, and his grandfather laughs hugely. Zack draws a deep breath, lets it go, draws another, and this time he barely exhales into the instrument, barely enough to set the reed vibrating.

Ah, says the old man, lovely subtone mode, don't stop.

Zack plays very softly, and strange sea creatures poke their heads above the surface of the lagoon to listen. Taken aback, he stops playing and looks at his grandfather.

The old man laughs. There is, he intones, no one knows what sweet mystery about this sea, whose gently awful stirrings seem to speak of some hidden soul beneath. He grins happily, reassuringly. Love that Melville! The water's fine, boy, go on in!

With a clarinet?

He arrived late. His parents' car and his sister's seemed to reproach him as he pulled into the driveway; the front of the big house was full of that silence of impatience which he knew so well, and the confidence he had brought away from Doctor Weiss' office in the science building began to ebb. There came a lowing sound, like the utterance of a perplexed cow: Melissa at her viola. Everyone looked up as he entered the music room. Father occupied his usual seat in the center of the room, facing Mother and Melissa. Mother sat at the piano; behind her viola, his sister looked gratified, or perhaps only relieved, that paternal wrath was not now directed at her. Father glared at Zack and said, "This afternoon we are rehearsing Mozart's Trio in E flat for piano, viola, and, if memory serves, but correct me if I'm wrong, clarinet."

"Heavy traffic, Zack?" his mother asked calmly.

Zack stammered an apology. "I came straight from campus. Doctor Weiss and I were talking after class, and I lost track of the time." Should I drop the bombshell now? he wondered, and wished that he had prepared a statement instead of merely anticipating a need to have one prepared. He avoided looking at anyone as he opened his instrument case and began fitting the wooden sections of the clarinet together. In spite of everything, the lacquered wood felt good in his hands. He smiled fleetingly at Mother, took the clarinet in his mouth, and ran through an arpeggio. Something occurred to him, the thought came from somewhere, I could do this in my sleep. He began to play the melody of an old romantic song. He did not remember the lyrics or even if he had ever known them, but he seemed to have known the melody all his life, and he understood that words had to have been written to go with it and that, whatever they were exactly, they must be filled with melancholy and longing. He played softly, and after a moment Mother picked it up and played along with equal delicacy. Melissa sat as one besieged behind her instrument, watching them with unconcealed resentment. She had virtually no conception of popular music, old or new, she did not approve of improvisation, and she had always been jealous of her brother's rapport with their mother.

Father sat glowering, but he let them finish a chorus before he said, "And *now* can we move along to Mozart?"

Mother gave him a mock-contrite look, Zack stammered an apology.

Mother said, "Dear, we're all just foaming at the mouth to get at that Kegelstatt," and punctuated the remark with a crashing chord.

Maybe I should say something before we begin, Zack thought. Mother smiled tranquilly back at him over the top of the piano. Melissa had her bow in position and an expression of intense concentration on her face. He did not say anything, and they began.

Father sat staring dourly at the ceiling as though awaiting answers to unvoiced questions. They all knew the questions: What have I done to deserve this? Why am I being punished? His expression's progress from dour to sour kept pace with their progress into the andante. Abruptly, he stood up, walked around Melissa, behind Zack. Zack knew from long experience what to expect. Nevertheless, he started when his father's hand shot past his ear and stabbed a bursitis-stiffened finger at a particular spot on the sheet music. "There," Father snapped, "right there is where your *mind* started to wander!"

Yes, thought Zack.

Father tapped the sheet music two or three times, then moved to stand before Zack. His scowl had become truly Beethovenian. "Your clarinet isn't going to play itself. You cannot set it going and then trust it to find its own way through the piece. It requires your presence. It requires your full attention from the *beginning* through the *middle* to the *end*."

Zack stammered an apology.

"Now," said Father, returning to his seat, "again."

They began afresh. It was worse than before. Zack exhaled in resignation and laid his instrument across his lap. Somehow, he met his father's eyes. "I'm sorry," he said, "I can't concentrate. I've got something on my mind, something important to tell you and Mother. Please try to understand."

And he dropped his bombshell.

Mother blinked and regarded him gravely, Melissa's slightly protuberant eyes became more so, and Father stared incredulously. When at last he did manage to speak he said, "You're giving up your studies, your instrument, for this, this fantasy?"

Zack shook his head. "That's not what I said. I'll still be studying music and playing. But I want to concentrate on geology."

"Geology! *Geology!* And if that wasn't nonsense enough—"

"Please try to understand."

"I am trying very hard to *understand!* I have been trying for years, in fact, to *understand* why anyone would prefer grubbing in rocks to performing music. And this other business, what's this, this business about time-travel expeditions?"

"It's true. They've found a—I don't know what exactly. A flaw in time, a rip or crack. It's something like that. I don't understand the first thing about the physics of it. Someone in the science department—"

Father laughed harshly. "Perhaps those physicists across the quad are having their little joke."

"It's no joke. The Association for the Advancement of Science made the announcement." Father's expression suggested that that organization meant no more to him than the Kiwanis, the Boy Scouts, the Justice League of America. Zack persevered. "People have already gone through and come back. It's real, this whatever it is, and they really can use it to travel back into distant prehistoric times. Back to the age of trilobites, four hundred million years ago."

"Pah! Not even to visit Mozart, Bach, Beethoven!"

"No," Zack said, smiling, "and just as well. My German stinks." His father did not return the smile. "Oh, for Heaven's sake, I'm talking about time-travel! Doctor Weiss said scientists are going to be going in droves, by the hundreds. After all, she says, it's easier and cheaper to get there than it is to go into space, never mind the moon or Mars. Everyone who can write a grant proposal is bound to get to go. There are already hundreds of people who're dying to go. Thousands, probably. Every institution in the world is going to want to send a team."

Now Mother spoke up. "Melissa," she said brightly, "would you please go make us all a cup of tea?" Something between a pout and a glower established itself on Melissa's face, and Zack resisted an irrational, resurgent urge, dormant since early adolescence, to tell her to pull her lip in because pouting made her look as though she had no chin. She got up suddenly and left almost at a run. Mother returned her attention to Zack. "If every Ph.D. and post-doc who ever found a bone is going—" she made a vague gesture "—back there, then why do you need to go?"

"Doctor Weiss evidently thinks I have the makings of a good geologist."

"Doctor Weiss, Doctor Weiss," Father said. "I think this Doctor Weiss should mind his own business."

"This is her business." Zack felt his temper suddenly trying to get away from him. Calmly, he told himself. He said, as calmly as he could manage, "Maybe I think I could be a better geologist than I am a clarinetist," and imagined that he saw lightning flash through his father's clouding expression. "It's not like I wouldn't keep up my playing in the meantime. I've never missed one of our gigs yet."

"And what about later, if you actually got to go? Would you practice when you're—" his mother gestured again, as vaguely as before "—back there?"

"Well, then I would have to give up playing for a while. It's hot and humid in the Paleozoic era. The climate'd ruin a clarinet. I probably wouldn't even get through my scales before the cork lining rotted. The pads would fall right out. I wouldn't be able to use a reed more than once or twice, and replacements would be difficult if not impossible to get."

"Just how long a while are you talking about?"

"I don't know. They're trying to figure a way to establish permanent camps. Where scientists could live and work for a year at a time, maybe more."

Now, definitely, lightning crackled across Father's face. "A year! You can't just put down the clarinet and expect to pick up it a year later! Unless you practice every day, you'll soon find yourself playing as badly as—as a child with a penny whistle! You'll lose your embouchure. Your fingers'll become stiff." Father held up both claw-like hands; the rebuke was unmistakable: Unlike you, *I* had no say in the matter. "What then?"

"You couldn't make your own reeds back in, back there?"

Zack answered his mother's question first. "There aren't, I mean, there weren't five ounces of good woody tissue in the whole Silurian period." Then he said to his father, "I can always take up whistling. Or learn to play spoons and Jew's harp. Maybe I'll just burst into song whenever the mood hits. The hills are alive, or I am the very model of a modern major general."

Father exhaled a consonant sound of exasperation, nnn! To Mother he said, "His head has turned to rock, I cannot communicate with someone whose brain has turned to rock. Talk some sense to him if you can. I am going out back to burst a blood vessel." He kicked out his chair out of his way and stormed out of the room.

Mother said nothing, merely looked expectantly at Zack. He made an effort not to appear abashed; the effort felt as obvious as his embarrassment. He said, "I know it means completely rethinking everything. But I have been rethinking everything. I was just going to take the earth-sciences course my sophomore year to keep my hand in. Keep up with my hobby. But it's not a hobby any more, not since this time-travel thing. It's not too late for me to switch majors." He paused to see what she would say; when she said nothing, he said, "Do you think you can get him to come around?"

Mother made a sound that could have been either a laugh or a sob. "What makes you think *I'm* going to come around? Just because I haven't blown my top or fainted dead away, don't suppose I'm any less astonished and dismayed by all this than your father is. All those years of music lessons, all those hours of practice, wasted."

"I said I'd keep my hand in."

"Keep your hand in! Your father was a good musician. When he could no longer play, he thought he could at least count on becoming the patriarch of a musical family."

"And he got Melissa and me instead. Semi-skilled musical laborers."

"That's a rather harsh judgment."

"Still, it's true, isn't it? I'm not going to presume to say what goes through Melissa's so-called mind when she's sawing away, but—"

"Don't be nasty. Melissa wants more than anything to please your father. Unlike you, she has no hobbies, no pastimes except the viola. She always plays at the absolute limit of her ability, which is adequate, and of course your father always insists that if she'd only push herself a bit more, she'd be brilliant. They break each other's hearts."

To avoid meeting her gaze, Zack put the metal cap on the clarinet's mouthpiece, removed the mouthpiece and the bell, broke the instrument down into its constituent sections, placed them in the instrument case. He regarded them thoughtfully. He loved the clarinet, and had ever since hearing—oh, what had it been? Oh, what did it matter? Learning to play had been for him a test of character; he had almost given up—for what seemed the longest time he could make the infuriatingly uncooperative black tube produce nothing but anguished squeaks.

And when had he first been drawn to the mysteries of the earth? Before I could tell the difference, he answered himself, between Mozart and mopop. He had been born and raised in Nashville and its environs, amid Ordovician strata thousands of feet thick, and introduced early to the joys, to say nothing of the sheer hard labor, of fossil-hunting by his maternal grandfather, a geologist for the State of Tennessee. He could remember vividly, for instance, the time and effort the two of them had once put into prying a big fossil arthropod out of the stone. All the while they had whistled and hummed and sung to each other, for his rockhound grandfather also loved music. His life had seemed always to embrace, encompass, serenely and easily, both interests, and he more than anyone had set the lexicons of science and music whirling in Zack's brain like worlds orbiting each other, separate, yet inseparable.

Until now.

He said, "I've had two dreams about Mozart this month. The first one was right after our last restaurant gig. You remember. I botched that passage. I could hear Father's eyes roll up in their sockets all the way across the room. Well, in this dream I was some kind of forensic archeologist crossed with a musicologist, and I had this crazy assignment. I was supposed to exhume the remains of some eighteenth-century aristocrat's wife. This aristocrat had commissioned Mozart himself to compose an original piece of music in her honor. Mozart composed the piece as ordered, but then, being the kind of fellow he was, he dedicated it to the lady's foot, which he thought was really beautiful. It upset the husband so much, he not only fired Mozart but also destroyed the only copy of the composition. Where *I* came in was, I had to dig the lady up, examine her foot bones, and from that somehow reconstruct this lost piece of Mozart music."

A smile flickered at the corners of Mother's mouth. "Perhaps it was your subconscious telling you you're on a mission from Mozart. That you should practice harder so you won't botch more passages."

"No, I don't think so. I knew in the dream I wasn't up to the job. I woke up in a panic. It was like I'd had an anxiety attack in my sleep. It wasn't a good dream. I think it was my subconscious telling me I know I just don't have it in me to be a great musician."

"Good or bad, dreams have only as much power over us as we give them," and for a moment it seemed to him that, without changing position in the least, she turned completely away from him and gazed at something far off. He almost did not want to say any more, but then she returned from wherever she had gone and looked at him. "You said there were two dreams."

"The second dream was early this week. In it—did you know Mozart actually died from exposure while exploring the American southwest? That his companions buried him in a cave? Nobody knows where the cave is. I learned this in the dream from Artie Shaw. The bandleader."

"I know who Artie Shaw was."

"Only he wasn't a bandleader any more. He was teaching a course in literature right here at the university. After class, he and I and one or two other people—maybe one of them was Doctor Weiss—we all piled into this old car and went looking for Mozart's final resting place."

"Interesting. And did you find it?"

"No. All that happened was I missed a lot of classes and a couple of gigs and—there was a lot of yelling and screaming after that."

"Mozart and Artie Shaw. Still. You picked another clarinetist to bum around with in dreamland."

"No, this was after he'd stopped playing. Shaw walked away from music when he felt it was time to go do other things. He was a big success as a bandleader, but he'd had enough, and he had other dreams. I'm not a success, Mother, but I've had enough, too. And I have other dreams."

"Not everyone's so lucky as to have more than one dream. Zack, you have the makings of a decent clarinetist."

"Decent. Solo or ensemble?"

"You have the capacity for large breaths," she said coolly. "Your tonguing is good. It is no mean thing to be a good ensemble musician."

Zack shook his head. "That's not much of an inducement. What we do is provide aural wallpaper at brunches and gallery openings. Nobody'd notice us at all unless we suddenly stopped playing in the middle of something. Maybe not even then. A hologram could do what we do, and you could edit out the fluffs."

"Better not let your father hear you say that."

"He doesn't hear anything he doesn't want to hear unless you get right up close to him and shout in his face. Don't get me wrong. I enjoy playing when I'm playing just to be playing. Aural wallpaper or not. I could go on enjoying that if only Father wasn't so determined to be a musical genius and have kids who're virtuosos."

"Zack, it's given only to two or three people in every hundred million to be geniuses. I've never met a genius. Not even your father. But I've known many more or less good musicians. Notice I do not say gifted. Good musicians, whether they're merely good or very good, are those people who can concentrate on their music to the exclusion of everything else. It's the price they have to pay to be good."

"But I don't want to be so good at just one thing that I'm no good at anything else. I love music, but I love geology, too. Like Granddad. He believed everyone needs art *and* science." How old had he been—six? seven?—the first time he had visited the seashore with his family? The sight, the idea, of such an immensity of water had paralyzed him with terror until his grandfather handed him a conch shell and told him to hold it to his ear; he had virtually forgotten to breathe as he stood listening to the ghostly echo, the ocean's music. All life came from the sea, Granddad had then told him, and as the old man spoke of the vastness of geologic time and the beginnings of life he stretched his hand indefinitely seaward, so that ever after Zack's concept of the past had been inextricably linked to the ocean and its unseen further shores. The eras and periods and epochs existed somehow simultaneously within and beyond the sea.

"About this prehistoric expedition," his mother said. "I'm sure you'd have to get all the way through to post-grad before anybody would even consider taking you along on any expedition. And there's no guarantee anybody would ever take you along."

"I know all that. But I want to try for it."

"Is it what you really want? Are you positive?"

"I believe I can do it. I believe it'll be worth all the work and waiting."

"You realize scientists make even less money than good ensemble musicians."

"Mother, it's—it's the greatest adventure anyone could ever have! Think of it!"

"Oh, God, I am. I'm thinking my only son wants to joyride in a time machine. I'm thinking he's going to get eaten by some prehistoric monster."

"There're no monsters there. Just shellfish and water bugs. Not even any stinging or biting insects." He knew better than to mention the Paleozoic arthropods likely to be encountered. But then he did say, "Even if we don't find anything pleasant, at least we'll find something new."

"You should be trying especially hard right now to make it all sound as safe as a high-school band trip."

"It'd just be field work. I was just repeating something Doctor Weiss said."

"You're awfully taken with Doctor Weiss all of a sudden. Until today, I'm not sure I ever heard you say her name. Is she pretty as well as smart?"

His necks and cheeks smoldered. "She must be in her thirties."

"That's not what I asked, but never mind."

"If Granddad had this chance, he'd've gone in a hot second."

"Yes," Mother said, "if he'd had the chance. Did you know he played in a jazz group when he was young?"

"Yes."

She appeared not to have heard. "He played piano and saxophone. The instruments in greatest favor, he used to say, among whorehouse musicians." Zack nodded mechanically. He knew the whole story, all the jokes, the titles of every song in Granddad's repertoire, which had run heavily to contemporary selections, "She Had Different Faces," "Joto Moto," but also included many old standards, "Goodbye Pork Pie Hat," "Something," "Moonglow." He had taught them to his daughter, who had taught them to her son, who had learned from both of them that all the best old songs were full of loss and yearning for that which was or that which may be. No one could write songs like that any more because no one had to give up anything or wait for anything any more. Yearning and instant gratification were mutually exclusive . . . .

Zack realized with a start that his mother had lapsed into silence. As she rested her fingers on the keys, he thought he saw on her face, in the lines around the eyes and at the corners of the mouth, a hitherto secret and inexpressible sorrow, even pain. It was there and then not there, but in that instant he understood, wrenchingly, that she was not and had never been merely the accessible, humorous, even-tempered parent who played counterpoint to the impatient, humorless, implacable one, that she was a more mysterious being than he had imagined. It was there, and then, when it was not, he sensed that they were passing from an accustomed state of being to another where she would have to accept that her child was no longer a child, and he, for his part, would never be able to forget his unsettling glimpse of the private self, the stranger who lived inside his mother.

When she spoke again, she did not look at him. "I'll see if I can't convince your father you have to go. For your own sake and for Granddad's, too."

He did not know whether to give her a hug and a kiss or thank her formally, adult to adult. Finally, he managed to gasp out, "Thanks."

"No promises."

"Thanks."

She slightly dipped her head in acknowledgement of both his gratitude and his uncertainty. She played a note and let it fade, leaned back from the piano, smoothed her dress across her lap.

Then suddenly she smiled at him. "Her foot!" The smile broke in soft laughter. "That's our Mozart, all right!"

Granddad, Zack says, this is a dream, isn't it?

There are dreams, and there are dreams. You either dream your own dream or dream someone else's. The old man spreads his arms in an ocean-encompassing gesture. Find out whose it is for yourself. Go *in.*

Yes. I will. Yes.

And, "O," Granddad sings in his cracked tuneless voice,

"I should have been a pair of ragged claws
Scuttling across the floors of silent seas!"

Zack wades in. Flat mats of alga glisten on the surface near the shore, but he moves easily through them, the water is warm and clear. He slips beneath the calm surface and discovers not only that visibility is excellent but also that what he took to be a clarinet is actually a snorkel that will enable him to breathe while underwater. Ahead, he sees flower-like crinoids, a meadow of them, waving in greeting and invitation. I accept, he thinks, and swims languidly toward them. There are moving glints everywhere he looks, and after a moment he identifies them as echelons of darting silver cephalopods, with shells as long and straight as pencils. The echelons keep forming and reforming around him, crossing and recrossing before him. They dart everywhere among the crinoid stems and rippling dark algal ribbons. Thus escorted, propelling himself with an occasional lazy kick, he passes above the lagoon's shallow bottom with all the eerie silent majesty of an airship. Below him are what seem like ten thousand kinds of shellfish, worm, and arthropod, clusters of rugose corals, strange seaweeds. The least flurry of activity on the bottom suffices to raise a small obscuring cloud, as when a swarm of trilobites the size of beans scatter before a tentacled predator. He does not see the outcome of the attack, but he does not care. He is too happy. He thinks, What sweet mystery. Humming far back in his throat, he swims away.

THE GIFT HORSE

Interviewer: Welcome back to the second half of our show, and thanks for joining us. For those who tuned in late, our guest is the noted physicist Nathan Cutsinger. Professor Cutsinger, you've always insisted this *isn't* a time machine you're talking about —

Cutsinger: I haven't even called what I'm not talking about a time machine.

Interviewer: Almost everything except, to be sure. But you can't expect the general public to know what you're talking about when you refer to "a closed timelike curve" or "a spacetime anomaly."

Cutsinger: I never expect the general public to know what I'm talking about, regardless of what I'm talking about.

Interviewer: Which in this case is not time travel, but travel from this universe to another. The theory being that there's a virtually infinite succession of universes, each different from all the rest. Some of the differences are so minor—occurring at the subatomic level—they make no difference at distances greater than a Planck unit.

Cutsinger: Listen to you. Planck unit.

Interviewer: I'm a fast study.

Cutsinger: Certainly faster than many people I could name. Differences above the subatomic level may include universes where humans never evolved on Earth, or any multicellular life at all. There could be Earths without moons, so there're no tides, so life never moved ashore in any meaningful way. I trust I'm not revealing as much ignorance about splash-zones here as biologists reveal about quantum physics. Some universes would be so weird, with laws of nature so different from those we know, that life never arose anywhere, stars and planets never formed.

Interviewer: That may well be, but everything about this particular universe you've tapped into matches what we know about our Earth in Paleozoic time. You've ruffled many feathers by insisting nobody should entirely trust any data the Paleozoic expedition collects.

Cutsinger: Ever since we discovered the anomaly, I've been hearing about what it means to the geosciences. Nobody in that broad field evidently paid attention when we physicists explained the profound implications of so-called time travel in accordance with the many-worlds theory. All we hear from that quarter are variations on "Wow, time travel, great, let's go collect live trilobites." Properly speaking, what they're going to collect are imitation trilobites, trilobite-like organisms. Trilobitoids.

Interviewer: Isn't that a rather fine distinction?

Cutsinger: Science is *about* fine distinctions. Somebody has to be responsible for yes-buts and reality checks, but nobody in the geosciences wants to make himself unpopular right now by asking the unanswerable questions.

Interviewer: Which unanswerable questions?

Cutsinger: For starters, how *close* a resemblance does this other earth in this other universe bear to our own? Why is it lagging four hundred and whatever million years behind ours? Is it really four hundred million years younger? What geoscientists know, what they think they know, about our world in Paleozoic time is based on a number of simplifying assumptions. Interpretations of fossil magnetism, based on the assumption that our planet's magnetic and rotational axes have always been more or less coincident. Predictions about the length of Paleozoic days, the number of days in Paleozoic years, based on the assumption that Earth's rotation has slowed at a constant rate.

Interviewer: Yes, but at some point, assumptions become necessary or the whole process is paralyzed.

Cutsinger: Scientists must retain the ability to question their own assumptions. Too many people in the geosciences and, unfortunately, in the greater scientific community are hot to confirm or disprove all sorts of assumptions *except* the biggest one of all—that events in this other universe, including the development of life on this other world, exactly parallel events in our own, to the smallest detail. I challenge anybody to say unequivocally that biological specimens from this other world are *identical* to Paleozoic organisms on our Earth.

Interviewer: Everything about those specimens, genetic evidence, RNA, DNA, protein sequence information, checks out perfectly.

Cutsinger: Maybe. Maybe researchers are on solid ground— semisolid ground—if they restrict themselves to testing only what has already been inferred from the geological record. But they're also breaking new ground on this other world. Finding things never seen before, that may have had no counterparts on our world. Undoubtedly, whatever data this other world yields will be fascinating. But they won't be trustworthy in the sense that they necessarily, absolutely apply to our world. Our own world and this other world are copies of each other, and at some level inexact copies.

Interviewer: Perhaps only at the subatomic level.

Cutsinger: *Probably* but not *certainly* only at that level. But how could you tell?

Interviewer: The stars in the sky above that other world are all mixed up, as astronomers say they would have been four hundred million years ago. But you can see a sun and moon and planets, and they're the same ones we know. If that world's a copy of our own, it's a very good one. I think—

Cutsinger: You think I'm splitting hairs.

Interviewer: Frankly, yes. Yes.
Cutsinger: Raining on the parade. Looking a gift horse in the mouth.

Interviewer: Yes. It *is* a gift. A wonderful gift.
Cutsinger: Emerson said Nature deals things out without fear or favor, after severe universal laws.

Interviewer: Do you intend going through the anomaly yourself and visiting that other world?
Cutsinger: I'm not an outdoorsman. The sad truth is, I have a horror of the great outdoors in any geologic age, even our own. Yet, the thought of going through the anomaly interests me, though I'm told it's an unpleasant experience. Still, it's possible I'll try it. And if it's at all possible, you know—even if *I* don't go, in the next universe over, I *do* go. That's the beauty of the many-worlds theory. There are no wasted opportunities.

PROMISED LAND

Tim's color had improved by the time Rene found him on the starboard catwalk under the helicopter deck. She gave him a solicitous smile and said, "Feel better now?"

"No. Just emptier."

"You're carrying on a great tradition. Charles Darwin was seasick most of the time he spent aboard the *Beagle*."

He looked sheepishly at the calm graptolite-choked sea; the surface glistened with sunlight reflected from the creatures' semitransparent and iridescent flotation bags. "I can't speak for Darwin, but I'm ashamed of myself. I feel like I've just defiled this place."

"You'll get your sea legs yet."

"It wasn't until this trip that I've ever been out of sight of land in my whole life."

"Well, perk up, we're almost there," and she directed his attention to a point off the starboard bow.

From that distance, the island looked like nothing so much as an immense heap of broken glass. Most of the Paleozoic real estate they had seen before now had tended toward dun, the grayish brown of barren, heavily weathered rock. This island was as black as tar, with here and there a gleam of sunlight on a ribbon of moving water. Rivulets rushed down from the interior; waterfalls cascaded directly into the sea or splashed onto scree at the bases of jagged cliffs. In places the cliffs dropped straight into the sea; elsewhere the waves had gouged out caves or carved away softer portions of the coast to create isolated irregular pillars. These sea stacks stoically endured endless battering while, behind them, the cliffs retreated across rocky wave-cut platforms.

Tim made a face. "Not really a place you'd want to bring the family."

"Oh, I don't know. That's prime pre-Pangaean ocean-front property. Grand view of Panthalassa. Put in a concession stand, some rides, a water park—people would come from eons around."

"Think Dick'll like it?"

Now more than ever before, she thought, Dick is incapable of liking anything. But she said, "He'd goddamn well better like it, after what we've done to get him here. And he's going to have it all to himself once we've come and gone. A whole prehistoric island to call his own."

"Where do you suppose it'll end up—plate-tectonically speaking?"

She shrugged. "Part of Scotland, maybe Ireland."

"Scotland and Ireland are good."

She glanced at her watch and turned from the rail. "They should be just about ready for us in the boat bay. You sure you've got everything?"

"Everything. Everything except breakfast, lunch, and dinner, that is. And my socks. Those came up right after dinner did. I wish we could fly over in a 'copter."

"Take it up with the Navy. Besides, I thought you said you suffer from airsickness, too."

"Airsickness, seasickness, carsickness. I can be utterly miserable on land and sea and in the air."

"You're certainly versatile."

"It's the hike once we get ashore that I'm not looking forward to."

They went below decks and waited until the bluejackets had finished stowing equipment and supplies into the boat. Then they stepped aboard and took their places under a canvas awning, and their Navy pilot deftly maneuvered the craft out into the open and made for shore. He put in to a cove where the sea had first created a small inlet and then, breaking through relatively soft rock, enlarged it. A second bluejacket had stationed himself in the bow as lookout. From time to time he raised his left or right hand, and the pilot gave the wheel a twist. The water here was smooth and clear, and on the bottom lay large, dark, irregular masses capable of holing the boat's hull. Two other Navy men, including an older one who was in charge, sat amidships. No one spoke. The only sound was the thrum of the boat's motor.

Within the cove, rubble from the crumbling cliffs encircled a muddy fringe of beach. One section of cliff had collapsed entirely. The landing party, comprising the two civilians and three of the Navy men, had to climb the steeply graded scree burdened with all their gear before they could at last consider themselves safely ashore. When they were about halfway up, Rene overheard one young sailor remark that "that skinny old lady climbs like a goat," and called a halt for rest. While the sailors caught their breath and looked on with varying degrees of interest and bemusement, she and Tim poked among the rocks and exclaimed in delight as they fished out wriggling primitive arthropods and insubstantial green plants. Tim showed the Navy men his muddy fingers.

"Ah?" said the one in charge.

"Dirt," said Tim. "Soil."

"Ah," said the Navy man. "That's good." He sounded tentative, almost dubious.

"Next time," said another, younger Navy man, "I hope you folks'll pick someplace closer to home and not so high out of the water."

The Navy man in charge nodded agreement. "What's so special about *this* island?"

"It's on the dark side of the world." Tim nodded toward the horizon. "All your major landmasses are thataway. From there all the way around to back of there is one big stretch of ocean with just the occasional crescent of volcanic islands wherever there's a subduction zone close by. And these isolated islands are the forcing houses for evolution. We can expect to find some very strange species here."

"Oh, thrill," said the young bluejacket. "Like there aren't enough strange species back at Stinktown. But why *this* island?"

"It was named for a colleague of ours. So, when we started planning this little field trip—well, we wanted a remote island, so we said, 'Why not *this* one?' It fit our needs. Isolated, yet not literally on the back side of the world."

"Well," the young sailor drawled, "if I was your colleague, I'd be more particular about what I gave my name to."

"He's dead. We submitted his name to the nomenclature committee. They applied it to this island."

"Sorry," the sailor said.

"He died a long time ago," Rene said, "or a long time from now, however you want to put it."

A nurse carrying a tray emerged from the room as Rene approached. They exchanged smiles, and Rene asked, "How is he? May I see him?"

"Go right in. His wife's with him. But he's not being polite to anybody today. You'll have to stand in front of the television to get him to pay you any attention. He's into one of his science things."

Rene ventured an experiment. "Do you know what it is, this science thing?"

The nurse lifted her shoulders in a meaty shrug. "I'm afraid I couldn't tell you if my life depended on it. Science isn't something they teach in nursing school."

"No. Of course not."

The nurse backed against the door and pushed it ajar, and through the tinny sound of television voices came a testy query, "What is it *now?*"

"You have another visitor."

"Kindly tell whoever it is to go away. Kindly tell him to go get stuffed."

"It's another lady."

"Then kindly tell *her* to go get stuffed. No, wait a second. Is she this dumpy bad-smelling thing with stringy mousy hair, wearing a too-small tee-shirt and too-tight jeans?"

"It's a tall brunette, the same one as ever."

"Send Doctor de Souza right in. I'll tell her personally to go get stuffed."

The nurse winked broadly at Rene and moved out of the doorway. Rene composed herself, then peeked around the doorframe. Dick lay amid a thicket of intravenous tubes and connections to monitoring devices; his wife, Judy, sat on the far side of the bed, holding his hand. The light coming through the opened blinds was cruel. Dick looked even more faded and shrunken than he had on the occasion of her preceding visit, a mere four days earlier. Judy looked puffy and tired, as though she had slept badly. Probably she had, Rene decided as she rapped on the doorframe and said, "Are you decent?"

"Sure, like I am *ever* decent. Come on in. You two have met, haven't you?"

"I hope I'm not intruding," Rene said as she stepped into the room. Judy appeared not to know what to say, to fumble for words, for a moment that lasted just long enough to make Rene acutely uncomfortable. Judy was somewhat of an unknown quantity to Dick's colleagues; he had always kept his professional and domestic lives well apart from each other, with the result that Rene could not now be certain that she and Judy had said two dozen words to each other in as many years. She could not even recall when she had last seen Judy—the last time Dick had been in the hospital, or the time before, or the time before that?

Finally, Judy said, "Dick's been talking back to the teevee, but I've lost track of the argument," and fixed a smile on the lower half of her face. It only accentuated the sag of her jowls and the smudginess of the flesh beneath her pale eyes.

Rene moved a chair close to the bed. She had always towered over Dick, but now, even seated, she thought he looked dwarfish. "Good thing you came now," he said. "Later this afternoon I'm scheduled to have my brain transplanted into the body of the Frankenstein monster."

"*That* would be a monster." Rene looked across him at Judy and said, "Don't ask me why, it's nothing I can really put my finger on, but I strongly suspect he's been giving the staff a hard time."

Judy worked on her smile. "The person at the desk got that look on her face when I asked how he was today."

"I know That Look. With two capital letters."

Between them, Dick growled. "What do you expect? It's not like I *want* to be here. You know, for what it's cost for me to be here these past few days, we could finance a major expedition into the Paleozoic. Maybe two."

"Ah," said Rene. "You've heard the news."

He gestured at the television screen, at a man who stood behind a podium and addressed himself to the camera. "Got it straight from the man of the hour."

"—Roman poet Seneca," the man of the hour was saying, "wrote that the fates lead the willing and drag the unwilling. He could have been writing about paradigm shifts."

"To hell with Seneca, then," Dick said, "quote from Thomas goddamn Kuhn. Showoff. Overeducated schmuck. God, I hate physicists!"

"Dick," Judy said, "you shouldn't let yourself get worked up."

"Hatred gives me strength, honey."

"Paradigm shifts," the man of the hour went on, "are by definition unsettling. In fact, they can be downright scary. Back around the turn of the century, when I was an undergraduate, the news media announced that someone had got a pulse of light to exceed the cosmic speed limit. Actually, they had done no such thing and hadn't claimed to do any such thing. It was science reporters in the mainstream media who'd misunderstood and misrepresented the facts. All the same, for just a moment or two, before reason kicked in, I felt the world tilt ninety degrees out of plumb. Everything I believed was wrong! I experienced exactly the same kind of unease, almost a frisson of terror—and I know I speak for my fellow researchers, too—that moment of vertigo when we actually realized what we had, what we'd stumbled onto—"

"Hear that?" Dick said. "'*Stumbled* onto.' He credits serendipity! It was all luck! He's trying to sound modest."

"Modesty is a becoming trait," Judy said, "even in a scientist."

"Especially in a scientist," Rene said.

"Hah. Any second now I expect to see him dig his toe in the dirt and say, 'Aw shucks.' But you can tell he *knows* he's next year's Nobel winner. And in the meantime he'll be beating female grad students off with a stick. Or maybe male ones. Fruity bunch, physicists. It's all Professor Schmucko there can do to keep from exploding with satisfaction."

"I can't say I blame him," Rene said. "He's entitled. It's his time machine."

"It isn't a time machine. It's a wormhole."

"Whatever it is, Dick, it's too wonderful a thing for such a slimy-sounding name."

"You're in the wrong line of work if slime upsets you."

"Oh, you know what I mean. They should call it a time warp, a space warp. Something—*grand*. Something science-fictiony."

"My distinct impression's that they're trying to make it sound as un-science-fictiony as they can. Anyway, what's in a name?"

"At least they should stop referring to its mouth. A mouth implies the existence of a nether aperture. Hardly an image to encourage explorers."

"Hah. It won't discourage a single one. I bet the line at the Directorate of Geosciences already stretches clear around the block. You should be in it instead of here."

"I'm there in spirit. Someone else is there in person. Don't think for one second we're going to miss out on this."

"Some of us are."

There was a moment of uncomfortable silence in the room. Finally, Rene asked, "How are you today?"

He grimaced, then worked the grimace into a tight smile. "I'm how I was a mere four days ago, only more so. I'm awful, thank you. Just bloody awful. I think this time is it."

Rene looked at Judy, who would not meet her eyes. She could read nothing in the woman's expression, no clue as to how to proceed. Rene weighed possible responses. Nonsense, you'll be out of here before you know it. Or: You mustn't give up hope. Or: I wish you wouldn't talk that way. But she had said those things to him on previous occasions and knew that he expected better from her now. She said, "You know, you don't *always* have to be the pessimist of the team."

"You angling for the position? Feh. Amateur. Rene'll deny this, honey, but deep down in her heart of hearts she always thinks the glass is half full. Me, I know it's half-empty. And dirty. And I'm the one who's going to have to wash it."

Judy said, "Dear, you don't have to do your whole comedy routine for us."

"Speaking of comedy routines," he asked Rene, "how did the conference go?"

Rene, grateful for the change of subject, said, "It went—it started out okay, but then the news broke—" she nodded in the direction of the television screen "—and after that it just became impossible to get anyone to stick to the program. It devolved from a conference to a bacchanal."

"And probably stopped just short of a panty raid. In other words, nothing out of the ordinary. Paleo boys loose in the halls. Booze flowing like wine. Poolside furniture tossed into the deep end. Someone making a pass at Tetyana Pylpiv. Tetyana passing out from the shock."

"Basically. On the other hand—do you remember Caroline Warren?"

"Paleobotanist from Cornell." For an instant, his eye sparkled mischievously. He turned his head toward his wife. "Redhead. Woof."

"See?" Judy said quietly. "Plenty of life left in you yet, old dog."

"As soon as the news broke," Rene went on, "and the implications started to sink in, Caroline Warren jumps up and says, 'Screw this conference,' and goes and shuts herself up in her hotel room. The next morning—"

"As the usual idiots are dragging around and comparing hangovers!"

"—she comes in with an entire study plan for determining the precise relationships of all those plants that're always lumped together as Cooksonia. 'Just give me one week in Paleozoic time,' she says. And of course she was all hot and bothered about some of the other specimens the probe brought back, the ones like nothing we've ever seen before."

"I would join in the celebratory jig," Dick said, "but under the circumstances . . . . "

"Everyone sent regards and hopes you get well very soon."

"Ugh. Tell everyone for me, 'Up yours very much.'" He grimaced again; this time, he let it remain a grimace. "I distinctly recall telling the head nurse to block all incoming regards and hopes. No flowers, no get-well cards. All visitors to be stripped and cavity-searched. All optimism, however guarded, to be confiscated on the spot."

"Don't we even get points for meaning well?"

"I hate to disappoint everyone. But like I said, I think this is it. The disease's led a merry chase all through me these last couple years. Bladder, lungs. Now it's holed up inside my head where you couldn't get at it with any instrument more delicate than an axe."

He glared suddenly at the television screen, which had bifurcated to show the man of the hour on the left, listening as an audience member on the right asked a question.

"That's enough of that crap," Dick said, "now let me show you something really cool," and when he spoke to the television screen an underwater scene instantly appeared. Shafts of sunlight slanted downward through green murk to illuminate patches of bottom mud. A shadowy form came swimming along just above the bottom, came head-on, purposefully, straight toward the viewer. Seemingly at the last moment, it turned sharply aside, affording Rene a glimpse of many pairs of bristly jointed appendages clustered on the underside of the blunt head. A long, flattened appendage extended oar-like from each flank. Halfway along its length, the segmented body narrowed, terminating in an affair like a dirty ice pick.

"Eurypterid," she breathed.

"E. remipes in the flesh," he said, "or its kissing cousin, anyway."

"That is just incredible."

"Lucky it wasn't one of the big eurypterids. Pterygotus would've tried to eat their roboprobe. Haven't you seen this already?"

"Not this particular clip."

"Want to see it again? Can you stand it?"

"Are you kidding?"

They watched the eurypterid a second time, and a third, in slow motion, and he told the television to freeze the image as the creature was halfway through its turn to the side, and to enlarge and enhance a particular section so that she could clearly see the underside of the head, the arrangement of the legs around the toothplate, the grisly orifice of the mouth. Then he let it swim on, and glowed with pleasure for a moment. Then his face clouded over again. "It moves," he said, "just like your computer models."

"Our computer models."

"Don't be generous. You did all the work. I began to die." He told the television screen to go away, and it instantly blanked itself. "At the risk of sounding really really bitter, this is as close as I'm ever going to get to going there, being there."

She took his free hand. It was cool in hers, the bones felt very fragile, and the blue veins showed prominently through the pale translucent skin. On the other side of the bed, Judy seemed intent on the hand she held.

"A week ago," Dick said, "I could've died happy and at peace with the world. I mean that. I'm tired and in pain all the time and I keep finding myself at the point of striking a bargain with some deity or other. 'Since you aren't going to cure me, God or gods, could you please just kill me a bit faster?' Don't either of you dare tell anybody I got religion on my death bed."

"I swear on a stack of Bibles," Rene said, "I wouldn't dream of it."

"Better not. I'll find some way to haunt anyone who tells lies about me. Anyway, at least till my brain turns to gleet, I've got to lie here and watch all this exciting stuff on television. Part of me's thrilled, of course. But the part of me that's dying, and it's the part of me that gets bigger all the time, crowding out the other parts of me, that part feels cheated, big time. That part's resentful as hell. That part of me feels like Tantalus in the old legend. In Hell he's hungry and thirsty and food and water are just out of reach. Whence, tantalize."

"I seem to recall Tantalus was being punished for his sins."

"That's what *really* pisses me off—it's a bum rap. If there's a God, I'm going to kick his ass for this. Here I'm coming up on the end of my life and after due reflection I'm deciding it's been a pretty good one. And then, suddenly, just out of reach, there's the thing that makes everything I've ever done pall. Time travel! Goddamn *time travel!* Brainboy on television's going to be one of the immortals of science, everybody'll get to jump through his wormhole, they'll make important discoveries and win fame and glory. And guess who has to stay right here at home and be worm's meat."

The women said, "*Dick,*" in unison and then looked at each other in embarrassment.

"Oh, both of you, don't look so goddamn stricken. I'm the one who should look stricken. I *feel* stricken. There's a party in the Paleozoic, and I can't go. I'm not going anywhere from here. Well, to the hospice, for a while, then it's off to the morgue. I wasn't afraid of dying—*as* afraid of dying—before all this. I'd already made it clear that no heroic measures are to be taken—what a stupid phrase! Heroic measures! Mock-heroic is more like it. But now I'd be grabbing at straws if there were any straws to grab at. I don't care what, untested drugs, yak dung extract. Anything as long as it promises recovery. No, not even recovery. Just a little more time. A year, six good months, so I, too, could go jump into that wormhole and see this prehistoric wonderland for myself."

Judy had let go of her husband's hand. Now, as she reached for it again, Rene studied her expression and after a moment realized what it was: That Look, with two capital letters—embarrassment and exasperation commingled with, and held in check by, resignation.

She started as the big nurse filled the doorway behind her and said, "Sorry to interrupt—"

Dick glowered at her past Rene. "What do you want now? No, wait, just let me take a wild guess. It's time for more unpleasantness, isn't it? Fresh indignities against my person."

"Dick," said Judy, "*be* nice."

"Why change my ways at this late date?"

Rene made a smile on her face and said to the nurse, "Allow me to apologize for my colleague's rude behavior. It never used to be a problem when we kept him chained in the basement."

The nurse chuckled and advanced into the room, radiating a kind of genial purposefulness. "Perhaps his problem is he always was too healthy till now. Someone who's never sick a day in their life doesn't know how to behave when they do wind up in the hospital."

"He doesn't know how to behave anywhere."

The nurse chuckled again and said to Dick, "Now are you going to let her talk about you like that?"

"Rene, if you're going to talk about me like that, please be a love and do it behind my back."

"Well," said the nurse, "I'm afraid visiting hours are over."

"Sorry," Judy said, "I—we lost track of the time."

Rene stood. "I'll see you tomorrow, Dick, if I can get away."

He effected part of a shrug. "You only have to bother with me as long as I remain lucid. Tell everybody to be brave."

Judy said, "We all have to be brave, don't we?" and leaned over the bed to kiss his cheek, near the corner of his mouth.

Rene patted his hand in farewell. "Don't make life too hard for these nice nurses. Try not snapping at just whoever's handy."

Dick peered around the nurse's bulging flank as she insinuated herself between visitors and bed. "If I only yelled at people I'm really mad at—life's too short for that degree of discrimination."

"Be good. Till tomorrow."

Judy stood no taller than Dick; as the two women walked slowly toward the elevators, Rene could not help hunching her shoulders and stooping slightly in an effort to compensate for the disparity in their heights. Judy glanced up at her and said, "He always did describe you as his tallest, slimmest, and most limbful colleague." Rene started to laugh, but then Judy added, "I feel like such a dumpling, waddling along beside you. Well, thank you for coming to see him. I'm sure you must be very busy with that—that time-travel business or whatever it is."

"Whatever it is, it is pretty exciting, isn't it? If I don't get on the team that goes through this wormhole, it won't be for lack of trying."

"I'm sure it won't."

"But, meanwhile—if there's anything I can do to help, anything any of us can do—"

"Yes. There is something."

"Dick is just—there's nothing we wouldn't do for him."

"I'm sure. Everyone tells me how much they've always liked and admired him."

They arrived before the elevator doors, and Judy dug a handkerchief from her purse. Her eyelashes glistened wetly. As she daubed at her eyes, she said, "If you want to know the truth, sometimes I have a hard time remembering him when he *was* likeable and admirable. You see how he's becoming extremely difficult to be with. Well, he's ill. And he's full of anger and self-pity. Anyway. I started thinking about what I have to say before you came. When he was watching television. I've never been good at talking to people. Not around Dick, anyway. It was always easier to fade into the wallpaper. But now I'm having to step into the foreground and take charge of everything, and it leaves me wide open for his famous caustic wit. The less of a sense of humor he has, the more caustic what he does have becomes. I go home in tears after every visit. But I guess a sense of humor's a lot to expect from a dying man. Especially one with a brain tumor. Anyway. I'd be very grateful if, from now on, you would downplay work when you come to see him. Particularly if it involves this new discovery."

"Well, I'm—"

The elevator doors slid open, and they stepped inside and rode down in silence with three other people.

In the lobby, Judy drew Rene to one side, out of the way of traffic, and said, "You saw how excited he is. It's not good for him. He needs rest and quiet from now on."

"Yes, of course, but—"

"He has a lifetime of valuable work to look back on. That ought to satisfy him. It ought to satisfy all of you. For all these years, I've had to share him with you. It was more like I had him on loan from you, when I did have him. When he was off in Australia or Antarctica, or even just off to a conference, I was at home with the children and my half of the bed. *We* were *only* his family—his real rapport was with his colleagues and with things that died millions of years ago. Well, now he doesn't have much time left. I want as much of that time as I can have. If I'm being horribly selfish, I'm sorry, I can't help it. But I am claiming my rights as his wife."

Judy turned abruptly and left. Numbly, dumbly, Rene stood and watched her go, then, after the better part of a minute, moved suddenly. She got out of the building as quickly as she could without breaking into a run. She was okay until she had come within arm's reach of her car. Then she felt as though all warmth had flowed from her, suddenly, in an instant, to disperse in some vast dark void. Her legs went rubbery. She staggered against the car, clutched desperately with both hands at its smooth surfaces. "Open the door," she said, and sounded thin and tremulant to herself, and when the car hesitated, she yelled, almost screamed, "Open the damn door!" and the door opened, and she got in.

The car said, "Please fasten your seatbelt."

She gripped the steering wheel and pressed her forehead against the backs of her hands. Her hands felt cold; her face felt hot.

"Please fasten your seatbelt."

She flung herself back in her seat, pummeled the steering wheel with her fists. She could not see for tears. Her fist collided with something less yielding than steering-wheel padding, and pain lanced her from knuckles to elbow. She clutched the throbbing hand to herself, curled around it.

"Please fasten—"

"*I know. Shut up.*"

She blindly fumbled with the seatbelt until she heard the click of the buckle. Then she wiped her eyes with her fingers and glared at the dashboard.

"*There*," she gasped. "*Happy?*"

The bluejackets helped Rene and Tim pitch camp above the slope and tested the radio for them, and then she expressed her gratitude to the United States Navy and said, "See you in six weeks."

The Navy man in charge said, "Happy collecting," and led the detail back down the slope to the waiting boat.

Watching them pick their way through the rubble, Tim sighed and shook his head. "Six whole weeks without cute sailors."

"You've always got me, big boy."

"Sorry. For starters, you're way too tall for me."

"You men. But at least you didn't say I'm too old."

Tim turned and surveyed the rocky jumble of the island. "Not that we came for the scenery, of course, but the view's scarcely worth all the effort we put into coming up."

"You'll feel better after you've collected a scorpion sting or two. Well. Shall we go ahead and get it over with?"

"Please, let's." Tim produced a metal canister from his backpack and set it on the ground. "I can't tell you what a relief it'll be not to have a dead man on my hands. I'm temperamentally unsuited for grave-robbing."

"We didn't rob a grave, Tim."

"I'm also temperamentally unsuited for smuggling. We *have* broken the rules."

"I appreciate your help."

"For chrissake, Rene. It's Dick. I wouldn't have done it for just anybody, you know."

"Me, either."

She unfolded the blade of an entrenching tool and began to dig a hole in the gritty earth. When she had finished, Tim handed her the metal canister. She gripped it firmly with both hands while he unscrewed and removed its cap. Then they knelt together over the hole, and he said, "Do you want to say something first?"

"I've been wondering all along what to say. All I've ever come up with is some lines from Housman. And an apology, I guess. 'Sorry it took us so long to get you here, Dick.' Ah, Tim. I never once told him I loved him. It just never occurred to me to say it in all those years we worked together. Then, at the end, I was made to feel I didn't have the right to say it. I didn't want to intrude."

"I'm sure he must have known. You two were best buds. Inseparables. There were *rumors*."

"That's all they ever were, just rumors."

"Of course. I never believed them for a second."

"To the best of my knowledge, he was absolutely faithful to his wife."

"Beats me how."

"Not nice, Tim."

"Well, maybe not, but even so."

"She was his wife." After a long moment, Rene added, "She just wasn't his first love. What a terrible thing, to be shut out like that. He felt cheated by fate, but she felt cheated by him."

She carefully upended the canister and poured its ashy contents into the hole. Then she recited:

"I see the country, far away,
Where I shall never stand;
The heart goes where no footstep may
Into the promised land."

"Nice," said Tim, "in a singsong kind of way. Housman, eh?"

"I would've recited it at the memorial service, but she was there, in full possession of the event, so to speak. I didn't want to make her resent us — resent *me* even more than she already did."

Tim waited a moment before taking the canister from her and returning it to his backpack. He watched Rene refill the hole. When she had finished, he said, "Well, that's that, at long damn last."

"After he died, someone suggested talking to the widow about bringing his ashes through the time portal and burying them here. I said, 'You'll never wring that concession from her.'"

"I'm surprised her children went for the idea. I'd've thought she'd've turned them against us."

"No, it was their wish. The whole time he was dying, they had to listen to him rant about not getting to come through the time portal. So they let Mom keep him on the mantelpiece. After she was gone, they brought him to me, and now I've brought him here."

"So she was happy, and now they're happy, too. Maybe she's still happy, now that she's got him for all eternity, if there is an eternity." Tim looked around in the failing light. "And I hope he's happy with his island."

She smiled wanly. "He didn't have a mystical bone in his body, but if he is anywhere, I'm sure he thinks we've taken an awful chance and are being horribly sentimental. He's probably pretty disgusted."

"And you?"

"I think we're being horribly sentimental, too."

"No, I mean, are you happy now?"

Rene gently smoothed the earth with her hand. "Is anyone ever really happy?

THE AGE OF MUD AND SLIME

It was another bright, balmy, beautiful morning, and their rocky perch above Stinktown afforded the three shipmates an excellent view. Haze and distance softened the outline of the eroded remnants of the Taconian highlands. That ancient range was now only barren hills. Its substance, reduced by wind and water to particles of grit, had washed down to form great banks of estuarine mud in the bays and inlets of the submergent coastline. Low tide at Stinktown exposed acres of glistening, iridescent muck.

It had no attraction for Walls, Berry, and McNiel. There was nothing to see out on the tidal flats except arthropods poking around in search of breakfast, scientists poking around in search of specimens, and other bored Navy men poking around just for the hell of it. Moreover, estuarine mud was glutinous and full of bubbles of gas produced by the decaying organic matter within it, so that one not only risked becoming mired with every step but also released a potent whiff of rotten eggs. The air on the heights was much sweeter.

Beyond the tidal flats was a broad, shallow bay where a Navy ship lay anchored amid its brood of auxiliary craft. The ship represented everything sailors came ashore to escape, but the consensus was that Stinktown itself had very little more to offer. Stinktown was a collection of tents and Quonset huts at the edge of a marshy area overgrown with tiny stem-like plants and infested, word had it, with centipedes the size of dachshunds. The approved pastimes available to enlisted personnel on liberty— soccer, softball, movies, virtual realities—were good for an hour or two each, if one was in the mood. There was 3.2 beer at the exchange; getting drunk on it entailed real work, but a determined man could do it. Hard liquor was difficult though not impossible for Navy men to obtain. Other illicit diversions were good only until one's stake was gone, or tempers flared, or the shore patrol hove into view. There were no women, unless one counted female officers and scientists, and there was no point in counting them. Female officers were, of course, strictly off limits. Scientists, male and female alike, belonged to an incomprehensible alien species. Each scientist seemed to be crazy in his or her own way, but all of them seemed to exist in a state of constant excitement, which naturally made them objects of both scorn and resentment to men hard-pressed to achieve even intermittent excitement.

All along the coast, longshore currents had cut the divides between neighboring valleys into headlands. It was to one of these low, steep cliffs that Walls, Berry, and McNiel had retired with their beer coolers. From atop the cliff they could look back into the drowned river valley, or down upon a narrow beach and the slender crescent of a tombolo linking an islet to the mainland, or out across the shimmering surface of the Iaepetus Ocean. They wasted little time admiring the view, however. They were men with a mission and went at their weak beer with fierce resolve. As morning passed quickly into midday, they went often, singly or en masse, to the cliff's edge and relieved themselves, to the accompaniment of much self-congratulation, onto the beach below. They had managed to get themselves somewhat beyond the feel-good stage of inebriation, if somewhat shy of the feel-nothing stage, when Berry vehemently declared that he had seen all the Silurian Period had to offer and would not give two cents for any of it.

It had been obvious to his buddies since coming ashore that he was building to an eruption. Therefore, when it came, Walls gave no sign of noticing it. He had opened his shirt, stretched himself out on a nearly level slab of rock, and pulled his cap down over his eyes. His wiry black arm dangled over the edge of the slab, and a beer dangled from his fingertips; he swung it gently, like a pendulum, keeping time as he hummed some indefinite tune. It was barely audible above the crash of waves breaking against the beach. For his part, McNiel took a long, unsatisfying pull on his beer, belched resonantly, and said, "Prehistoric times sure suck, all right."

"Five billion years of earth history," Berry said, "and this has got to be the wettest and dullest stretch of all."

"Can't even watch the grass grow," McNiel said mildly.

"What I'd give to have a dinosaur in my sights right now."

McNiel asked, "What sights?" and when Berry took aim at an invisible target with an imaginary rifle, "What dinosaur?"

"Like it goddamn matters. This is the first tour I've ever done where a seventy-two-hour liberty's actually bad for the morale of enlisted personnel."

McNiel grinned. "You think it's just bizarre coincidence the enlisted women never come ashore when the enlisted men do?"

Although he continued to swing his arm in time, Walls left off humming to say, "The Navy doesn't want you unmarried fellows getting laid. Might dull your fighting edge."

"We might's well go queer," McNiel told Berry. "That'd show the Navy."

Berry's mouth twisted with disgust. "All I know is, I've never been so bored in one place in my whole life."

"Beer's pretty lousy, too," said McNiel.

Walls interrupted his humming again. "Beer doesn't time-travel well. It's all that shaking up it gets when it comes through the hole. Knocks the fizz right out of it."

"Izzat a fact?"

"Well, it's a theory." Walls went back to humming.

"I got my own theory," McNiel said. "Some contractor back home's selling the Navy canned horse piss." Nevertheless, he sucked out the last foamy mouthful before crumpling the can and flipping it into the cooler nearest him. There was an entire stratum of crumpled cans in there; he started to dig down through it with both hands.

"I can't believe," Berry said to Walls, "this is your second tour."

"What's not to believe? Here, you get most of the perks of submarine duty and none of the claustrophobia."

"Uh oh," said McNiel. "We're about out of brew. How'd that happen?"

"Three coolers full of bad beer," Walls murmured, "divided by three desperate sailors. Take the rest of mine if you want it. I'm so full now I'll be pissing like a freight train for days to come."

"You only got one left."

"Drink it."

"Then what'll we do?"

Walls yawned. "Sober up, I guess."

"Unless," Berry said to McNiel, "you wanna haul yourself down to Stinktown and bring back another cooler. I'm so looking forward to spending more time up here, trying to get shitfaced on three-two."

McNiel actually appeared to consider it for a moment. Then he cast a doubtful eye skyward. "Be getting on towards dark by the time we got it back here." He slightly emphasized the pronoun.

Berry sighed profoundly. "Christ, I hate this place. We might as well've stayed on the ship."

"Bite your tongue," said Walls. "Yesterday, you couldn't get ashore fast enough."

"Yesterday, I just wanted to get away from the chief. Him and that new butthead jay-gee we got now."

McNiel took aim with an imaginary rifle of his own. "What do you need dinosaurs for, when fuzz-faced lieutenants infest the prehistoric world?"

Berry scowled. He had fine, curly blonde hair atop a round, smooth face. It was almost a baby face, and the scowl made him look merely petulant rather than formidable. "That little bastard won't let up on the chief about that tool belt I lost over the side. So the chief won't let up on me. It ain't like I deliberately threw the damn thing overboard. Christ Awmighty, court-martial me for losing Navy property, but stop *scolding* me like I was a little kid. You'd think it was the end of the world because a lousy tool belt fell overboard."

"Sounds to me," Walls said, "like the jay-gee's worried about the butterfly effect."

"The what?"

"It's one of the paradoxes everybody used to worry about." Walls raised himself on one elbow. "I thought they stopped giving the paradox lecture when they stopped making everybody wear those spacesuit—looking getups, but maybe young lieutenants still have to listen to it. Ah, God, those suits. Count us lucky, boys. Even after they stopped wearing the things, it used to be that if a guy so uch as farted, he had to write it up in triplicate. Damage-assessment specialists'd carry on about how one poot was going to unbalance the whole Paleozoic ecosphere. Anyway, maybe the jay-gee just saw the same science-fiction show I did. It was about this guy who travels to the dinosaur age and accidentally steps on a butterfly. The butterfly's an important link in a chain of events stretching across the eons. It's the ancestor of thousands of generations of butterflies that would've been food for animals that would've been food for other animals, et cetera. On and on, right up until it's our own distant ancestors who're going hungry and dying off before they're supposed to. When the guy gets back to his own time, everything's different. Because of that butterfly, that one little death millions of years earlier, history's been changed, Hitler won World War Two or became a painter or something. Maybe the South won the Civil War, I don't know."

"That'd sure settle your hash, Walls."

"Wouldn't it, though? So, let's say the jay-gee saw that show. Then he hears you've dropped your tool belt into the bay, and he thinks, Omigod, what if it brains the one fish that's going to give rise to amphibians and reptiles and us? He thinks, This dumb rating's maybe erased the dinosaurs and cavemen, Egypt and Rome, the Bible, everything."

Berry's scowl had deepened and his complexion had reddened as he listened, improving his resemblance to a cranky toddler. "Somebody oughta tell him the future already exists. It can't be changed."

"How do you know? Who says it can't be changed?"

"The scientists. Physics."

Walls laughed. "Now what the hell do you know about physics? For that matter, what do physicists know? They used to say time travel was impossible, and had the figures to prove it. Then they found a hole in time big enough to steer a ship through. Zap, and here we are, having the time of our lives four hundred million years before we're even born!"

"Well, notice," said Berry, "we *ain't* having to do it dressed up like spacemen. And I don't think the scientists worry much about killing something they shouldn't. They ain't been making pets out of the specimens they collect."

"Maybe," said Walls, "it's like the lottery. Only one ticket in ten million matters. The rest are just waste paper. The odds must be a trillion to one somebody's actually going to catch and cut up the animal that's the linchpin of our entire history."

McNiel scratched his jaw thoughtfully. "Maybe the animals that're part of your chain of events *can't* get killed before they're supposed to. Like, they have to survive."

"Sounds too much like predestination to me."

"I have got to remember every word of this," Berry said with fine sarcasm, "so the next time the chief gets after me, I can talk rings around him."

Nobody spoke again for several minutes. Berry stood glowering at the sea. Walls hummed. McNiel stretched out on his side and drank the last beer. When he had finished, he began tracing a pattern on the ground with his finger. He said, "This isn't even real dirt."

"What?" Berry looked wonderingly at him.

"This place—this time, it doesn't even have real dirt." McNiel took a pinch of grit between his fingertips, rolled it there for a moment, flicked it away. "It's just sand. No organic matter in it at all." He saw the look Berry was giving him. "I was just thinking, there's probably not more'n a ton of decent topsoil in the whole world right now."

"This is the age of mud and slime," Berry said, "and I can't believe I volunteered to come to it because I thought it'd be exciting."

"That does it." Walls sat up, stretched, and swung his legs over the edge of the slab. "If you're about to launch into a whole new cycle of grousing, I'm heading back. Coming, Mac?"

"I'm not sure I can get up from here."

After a while, however, they noticed that the tide was coming in and how the shadows had deepened and lengthened across the valley. It really was time to go. They lined up to send a final golden cascade onto the beach, then shouldered the coolers and began picking their way through a jumble of stony debris. It was not an especially hazardous or even an arduous trek unless one were burdened with a beer cooler or awash with the beer itself, or both. Finally, sweaty and winded, they paused to rest on a shelf or rock that formed the rim of a muddy basin. The basin drained into the marsh through a gap directly opposite the men; they had arrived at the edge or life's domain. The shelf sat atop a layer of porous rock from which water seeped. A film of algae covered the damp rocks. Scum floated in shallow pools that had collected in the basin, and each pool bordered a dense, bristling mat of greenery barely an inch thick. A band of desiccated plant matter around the basin's sides showed where life had fatally overreached itself.

Berry suddenly cried out, "Hey!" and pointed at something on the ground before him. "Come look at this."

Walls and McNiel looked. Not far from Berry's foot, two millipedes writhed, entangled, on the detritus. It was hard to tell how long the creatures were or where one ended and the other began. They had purplish brown segmented bodies as big around as a man's thumb and scores of rippling orange legs.

"Prehistoric monsters going at it tooth and nail," Berry said grandly, "in a battle to the finish."

Walls shook his head. "No. They're making baby millipedes."

"First you're an expert on physics and now you know all about bugs. Where'd you get so educated, Walls?"

"Look at 'em. What else could they be doing?"

"Trying to kill and eat one another."

Walls shook his head again. "They're plant-eaters. That much I do know."

"You'd know it, too," McNiel told Berry, "if you weren't always jerking off in briefings."

"Get stuffed, Mac."

"Even the big ones are plant-eaters," said Walls. "Can you imagine a millipede as long as a cow?"

Berry snorted derisively. "You believe that stuff? You ever seen one that big? You, Mac?"

"No, but they say they're around."

Berry laughed outright at that. "Those scientists started that rumor just to keep us poor ignorant sailors from tracking up their precious swamp."

McNiel made a shushing sound. "It's kind of fascinating," he said in a low voice. "So that's what sex is. I almost forgot, it's been such a long time."

"What're you whispering for?"

"How'd you like someone yelling when *you're* having sex? I'm glad somebody around here's getting a little."

"Christ," Berry said, "even the goddamn bugs here have more fun than us." He reached down suddenly, scooped up a flat rock in his left hand, and held it menacingly over the oblivious millipedes.

"Hey," said Walls, "don't do that."

"Hell, Walls, they're only bugs."

"Just the same, don't."

"What's the matter, you scared of that butterfly effect?"

"Maybe."

"Well, I say it's a load of crap. Those scientists probably started killing and cutting up everything they could get their hands on the minute they came through the hole. Suits or no suits. They sure's hell started sometime. They've been doing it for years now, and it hasn't made a damn bit of difference in the twenty-first century. Not one damn bit."

Walls shrugged. "Not that we know of, anyway."

"What's that supposed to mean?"

Walls straightened and folded his arms across his chest. "Just a thought I had. What if—what if every time they kill a trilobite, or dig up some puny little plant, or scoop up another sample of plankton, they do change history? I mean, *every* time. For every single little premature death they cause here in the Silurian, the future becomes something other than what it was. And how would we ever know?"

"We'd go back," Berry said, "and see how different everything was."

"No. We'd go back, and everything would seem perfectly normal to us. We're from the future that's always being changed. We're inseparably part of it, so, if it changes, we change right along with it. Moment to moment, on and on. Who knows, the first people to come through the hole might not've been human beings at all. They might've been the intelligent descendants of—of raccoons, or squirrels, until something happened here in the Silurian that took raccoons and squirrels out of the running. Originally, there might not've been apes to give rise to human beings. Then something happened to change that. Or maybe the changes are a lot more subtle. Mac, instead of joining the Navy, you suddenly find yourself farming back in Kansas."

"You're beginning to creep me out," McNiel said.

"Maybe," Walls said, "maybe I never meet a certain girl back in Houston, so I can't very well marry her, and she and I can't very well have a baby. Maybe I marry somebody else, or don't get married at all. Maybe I don't even get born." He smiled at Berry. "What could your life become if you drop that rock?"

"What an utter load of crap!" Berry said, but the hand holding the rock wavered.

"Go ahead and do it if you're going to."

"Aah." Berry lowered the rock. "This is stupid."

"Come on, Berry, let's go." McNiel gave him a comradely slap on the arm. "Haven't eaten since breakfast, and I'm getting real hungry."

"Me, too," said Walls.

"Yeah. Me, too." Berry weighed the rock in his hand, then cast it aside. It clattered along the limestone shelf. They saw it go over the edge and heard it land wetly in the basin.

"Ah, God," Walls said in a hushed voice, "now you've done it!"

"What?"

Walls peered intently at Berry, drew back with a perplexed expression on his face, and looked significantly at McNiel. A frown slowly creased McNiel's forehead.

"Well?" Berry demanded. He looked from Walls to McNiel and back to Walls. There was the faintest note of unease in his voice when he spoke again. "What is it?"

They continued to stare at him for several seconds. Then Walls cleared his throat, grimacing as though it hurt to do so or as though he did not want to say what he was about to say, and solemnly asked, "Berry, weren't you a raccoon just a minute ago?"

For the space of a heartbeat the only sound was a gentle plash of water from below. Then Berry closed his mouth with an audible click of back teeth and lunged at his two shipmates as they retreated laughing across the shelf.

"You assholes! Assholes!"

"That look in your eyes," Walls gasped, "that quaver in your voice—"

All of them were still too full of beer for sustained running about. They collapsed onto the limestone. They caught their breath.

Berry glared hard and said, "Very funny. Ha, ha. Assholes."

Walls grinned, looked around at the coolers, sighed. "We better get going. On the count of three, everybody. One. Two. Three."

Neither Berry nor McNiel moved, or even tried.

"But, fellows," Walls said, "we've still got—" he glanced at his watch "—forty hours and thirty-seven minutes of liberty left, and, ooh la—" he kissed his fingertips "—Stinktown by night!"

McNiel laughed. Berry tried not to laugh but laughed anyway. It was sharp, bitter, and short-lived, but it was laughter nonetheless.

THE WIND OVER THE WORLD

The attendant barely looked up from the clipboard cradled in the crook of his arm when Leveritt came in. The room was devoid of personality, but just as she entered through one door, a second man dressed in a lab coat went out through a door directly opposite, and in the instant before it swung shut, she glimpsed the room beyond—brightly lit, full of gleaming surfaces—and heard or thought that she heard a low sound like a faint pop of static or the breaking of waves against a shore. She shuddered as an electric thrill of excitement passed through her.

"Please stretch out on the gurney there." The man with the clipboard continued writing as he spoke. "You can stow your seabag on the rack underneath."

Leveritt did as he said. She said, "I feel like I'm being prepped for surgery."

"We don't want you to black out and fall and hurt yourself." He finished writing, came around the end of the gurney to her, and turned the clipboard to show her the printed form. "This," he said, offering her his pen, "is where you log out of the present. Please sign on the line at the bottom there."

Leveritt's hand trembled as she reached for the pen. She curled her fingers into a fist and clenched it tightly for a second. She gave the attendant an apologetic smile. "I'm just a little nervous." She tried to show him that she really was just a little nervous by expanding the smile into a grin; it felt brittle and hideous on her face. "I did volunteer for this," she told him. I am more excited than scared to be doing this, she told herself.

The attendant smiled quickly, professionally. "Even volunteers have the right to be nervous. Try to relax. We've done this hundreds of times now, and there's nothing to it. Ah!"

His exclamation was by way of greeting a second attendant, so like him that Leveritt felt she would be unable to tell them apart were she to glance away for a moment, who escorted a slight figure dressed in new-looking safari clothes and carrying, instead of the high-powered rifle that would have completed his ensemble, a seabag and a laptop. He stowed the bag and climbed onto the gurney next to Leveritt's without being told, signed the log with a flourish, and lay back smiling. He turned his face toward Leveritt and said, "Looks like we're traveling companions—time-traveling companions!" He talked fast, as though afraid he would run out of breath before he finished saying what he had to say. "Allow me to introduce myself—Ed Morris."

"I'm Bonnie Leveritt."

"Pleased to meet you, Miz Leveritt—or is it Doctor?"

She wondered if he could utter sentences not punctuated with dashes. "Miz," she said, "working on Doctor. I'm on my way to join a field team from Texas A and M."

One of the attendants consulted his wristwatch and nodded to the other, and each picked up a loaded syringe. The man looming over Leveritt gave her that quick, professional smile again. "This is to keep you from going into shock."

She had no particular horror of needles but turned away, nevertheless, to watch Morris, who lay squinting against the glare of the fluorescent lights. She heard him grunt softly as the needle went into his arm.

"It'll be another few minutes," said Leveritt's attendant. He and his twin left. Leveritt and Morris waited.

After a minute or so, he asked her, "How you holding up?"

"Fine." Her voice sounded strange to her, thick, occluded, like a heavy smoker's. She cleared her throat and spoke the word again; improvement was arguable. "Actually," she confessed, "I'm nervous as hell. This is my first time. It wouldn't be so bad if I didn't have to lie here waiting."

"Supplies go through first—we're down on the priority list, below soap and toilet paper. My first time, I was nervous as hell, too. Nobody gives people in my line of work credit for much imagination. Except—" he made a breathless kind of chuckle "—when it comes to creative accounting. Yeah, I'm one of the bean-counters. But let me tell you—the night before my first time, I didn't sleep a wink. Not a wink. I kept imagining all sorts of things that might go wrong—plus, it all seemed so unreal, it was all so thrilling—and it was going to happen to me. Man! Oh, sure, the concept's more exciting than the reality. There's not much to where we're headed—a little moss and a lot of mud. Beats me why they couldn't've made a hole into some more interesting time period."

"I suppose that depends on your definition of interesting. Besides, as I understand it, they didn't make the hole, they sort of found it. We're lucky it didn't open up on somewhere we couldn't go or wouldn't want to."

"You mean, like my hometown—Dallas?"

Leveritt smiled; she was from Fort Worth. "Worse. For all but the few most recent hundred millions of years, the Earth's been pretty inhospitable—poisonous atmosphere, too much ultraviolet light, things like that."

"Spoken like a true scientist!"

"Not quite a full-blown one yet," she said, "but I guess I've got pedantry down."

"Ah. Well, anyway, as I was saying—I was nervous before my first time. Scared, in fact. You might not think it to look at me," and he paused long enough for her to realize that she was now to take a good look at him, so she did, "but I am no shrinking violet. I have a real active life-style—mountain climbing, sky diving. I guess I like heights."

Leveritt was willing to give Morris the benefit of the doubt, but he was a balding little fortyish man whom she could not imagine working his way up a sheer rock face. Dressed in his great-white-hunter outfit, he lay clutching the laptop to his narrow chest, drumming his middle, ring, and little fingers on the case. He looked as calm as though he were waiting for an elevator, but he also looked like what he was, an accountant.

"Still," he went on, "it's one thing to jump out of a plane at ten thousand feet—another to jump through a hole in time. Straight out of the twenty-first century—straight into the prehistoric past! So, I didn't get any sleep. The next day, when it came time for me to make the jump, I was a wreck—all because I was scared, see. But I hid the fact I was a wreck—and you know why? Because I was even more scared that if anybody found out, I wouldn't get to make the jump—getting to do it meant that much to me."

Leveritt gave him another, more heartfelt smile. "It does to me, too. But was it rough? The jump itself? I ask everyone I meet who's done it."

Morris screwed up his face and gestured dismissively. "It's no worse'n hitting a speed bump when you're driving a little too fast. Oh, sure, you hear sometimes about people who got bounced around kind of hard, but—speaking from personal experience—I honestly think I could've walked right out of the jump station afterwards with nothing more'n a headache and upset stomach. It was nothing. Now I'm less nervous about making the jump than I am about talking funding to this group of entomologists when I get there. Uh, you're not an entomologist yourself, are you?"

"Geologist."

"You ever tried to talk to an entomologist about anything but bugs?"

"Not knowingly, no."

"Then you've never had to pretend to listen to whatever gas some guy wants to vent—"

Leveritt had to laugh. "You obviously have never dated some guys!"

"Ah?" Morris frowned. "No. I sure haven't." Then he got it, or got part of it, anyway, and made another breathless chuckle. "Anyhow, I have to go talk to these entomologists, and they never can—I deal in the definite, see. All they can talk about is the great contributions they're making to science—how vital their work is. I know they're making contributions to science—that's why they're there, right? They understand all about bugs. I understand all about money—and never the twain shall meet . . . . "

Leveritt found herself tuning out the sense of the words, but she could not tune out the sound of them. The drugs were taking effect; she wanted to relax and drift, but Morris' voice would not let her. She closed her eyes. Scarcely five seconds later, the attendants suddenly returned, one of them announced, "Time to go, folks," and Leveritt's gurney struck the door sharply as it lurched into motion. The air in the jump station had an unpleasant tang to it. Leveritt saw people moving briskly about, heard them muttering to one another, heard that low sound of static or surf again. A technician seated behind a console said, "One minute to next transmission."

"Doesn't matter which one of us goes through first, does it?" Morris asked his attendant, who answered with a shake of his head. The little man grinned at Leveritt. "Then I'll go first and wait for you on the other side."

"No. Please, I need to get this over with. Let me go first."

"Well, guys—you heard the lady."

Leveritt's attendant pushed her gurney quickly past Morris', past a metal railing, onto the sending-receiving platform. He lightly touched her arm with the back of his hand. "Have a nice trip."

"Thanks."

"Deep breaths, now," he said as he stepped back off the platform.

"Stand by to send," said the technician at the console. "Five seconds. Four."

Leveritt inhaled deeply.

"Three."

Morris caught her eye through the bars of the railing. She was touched by and grateful for his wink of encouragement.

"Two."

She started to exhale. Everything turned to white light.

The Navy doctor held her eye open between his thumb and forefinger and directed the beam from a penlight into it. She moved her tongue in her mouth, swallowed, and managed to say, "Where'm I?"

"Sickbay."

"I made it? To the Silurian?"

The doctor put away the penlight. "Now, what do you think?"

Leveritt moved her head experimentally and at once regretted it. When the pain had receded, she carefully took stock. She was still on the gurney. There were exposed pipes overhead and a muffled throb of machinery. The ship, she thought, I'm on the ship, in the Silurian, and after a second or two she realized that she was disappointed. She had wondered if being in Silurian time would feel somehow different. Thus far, it felt just like a hangover.

The doctor held up a knuckley finger in front of her face. "I want you to follow my finger with your eyes. Don't move your head."

It hurt her even to think about moving her head again. She watched the finger move to the left and back to the right. She said, "My head's killing me."

"You'll be fine in a little while. You're just a little shaken up. Here." He gave her two aspirin tablets and some water in a paper cup. "Stay on the gurney till those take effect. Then we'll see about getting you up on your feet."

"How soon can I get ashore?"

"We generally like to keep new arrivals under observation for at least six hours." Leveritt groaned when he said that, and he gave her a mildly reproachful look. "You can only get ashore by boat, and the next one doesn't leave until late this afternoon."

"It's just that I've been looking forward to this so long."

"Uh huh. Well, the Silurian Period's still got five or ten million years to run. You aren't going to miss out on it."

The door opened behind him, and a khaki-clad officer leaned in and asked, "Doctor White, may I talk to her now?" Visible in the passageway was an unhappy-looking man in civilian clothes.

"These gentlemen," said the doctor, "have some questions they want to ask you. Feel up to it?"

Before she could reply, the officer said, "Just a couple of routine questions."

"Sure."

The officer moved quickly toward the gurney with the civilian in tow. Doctor White said, "Miz Leveritt, this is Mister Hales—"

"How do you do?" said the officer, rather too impatiently, she thought.

"—and this is Doctor Cutsinger." The civilian slightly inclined his head in greeting and repeated her name. "The lieutenant is from our operations department. Doctor Cutsinger is one of our civilian engineers."

"Physicist," Cutsinger said, and smiled tightly.

Leveritt tried to sound good-natured. "I was hoping you were the welcoming committee. Isn't anybody going to welcome me to the Paleozoic?" Evidently, no one was. Lieutenant Hales regarded her as though her show of good-naturedness were somehow in poor taste. Cutsinger continued to look unhappy. The doctor nodded at the two men and went out, closing the door behind himself. Leveritt repressed a sigh of bafflement and said, "Well, gentlemen, ask away."

Hales said, "Miz Leveritt."

"Lieutenant?"

He was obviously uncertain as to how to proceed. The lower part of his expression suddenly twisted, rearranging itself into an approximation of a smile; at the same time, a frown intensified the upper part. Considered with his deep-set eyes and hook nose, the effect was ghastly and alarming. Finally, he said, "The, ah, experience of time-travel is never exactly the same for anyone. We like to find out, ah, make a point of finding out how it was for each person each time. Can you describe your experience in detail?"

Leveritt's eyes met Cutsinger's. He blinked and shifted his gaze to a point slightly to the right of her ear. She refocused on Hales and said, "I'm afraid there were no details, just a blinding flash of light."

Hales seemed disappointed by her answer. "What about before the jump? Did anything in the jump station strike you as unusual?"

If you weren't so intense, Leveritt thought, that question would be funny. "It was all unusual to me, because, as you surely must know already, this was my first jump."

"Of course. We want your impressions, though. Anything you can tell us, anything at all. Before the flash of light, when they took you into the jump station—you and Ed Morris. Do you know him well?"

She saw something shift in Cutsinger's face as he glanced at the lieutenant, saw his expression of general unhappiness sharpen into one of very particular contempt. To the oblivious Hales she said, "I don't know him at all. We met a few minutes before the jump, and he talked my ear off. I think you'd do better to ask him these questions. As you surely must also know, Mister Morris'd made at least one jump before this. He can tell you if anything was unusual or not. As for me—" she swung her legs over the edge of the gurney and sat up "—if I'm going to answer any more questions, it's going to be in an upright position."

After a second's hesitation, she slid off the gurney, onto her feet. Cutsinger said, "Are you all right?"

"A little rubbery in the knees, like I just came in off the jogging trail. Otherwise—" She stepped away from the gurney, quickly stepped back, leaned on it for support, admitted, "Still a little wobbly." She locked eyes with the lieutenant. "What is it in particular you're driving at? I somehow can't help feeling you know something and are dying to know if I know it, too."

Hales turned the full force of his grimace on her again, and she realized with a jolt that he now intended it to be a look of reassurance. "As I said, these are just routine questions."

And possibly excepting my six-year-old nephew, you are the worst, the most unconvincing liar I've ever known. She almost said it aloud. What stopped her was the thought of all the time and effort she had put into getting this far—to a room, as she saw it, adjoining the prehistoric past—and how much farther there was to go. Fist on hip, she waited.

Hales, however, clearly was at a loss. He turned to Cutsinger, who, no less clearly, was close to losing his temper. "Anything you can think of to ask her?"

"I told you there was no point to this!"

"I wish to God," said Leveritt, "one of you would tell me what this is all about." Neither man spoke. "Fine. Have it your way. But if I don't get out of this room, I'm going to go insane. The doctor said I wouldn't be able to go ashore for hours, but if you're through, I'd at least like to take a look outside. Okay? Please?"

Cutsinger brushed past Hales. He said, "permit me," and offered Leveritt his arm.

A romantic, she thought, taking it.

"I think," Hales said, "Miz Leveritt had better remain in sickbay."

Not looking back at him, Cutsinger said, "Take a flying leap."

"Master-at-arms!"

A bluejacket with a sidearm suddenly filled the doorway. Cutsinger sighed, shrugged, and said, "Sorry," as he directed Leveritt to a chair.

"I'm sorry, too," said Hales, "but this is a United States Navy ship, and the rules of security are in force. Miz Leveritt, I want you to understand that this interview is confidential."

"So much for the subtle approach!" Cutsinger said sourly.

Hales ignored him. "You're not to repeat any part of our conversation to anybody or make any record of it without express authorization. Any breach—"

"I'm sure she gets the idea, Lieutenant."

"Not at all," said Leveritt. "What am I not supposed to talk about?"

"We have a situation," Cutsinger said quickly, before Hales could open his mouth to answer her, "an unprecedented one, I might add, which is why Hales here's so rattled, why he's handling it in such a ham-handed manner. Ham-headed, too." The lieutenant's mouth did open now, in a threat display. Cutsinger met it with a glower and continued talking. "About all he's really going to accomplish by invoking security is to make it impossible for you to do the work you came here to do."

Leveritt gave Hales an even look. "I didn't come all this way just to fight the Navy."

"There're some thousands of people living and working here," said Hales, "and in the interest of general morale, we have got to keep rumors and misinformation from spreading and panic from breaking out."

"You're the one who's panicked! Either leave her alone or tell her. She'll hear all about it soon enough."

"Don't underestimate Navy security," Hales said stiffly.

That elicited a harsh laugh from Cutsinger. "I bet you anything it was all over the ship inside of five minutes. I bet you it's already gotten ashore, some version of it, anyhow. All you're doing is putting Miz Leveritt in a very awkward position. She'll be the only person in the whole expedition who won't have an opinion on what everybody else is talking about."

"Master-at-arms, Doctor Cutsinger is needed back at the jump station."

"Aye, aye, sir." The bluejacket stepped to Cutsinger's side.

"Tell her," Cutsinger said over his shoulder as he went out, "for God's sake, tell her."

The bluejacket closed the door behind himself, and Hales said, "Well." He looked at Leveritt; his features relaxed; he almost smiled a real smile. "Please accept my apologies on Doctor Cutsinger's behalf. As a civilian aboard a Navy ship, he naturally finds working under Navy supervision irksome at times."

"By supervision, do you mean armed guard?"

"I mean—I am not a martinet or a horse's patoot." He took a step toward the door. "Please come with me. I have enough to worry about without you going insane."

He led her down the passageway and opened a heavy steel door at the end of it. As Leveritt stepped through the doorway and onto a catwalk, a breeze touched her face and ruffled her hair. Her first, quick 180-degree survey took in the fact that the ship and some lesser vessels lay off a rocky coast. She gripped the railing with both hands and inhaled the scent of sea salt and the faintly oily smell of the ship. From a deck overhanging the catwalk came the sounds of a helicopter warming up its motor and spinning its blades. Below, waves smacked noisily against the hull. The mid-morning sun was behind the ship, in whose great angular shadow the water was blue-black, almost slate-colored. Close by, two auxiliary craft rode at anchor, and beyond them a glittering expanse of blue-green water stretched to a line of sea cliffs. Even as she stared, transfixed by the sight of that shore, another, even smaller craft—not a Navy vessel at all, but a sailboat—came into view around the headland. Against the somber cliffs, its sail looked like a blazing fire. "Oh, my." She breathed the words.

Hales had followed her onto the catwalk. He rested his elbows on the railing and did not look at her when he spoke. "Doctor Cutsinger did tell me there'd be no point in questioning you. If there'd been any way to find out what we need to know without actually asking you . . . . "

She realized after a moment that what he was saying must be important, but it took an effort of will to turn her attention from the Silurian vista, and she was scarcely able to say, "I beg your pardon?"

"He also talked me out of sending you right back to the twenty-first century. He may have talked me out of confining you to the ship until we get this, this situation straightened out. "

Now Leveritt could not take her eyes off him. "I swear to you, I don't know anything and won't talk to anybody about anything, please just let me go off into the hinterlands and collect rocks like I'm supposed to."

Hales almost smiled again. "He said I'm treating everyone here like children. I'm not trying to, I'm really not. I see his point." He made a gesture that seemed meant to take in everything around them. "This is the greatest thing since the moon landings, and a lot less exclusive. Every single person here, Navy as well as civilian, wants to be here and volunteered to be here. Doctor Cutsinger's view is, we're all grownups and deserve to be told the truth like grownups. All the truth all the time."

Leveritt asked, "And what's your view?" and when he did not answer immediately, "Or doesn't the Navy let you have one?"

"Right the second time. All of us here, we're an extension of our nation. There're all these little communities of scientists scattered about, and there's the Navy, delivering supplies, providing transport, holding things together. The Silurian Earth's a United States possession, Miz Leveritt, American territory, and the Navy's here to guard our national interests. It is in the national interest that the Navy decides what is classified matter. Only persons who need to know about classified matter to perform an official job for the Navy are entrusted with the information. That's rule number one, and it leaves you out. Rule number two is, persons to whom classified matter is entrusted are responsible for protecting it against unauthorized disclosure. That hems me in."

"Fine. What're you going to do with me?"

"Escort you back to sickbay. Later, I hope, see you on your way to go collect rocks."

It was late in the short Silurian day when Hales guided Leveritt through the ship to the boat bay. From a platform above that noisy grotto, she watched as the last supplies were loaded, then, with a nod to the lieutenant, descended to the boat. The coxswain helped her aboard. Hales surprised her by climbing down after her. He gave no sign that he heard her when she asked, "Are you going to keep watch on me from now on?" She found a seat amidships; he gave her a nod as he took the one next to hers but said nothing.

She was too excited, however, to resent his presence. She had had sleep, a shower, and her first food in almost twenty-four hours, and the morning's frustrations and mystifications were falling away behind her. When she ran her eye over the neatly stowed boxes and crates, the words BATHROOM TISSUE prompted something too fleeting to be called a memory. The bay's gates opened. Leveritt looked up, caught a glimpse of someone who could have been Cutsinger on the platform, and glanced at Hales to gauge his reaction. His attention, though, was directed forward rather than upward. The boat slid out, sliced across the ship's lengthening, darkening shadow, and emerged suddenly into sunlight. She gazed shoreward, at the drowned valley's rocky walls, and felt that at last she truly was entering Paleozoic time. Not even the sight of the pier, jutting out from the near shore below a cluster of Quonset huts and tents, dispelled the feeling. She spared the ship a single backward glance. Everything in its shadow, everything aboard it, contained by it—even the air circulating through it and the seawater sloshing within the confines of its boat bay—belonged to the twenty-first century. She looked shoreward again and thought of the great steel monster no more.

Several boats, including a tiny blue-hulled sailboat, were tied up at the pier. Indistinct human figures waiting there gradually resolved themselves into a small party of Navy men in tropical khakis and two civilians who stood apart both from them and from each other. Both civilians wore white suits, but one man was short, stout, and sunburnt, and the other was tall as well as thickset, tanned rather than burnt, and had a Panama hat with a purple hat band set at a rakish angle atop his squarish head. It was clear from his bearing that he considered himself to be a vision. Leveritt laughed when she saw him, waved, and called out, "Rob! Rob Brinkman!"

Brinkman waved back, and when the boat had been tied up he reached down and offered Leveritt his enormous brown hand. She was a medium-sized woman, heavier in the hips than she cared to be, but he seemed to lift her right out of the boat and onto the pier with only minimal assistance from her. His grin and voice were as big as the rest of him. "Welcome to the Silurian!"

Leveritt hugged him. She could not quite encircle his torso with her arms. "It's about time someone here said that to me. What a suit! What a hat! Is this what you wear on collecting trips now?"

"Only if pretty grad students are going along."

Behind her, somebody peevishly said, "I'm supposed to meet Ed Morris. I'm Michael Diehl, from the San Diego Natural History Museum."

As Brinkman stepped around Leveritt to ask a bluejacket to hand up her gear, she saw the other civilian peering anxiously into the boat, as though he expected to spot Ed Morris trying to hide from him among the cargo. The party of Navy men had got immediately to work unloading the boat, and their interest in Diehl did not extend beyond his keeping out of their way. Hales, however, introduced himself and said, "I regret that Mister Morris is unable to come ashore at this time."

"Eh? Why not?"

"Side-effects of the jump."

"Oh. Well, you could've radioed that piece of information and saved me an hour's wait for nothing. Could've saved yourself a boat ride, too."

Hales noticed Leveritt watching him. He favored Diehl with a mild version of his frown-above, smile-below expression. "Boat rides're what the Navy's all about."

Brinkman turned with Leveritt's seabag on his shoulder and said, "Okay," and the two of them walked away. The pier came straight off the camp's main thoroughfare, which was paved with metal matting and lined with huts. Tents had been erected along intersecting streets. There was a good deal of pedestrian traffic, both civilian and Navy. Brinkman led Leveritt past supply, generator, and administration buildings, the dispensary, the exchange, the mess—"the Navy part of camp," he told her, adding, "But we get to use the facilities, of course." Civilian personnel lived in and worked out of a group of tents he called the suburbs. "Our people're already upriver, so, tonight, you'll be the guest of a bunch of centipede enthusiasts."

"How charming."

"It'd probably be a good idea to shake out your shoes in the morning. Want some dinner?"

"I think all I want tonight," she said, "is to walk a little way past the last row of tents, where I can see pure and unadulterated Paleozoic."

"Care for a guide?"

She gave him a sidelong mock-wary lock. "Not if it's some notorious lady-killer in an ice-cream suit."

Brinkman laughed. "Just make sure you keep the camp on your left when you go out, or you'll wind up in the marsh. And don't go out too far, either. And don't stay up too late."

"Yes, Mother."

"We leave right after breakfast, and around here breakfast is at sunrise."

He showed her where she was to spend the night. None of his centipede enthusiasts was about, so Leveritt put her seabag just inside the door, bade him good night, and with no further ado set out on her walk. Not far beyond the last row of tents, the ground rose sharply; the going was not especially rough, but she did not push her luck—the sun was going down fast, and she did not fancy making her way across unfamiliar ground in the dark. Just as she reached a ledge from which she could look down into the camp, a thin bugle call announced the commencement of the evening colors ceremony. Electric lights illuminated the camp, and she had no trouble spotting the flagpole. There came a second bugle call, followed by the national anthem. The flag sank slowly out of sight behind a Quonset hut. Out on the water, the shadow of the Earth itself swallowed up the ship. Leveritt sat down on warm smooth rock, lay back to look up at the purpling, then blackening, sky, and finally felt herself part of Silurian reality, in Paleozoic time and space. Contentment filled her.

How long she remained thus, she did not know. The moon rose, the unrecognizable stars slightly shifted their positions. Eventually, she became aware that the rock had cooled without getting any softer. She got up and walked slowly toward camp.

As she came among the tents, she heard voices and music from some of them and noticed that traffic had thinned. No insects orbited the lights, unexpectedly reminding her that no birds had wheeled and screeched over the bay. She knew, of course, that the Silurian was too early for birds and insects—flying insects, at least—but until this moment she had not appreciated their absence.

Just before she reached her tent, she saw Michael Diehl approaching. His face held a sickly cast, and he appeared to have his entire attention focused on the ground before him. When she started to go inside, however, he called out, "Excuse me, these tents're reserved for the San Diego Natural History Museum."

"Rob Brinkman said there's an extra cot. He's the—"

"Brinkman. Texas A and M." Diehl was near enough now for her to catch a whiff of what he breathed out. His red complexion, she decided, was not wholly the result of too much sun.

"We're on our way upriver in the morning," she said, "so it'll only be—"

"You're the woman who came in on the boat with Lieutenant Hales. Leveritt, isn't it?"

"Yes. And your name's Diehl. Look, if there's a problem, I'm sure Doctor Brinkman can—"

"You made the jump this morning. With Ed Morris."

"Yes." She said it quickly and said no more, not wanting to be cut off again.

Diehl glanced to left and right. "I think you better come with me. I know where we can have a drink and talk in private."

"Um, thank you for the offer, but I'm very tired, and I need to—"

"You're the only one I can talk to about what's happened to Ed Morris!" There was a note of pleading in the whiskey-scented voice. "And I'm the only one you can talk to."

"What? What's happened to Ed Morris?"

Diehl looked closely at her. "You don't know? No, I can see you don't. You didn't really see it happen. I guess nobody really saw it. And Hales didn't tell you, did he? No, of course he didn't. He laid that Navy security stuff on me, too. Tried to hand me some crap, and when I raised holy hell and threatened to go straight to his commanding officer—"

"What about Ed Morris?"

"There was an accident! Come on, let's go where we can talk. We're too close to the Navy here."

She hesitated as he walked past, got as far into a protest as "I don't think I'm supposed," then followed him back the way she had just come, up the slope behind the camp, to the ledge. Diehl wiped the mouth of a small flask on his coat sleeve and offered it to her. She declined to accept. He took a drink, gasped, and replaced the screw top.

"Ed Morris," he said, "didn't come through the hole today like he was supposed to."

"What do you mean?"

"Just what I said. Hales told me—after I made him tell me—Morris made the jump one minute after you, but he never arrived here. He's gone. Lost."

"Gone, lost—where?"

Diehl shook his head. "They don't know."

"But—"

"They don't know! They honestly don't. Maybe it was some glitch in the machinery that did it, or sunspots. Maybe some quirk of the hole itself, something they don't know about. I frankly don't think they know much more about the hole now than they did in the beginning."

"But how do you *lose* somebody?"

"You gotta remember what a strange thing the hole is. When they first stumbled across it, all they knew was, here's this strange thing. This anomaly. They sent in robot probes to get specimens, photograph everything in sight. By and by, they figured out what they had was this doorway into the past. But it didn't just open up on a place on a day. It wasn't that stable. There was a sort of flutter, and it caused what they call spatial drift and temporal spread. So, two probes might go through together on our side, the twenty-first-century side, but come out miles and years apart on the Silurian side. That's why they built the jump stations. They built one of them aboard that ship and pushed the ship through the hole so they could keep things synchronized on both sides of the hole. It all worked perfectly, until today. Today, Ed Morris may've been plunked down anywhere. Far inland or far out to sea. He may've arrived a hundred years ago or a hundred years from now."

"Alive?" She was barely able to ask it.

"Not for long. Not unless he's a helluva lot smarter and luckier'n Robinson Crusoe. And if he was hurt—"

"How awful. That poor man."

"If he was really lucky, he never knew what happened. Never felt a thing. Hales says he may just've been scattered across four hundred million years."

Leveritt felt a chill of horror, though she could not have said what being scattered across four hundred million years might entail.

"He says everything's working again," Diehl went on, "they're sending and receiving again, but until they figure out what went wrong—" He abandoned the sentence to take another drink. "Everything we use here, food, supplies, it's all gotta come through the hole. And the hole—"

Leveritt knew what he was about to say and said it for him. "The hole's the only way home."

"You got that right! The only way!"

She looked upward. The moon was slightly higher in the sky than when she had seen it—how long before? Half an hour? Then, she had experienced happiness greater than any other she could remember. Now, she felt oppressed, weighed down.

They were silent for almost a minute. Then, as Diehl tilted his head back to drink, Leveritt said, "Well, what can we do about it?"

Diehl smacked his lips. "Indeed, what? Doesn't seem right. It isn't right. A man dies, vanishes—whatever's applicable in this case. He's got no family or friends far's I can find out, and there's nothing to bury. And nobody's supposed to talk about him, so he won't even get a memorial service. Not even if he did have family and friends."

"M-mister Diehl, I don't think we should—"

"It isn't right! Know what really sets us apart from the animals? Never mind what religion says about souls. Souls're just puffs of air. The only thing makes a man's death meaningful is remembrance. Without remembrance, he's just a wind that blew over the world and never left a trace."

"Mister Diehl! I don't think we should talk about him any more. I don't think we should meet again, either."

"Huh? Why not?"

"If Lieutenant Hales finds out we've had this conversation and that I know about Ed Morris—"

"To hell with Hales! Don't be scared of him, stand up to him like I did!"

"He may not be able to make trouble for you," Leveritt said impatiently, "but I think he can make a lot for me. It's already occurred to him to either send me back home or lock me up. Will you give me your word you won't let him find out?"

"Bastard's not gonna hear a thing from me. And if you're upriver, he can't bother you any."

"I wish I could be sure of that. I'm—listen, from the moment I learned about the hole, I wanted to join this expedition. I worked hard to get here. Now that I am here . . . . "

Her voice trailed off in a sob; her throat constricted as she sensed impending, insupportable loss, and tears gathered on her eyelashes. She clenched her jaw and fists and held on, somehow, to her composure. Beside her, Diehl coughed and said in his thickened voice, "Still some left, how 'bout it?" and when she had blinked away the tears, she saw him holding the flask out to her again.

"No," she said, "thank you."

"You ever drink?"

"Hardly ever."

"Same here," and he raised the flask to his lips.

"Well," she said, and went carefully down the slope and directly to her tent. The camp had grown quiet, and most of the electric lights had been extinguished. A middle-aged woman answered her knock and let her get barely one sentence into an explanation before inviting her inside and introducing herself as Carol Hays.

"Rob Brinkman met me in the mess tent," Hays said, "and told me to expect you. Sorry nobody was here earlier, but we were probably still sluicing the mud off ourselves. We've been slogging around in the marsh all day."

Leveritt let Hays introduce her to a sleepy-looking young woman. She instantly forgot the woman's name but managed to smile and say, "Doctor Brinkman told me you're centipede enthusiasts."

Hays made a mock-horrified face and then laughed, and the young woman, affecting a tolerably good Dixie-belle drawl, said, "We have found that gentlemen do not look at us quite so askance if we refer to ourselves as entomologists."

Did either of you know Ed Morris? Leveritt wanted to ask. She was grateful that they were very tired and not such good hosts that they would stay awake on her account.

Soon, on her cot, in the dark, she lay listening to their soft, regular breathing and trying to resist falling immediately asleep. She had realized as soon as she lay her head down that she was exhausted, but she felt herself under obligation, at the end of a day she regarded as the most momentous of her life, to spend some time sifting through its events, analyzing and categorizing, summing up. She could not, however, keep everything straight on the ledger page before her mind's eye; Ed Morris kept shoving everything else aside. Then, when she thought pointedly about what must have happened to him, her imagination was drawn not to visions of accidents resulting in death, but to one of a human figure stretched like a rubber band from the top of the geologic column toward an indefinite point at the mid-Paleozoic level. The figure was alive. It writhed across almost half a billion years.

She recoiled from that image, and another promptly presented itself: Ed Morris as a straight line continually approaching a curve but never meeting it within finite distance.

But perhaps, she told herself, he met a real death instead of some exotic asymptotic fate. Perhaps he's at the bottom of the bay . . . .

If I'd let him make the jump before me, it would've been me who . . . .

And Morris might've been sitting out there with Diehl tonight, trying to think of something to say about a person he'd barely known for five minutes.

Or maybe not. Diehl wouldn't even have known who Morris was talking about . . . .

She awoke remembering no dreams. The sky had only begun to lighten; she showered and dressed and was packed and waiting to go when Brinkman came for her. He wore old khaki now, and a hat that needed blocking. After a quick breakfast, they went directly to the pier. There was fog enough so that, viewed from the pier's end, the camp seemed obscured by curtains of gauze. Nothing could be seen of the vessels in the bay.

Leveritt and Brinkman stepped aboard the boat that was to carry them upriver. There was no ceremony, no one to see them on their way, and they were the only passengers. They sat under a white canopy and drank coffee from a thermos bottle as the lines were cast off and the boat nosed into the current. Pier and camp receded and were soon lost from sight; by the time the fog lifted, they lay behind a bend in the river. The view from the boat was of barren heights and marshy borders. Dense Lilliputian forests of primitive plants covered the low, muddy islets. At length, Brinkman put his face close to Leveritt's and said, "Hello."

She started, drew back, looked at him in astonishment.

"I said hello, Bonnie. Before that, I said I think it's going to be a beautiful day." He aimed a finger vaguely skyward. "You know, dazzling blue sky, fleecy white clouds."

"Sorry. I must've—I was in a trance."

"I'll say."

She nodded toward the marsh. "I guess I've probably seen nearly every documentary ever made about the Silurian. But I never imagined how quiet it is here. Life on Earth hasn't found its voice yet. Hasn't hit its stride." She broke into a grin. "I think I'm quoting from one of those old documentaries."

"I doubt it," said Brinkman. "I bet everybody here is secretly, mentally narrating a documentary every second of the day."

The boat bisected the silent world. Brinkman pulled his hat down over his eyes, folded his arms, and slept. After a time, Leveritt realized, and was by fast turns surprised and appalled to realize, that the vista bored her.

It can't be! she thought in panic.

It isn't, she thought a moment later. It's something else. I'm distracted.

By Ed Morris.

Leveritt sprawled on her cot, arms and legs dangling over the edge because she could not bear her own blistering touch. It was a hot evening and humid, so sticky that her face stung and her tee-shirt and boxer shorts adhered to her skin, pasted to it with perspiration. Her tentmate, Gilzow, lay on the other cot, a wet handkerchief over her face. The flaps were drawn at both ends of the tent; from time to time, the air between the two women stirred discreetly, trying, it seemed to Leveritt, to attract as little attention as possible when it did so.

Finally, she delivered herself of a theatrical groan to signal that she was giving up on the notion of falling asleep. She sat up, lighted the lantern, and wiped her face and throat with a damp cloth. She said, "And I thought Texas summers were miserable."

Through her handkerchief, Gilzow said, "Look at the bright side. No mosquitoes. No fire ants, either."

"But no shade trees to sit under, and no grass to sit on. And no watermelon to eat out on the grass, out under a tree."

Gilzow lifted a corner of the handkerchief and peeked out. "You know what'd really be nice right now? Cold beer. Not that awful Navy stuff, I mean, real beer. Fine, manly beer so cold it's got ice crystals suspended in it. Or rum and Coke, in a big tall glass, with lots of ice cubes. Mm hmm. Cool us off and render us insensible at the same time." She let the corner of the handkerchief fall back into place. "I cannot believe there isn't a drop of anything to drink in this whole camp."

"Well, at least we can get Cokes and ice at the supply tent."

Gilzow sighed, barely audibly above the lantern's hiss. Then she plucked the handkerchief off her face and sat up. "I'm willing to forego insensibility," she said, "if I can only cool off. Just let me find my sandals."

Leveritt slipped outside and waited, listening. The camp was on a low bluff overlooking the river valley. Behind the bluff was a rocky flatland extending to distant hills. By day it stood revealed in all its stark desolation; nothing moved on the plain that wind or rain did not move, for only down in the valley, along the river's winding course, was there life. Between sunset and sunrise, the flatland lay vast and black, as mysterious as sea depths, while the night resounded with the cracking of cooling rocks.

Gilzow emerged. Theirs was the one undarkened tent, and the sky was overcast, but the obscured full moon cast enough light for them to see their way through the camp. No one else was about. The tents were open, however, and out of them came snatches of conversation, murmurings about heat and humidity and the day's work and the next day's prospects. When they overheard a man say, "Roger, where's that rain you predicted?" They paused, Gilzow literally in mid-step, balanced on one foot, until Roger answered, "I think the rain clouds must've gotten themselves snagged on those jumbly old hills." Leveritt walked on, Gilzow hopped and skipped to catch up, and her soft laughter hung in the unmoving air.

"Jumbly old hills!" She glanced back over her shoulder at the tent. "I don't think Roger's actually supposed to be doing what he does. I think he's a meteorologist who got lost on his way to becoming a poet."

"Listen to you!"

"It's true. He once showed me some poems he'd written, and I memorized one of them." Gilzow stopped walking, struck a pose, and recited:

"Australopithecus' sleep
is fitful, for it seems
that Australopithecus
isn't used to having dreams."

"That's not poetry," Leveritt said, "it's doggerel. And besides, I'm sure australopithecines could—"

"Oh, get a sense of humor, Bonnie."

Stung, Leveritt opened her mouth to reply, but no retort occurred to her.

"Sorry, Bonnie." Gilzow sounded sincerely contrite. "This heat and humidity—"

"It's okay," Leveritt said stiffly. "It's—I'm a born pedant."

On their way back from the supply tent, carrying a cooler between themselves and each holding an opened soft drink by its throat in her free hand, they came upon two men. Gilzow said, "Mike, Roger."

Mike Holmes and Roger Ovington turned, and the former said, "Hi, Lou. Bonnie. Hot enough for you?"

"Blah. About that rain, Roge."

"Paleozoic weather's as capricious as Cenozoic." Ovington nodded toward the hills. "But it's coming. We just saw some lightning flashes way off on the horizon."

"Bonnie 'n' I're going to have to drown our sorrows in straight Coca-Cola—unless somebody around here's got some rum or something he'd consider swapping for bizarre sexual favors."

"Sorry," said Holmes, "sorrier than I know how to tell you," and he gave a little laugh obviously intended to show that he might not be kidding. Gilzow laughed, too, to show that she definitely was. Leveritt could only marvel at her tentmate's self-possession. She herself could think of nothing to say, could think nothing, in fact, except, We're all four of us standing here in our underwear.

"Well," Gilzow said, "come sit on the cliff with us anyway. We also grabbed some crackers and a can of chicken salad."

"Then stand back, girls," Holmes said, "because we take big bites."

They sat among the rocks at the edge of the bluff and dangled their feet over an inky void—by night, the valley was abyssal. They ate and spoke of nothing in particular. All four of them started at a very loud pop of fracturing rock, and Ovington said, "It doesn't take much imagination to populate the darkness here with giant crustacean monsters clacking their claws."

Gilzow leaned close to Leveritt and said in a low voice, "I rest my case."

Holmes said to Ovington, "Sometimes you are a weird person."

Ovington laughed. "To me, prehistoric still means big ugly monsters. Hey, I'm just a weatherman, okay? I can't tell a psychophyte—what is it?"

"*Psilo*phyte," said Gilzow.

"I can't tell a psilophyte from creamed spinach. To me, a trilobite's just a waterlogged pillbug. And it doesn't matter what time period I'm in, meteorology's the same here as it is back home. Trade winds blow from the east, a high-pressure system's still— everything's different for the rest of you."

"Not for me and Bonnie," said Holmes. "Rocks is rocks."

"Still." Ovington gestured at the overcast sky. "The Milky Way's different, yet it looks the same to me here as it does back home. One of the astronomers told me once that in the time between now and the twenty-first century, our little solar system is going to travel all the way around the rim of the galaxy. A complete orbit and then some, as a matter of fact."

"You try to imagine that," Leveritt said quietly, "but you just can't."

"When I was a kid," said Gilzow, "I drove myself just about nuts trying to deal with geologic time and cosmic immensity. I started collecting models of geologic time, copying them out of science books and science-fiction novels, into a notebook. I must've ended up with a couple or three dozen. Like, if the Earth's age were compressed into twelve months, or twenty-four hours, or sixty minutes. Or how, if you put a dime on top of the world's tallest building, the height of the building would represent the entire age of the Earth, and the thickness of the dime would represent how long humans've been around."

"I like that one," Ovington said, and laughed. "I like it a lot!"

"My favorite," said Holmes, extending both arms out from his sides, "has always been the one my dad taught me when I was ten. The span of my arms, he said, was how long life had existed on Earth. And all of human history and prehistory fit on the edge of my fingernail."

"Dang," said Gilzow, "where's my notebook?"

They fell silent. Minutes passed, irregularly punctuated by the sounds of splintering rock and faint, unmistakable thunder.

"Do you suppose," Leveritt said suddenly, and tried to keep herself from asking the question that had been forming in her for weeks, since the night before the boat had brought her from the camp on the estuary, tried to make herself stop, but it had to come out now, had to, now, "do you suppose that if somebody came from the twenty-first century and died here in the Silurian, he'd cease to exist back in the future?"

The others' faced turned toward her. She could not see their expressions clearly but did not think she needed to see them to imagine their collective thought, What a truly *stupid* question!

Holmes said, "Whoa," but not sarcastically, and then, "Run that by me again."

Encouraged, she said, "I mean, would that person still be born and grow up to come back through time and die four hundred million years before he's born? Or would he be erased from existence? Would he have never been?"

"Actually," said Ovington—it was, Leveritt realized with gratitude, his kind of question—"there's a story about someone who decided to tackle that very matter. This was back in the early days of the expedition, when everybody was jittery about creating paradoxes. All this person did was bring back some lab animals and kill them."

"What happened?" Leveritt said.

"Nothing happened. You could say the experiment annihilated the animals but didn't annihilate them from having been. Or so the story goes. It may not be a true story."

"What if—" Leveritt cut herself short. What if *what?* What if somebody were to be scattered across four hundred million years, what then? "Nothing. Never mind."

Gilzow turned back to Ovington. "What you're saying, if that story's not true, is that the matter hasn't been settled."

"Well, by now, it surely has. People've been in Paleozoic time long enough."

"Long enough, anyway," said Holmes, "so nobody can tell the true stories from the weird rumors. All these myths're building up. Everybody repeats them, nobody knows if there's anything to them or not. Like the one about the government's secret plan to dump reactor waste in the Silurian."

"Actually," Ovington said, "the way I heard that story, if it is the same story, is that some generals tried to figure out a military application for a hole into the Silurian. Their plan was to sow Eurasia and Gondwanaland with nukes, so, later on, whenever the infidels and darkies got out of line—"

Holmes guffawed, and Gilzow said, "It's got to be true!"

"No," said Holmes, "it can't be, it's too stupid."

"It's so stupid it has to be true."

"Maybe it is," said Ovington, "and maybe it isn't, but this much is certain—the United States isn't sharing the hole with anybody!"

Then, Leveritt thought, there's the story about the man who jumped through—into? across?—time and never came—out? down? Anyway, he vanished as though he'd never been. No one could tell he'd ever been, because nobody was supposed to talk about him.

And there's a woman in the story who worked hard to get someplace, do something, be somebody. She found true happiness for maybe a whole hour. Afterward, she kept wondering what had happened to it, what had gone wrong. She was no quitter, never had been, but her work somehow wasn't as fulfilling as she'd expected, and everyone around her thought she was a humorless prig.

But those were just symptoms. The problem—

Thunder rolled across the flatland, louder than before. Leveritt looked and saw a lightning-shot purple sky. The air suddenly moved and grew cool, eliciting a duet of ahs from Gilzow and Holmes and a full-throated cry of "Yes!" from someone in camp. Ovington rose and shouted in that direction, "I told you it was coming!" To the others on the bluff, he said, "Gotta run, work to do," and rushed off.

"Guess we'd better go batten down," said Holmes.

"Just toss everything into the cooler," Gilzow told him. "Bonnie 'n' I'll clean it up later."

He did as she said, and then they picked up the cooler between themselves and hurried away.

Leveritt did not follow. The problem, she sat thinking, really was that the woman thought she was in a different story, her own, instead of the one about the man who vanished. Every time she turned around, there was his ghost. She couldn't make him go away. There was no place else for him to go, no one else who would take him in. No one else knew who he was because she wasn't supposed to talk about him.

Stop haunting me, Ed Morris. Stop.

The first heavy raindrop struck Leveritt on the back of the hand. She got to her feet and found herself leaning into a stiffening wind, squinting against airborne grit, in some danger of being either blown off the bluff or else blinded and simply blundering over the edge. She saw a bobbing point of light that had to be a lantern and concentrated on walking straight at it.

The rain started coming down hard. She found her tent, but as she bent to duck under the flap, she smelled ozone and felt a tingling all over her body, a mass stirring of individual hairs. Everything around her turned white, and she jerked back. For a timeless interval, she saw or imagined that she could see every upturned, startled face and wrinkled square inch of tent fabric in camp, every convolution of the roiling clouds above, everything between herself and the faraway hills, every rock, every fat drop of water hurtling earthward. At an impossible distance from her, yet close enough for her to see his safari garb and the dark flat square object he held, was a slight man whose expression both implored and accused.

The thunderclap smashed her to the ground. She came up on hands and knees, blinded, deafened, screaming, "I *remember* you, goddammit, what do you *want?*"

Strong hands closed around her wrist and forearm and dragged her out of the rain. Someone wiped her face with a cloth. At first, she could see nothing and heard only a ringing in her ears. Gradually, she made out Gilzow's face, saw the look of concern, even alarm, in her wide blue eyes, saw her lips move and heard the sound of her voice though not the words she spoke. Leveritt shook her head. Gilzow stopped trying to talk to her and unself-consciously helped her remove her wet underclothes. There was a second lightning strike close by the camp, and thunder as loud and sharp as a cannonade. Leveritt toweled herself dry, pulled on khaki pants and a flannel shirt, found her voice at last.

"I'm fine."

"You don't sound fine to me."

She did not sound fine to herself. "I was just dazzled by the lightning."

"You're lucky you weren't fried by it. I don't guess you'd've been yelling bloody murder if it'd hit you, but it must've hit right behind you. I'd swear I saw your silhouette right through the tent flap."

"Really, I'm fine. Really."

"Well, you lie down." Gilzow made a shivery sound. "I'm breaking out the blankets. First it's too hot for sleep, now it's too chilly."

Leveritt stretched out on her cot, and Gilzow spread a light blanket over her, tucked it around her almost tenderly, and extinguished the lantern. Leveritt lay listening to the rain's arrhythmic drumming. It shouldn't be my job, she thought, to have to remember Ed Morris. The storm passed. She slept.

The following morning was as warm and humid as though there had been no rainstorm. The normally clear and placid river had become a muddy torrent. Erosion was rapid in the Silurian; the steaming flatland, which drained through notches in the bluffs, looked the same and yet subtly changed. The camp's denizens, ten people in all, stood about in twos and threes, surveyed the valley and the plain, and talked, depending on their specialties, of turbidity or fossiliferous outcrops or possible revisions in topographical maps.

Leveritt and Holmes spent the day in a tent with the sides drawn up, consolidating survey data and incorporating it into a three-dimensional computer model of the region from the valley to the hills. Over tens of millions of years, the land had been repeatedly submerged, then raised, drained, eroded. "Up and down," Holmes said, "more times than the proverbial whore's drawers." Leveritt, her fierce concentration momentarily broken, shot him an oh-please look. They barely noticed a brief mid-morning cloudburst, barely paused for lunch, and might have skipped it but for the noise made by a couple of campmates returning muddy and ravenous from a collecting sortie into the valley. The sun was halfway down the sky when Holmes abruptly switched off his laptop, stretched, and declared that they could continue that evening, but right at that moment he needed some downtime. Leveritt glared at his retreating back until he had disappeared into the next tent; she found herself looking past the tent at the barren plain and the distant hills, and after a minute she resigned herself to thinking about Ed Morris and wondering what had become of him.

Ed Morris. Ed Morris. Maybe you arrived high and dry and unhurt out there on the plain . . . .

Her catalog of the possible fates of Ed Morris had grown extensive. It occurred to her now to record them in a notebook, like Gilzow's models of geologic time. Then she remembered Lieutenant Hale's injunction against writing anything that had to do with Ed Morris. She still did not feel safe from Hales.

Ed Morris. You arrived and—what? You wasted at least a little time and energy being confused and frightened. But after a while, you gathered your wits and took stock of your predicament. And what a predicament. You've got no food, no water, no idea of where you are. You know only where you aren't. You have only the clothes on your back and the laptop in your hand.

If it's night, you learn immediately that the stars are no help at all. The constellations you know don't exist yet. You wander around in the dark, fall into a ravine, break your neck and die instantly . . . .

Or break your leg and expire miserably over the course of a couple of days.

Back to the beginning. You find water, a rivulet, and follow it to a stream and follow that to the river and follow the river to the sea and find the main camp . . . .

Or find nothing, if you've arrived before there is a camp.

Or you don't find water and don't fall and break any bones. You just wander around until your strength gives out.

No. You do find water, you reach the river, but you realize your strength will inevitably give out, that you're lost and doomed to die in the middle of nowhere and no two ways about it, unless you take a chance, eat some of the local flora or fauna, shellfish, millipedes, whatever you can grab, anything you can keep down. You eat it raw, because you don't have any way to make fire, but don't get sick and die. You—what do you do if you live?

You live out your life alone, Adam without Eve in paleo-Eden. Robinson Crusoe of the dawn.

Alone with your laptop.

Best-case scenario, Ed Morris. You walk into camp just around dinnertime tonight, ragged and emaciated after an epic trek, and tired of subsisting on moss and invertebrates, but alive, whole, and proud of yourself.

Not-as-good scenario, at least not as good for you, but it'd let everybody give you your due and let me be done with you. We find the cairn you built with the biggest rocks you could move. Inside the cairn, we find your laptop. The seals're intact, the circuitry isn't corroded. We can read the message you left for us . . . .

Lot of work for a dying man.

Okay. First, you figure out how to survive. Then you build a cairn. You wander around building cairns all over the place, increasing the chances we'll find at least one of them.

Leveritt went quickly to her tent. She hung a canteen from her belt, put a wide-brimmed straw hat on her head, and started walking toward the hills. The wet ground crunched underfoot.

The levelness of the flatland was an illusion; the ground was all barely perceptible slopes, falling, rising, like the bosom of a calm sea. When she could no longer see the camp, she planted her fists on her hips and stood looking around at the rocky litter and thought, Now what?

Take stock, she told herself.

I've eaten, I'm not lost, my life isn't at stake here. None of which Ed Morris could say. I'm not confused and scared, either, and I haven't been injured. Besides not having eaten for ten, twelve hours before the jump, he didn't look like he had a lot of body fat to live off. On the plus side, he was a mountain climber and a skydiver, in good shape and not a physical coward.

How long would it have taken him to get over the confusion and fright? Give him the benefit of the doubt. A career in accountancy implies a well-ordered mind.

How much more time would've passed before it occurred to him to build a cairn? Then he'd have had to pick a site where a cairn would have a chance of being found, where it wouldn't get washed away, where there was an ample supply of portable rock. If he was back toward the hills, he'd have found the streambeds full of smooth stones of a particularly useful size. Out here, he'd just have had to make do with what's at hand.

How much rock could he have moved before his strength gave out?

Leveritt picked up a grapefruit-sized chunk of limestone, carried it a dozen feet, and set it down next to a slightly larger chunk. She worked her way around and outward from the two, gathering the bigger stones, carrying them back. After laboring steadily for the better part of two hours, she was soaked with perspiration, her arms, back, and legs ached, and she had erected an indefinite sort of pyramid approximately three feet high. Increasingly, she had expended time and energy locating suitable stones at ever-greater distances from the cairn and lugging them over to it. She squatted to survey her handiwork.

Ed Morris, she told herself, wouldn't have stopped working at this point, because he didn't have a camp to return to when he got tired. Still, it's a respectable start, stable, obviously the work of human hands.

She rose and walked in the direction of the camp. She paused once to look back and wonder. How long before it tumbles down?

No one in camp seemed to have noticed her absence. Typical, she thought. She discovered, however, that she could not maintain a sour mood for very long. She and Holmes worked together for an hour after dark, and then she retired to her tent and, soon, to her cot. Despite the mugginess of the evening, she had no trouble falling asleep.

For the next two days, work thoroughly involved her. On the afternoon of the third day, she returned to the cairn. She started to add to it, decided, No, moved off a hundred yards, and built a second cairn. Thereafter, she spent most of such free daylit time as she had piling up stones. She never returned to any site.

Now her absences did attract notice. Holmes trailed her past two abandoned cairns to her latest site. She answered his questions with monosyllables or shrugs or ignored the questions altogether, keeping on the move the whole while, finding, prying up, carrying, setting down stones. She refused his offer to help. Finally, he said, quite good-naturedly, "You need a hobby, Bonnie."

"This *is* my hobby, Mike." She wished aloud that he would go away, and he did.

That evening, over a dinner that tasted better than dinner usually did, Gilzow asked her what she was doing, and Leveritt replied, "Pursuing mental health." Later, she was almost unable to keep herself from laughing at one of Holmes' stupid jokes.

Two weeks and seven cairns after she had begun, as she lay on the edge of sleep, she realized with a start that she had not thought about Ed Morris all that day.

Four days later, when she had returned from building her eighth and last cairn, she asked around for a copy of *Robinson Crusoe*. Nobody had one. Gilzow offered her *Emma*, by Jane Austen. "Close enough," Leveritt said.

A month passed.

The supply boat arrived three days ahead of schedule. Everyone turned out to carry boxes; the first people to reach the boat yelled to those following, "Brinkman's here!" The big man, who had been downriver for ten weeks, stood in the bow, waving his shapeless hat. It transpired that the loud, sincere welcome was not entirely for him. He had brought a mixed case of liquor.

When the supplies had been unloaded and the camp had settled down for a round or two of good stiff drinks, Brinkman sought out Leveritt and asked her to walk with him along the bluff. They had scarcely put the camp out of earshot when he heaved a great sigh, his ebullient humor fell away from him like a cloak, and he suddenly looked tired and pale under his tan and more solemn than she could recall having seen him.

"I really came all the way up here," he said, "to tell you this personally. Two days ago, they dug something out of the marsh down by the main camp. It was one of the—part of one of the gurneys they use in the jump station."

"Ed Morris," Leveritt said bleakly. She had not said the name aloud since her conversation with Michael Diehl. Now, as though invoked by her speaking it, a humid wind swept up the valley, bearing a faint fetid breath of the estuary.

Brinkman said, "A Navy security officer named Hales told me about it."

"More surprises. I'd've thought he'd be swearing everyone to secrecy."

"It was too late for that. Everybody in camp knew it by the time he heard about it. Everybody."

"What about Ed Morris himself?"

"They're digging around. They haven't found anything else yet, and God knows if they will. The gurney's all twisted up like a pretzel, and one end's melted. God knows what that implies— besides the obvious, terrific heat. The thing was buried in a mud bank. Impacted. A botanist tripped over an exposed part."

"How long had it been there?"

Brinkman shook his head. "They're still working on that, but even the most conservative guess puts it before the manned phase of the expedition. As to how it got there—there has to be an inquest. You have to be there for it."

Leveritt groaned. "I don't have anything to tell."

"So Hales said. But people higher up're calling the shots. Everything's got to be official, and you've got to be part of it."

"I cannot get away from this thing!" Leveritt sat down on a knob of rock and angrily kicked at the ground. "Not from Hales and the Navy, and, most of all, not from Ed Morris. I thought I'd done it, finally worked it out by myself, but—"

"I'm sorry, Bonnie. You have to go back with me in the morning. I can find work for you to do until this thing's over."

"Making coffee?" She could not keep the bitterness out of her voice. "I want to be *here*, Rob."

"I've never known you not to be willing to do what you had to do so you could do what you want to do. While you're there—the San Diego bunch has talked about holding a memorial service. I kind of gather none of them knew Morris all that well, or liked him, or something. But he is the expedition's first casualty. Since you were almost the last person to see him, perhaps you could—"

Leveritt shook her head emphatically. "No."

"Bonnie, the man is dead."

"I couldn't eulogize him if my life depended on it. What I know about him wouldn't fill half a dozen sentences. He talked too fast and dressed like Jungle Jim. He said he liked mountain climbing and sky diving. And I'm very sorry about what happened to him, but it wasn't my fault."

"Who said it was your fault?" Brinkman knelt beside her and picked at his cuticle. "There has to be one meaningful thing you could say about him."

Leveritt sighed. She looked down at the supply boat and imagined herself on it again, sitting, as before, under the white canopy with Brinkman, drinking coffee from a thermos bottle, and glimpsing the pier and the cluster of tents and Quonset huts through the fog. She saw it all as though it were a movie being shown in reverse. She would have to go back and back and back, until she reached a point before Ed Morris had taken over her life, and start anew. This time, she told herself, I will make things happen the way they're supposed to happen. I will be the hero of my own story.

She said, "When he found out how nervous I was, he gave me a pep talk. And just before I went through the hole, he gave me a wink of encouragement."

"Well, then, if nothing else, you owe him for that wink." Brinkman could not have spoken more softly and been heard.

Leveritt closed her eyes and thought of the scene in the jump station, the purposeful technicians, Ed Morris' face framed by the bars of the railing. She looked helplessly at Brinkman, who said, "What?"

The humid wind moved up the valley again, and again she smelled the estuary's attenuated fetor of death and of life coming out of death. She exhaled harshly and said, "Nothing." She had meant to say that she could not recall the color of Ed Morris' eyes. "Never mind. I'll think of something." The wind passed across the rocky plain, toward the ancient crumbled hills and beyond.

THE TORTOISE GROWS ELATE

SeePee and I were sexing eurypterids when one of The Paleo Boys, the mycologist I call Fungus-Among-Us, waddled up, looking more than usually sweaty and smirky, and said, "You'll never guess."

I know you're going to ask, so before I go any farther: sexing eurypterids isn't nearly as much fun as it sounds. These were small eurypterids, to be sure, only about as big as your hand, and both SeePee and I wore dense-mesh gloves, but we still had to reach down into the big tank and grab the critters. Now, eurypterids of any size react to being grabbed by lashing out with their telsons, those spikes on their tails; get stabbed enough times on an unprotected patch of forearm, you start feeling as if you've been tattooed with a nail gun. Anyway, when you've got your eurypterid firmly in hand, you check its underside, and then, depending on what you see there (sexual dimorphism in eurypterids being blessedly obvious, you *don't* have to *touch* anything down there), you chuck the animal into one of two small tanks. We were, SeePee and I, compiling statistical data on male-to-female ratios in local populations.

There were five of us, SeePee, *moi*, two Paleo Boys, and our glorious leader herself. She had picked us, but only SeePee and I had met before she called us together to begin planning our field trip. We would barely have a chance to learn names and match them to faces before the transition from the Holocene to the Silurian.

Not that The Paleo Boys wasted any time cornering me. I knew from the moment I laid eyes on them they were jerks; it's this talent I have. The giant stinky one offered me his hand (clammy, as it turned out—big surprise there), and neither of them had to say a thing because their thoughts couldn't have been plainer if the words had been printed on their foreheads in block letters—Oh boy, a hot young Paleo chick, I want to be teamed up with the hot young Paleo chick!—but the other, weedier Paleo Boy, Centipede Sam, went ahead and said, "Hey there, you're the only woman."

"But, sirrah, false," I said, or words to this effect, "for is not our own glorious team leader The Wasp Woman?" That's what we called our glorious team leader, though not to her face.

Centipede Sam giggled, my first experience with this particular annoying habit of his, and said, "Well, I mean, among us troops. I've always felt that the earth sciences could do with the woman's touch."

Ha ha and ha. "By the time this thing is over," I said, "my legs'll be as hairy as anyone else's, and my socks will smell as bad." Probably a mistake, I thought as soon as I said it: some guys are into that kind of thing.

"Do you know our other teammate?" said Fungus, breathing at me.

"Probably not even as well as I know you. Probably not even enough to say 'get lost.'"

"His name's Bon-bon Chitty-chitty-bang-bang or something like that."

"SeePee!" I yelped. "Yes, I do know him!" *Praise be*, I thought, *I am saved*. SeePee B—(the first letter of a Laotian name on which, born 'n' bred Midwesterner that I am, I could never get a grip) Chittaphong-Phommahaxay. We had met as undergrads at Cornell. He was the ugliest human being I'd ever seen (Paleo Boys not counting as human), frog-faced, round-bodied, and long-limbed, as well as one of the smartest and most considerate people I'd ever met, and the only man I'd have done anything in the world for. Short of sleeping with him, that is.

"Well, whoever he is," said Fungus, "The Wasp Woman knows her stuff. She recognizes talent."

After seeing these Paleo boys, I would have begged to differ, but SeePee made up for a lot.

"What did you bring to do," asked Fungus, "when the weather turns bad on us or it's just time for a break?"

Probably he hoped against hope I'd say something titillating like, A vibrator and a big stack of girl porn, but if so I devastated him by saying, "I never travel without a great fat Russian novel. By the way, I'm a dyke."

Fungus's eyes got big and Centipede Sam said, "Interesting conversational gambit," and they did me the honor of shambling away and gradually taking their miasma with them. I knew their tiny brains were afire, though, or at least smouldering with groundless hope and fanciful speculation. My heart sank when I calculated the prospect of getting teamed up with either of them.

Well, I figured sisterhood is powerful and The Wasp Woman, being arguably as much woman as wasp, would understand if I went and told her I might have a problem with either Paleo Boy and could I please be teamed with SeePee, whom I knew to be cleaner and more socialized and had long suspected might even be gay. After all, I figured, she was an old hand at this sort of thing, she surely knew the rules of fieldwork and would never try to violate them. One of the most important rules is, The second-best combination for pairs is a homosexual man and a heterosexual woman (*the* best, a homosexual man *and* woman, is just too much to hope for); the worst pairing is a heterosexual man and a homosexual woman.

So I did go and tell her, and she said, without a whole lot of sympathy, "I have to assign you a partner on the basis of your specialties, not personal compatibility. All of you have valuable careers ahead of you—that's why I want you to go with me," and as she went on she got this very slight edge in her voice, like, Don't start bothering me with trivialities or my full waspishness will come out. I had had some experience with that. "We're on a shoestring budget, we have a certain amount of work we're supposed to get done within a certain period of time. Everything else, and I mean everything, is secondary. I expect you and your assigned partner to hammer out some kind of relationship in the field that permits you to complete your assignments in a professional manner, and incidentally does not conclude with your killing each other. Luck of the draw. Sometimes you click, sometimes you clash. Is there anything else you want to talk about?"

No, I said, and thought sniffily, *So much for sisterhood*, and effected my retreat in semi-good order. Being asked to go on this Paleozoic jaunt was a major deal career-wise and you can bet I had no intention of jeopardizing my chances by being a pain in the boss's skinny ass.

One day before we were scheduled to report to the jump station, The Wasp Woman took me aside and said, "I'm going to put SeePee in with you." How much my going to her before may have influenced her decision, I can't say. I didn't care. Right then I could've kissed her, but didn't, because I wanted to keep the Paleo Boys guessing.

I was still congratulating myself when the five of us reported to the jump station. While we were standing around waiting to go through, Fungus sidled up out of nowhere like The Thing From Beyond and gave me a crooked smile like The Thing From Beyond With Sex On The Brain. "Just curious," he said, trying very very very hard to be ingratiating and failing most wretchedly, "are you really a, you know?"

"That's for me to know and you never to find out," and away he shambled again.

Just before I went through the jump station, third in line after The Wasp Woman and SeePee, Fungus and Centipede Sam staged a little bragging contest, exchanging amazing facts about their specialities to impress me.

As the jump-station tech started to take me in, I looked at the Paleo boys and told them, "Wow. Listening to you two talk about mold and poisonous arthropods really makes my nipples hard."

Well, the other rule about assembling field teams is, Don't send three people out together because invariably two of them form an alliance against the third. I should have known my luck wouldn't hold: Centipede Sam got a mild concussion making the jump and landed in sick bay aboard the big Navy ship that services the Paleozoic expedition; The Wasp Woman delivered herself of some inspired cursing and told Fungus to stick with SeePee and me until Centipede Sam could rejoin us. And so, SeePee and I did in fact form an alliance against him.

Not without good cause, you understand.

This happened on our fourth night ashore. We had pitched our tents far back along one of the headlands bracketing the marsh that gives the base camp its nickname: Stinktown. The Wasp Woman being excused menial labor, we three underlings drew straws to determine the order in which each of us had to play chef. We'd all been in the field before, so we all knew not to expect haute cuisine; generally speaking, as long as the food's edible and nourishing, you put up with it. Then, four nights into the first week, I'm walking by the cook tent we'd set up, it's Fungus's turn to cook, and he's sitting on a camp stool picking at his foot.

Without preamble, he asks, "What's your opinion on Objectivism?"

"Isn't it that philosophy that's tailor-made for narcissistic sociopaths?"

Fungus frowns, catches himself, goes back to grinning as though he still somehow expects me to fall down in front of him at any moment and start lubricating at the prospect of eight seconds' worth of bucking and grunting.

"Rather a harsh and ignorant judgment," he says, "on the most influential system of thought ever conceived."

"Some system. 'I, me, myself, I've got mine, Jack, hounds bite the laggards, devil take the hindmost.' I know quite enough men who make a practice of selfishness. I don't need to know any who're selfish on philosophical grounds."

"But you're so intelligent. You—"

"Don't try to neutralize me with niceness."

"Well, I think you're just wrong. Perhaps we can discuss it at length sometime. I'm sure I could show you the error of your thinking."

"That would be really altruistic of you," I say, "but altruism is immoral." And then I finally ask him, "What are you doing to your foot?" and he says, "There's a type of fungus here that grows on everything. Plants, animals, other fungi, metal, my person. My very own very particular person. Ointments and ultraviolet lamps don't bother this fungus nearly as much as they ought to. I've come four hundred million years to fall victim to the great-grandpa of athlete's foot."

"Thanks so much for sharing that with me." I look around at the cooking utensils, the half-prepared dinner, and my stomach is starting to roil, because Fungus just keeps talking and picking at his foot.

"You'd think," he goes on, "Silurian-vintage fungi wouldn't know what to do with mammalian tootsies. Must be some weird mutant preadaptation."

"Did you just now actually say 'tootsies'?" And I reach into a trunk and grab a couple of meat bars—making sure the seals are intact. I go and find SeePee and hand him one of the bars and sit down beside him. "Dinner's on me tonight," I say.

"I don't understand."

"Eat first. Horror story later."

Okay. So, taking it from the top, Fungus waddled up and said, "You'll never guess."

SeePee barely glanced at him. I let the silence drag itself out for several beats, though I knew a Paleo Boy couldn't be put off by anything as subtle as an obvious, total lack of interest. In case you're wondering why, given a choice between eurypterids and Paleo Boys, well, it's no choice. But Fungus stood there giggling like a big mutant squirrel and finally I had to say, "What?"

"The Wasp Woman's got a boyfriend. She's in love!"

I said, without conviction, never mind enthusiasm, "Good for her," and reached for another eurypterid.

"You'll never guess with who."

"Whom." I took my time examining this particular eurypterid before dropping it into the tank for females.

Fungus pretended we were begging him for details. He said, "The Acid Drip!"

Short for Mister Post-Nasal Acid Drip Himself.

SeePee shot me a look from under his eyebrows that was as skeptical as I felt. I glared hard at Fungus. "You are talking about the head of the astronomy team?"

"None other."

"And our own glorious leader?"

"The same. The one and only."

"Together. The two of them."

"Yeah, can you imagine?"

I wanted to say "No way!" but also didn't want to give Fungus the satisfaction of knowing he had aroused my curiosity. Just having to use the word "aroused" in any context involving Fungus made me nauseated, so I reached for another eurypterid. The Wasp Woman and The Acid Drip weren't merely the respective heads of the paleontology and astronomy teams, they were their twin terrors. She was a demanding taskmistress and a prickly perfectionist, with a tongue that could strip the asphalt off a mile of two-lane blacktop. He openly despised geoscientists, biologists, and everybody else this side of celestial mechanics. His group had staked out the heights of the headland, where they could literally as well as figuratively look down on everyone else.

To SeePee I said, "He's making this up." I wouldn't have put it past a Paleo Boy.

"I got it," Fungus said, "straight from the horse's ass's mouth."

"Brilliant if labored metaphor."

"The Acid Drip and me were both down at the pier, waiting for the supply boat. When it comes, there's our own glorious leader in it, and she waves to us, you know. Waves. And The Acid Drip waves back."

"Now I *know* you're making this up."

SeePee said, "That doesn't seem like her at all. Or him." He sounded fairly weirded out, which was just how I felt.

"Lemme finish," said Fungus. "I sort of half-turn to him, he's standing right next to me, see, and I say something about how she always makes me think of a strip of beef jerky."

"Gallant as ever."

"Yeah, well, he gives me that look of his. You know that look of his."

"Like he turned over a rock," I said, "and you crawled out."

SeePee grunted softly. "Like Darcy in *Pride and Prejudice*?"

"Huh?" Fungus and I said in an isolated incident of fellow feeling.

"Darcy," said SeePee, "in *Pride and Prejudice*."

(Later I asked SeePee to tell me who Darcy was in *Pride and Prejudice*. He looked at me reproachfully and asked, "Have you never read Jane Austen?" and I looked back at him defensively and said, "No, but I'm not some illiterate, you know, I have read the Brontës." He laughed. "The Brontë sisters were crazy women who wrote about crazy people, but, ah, Miss Austen," and he pulled this really ratty-looking printed-on-dead-tree-matter book out of his seabag and flipped a few pages and showed me the part where catty Miss Bingley disses Elizabeth Bennet to Mr. Darcy, whom both young women have the hots for. Miss Bingley teasingly reminds him that he thought Elizabeth rather pretty at one time.

> "Yes," replied Darcy, who could contain himself no longer, "but *that* was only when I first knew her, for it is many months since I have considered her as one of the handsomest women of my acquaintance.")

But right then, for maybe six, seven, eight seconds Fungus and I just gaped at SeePee, and then Fungus finally managed to nod and said, "Yeah, whatever, it was his look. And he's just as stiff as if he had a ten-foot iron rod up his butt. And he moves off, and as the boat ties up, he gives her his hand to help her out of the boat, and they go off chitchatting, arm in arm, happy as can be. It was like she didn't even notice I was there."

"Well, you are beneath notice," I said. "Beneath contempt, at least."

"Funny, Tammy."

"Don't call me Tammy. Tammy is not a diminutive form of Tamiko."

"Sure thing, Tam Ee Koh. Well, to continue. As they went off, I heard him ask her was she still going to visit him at the observatory tonight."

"Some observatory," I said, "a big hole in the ground"—which was true. The big hole in the ground was the future site of the radio observatory, a natural depression back on the ridge currently under improvement by a construction team. But I really only said anything to buy myself a couple of moments in which to think.

"My guess," said Fungus, "is she's going to let him show her the stars, if you follow what I'm saying."

"Get out of here," I told him. "SeePee and I have work to do, and we can't do it if you make us puke more than usual."

Fungus grinned and sauntered away with a "Check with you later."

"I don't believe it," I said to SeePee.

"But," he said, absently regarding the tanks, "she has been acting strangely all this week, now that I think about it. I've hardly heard her snap at anyone."

"Even if it wasn't her and that stargazer, what can a paleontologist and an astronomer find to talk about?"

"The same thing men and women always find to talk about," he said. "The beginnings of things."

"But—"

He gave me a reproving look and as he stuck his hand back in among the eurypterids he said, "In June the tortoise grows elate and walks on the tips of his toes."

"Huh? Is that Darcy again?"

"Gilbert White."

Day followed day without further untoward incident, Centipede Sam recovered from his time-travel-induced headache and joined us in the swamp, and SeePee and I, relieved of Fungus's constant presence, fell to our work with a will. Then The Wasp Woman asked me to accompany her back to the base camp, which sat about a half-mile away on a sliver of dry land squeezed between the rocky headland and the broad, stinky estuarine marsh. We had spent the night before crating specimens and loading them on a cart which we would have to lug ourselves, like medieval French peasant women. The menfolk evidently had more important work she wanted them to do.

It was early evening. After much huffing and puffing, we delivered our crate to the pier, signed a slew of forms, and then The Wasp Woman turned to me and asked, with what was, for her, unnatural friendliness, "Are you hungry? Do you want to eat Navy chow for a change? Ogle a sailor or two?"

"Well, the chow will be a change."

"Go on. I'll catch up with you later." Just like a big sister telling a little sister to go on, have fun, I trust you, be home by midnight.

I sat in the mess tent for a while after I had finished eating, then walked out and looked around. She had made herself scarce. Fortunately the camp is laid out on a square grid, and there are lights strung on poles to help folks avoid blundering off into the marsh. There is also a path up the side of the ridge, leading over the crest to the observatory, and some thoughtful individual had even strung a line along it you could use as a hand rail, and lights so you wouldn't blunder off the path and roll down the side of the ridge into the marsh.

And coming along the path was The Acid Drip.

Now, I am not by nature a snoop, but I confess: I was on fire with curiosity. I hung back and let The Acid Drip pass me in the twilight, and then I slipped along behind him.

He went past the verge of the camp, where the ground slopes off into muck and green slime, and there was The Wasp Woman, waiting for him. She extended a hand which he took, and they moved together, kissed enthusiastically, and then turned to watch the sun slipping down behind the headland on the far side of the estuary. I didn't care to eavesdrop, I had already seen all I needed to see, but just as I started to turn away I saw The Wasp Woman lean her head against his shoulder and saw him put his arm around her.

Then I felt a bad sneeze coming on, and clapped a hand over my nose and mouth, and faded well back in among the tents before letting go.

After dinner the next night (it had been SeePee's turn to cook, always a plus) and several drinks, I made bold enough to say, "It's true."

Quizzical looks from SeePee, Fungus, and Centipede Sam rewarded my observation.

"I saw them last night. The Wasp Woman and The Acid Drip. I guess they thought they were being discreet, but it was obvious they're dead goofy gone on each other."

Fungus looked smug. SeePee looked uneasy. He said, "Should our team leader's private affairs become the conversational topic *du jour*?" but he had had about as much to drink as I, and if he was thinking of shoving off and leaving us low-lifes to wallow in gossip, he couldn't quite act on the thought.

Centipede Sam ignored him anyway and said, "Look at the bright side. This could mean The Wasp Woman's waspier aspects will yield to her womanlier aspects. Result: things get better for everyone."

I responded to that by pretending to stick my finger way into the back of my throat.

"I still can't imagine the two of them," said Fungus. "I mean, it must be like, I dunno, scorpions mating or something."

Centipede Sam said, "Have you ever seen scorpions mate? The difference between those two and scorpions is just a matter of degree. Scorpions have more primitive wiring and plumbing."

"Count on you," I said, "to reduce love to wiring and plumbing."

Centipede Sam shrugged to show what he thought of my opinion. "When my old cat Sophie had a litter—I let her have one litter before I got her fixed—she let me examine them a couple or three days after they were born. I'd stroke 'em on their bellies, and they'd go into nursing mode. Extending and curling their tongues. Their wiring was in such an undeveloped state at that point in time that if something felt good to them, they automatically responded to it as though they were nursing."

Then SeePee astonished me by taking Centipede Sam's side. He said, "Love comes out of all that wiring and plumbing. The brain's limbic system is where the electrical and chemical disturbances occur that produce the basic emotions. Love, joy, sadness, fear, and so forth are the effects of phenylethylamine, norepinephrine, dopamine, and so forth."

"I'm sure," I said, "and I don't care. I much prefer to think of love as Laberius did."

"Who?"

"Laberius."

"Laberius!"

"Hey, I read a poem every now and then myself. Laberius compared falling in love to a cockroach falling into a basin."

"Sounds like a poet all right." From the way Centipede Sam said it you'd have thought "poet" was a synonym for "pedophile".

SeePee shook his head solemnly. "Love isn't some external thing that ambushes people. The phrase 'falling in love' always annoys me. You create love within yourself. Infatuation is just chemistry. The ingredients are brain chemicals. The turtle cannot sing, yet it knows love."

"Is that Gilbert White, too?"

SeePee shook his head. "No, some poet. White was a naturalist."

"Whatever."

Fungus said, "Maybe they can't help themselves. SeePee talks about brain chemicals. Consider the possible effect on brain chemicals of a primitive fungoid organism that produces a hallucinogen when taken into the system, resulting not just in mild hallucinations, but also shed inhibitions. I think there could be such an organism here."

"You are the only primitive fungoid organism here," I said, "and also the only one hallucinating. And don't even think about shedding your inhibitions, whatever they may be."

"No, no," Fungus persisted, "think about it."

"If that were the case," Centipede Sam put in, "it wouldn't be just The Wasp Woman and The Acid Drip who'd gone nuts. Everybody's brains would've turned to crap."

"Some people are ahead of the curve on that one."

"It could affect different people in different ways."

"Fungus," I said, "you are so lame."

Just then, The Wasp Woman appeared out of the darkness from the direction of the base camp. She walked quickly, almost stalking, and as she entered the circle of light surrounding us I saw that she had both hands clenched into tight hard fists and a look on her face that told me something had gone distinctly wrong in the shining city of love.

"It's *late*, people," she snapped, "and we have another busy day ahead of us."

Suddenly, unexpectedly, things were back to normal.

I never found out what had happened between her and The Acid Drip, and didn't try, but a couple of days later, apropos of I'm no longer sure what, she happened to mention him and astronomers generally in unflattering terms. "Conceited," "arrogant," and "unpleasantest people I ever met" were the mildest terms she used.

When, later, I discreetly relayed this to SeePee, he clucked his tongue and said, "It's Jane Austen in reverse. The happy ending came before the unhappy beginning."

"What?"

"On first meeting Mr. Darcy, Elizabeth Bennet and the other female Bennets decide that he is a most disagreeable, horrid man, not at all worth pleasing."

"SeePee, may I borrow that book you showed me?"

"Of course. It is my favorite work of fiction. I hope you'll like it."

And I did, too, and asked for more, and SeePee supplied it: *Sense and Sensibility, Mansfield Park, Emma.*

And during the long course of our year in Paleozoic time I found myself looking at him differently. Oh, nothing really changed. Just as The Wasp Woman and the Paleo Boys went on being their respectively waspish or primevally male selves, so, too, SeePee remained frog-faced, round-bodied, and long-limbed. But something beautiful began to radiate from within him. Finally, not long before we were to wrap up and go home, he and I took half a bottle of rum with us to a nice perch on the ridge overlooking the bay, and we watched the sun go down together, and I heaved me a great sigh and said, "SeePee, if only you weren't gay."

He looked at me in obvious surprise. "But I'm not."

Reader, I married him.

Just kidding.

CLOUD BY VAN GOGH

Bearden had not slept on her cot. Well, Wheeler thought sourly, I'm glad somebody around here's got a love life, and she kicked her blanket into a loose wad at the foot of her own cot. She peeked outside at the lightening sky. Maybe I can do some painting today. The prospect immediately sweetened her mood. She felt the familiar itch for the brush in her fingers, and something more than that, the vital connection of hand to brain and eye. Today, by God, she promised herself. She dressed quickly in old fatigues, slipped the strap of her specimen case over her shoulder, and stepped outside, into air thick with estuarine fragrances.

The camp was quiet; she saw no one. She soon passed the last line of tents, walked briskly to the spongy edge of the marsh, and then proceeded upstream, keeping to the left of a broad, dark, algal band that marked the frontier of habitability—unless, she reflected, one were either human or a lichen.

And, of course, one couldn't be a lichen, because lichens were symbiots.

Ugh, she thought, botanical humor. Better not repeat that to anyone in camp.

Well, maybe to the botanists . . . .

The sun rose quickly behind her, illuminating the featureless black expanse of the marsh by degrees. Plant growth at the edge, of the marsh was patchy, struggling—brave little plant pioneers, as she regarded them, delicate as hairs, sprouting wherever a film of moisture held together a crumb of dirt. She knelt, measured, carefully dug out an intact brick of earth.

As she put it into the specimen case, she heard a rustling, crunching, crinkling noise coming from nearby. She looked down and glimpsed something elongate slithering across the toe of her boot, and then she found herself two or three feet away: she could not have said whether she had teleported across that distance or merely broadjumped backward from a squatting position. She could not have said her own name right at that moment. Her entire attention was fixed on the monster nosing among the psilophytes. It was one of the biggest land animals she had seen since her arrival in Paleozoic time—as long as her forearm, as big around as her finger. Two, possibly three, seconds elapsed before the monster's common name came back to her: millipede. Then she laughed nervously. A harmless ol' millipede, she thought, and I nearly jumped out of my skin. Granted, it's an enormous harmless ol' millipede, but, still . . . .

The scientist in her took over; she crouched over the animal, peered at it, debated taking it back to camp. The artist in her decided to let it be: it was too lovely where it was. Its flattened and segmented body was like a string of fat, polished beads, and its scores of legs rippled like water. The rustling, crunching noise was the sound it made as it propelled itself through the psilophytes. It ate its way through them as well. The crinkling noise was the sound made by smaller arthropods as they scrambled in search of still smaller arthropods, and of any other edible thing, amid the organic rubble left by the millipede's passing.

Catch you next time. Wheeler thought as the millipede and its entourage moved off into the marsh. She began walking back.

The camp had by now begun to awaken, and the Navy as well. She saw people moving among the tents and Quonset huts and thought that she could even make out tiny human figures moving about on the big Navy vessel anchored in the bay. A helicopter turned far out over the water and bore away to the north. The sky was lightening to a clear, brilliant blue, and, drifting serenely through that sky, was an omen—a beautiful fat cumulus cloud.

Back at the tent, there was still no sign of Bearden. Wheeler put the earth sample she had collected into the tullgren funnel, which consisted of a container, with a sheet of gauze affixed to its base, mounted over a funnel. Above the container was a lamp. Heat from the lamp would cause the animals to move away from the top of the soil sample; though complete extraction might take two or three days, most animals in the sample could be expected to move through the gauze and into the funnel during the first couple of hours. Then Wheeler would collect, categorize, and count them.

She turned on the lamp, then left for the mess tent. A Navy cook served her breakfast. The only other people present were the astronomy team. Gabbert, the leader, sat with his eyes closed and his long chin propped up on his hands. He looked as though he had been up all night; probably he had. Between his elbows on the table, a cup of coffee cooled and a plate of eggs congealed. His two assistants, Manning and Hayes, were rising to go, but they lingered as Wheeler sat down across from Gabbert. She ignored them and bade him good morning; he barely opened his eyes, croaked a hello, and reclosed his eyes.

Manning said, "Big news. The satellite's up."

Wheeler nodded. "That is big news."

Manning smirked. "Are you rooting in the dirt this fine morning, or painting."

"I've done my rooting for the day," she said evenly, "maybe I'll paint later."

His smirk approached to within a millimeter of becoming a sneer. "You're the only person here who has a hobby."

Hayes took that as her cue and said, "You're the only person here who needs a hobby," and smiled to show that she was just kidding, really.

Wheeler smiled back, thinly, and thought, Bite me. She said, "Science and art make for a well-rounded life." They departed.

"Gab," she said, "tell me something. Why are astronomers such gruesome dweebs?"

Gabbert opened both eyes; they glittered with amusement in his otherwise saturnine face. "What you mistake for dweebishness is actually an aristocratic disregard for inferiors. We're higher in the pecking order of science. Astronomy is clean and cool and cerebral. You root in dirt and stick your fingers into dead trilobites and things."

"By the way, congratulations. On the satellite."

He shrugged and turned down the corners of his mouth. "I had nothing to do with it. I wasn't even asked for my opinion."

"Are we going to have to look through your spy-glass to see it when it passes over?"

"Nope. I'll point it out to you. Come before midnight."

"I'll be there, if I'm conscious at all. But I've got lots of work to do today, and I want to get in some painting, too."

Gabbert clucked his tongue at her. "It seems to me that the Silurian Period can't have much to offer you as a painter. If you'd stayed in Austin, you could still be teaching at U.T. and making a few bucks on the side selling paintings of bluebonnets." The moue she made only encouraged him. "Some flowers would enliven your masterpiece."

"When have you seen it?"

"Got a good look," he said, "when I stopped by to make a pass at your tentmate."

How could you? she thought, but she knew. She said, "No wonder she's been in a bad mood."

"She's been in a bad mood because of the smell. Our Miz Bearden is a bit of a princess. She's always complaining about smells."

"Then she's in the wrong line of work," Wheeler said, more harshly than she had intended. "Anyway, I am going to finish the painting today."

"Uh huh. She says you say that every time. You go out, slop some paint on, come back, scrape the paint off. And the whole tent ends up reeking of turpentine."

"Mineral spirits."

"Same difference. It's put her off sex. What you're doing with that poor painting is beyond pathetic. It's Sisyphean."

"Like Sisyphus, I have no choice. Gotta keep rolling that rock up the hill. Gotta keep believing that one of these times it won't roll back down."

"You know," Gabbert said, "if you really want to make pictures, you can do it faster with a computer, and without the smelly mess. You'd be happier with the result, too."

"Gab, you just don't understand about artists."

"Artists!"

"Oh, never mind." She attacked her breakfast.

He let her eat for a minute, then said, "Come on, tell me. My interest has been piqued. Tell me about artists."

"Oh-kay. Listen. I sneaked in art history and music appreciation whenever I could while pursuing a degree in agriculture. One summer I got to go to Europe, and I hit all the art museums. I was looking at this one van Gogh one day—are you at all familiar with van Gogh?"

"I only ever saw the movie about him. A seriously disturbed man. Cut his own ear off."

"I was looking at this van Gogh painting of a rustic drawbridge. It's just called 'The Drawbridge.' He painted it in Aries in May of Eighteen Eighty-eight. I'd seen reproductions of it before, but you can look at a thing for hours or years before you actually see it. And here was the original painting, and there I was, when my attention was drawn to a fat cloud off to one side. And as I looked at it, I suddenly had this, this insight—"

"Whoa," Gabbert said mildly, "jump back."

"Make fun. But for just an instant, I saw that canvas exactly as Vincent van Gogh himself must've seen it when he was working on it. I was so conscious of the power, the sheer responsiveness of his hand. I saw how he'd dabbed on a big glob of white paint, swirled it just so, and—voila! Cloud by van Gogh. He made it look so easy, and yet—" Wheeler smiled ruefully. "Ever since, I've been trying to reproduce that cloud. No, that's not quite it. I don't want to copy it. Van Gogh only painted what he could see right in front of him. He didn't trust memory. He painted a thing the way he saw it. I want to do that. Paint a thing the way I see it. I want to feel what van Gogh felt when he looked at a cloud, and his eye transmitted what it saw to his brain, and his brain passed it along to his hand, and his hand made it, made, you know, art."

"Sounds like pure obsession to me."

"If I was truly obsessed, I'd've gone around doing whatever van Gogh went around doing. Retraced his steps, dug up my own cadmium."

"But kept both your ears, I hope."

"All I want is to have what goes in here—" Wheeler pointed at her eyes "—to come out here," and she waggled the fingers of her right hand. "Just one time, I want the brush to be a direct, spontaneous extension of myself. Van Gogh wrote once, 'What a queer thing touch is, the stroke of the brush.' I know I'm a dud as a painter, even as a Sunday painter. But just one time in my life, I'd like to brush on some flake white and have it magically become a cloud."

"I hope you'll let me know when it happens."

"Maybe today. The light's going to be perfect. And I've had an omen. A beautiful cumulus."

"The light's always perfect here. And there're always clouds."

"Clouds gone to waste. Gab! Clouds that formed and dissipated in vain. But today I've had a sign."

"From whom? God? Or the Impressionists?"

When Wheeler got back to her tent, Bearden was there, freshly scrubbed, dressed in a terry-cloth bathrobe, with a towel wrapped turban-fashion around her head, and looking about as out of place as—Wheeler could not think of anything sufficiently inappropriate.

She settled for saying, "You're late."

Bearden removed the towel, and as she began combing out her hair, she said, "I am not late. I just didn't leap out of bed at the crack of dawn."

Wheeler resisted the impulse to ask, Gab's bed? "The sun's a third of the way up the sky."

"That sun hurries too much to suit me. No wonder I've been starved for sleep ever since I got here. I can't adjust to these shorter days."

Wheeler breathed deeply, slowly. Do not wreck your whole day, she warned herself, otherwise she'll get into one of her moods and there won't be anything you can do to get her out of it and you won't be able to do your work, never mind any painting. Make an effort now, or the day is lost. Wheeler put a smile on her face and said, with all the good humor she could muster, "I have only minimal sympathy for the problems of anybody who's as slim, graceful, blonde, and sought-after as yourself." Bearden managed a pinched sort of smile in return.

Bearden sat down at the work table and examined the tullgren funnel. The first refugees from the lamp-heated brick of dirt had begun tumbling down the funnel. By now she knew them all: worms and mollusks the size of rice grains, wingless, unfinished-looking insects, some tiny, primitive spiders, and one small, modern-looking, thoroughly annoyed scorpion. As she sorted them, she kept hoping to see a new, unfamiliar face. Then she remembered the painting, and she told herself, Never wish for more than one good thing at a time.

Bearden, her toilette completed, sat down at her own end of the table and went to work.

Finally, Wheeler thought, her mouth set in a thin, firm line.

Can't let things go on this way for much longer.

Yeah, like you can really do anything about it . . . .

She and Bearden had been assigned to a team by their expedition leader, with no regard for personal compatibility. In a small, isolated camp off in the hinterlands, the arrangement probably would have worked; with no place to go, no way to get there, and nothing to distract them from the job at hand, they would necessarily have developed, out of their common interest in Paleozoic biota, a superficial but sustainable, and mutually sustaining, relationship long on technical talk and devoid of intimacy.

Here at the base camp, however, distractions abounded. Bearden did not need to be sustained by Wheeler: several different expeditions used the base camp; at any time, it contained hundreds of researchers and hundreds more Navy personnel. Consequently, Bearden's work was becoming sloppier all the time. Wheeler, who took her own work quite seriously, could not help feeling puritanical.

Another consequence—Wheeler looked at the situation honestly—was that, here, unfairly, she herself could not simply ignore Bearden and concentrate on her own work. She found herself struggling constantly with personal insecurities she had imagined were not merely laid to rest for good but laid to rest four hundred million years away.

Bearden was precisely the kind of woman who had always made her feel fat, graceless, unattractive to men. Rationality was suddenly and unexpectedly no defense against this. It did not matter that Bearden, by slacking off—whether consciously or because she was dissipating her energy—was surely destroying her own chances for a career in the field, while Wheeler's conscientiousness would surely pay handsome dividends in both a scientific and a professional sense. It did not matter that Wheeler would not have wished the acidulous Gabbert on anyone as a lover. It did not matter that it did not matter. The discovery that she was still capable of sexual envy and jealousy came as a very rude shock to Wheeler. She did not regard these as worthy states of mind; they made her ashamed of herself. For years she had been content in the conviction that her interest in men as men was safely defused. Her experience of men and of love, though not broad, had been deep, and so disappointing in its outcome, so distressing and even disgusting, that her libido had, so to speak, cleared out in the dead of night without giving notice—without, in fact, calling any attention to itself whatsoever. Months had passed, then a year, then another, before she abruptly understood that her work and her private interests, art, music, gardening, nieces and nephews, had expanded to fill the extra space in her life. It had been one of the great liberating moments of her life . . . .

I enjoy my work, she thought as she sat segregating arthropods. I am overjoyed by it. This is not one of the glamorous geologic ages, for every one of us who's thrilled to death to be here there're hundreds back home, thousands, who curse spacetime for not opening up in the Mesozoic or the time of the early hominids or whenever, sometimes I even catch myself wishing I could step backward or forward several million years to get some quick answers to questions. But I'm happy with what I've got to work with here. I hope—

Something unfamiliar dropped through the funnel.

Well, well, look at you. Wheeler thought. She recognized the creature as a trigonotarbid, a ten-legged arthropod that somewhat resembled, but was not, a spider. I hope I haven't just now used up my quota of good luck for the day. I hope I still get to paint.

Hope, she believed, was unaimed prayer.

The exodus of invertebrates through the funnel slowed. Wheeler leaned back on her campstool and peered longingly through the gap between the tent flaps. She stretched her arms above her head and made a decision and looked over at Bearden. "Go get some lunch if you want." Or get laid or whatever. "I'm going to knock off for a couple of hours and go paint." She could not resist adding, "I haven't taken any time off in days."

Wheeler opened her footlocker and drew forth a box containing brushes, tubes of paint, and other paraphernalia. A rectangle of masonite hung from the tentpole; she took it down, uncovered it, held it at arm's length, regarded it with a particular mixture of affection, embarrassment, and resolve. Depicted in oils on the board was a drab Paleozoic landscape, all greens, grays, and browns, stretching uncertainly to a leaden sea; above was a cerulean expanse marred by white blotches that might have been fungoid growths. An upper corner of the board had been scraped off and re-gessoed. She slipped the board into a carrying case, strapped her collapsible easel to her paint box, and left the tent with the case under one arm and the bundle over the other shoulder.

She lugged this cargo, panting and perspiring, to the heights behind the camp and erected the easel on a finger of rock that pointed seaward.

The sun was high and hot, so she did not fall immediately to work but sat with her legs dangling over the edge of the rock. She breathed languorously. Lichens discolored the rock; she covered one with her hand. Lords of the highland, she thought. For now.

From her vantage point she could see clear across the estuary. The crumbling headlands were striped white, gray, brown; the turbid mocha-colored river bisected the vividly, succulently green marsh and spilled into the bay. Van Gogh, she thought, cannot have loved Provence more than I love this. When she looked out to sea, her heart was lifted higher still by the sight of two separate cloud masses, great fat billowy things approaching from the horizon. Like they want to audition. Only need one of you, but thank you both for showing up.

She got up. Time now to put all thoughts of work and jerks out of your mind. Time to paint a cloud.

She studied the masonite board as clinically as she could. It would be pleasant, she thought as she prepared her palette, to be able to blame my picture's dreariness, its lifelessness, on the Silurian vista. This world's so quiet, sometimes it does give me the creeps. Its colors are so drab, so monotonous, sometimes I ache for a bird with scarlet plumage, or some sunflowers. Impossible, of course, I'm a long way off in time from birds and flowers. It would be nice to get flowers—

Stop that. You're going to paint only what is here. This is Earth on the verge of erupting with riotous life, and the only reason you can't paint it is that you can't paint. Nevertheless, as she carefully scooped up a glob of flake white on her brush, Wheeler thought. God, you know how much I love art, how much I enjoy painting, and you also know that I don't think for one second that I actually have talent. I know I'm utterly devoid of it. All I want, Lord, just this once, is a cloud.

And, as usually happened when she began thus, she thought. Why am I asking God to help me paint a cloud? If I can get things from God just by asking for them, shouldn't I ask for something like world peace or at least more funding—

Stop. It.

Don't think about anything except the cloud. Not about whatever you're not thinking about but about the cloud. Push everything except the cloud out of your mind and think only about the cloud. Think about the cloud.

She began to get into it. She stepped closer to the easel and moved the tip of the brush toward the scraped-off, re-gessoed spot on the masonite board where she had tried and failed, tried and failed so many times, to paint a simple cloud—

—don't think about failure don't think about anything except the cloud. Think—

Cloud.

Now something in her did seem changed: she looked at one of the clouds out over the sea, the one she had chosen without having to think about it, and she let everything that was not essential to the moment fall cleanly away from her, work, Bearden, the hot sun, time, space, until all that remained were cloud, eye, hand, and she felt, believed in, the connectedness of eye to hand, so that the sight of the cloud whirled inside her head and flowed out, down, along her arm, into her fingers. The brush untremblingly approached the masonite board. She took a deep breath and held it. She dabbed the paint on the board and gave it a swirl. What a queer thing touch was. She said, "Voila!" Then she almost cried.

Walking down to the camp, she thought. Do I dare hope for anything good again? Ever?

She found Gabbert sitting on a campstool in front of his tent, pecking at a laptop. She set her equipment on the ground.

After a moment, she said, "Did I tell you," and she held her hands about a foot apart, "this morning I saw a millipede this long?"

"I don't know whether to be thrilled or horrified, but I'm sure it'll chap Curray's butt." Curray was a widely disliked entomologist.

"I found my first trigonotarbid today, too."

"Ah. Did you?"

"About tonight. Satellite-watching. Can I bring a date?"

"Can you?"

"May I bring somebody? I think I'm going to set my cap for a Navy man."

"Bring the whole Navy if you like. It's an occasion."

She sat on the ground before Gabbert, took the masonite board from its case, and placed it across her knees.

He looked over his laptop at her in a questioning way. "And? Did we do art today?"

Wheeler glowered. "It's not as easy as it looks, you know." With her knife, she began to scrape a white fungoid blob from a corner of the board, disconsolately at first, then with the resurgent conviction that it would all be made right one of these times.

HALF A LOAF

"Are you sure," someone asked, again, in a liquor-thickened voice, "we'll be able to see it?"

Gabbert answered, for what seemed like the hundredth time, "Yes," clipping off the word with his teeth. He was tall and thin in the moonlight, and his expression suggested that he found the night sky, or perhaps the company in which he viewed it, somehow displeasing. Few other people, nothing like the number he felt should have turned out for the occasion, had climbed the stony slope above the camp. Gabbert sighed and shifted his gaze to the summit. A structure of indeterminate but vaguely skeletal shape and considerable size gleamed dully far back among the rocks on the ridge top. The sight did not have an entirely calming effect on him, and he looked hurriedly away. Tonight he felt conflicted about nearly everything.

Two human figures detached themselves from the camp and began to ascend the slope toward him. There was no mistaking the thickset Helen Wheeler, but Gabbert did not recognize the person accompanying her. She called up, "Tom's not coming. I tried to get him up, but he told me to go away and turned over and went back to sleep."

Typical, Gabbert thought. Most expedition members who had spent the day collecting botanical specimens along the margin of the mudflat, or digging invertebrates out of the mudflat itself, or prying fossils from the cliffs back of the camp, now slept the profound, justified sleep of people who had physically exhausted themselves doing work they loved. Tent flaps were opened, tent sides furled, to give the sleepers the benefit of the least breath of wind, but the air hardly moved at all, as though it were weighed down by the damp rank smell of stagnant mud. The Quonset huts which formed the relatively permanent part of the camp were darkened. The surface of the bay lay so smooth and black that the large Navy ship and its brood of auxiliary craft appeared to rest on a slab of obsidian.

Wheeler reached him puffing and sweaty. Her companion was a wiry middle-aged man dressed in Navy tropicals. She gasped, "Like you to meet Navy Chaplain Madiel."

"How do you do?" Gabbert perfunctorily shook hands, then, after a moment's hesitation, turned and indicated a man sitting nearby. "Helen, this is Roger Ovington. Meteorologist. Helen Wheeler. Her specialty is dirt or bugs, I forget which."

"Gab's," said Wheeler, "is hot gas."

"Oh," said the chaplain as he shook hands with the meteorologist, "you're Roger Ovington. Your reputation precedes you. Somebody told me you're the best-read person in the Paleozoic."

"How do you find the Paleozoic?"

Madiel recited:

"The sea was wet as wet could be,
The sands were dry as dry.
You could not see a cloud because
No cloud was in the sky.
No birds were flying overhead—
There were no birds to fly."

Gabbert and Wheeler regarded him in astonishment. Ovington merely grinned. "Lewis Carroll!"

"A Navy man who quotes poetry," Wheeler said, "and a weatherman who recognizes it'"

"God bless liberal arts," Gabbert said dryly. "Roger's on his way home tomorrow, fortunately."

"That's too bad," said the chaplain. "It's been a while since I got to discuss books with anyone. I suppose it serves me right for waiting this long to come ashore. This is my first time."

One of two shaggy individuals sitting a little farther up the slope said, "Well, padre, what kept you?" and laughed raucously and swung his arm in a gesture obviously intended to take in everything, the camp, the marsh, the barren heights.

The other shaggy individual said, "What brought you?"

Gabbert repressed a shudder. "The paleo boys were let out of their cages, and have consumed their entire whiskey ration tonight."

Madiel peered up the slope at the paleo boys. His tone of voice was friendly, unprovocative; he sounded, Gabbert decided, as though he were addressing strange dogs. "If you mean, what am I doing here generally, I'm a volunteer like everyone else. I willingly let myself be dropped, shot, or in any case transferred through a spacetime anomaly for the purpose of tending to the spiritual needs of several hundred officers and enlisted personnel of the United States Navy. But I wanted to see more of this place than you can see from the deck of a ship."

"Well, here's to you, padre!" and there was a faint clink of bottles.

Gabbert turned his back on them, and to fill the silence he asked the chaplain, "How long've you been here?"

"I could probably tell you," said Madiel, "if they hadn't given me that lecture about how the days're a couple or three hours shorter here, and the year's a few dozen days longer. I learned that the length of days will increase as the Moon moves away from the Earth, but I couldn't tell you why to save my life."

Ovington exaggeratedly drew a breath and said, very fast, "Conservation of angular momentum requires that the Earth must accelerate if the Moon approaches—and vice versa!"

"Don't mind him," Wheeler said, "we've all learned to say that, but Gab's the only one here who knows what it means."

Gabbert nodded in acceptance of this tribute. "In consequence of the Navy's unfortunate decision to stick to the twenty-four-hour military clock and the Gregorian calendar, everybody is hopelessly confused."

"Well," said the chaplain, "the standard clock and calendar may not be adequate here—"

"They're hardly perfect back home."

"Yes, but they're familiar. They help to keep us anchored. I've heard that somebody, one of you astronomers, devised a clock for a day lasting twenty-one hours and twenty-some-odd minutes, and a four-hundred-day calendar."

"Yes," said Gabbert, sourly, "and just about got tarred and feathered for his trouble, too."

Ovington said, "I found the easiest thing to do was to just not worry what day it was or what time it was. A lot of the time, I couldn't even remember what month it was according to the standard calendar. Hardly makes a difference here. It's not like there're seasons."

"It's almost—" Madiel stopped, stumped for a word to describe what it was almost.

"I just go by the sun," said Wheeler. "I get up and eat breakfast around sunrise. I work till sundown, eat dinner, hit the sack. Tonight's the first time in ages I've looked at a clock. Every seven or ten days, I take a day off. Tomorrow, for example, is my day off. I think it also happens to be Sunday."

"What does a soil scientist do around here for fun on her day off?"

"Pretty much what everybody else does. I go for walks, listen to music. Oh, and I'm a perfectly lousy landscape painter. But my work here's really the most fun I've ever had in my life. It still amazes me I'm here. I was a Tennessee farm girl. F.F.A. in school. Other girls wanted to be prom queen—I thought I'd arrived when I made the Soil Judging Team in my junior year. If I could've seen into the future, this would've blown my mind."

"I'm afraid most Navy men find it pretty unexciting. It's not what they expected. I guess it's exciting if you're a scientist."

"You'd never know it from Gabbert here," Ovington said, "but the astronomers are the giddiest of the lot. I've only had to be around them since I came downriver two days ago, and they already drive me crazy. They sit around all night asking each other questions like, Where are the stars we know? And, What are conditions like on Mars, on Venus? Actually, the questions are more along the lines of, What's going on with that massive black hole at the center of Galaxy M-eight-seven, in the constellation Virgo. And, Where *is* the constellation Virgo?"

The chaplain said, "Well, whatever's going on, wherever—it's quite a sky."

"Personally," Wheeler said, "I miss the constellations."

"They're there." Ovington aimed a forefinger upward and drew an invisible line from some point to some other point.

"Well, are they Paleozoic or twenty-first-century constellations? Trilobites or Moon rockets?"

"I don't think anybody knows yet what they are, but they're there."

Gabbert said sharply, "The kind of world view—cosmic view—necessary to arrange stars into constellations doesn't exist any more. Except maybe in Papua or the Australian outback, nobody believes in gods and heroes any more."

"I, of course," said Madiel, "beg to differ. Slightly."

"When I get back," Ovington said, "just one of the things I'll be glad to see again is a familiar sky at night. I miss the Dippers and Orion and the rest. This just adds to my disorientation. Time isn't right, and the stars aren't right. And I miss things—places—that have names. This world needs names. We brought along a few. We've got names for the major landmasses, bodies of water, divisions of time. We're in Laurentia, and out that way—" he pointed seaward "—is the Iaepetus Ocean, and beyond the sea is Gondwana. We're straddling the Devo-Silurian boundary. One day this spot we're standing on will be Pennsylvania or Ireland. But we can't go on calling it the part of Laurentia that's going to be Pennsylvania or Ireland. We're making maps of this world, and maps of this sky, and we need names for every island arc, peninsula, bay, river, mountain, and the stars and galaxies. And sooner or later we're really going to have to make up our minds whether it's Thursday and we have to work, or Saturday and we get to sleep in. We're the species that puts names on things. We're a tool-using species, and names are tools."

"Any suggestions, then?" said Gabbert. "I can show you Mars and Venus and Jupiter up there in the sky. I'm afraid we pretty well used up mythology naming everything in the solar system."

"Classical Greek and Roman mythology. So we'll use some other mythologies. We can use H.P. Lovecraft if we have to."

"There are hundreds of saints," the chaplain said, "and thousands of angels and devils. Skyfuls of them."

"This is the world before the Fall," said Wheeler. "Why set good and evil on each other ahead of schedule? Why not just do what they did when they named craters on the Moon and planets? Name things after scientists. Especially geologists. The Hutton River, Wegener Bay—"

"Wegener was a meteorologist," said Ovington.

Wheeler shrugged. "Mount Murchison. Or even the Murchison Mountain Range. Murchison was a jerk, but he—"

"Was he as big a jerk," asked Ovington, "as Newton?"

"Nobody," Gabbert said crisply, "was as big a jerk as Newton. Or was Murchison a vindictive schemer, too?"

"Well, even if he was, he identified and named the Silurian system. If anyone deserves to be immortalized here, Murchison does."

They lapsed into silence. After about a minute, the paleo boys launched themselves into song.

"Sin," Gabbert said, "has entered the world."

Wheeler said, "I think what I miss about the twenty-first century are flowers and trees. Oh, and the heavenly scent of new-mown grass. Every now and then, I think it would be nice to plant a little garden here. And to have a pet, a cat or a small dog. Something furry and well disposed, anyway. On my days off, I could lounge around with a sketchbook and a cat and a cup of tea and know that civilization is a good thing. Only, we're hundreds of millions of years shy of the first flowering plants and the Age of Mammals, and even if it weren't for regulations I wouldn't want to be the party responsible for complicating life for future paleontologists by having my pet's fossilized poop turn up in Paleozoic strata."

"I miss concerts in the park," the chaplain said, "and birds. I'm a bird-watcher. And I miss going to church."

"Well," said Gabbert, "I never saw that coming."

The chaplain appeared not to take offense. "God is everywhere, of course, and worship is meaningful whether it's done on the quarterdeck or in a church. Or at the bottom of a coal mine for that matter. But for me the experience of being in a church has always been tremendously moving."

"I'm afraid," Wheeler said, "I haven't been to church in years. I was brought up Southern Baptist, but it didn't take."

"Same here," said Ovington, "only I'm a lapsed Unitarian," and he laughed softly.

The chaplain looked at Wheeler. "Why do you say it didn't take?"

"I—I was always told you had to get right with God. That was the way it was phrased. That, and—Accept Jesus as your savior, give your life to God, live your life according to his will. If you could do those things, you would find salvation. But I realized at some point that I had no idea what those phrases meant. I tried to live according to the commandments, went to church, said my prayers, but I never felt the presence of God. In fact, I found myself getting farther and farther away from whatever it I was trying to get closer to. God. The Cosmic Oneness. I said, here I am, ready and waiting, come and get me. I'm still waiting. But the funny thing is, since I came here, I've become more convinced of God's existence than I ever was before. Sooner or later, I think, I'll make his acquaintance."

She seemed particularly abashed when she made eye contact with Gabbert, who said, "Well, don't look so taken aback because I don't look taken aback. There's always been practically the whole range of believers and non-believers here."

"Except," Ovington said, "creationists, I bet. Now that would be interesting." He turned to Madiel. "I've got a poser for you, Chaplain. What if the second coming of Jesus Christ happens back in the twenty-first century while you're here in the Paleozoic?"

"Ah, well, I believe I'd be wise to leave that to a committee of theologians and physicists to ponder. Even if they couldn't, I'm sure God's figured it out."

"Optimist. I've got another."

"Don't torment him," Wheeler said, "he's a guest."

"Let's say there's a scientist here who's a devout Muslim. We'll call him Hossein. Hossein's supposed to pray several times a day in the direction of Mecca, which won't exist for another four hundred million years. He can't even pray in the direction of Mecca-to-be, because the landmasses are all moved around, the poles are different. The stars are obviously different. There just aren't any referents, so, for practical purposes, this isn't Earth at all but an Earth-like planet. The planet Mer."

The chaplain shook his head, and Gabbert told Ovington, "You can come up with the weirdest crap."

Madiel said, "I'm not an expert on Islam. But Hossein, being a man of faith, must know that even if Mecca doesn't exist yet. God does. Perhaps Hossein prays due south, because somewhere down that way is proto-Arabia and the future site of Mecca. But the important thing is, Hossein prays. He places his trust in God's understanding, just as I do. God is eternal understanding. God knows what's important and doesn't sweat the small stuff. He understands if we sometimes have to forego the niceties of worship."

"Like going to church regularly?" said Wheeler.

"He hopes we'll make every effort, of course."

They grew quiet again, all except for the paleo boys, who suffered fits of giggles. Gabbert kept checking his wristwatch. Then he startled the others by saying, "Do you want to know what I really miss about the twenty-first century?"

"Besides family and friends?" said Madiel

Gabbert exhaled dismissively. "There's no family—no wife, no kids, and my parents're both dead. No. What I miss is having the right tools for the job. Like every other scientist here, I've been given an extraordinary and unprecedented opportunity to probe into all sorts of ancient mysteries. But I'm having to do it the hard way, on a shoestring budget, using a lot of old-fashioned technology. Cheap rotary rockets capable of lifting satellites into orbit have been around for decades, and we've just now put up one lousy satellite here. We've got a whole new sky to map, and—" he gestured angrily toward the structure atop the ridge "—we're practically having to build a radio telescope out of old screen doors and extension cords!"

"Some folk." said Ovington, "want their luck buttered,"

"And why the hell not?"

"It's human nature," the chaplain said to Gabbert, and his voice was different now—it was the voice he had used before to talk to the drunken paleo boys—"to always want a little more that we're given. More money, more love."

"More faith," said Wheeler, "and more talent."

"More life, more life after life."

Gabbert checked his watch again and stepped around the others. "Up yours, Ovington," he said, casually bitter, "and yours, too, Chaplain. I want to do good work here, great work, impeccable work if I possibly can. I want it to outlast me. I want the papers I write to be the best ones I can write. This is the work of my life. I want it to be worthwhile."

Gabbert abruptly directed their attention to a particular sector of the heavens. Everyone peered; it took those with untrained eyes several seconds to pick out the small point of silvery light that moved slowly but perceptibly across the black sky. The drunken paleo boys whooped in derision and in unison.

Ovington said, "Tiny little thing."

"It's beautiful," Wheeler breathed.

"It's a start, anyway," said Gabbert.

Ovington gave him a searching look. "Doesn't seeing it up there at last make it the slightest bit harder for you to be pissed off about things in general."

"Harder, but not impossible."

"You're impossible. My fellow meteorologists will be ecstatic, and the mapmakers, too. And communications. No more futzing around with atmospherics. The Paleozoic Era's finally entering the twenty-first century!"

"It's a start," Gabbert insisted. "Belated, half-hearted, and rather half-assed, too—"

"But a start."

"That thing doesn't do me much good. I need something that looks up, not down."

"When you get back," said Wheeler, "remember to let NASA and the N.S.F. and everyone know exactly how you feel. Then you're sure to get absolutely everything you want." To the chaplain she said, "Gab's just not going to be satisfied until he gets his own vee-el-bee—are you. Gab?"

"Nope. Not until there're radio dishes stretching clear to Gondwana."

After a moment, the chaplain sheepishly asked, "What's a vee-el-bee?"

"Very-long baseline array," Ovington said. "It's this big radio-dish link-up stretching from Hawaii to the U.S. Virgin Islands. It acts like a single radio telescope."

They watched as the small point of silvery light continued in its leisurely passage across the sky. The moon looked crisp and sharp and close. The Milky Way looked like lace and frost.

It was Gabbert who broke the silence. "If ever we reached a state where we actually felt we had enough of everything—" He glared around at them. "What would've become of life on Earth if organisms had ever become content?"

"Oh, Gab," Wheeler said, "put a sock in it."

CHAOS AND THE GODS

"We have encountered and passed the spirit, which broods on these immense waters. There is no fear left now of chaos."
—Lawrence Durrell, *The Black Book.*

"Now that Gab's insulted everybody at least once," Helen Wheeler told the Navy officer, "the stargazing party's properly over."

Navy Chaplain Madiel came out of a half-doze to see her carefully smother a yawn.

"I've put in a long day," she said, "and I'm tired. But it's a sort of delicious, dreamy tired."

"Best kind," the chaplain murmured. "I'm up way past my bedtime, too, and I have to hold services in the morning."

Yet neither he nor she made any move to emulate the people now descending the slope, by ones and twos and threes, to the camp, to their waiting beds. Helen and the chaplain sat on a limestone bulge. Gabbert, a stick-figure of a man, stood a short distance away; he appeared to the chaplain to be gazing raptly upward. By day the heights afforded an unobstructed view of an estuarine marsh, tents and Quonset huts neatly laid out on a grid plan, and a bay opening onto the great Paleozoic sea. By night, with the camp darkened and the moon vanished into clouds, the men and the woman hung suspended in an infinite black void. At some indeterminate distance, the sea's oily blackness merged with that of the sky. The stars blazed. A meteor cut a fine straight streak toward the invisible horizon. Nothing else in the world moved or made a sound until Helen delivered herself of a deep, contented-sounding sigh and said, "How could anyone look at this sky and not feel the presence of God?"

Madiel said, "It's certainly quiet here. I've never heard such quiet before. And lovely and strange. The moon, most of all. It's the same moon, yet it isn't. It's—let's see if I can recite this correctly—it's inclined only about five degrees to the equator, and it's only about fifty earth radii away. It's sixty radii back home."

"Excellent, Chaplain," Gabbert said crisply, "go to the head of the class," and, after a moment, "Are you by chance an amateur astronomer?"

"Oh, no. But the subject interests me. I talk with the team on the ship sometimes, about navigational applications. Pretty small potatoes, I guess, compared with the radio telescope you're building."

"The radio telescope's pretty small potatoes, too. But it will double as the world's biggest colander."

Helen groaned. "Oh, please don't get Gab going about the radio telescope again! Gab, don't you dare start. Nobody wants to hear any more about it tonight or for the next month."

"If I'm an amateur anything," said the chaplain, "it's a mythologist. My parents raised me on the Bible *and* Bulfinch."

"Weren't they at all worried that the two would work at cross-purposes?"

"Evidently not. I became quite the connoisseur of myths and folk tales from around the world. We lived in Nashville, Tennessee. The centerpiece of Centennial Park there's a permanent full-size replica of the ancient Parthenon. Inside is a huge statue of Athena in full regalia. *Not* the sort of thing you expect to find adorning the buckle of the Bible Belt. But I liked the old gal just fine. Still do. She was the goddess of wisdom, the arts, cottage industry, defensive war—things that appeal even to a modern Christian sensibility. Also, her morals were better than Aphrodite's, and she wasn't insanely jealous like Hera."

"Or Jehovah?"

"Gab," Helen said in a warning tone.

"I can see how an interest in mythology might be very useful in your line of work. Even essential."

"Mythology's interesting in its own right," the chaplain replied easily, "especially the creation myths."

"You're not a stealth creationist, are you?"

"Not any kind of creationist. Only fundamentalists find faith and reason incompatible."

"Ah. Personally, I have nothing against faith except reason. I always found the Biblical story of the creation pretty childish."

"Creation stories come out of our species' childhood. They may be wrong, may tell us nothing about how the world really began, but they do tell us that people have always believed that it began for a reason, so our lives are not purposeless." Madiel realized after half a dozen heartbeats that the scientists were waiting for him to continue. He was not sure, however, which way they expected for him to go. He said, "A relative handful of creation myths admit to total ignorance of how the world came into existence."

"Decent of them."

"They're concerned only with the origins of people. Otherwise, there's broad agreement—between Eskimos and the *Rig-Veda* and from the Congo to Siberia—that in the beginning there was chaos. From the Greek for chasm. The disorder of formless matter and infinite space before the ordering of the universe. Pre-Big Bang, in your patois. Chaos is sometimes described as mere nothing, empty darkness. But the human mind can grasp *nothing* only if it surrounds or is surrounded by *something*. Try as we might, we're stuck with spatiality and temporality. So, often, chaos is described as darkness and empty ocean. You'd almost think the story-tellers were precursors of eighteenth-century European Neptunists, who theorized that all rocks had been precipitated from seawater. Unsurprisingly, Pacific islanders said there was only open ocean in the beginning. Very surprisingly, to me, anyway, Crow story-tellers living on the Great Plains said the same thing. Among the watery creation myths you occasionally find a neat embellishment. The Maya-Quiché of Central America said that at first there was no motion and no sound. Stasis and silence. The Jicarilla Apaches insisted on darkness, water, and *cyclones*. Somewhat more evocative of roiling chaos. Green slime floated on the Mixtecs' version of the primeval waters."

"Sounds almost like they had the Silurian Period in mind."

"A single rock jutted above the primeval Haida sea, providing a resting place for Raven, who, having rested, set about making the world. The Yokuts' great sea had a stump sticking up out of it, and more than one creator was involved in making everything—Eagle, Coyote, Duck, Lizard."

"Art by committee!"

"At length, of course, something or somebody disturbs the status quo. As the Egyptians told it, the primeval hillock rose from the waters of chaos. As others told it, Raven found a clamshell, and inside it were the first people. Without much prompting, Bumba vomited up the sun, moon, stars, and everything else. The Winnebago Earthmaker gradually became conscious and found himself sitting in nothingness."

"What was he sitting *on?*"

"The story doesn't say, but he nevertheless takes a piece of it and fashions the world from it. In some stories, the first deity grows out of primeval chaos, or ocean, and duly sets forth imposing order, creating the familiar world by utterance, from part of the deity's own body, or from some other deity's body. Or that of a slain giant, like the Norse Ymir. Ymir was spawned in Ginnungagap, the cold, fathomless void that yawns at the center of the earth and into which the rivers of the universe empty. The brothers Odin, Vili, and Ve, kill Ymir, whose bones become rocks and mountains, and his blood, the seas. Plants sprout from his hair. His skull forms the dome of the sky, his brains become fog and clouds."

"Waste not," Gabbert said, with arid humor, "want not."

"Gab," Helen growled, "be nice."

"Why, Helen, whatever do you mean?"

"I can't actually see the expression on your face in this light, but I know you're sneering."

"*Au contraire.* I'm fascinated. Tell me, Chaplain, do you ever wonder about life on other worlds?"

"Of course."

"Though your Bible doesn't mention it? Though it claims God created the moon and the stars to glorify his name, and incidentally to aid us in navigation?"

"The Bible doesn't mention the Americas," Madiel said, "or butterflies, or spacetime anomalies. Yet they exist."

"Patently."

"Take another look at this sky, Gab. Then tell me it doesn't say something about the glory of God."

"I'm surprised at you, Helen. Don't argue from design. You ought to be ashamed of yourself."

"*You* should be ashamed. The sight of this sky doesn't move you? And the fact that it's a *Paleozoic* sky, and you, almost alone of all the astronomers who've ever lived—by a miracle, you've—"

"By the grace of physics, Helen."

"By a *miracle* of physics, you've been allowed to cross hundreds of millions of years and stand here and look at this."

"I can be profoundly moved without believing in the supernatural. Allow me to issue the following official statement." He struck a pose. "Yes, I do feel awe and wonder whenever I contemplate the vastness and splendor of the universe. We astronomers are humble people."

Helen erupted into laughter. "Astronomers are the snidest, snottiest, most stuck-up people here. You call us earth-science types grubs."

"And worse, dear Helen, when you're not around. But when our attention is directed upward to the heavens rather than downward to our inferiors, when we ponder the mysteries of energy and matter and distance, why, we wax positively poetical."

"And," asked the chaplain, "that's all it is, in your view, nothing more personal than energy, matter, and distance?"

"I don't believe the universe is personal. We take it personally and tell ourselves that we're the consciousness of the cosmos, but the fact of the matter is, we're isolated local phenomena. Temporary aberrations—in gross violation of the second law of thermodynamics. We're infinitesimal specks of matter and sparks of energy, arranged in such a way that we're aware of ourselves and our surroundings. Some of us look around and say, 'Oh, my God,' as if that explained everything. But some of us aren't satisfied with that. We want to find out as much as we can in the little time we have, and not take anything on faith. Better insignificant but informed sparky specks than ignorant and arrogant ones. If you buy the physicists' theory of multiple universes, we shrink even further in significance, down to the sub-micro-infinitesimal. Can even the one true God Almighty pick us out amid the infinite details of an infinite series of universes? Or do you suppose each universe has its own one true God Almighty?"

"I'm sure that God, being God, is big enough to cover all the bases in any number of universes. My job's a lot easier if I concentrate on just the one God and the one universe."

"Ah. Well, even if God is in his Heaven, or God *is* the heavens—the universe, spacetime, spacetime—is he subject to the laws by which spacetime works?"

"Aquinas said God exists outside time."

"I said spacetime. Spacetime's indivisible. Let's assume Aquinas was full of it and God and spacetime are indivisible."

"Immanent rather than transcendent."

"Right. God and spacetime are one. Spacetime is bound by physical laws. God, being everywhere in spacetime, obeys its physical laws, including the one that sets the cosmic speed limit, which nothing with mass can exceed."

Helen yawned noisily, without trying to smother it. "Gab, it's late, I'm sleepy, and I have the feeling you're about to unleash a brain-teaser. Chaplain, we should go before he—"

"Hear me out, Helen, then I'll escort you to your tent and tuck you in personally."

"Bad enough, brain-teasers. Now you want to give me nightmares."

"Hear me out. By definition, the omnipresent, omniscient God must be simultaneously aware of everything occurring everywhere. Yet, if nothing, and that includes information, if nothing can travel across the universe faster than light—"

"God *is* everywhere," Madiel said, "and *locally aware* of everything everywhere."

"That doesn't solve the problem. Even if part of God takes care of business in the Andromeda galaxy while part keeps tabs on us here on Earth, since information can't move any faster than light, one hand of God doesn't know what the other's been up to until a million years after the fact. And we haven't even touched on how God manages to be both in the twenty-first century of the Christian era and here in the Paleozoic—"

"And we're not about to, either," Helen said sharply, but the astronomer ignored her.

"—unless there *is* something to the many-worlds, many-gods hypothesis after all."

"However he manages it," said Madiel, "God *is* here."

"Ah. Well, I imagine if there's a god here, it's not any kind humans ever worshipped. Not one they'd want anything to do with. Don't gods evolve as well as organisms? In five thousand years of human history, elemental forces evolve into cat-faced Bastet and goat-assed Pan, thence, into the old man with the long white beard and his son and that ghost. No, our paleodeity isn't just unhuman, it's probably unsympathetic to chordates generally. It's the eldritch ur-god of trilobites and sea scorpions."

"The sea has many voices," said the chaplain, "many gods and many voices."

"Bible verse?"

"T. S. Eliot. You raise many interesting points, Doctor Gabbert. I'm glad I never had you in my Sunday school classes. You might've have caused mass apostasy."

"Is faith so fragile?"

Helen growled again and got heavily to her feet, "That's it. It's time to call it a night, Gab, and tell you you've behaved perfectly horribly to our guest."

"Not at all," Madiel said as he stood. He and Gabbert shook hands. "I've enjoyed myself."

"So," said Gabbert, "have I."

"Good *night*, Gab. We're leaving. I hope you're satisfied now you've run everybody off. Thank you for the part of the evening that was lovely, you jerk."

Gabbert bowed slightly. "Always a pleasure to see you, Helen. Do be careful on the path going down."

Halfway down the slope, Helen said to the chaplain, "Allow me to apologize for certain of my less socialized colleagues in the scientific community."

"He didn't offend me."

"He was trying to with all his might. If we'd stayed he'd have kept trying till he succeeded."

"I had a good time. It reminded me of bull sessions back in school. Next time, of course, I'll *expect* to find myself under attack and give as good as I get."

"You didn't do badly. Still. He was attacking your faith."

"My faith can withstand attacks. What would faith be worth if it was fragile? And, really, he did hold my interest the whole time. He's quite a stimulating talker, your friend."

"He's not—well, he is my friend. But it's in spite of the way he is, not because of it. If you were the pope, he would have tried to get your chasing your own tail about papal infallibility."

Madiel laughed. "I don't think that's much of an issue among Catholics any more."

"Whatever. If you were an atheist, he'd have figured out some way to attack your lack of faith."

"Are you a Christian, Doctor Wheeler?"

"Thinking about it."

"Then you know that Jesus died for everyone, even people who disagree with you and are disagreeable to you."

Just as they arrived at the edge of the camp, the black sky turned a creamy purple, and the moon peeked around the edge of a backlit cloud at the world. The cloud withdrew with unhurried dignity.

"And here around us," Madiel said softly, "is the rolling primeval sea, the begetter. The dragon of the deep, the deep itself, the salt sea, the mother who gives birth to the gods. Or whom the gods and the first heroes of men, Nun, Apsu, Tiamat, slay and from whose disorganized substance they fashion the world, bringing order out of chaos."

The purple sky became creamier. The surface of the sea sparkled as the moon, bowed like a wind-filled sail, beat its course along the horizon.

"Wow," said Helen. "They do *good* work."

When they reached her tent, they shook hands, she entered, and he walked slowly through the camp. The windows of the communications hut were illumined from within, but he saw no sign otherwise of human activity, and between the time he bade Helen Wheeler goodnight and the moment he came within sight of the dock he saw no one, overheard no conversation.

He returned the petty officer's salute and wordlessly, almost inaudibly, answered the needless comment that this would be the final trip of the evening. He sat down in the boat and waited with his elbow on the gunwale and his chin propped up in his hand. All sound was muffled, as though it crossed a vast distance. His eyelids insisted on drooping. He shook his head to clear it, looked first at the moon, then across the black water of the bay, bisected by a shimmering silvery path that pointed to the horizon. The boat rocked slightly, the path beckoned, and after considering the matter for a moment he made up his mind and stepped out of the boat, onto the moonlit path. It was yielding yet firm. When the moon momentarily disappeared into clouds again, the path dulled but still supported him. Uncertain of the way to go, he waited for the moon to reemerge, and while waiting looked down through water now suffused with pale light from no obvious source. Beneath his feet, crimson fish and amber-backed sea scorpions with ebony claws went mindlessly about their business. When the moon reappeared, he had the sensation, unexpected but not unpleasant, of being drawn forward by some external agency—by the moon itself, he decided after reflection. It was some hitherto undiscovered tidal effect. Or something. He accelerated along the path toward the invisible seam of the horizon that held sea and sky together, and then the moon swept him right off the earth, bound him somehow to itself, so that the planet fell away sharply, lost definite shape, became indistinguishable from a starless darkness and he could no longer tell where anything below him left off and anything else began. He turned his gaze upward and saw only the moon. Satellite and satellite, the greater and the lesser, rushed through the darkness, closing the distance between themselves. It occurred to him after a brief interval that he really was approaching the moon at tremendous speed, that it might be a good idea to slow down, but before he could begin to wrestle meaningfully with the problem of braking, he had abruptly plunged through the surface of a mare and come to a full stop, without suffering any harm whatever from the sudden deceleration. He found himself teetering on the brink of a precipice. The edge curved to left and right and met at a point opposite him, but distant, so distant. He had, he somehow understood, flown not to the moon but beyond spacetime itself. He stood on the rim of a vast hole, perfectly circular, in the floor of Heaven, and ranged with him around the rim were presences or beings or in any event gigantic and strange awfulesses, the first inhabitants of Heaven. There was none among them even as familiar-looking as a hawk- or cat-headed god, nor even the naked writhing ropy horrors of less formal pantheons. These beings paid him no attention; they had important matters before them. Within the hole lay a roiling infinite darkness like a heavy sea of petroleum, the primordial chaos, lightless, noiseless, formless, substanceless, and yet *there*. The things ranged around the rim were trying to reach some agreement concerning the disordered state of affairs below. There were irreconcilable factions of introspectionists, extro-, proto-, and even daring abstract retrospectionists. One faction desired a universe in which everything would happen exactly as it should and only as it could, from beginning to end, on grounds that they might then trust it to operate by itself while they pursued other interests. Another faction wanted a universe in which nothing was predetermined, on grounds that it would remain eternally interesting, thereby obviating the need to seek outside interests. Some who aspired to immanence, who wished to suffuse and pervade the universe with their essence, maintained that order could be brought out of chaos, summoned forth from it. Others, whose ambition it was to transcend, to exist apart from, the material universe, held that order must be, could only be, imposed upon chaos, from on high or in any case from without. Still others liked things just the way they were and saw no reason to tamper with a system that obviously worked. As those of a legalistic twist of essence discussed the sameness or differentness of otherness and outsideness, the debate raged and flamed into argument, and accusations began to fly, accusations of timid orthodoxy, counter-accusations of reckless unorthodoxy, of incorrectness, heresy, and apostasy, of uncommunicativeness, uncooperativeness, and obstructionism, of imbecility and rationality, of speakable horridness, of inunhumanity and uninhumanity, of general indivinity and all which it implied, from divisibility to visibility to viscosity. The factions began to jostle one another. He felt himself in danger of being trampled and hopefully invoked the protection of his own god. The paleodeities paused and regarded the presumptuous *creature* perplexedly or with more or less indifference, more or less antipathy, each according to its nature, and then collectively and unceremoniously dismissed him, through the simple expedient of crowding him over the edge of the rim. Tumbling toward chaos, he choked down his terror and closed his eyes and prayed. And after a timeless interval the prayer was answered, and he felt something yielding but firm underfoot. He stood on the moonlit path again. He saw that the stars had been

carefully reset in the black sky. He offered up thanks to the only god who knew him, and followed the moon's elongate reflection home to his dreaming self and the rest of dreaming humanity.

FOODSTUFF

The boat taking me upriver broke down the first afternoon out of Stinktown. Doug, the boatman, ran in close to the bank, apologized for what he said would be only a slight delay, and disappeared belowdecks to fuss with his malfunctioning motor or balky galley slaves, whichever.

Till now, I'd kept pretty much to myself, and so had the other passenger. Which suited me just fine. I'd been bunged up on arrival and spent some time in sickbay—jumping through a spacetime anomaly is about as much fun as riding in a spin dryer full of rocks—and I still felt rotten. I was behind schedule, too, which made me feel rottener. There had been a third passenger when we set out, a bland-looking fellow who got off before we even left the marshes behind. The whole time he'd been aboard he just sat on a crate and played a recorder, with a beatific look on his face. He played well, coaxing out of that simple instrument of his what I supposed was something by Mozart, or maybe one of the B's. Given my druthers, he'd've stayed and played, and the other passenger would've gone over the side. As soon as he'd gone, though, The Other Passenger approached with a sort of ducking and bobbing movement, like a stray dog wanting to make friends. There was no way I could pretend not to notice him, so I made a show of pausing in the insertion of my earbook and let him introduce himself as Ellis something or something Ellis (he mumbled), tell me his specialty (something botanical), and make a joke appropriate to our situation (never mind). I replied in kind, skipping only the joke. It really was like feeding a stray dog: he brightened appreciably and stopped mumbling.

He said, "I found the propelling idea for my own line of research in one of Kelly's early monographs."

"Whose?"

"Ivan Kelly. He did a lot of pioneering work here on the evolution of soil and the part mid-Paleozoic terrestrial organisms played in the transformation of sterile regolith into real soil."

"Oh," I said blankly, "him."

"But Kelly also got stranded far inland once and had to eat whatever he could find for a few days. You know, primitive plants and invertebrates. I want to prove that people could live off the land here indefinitely if they had to."

I gave him my best look of mild disapproval. "It's not just the thought of eating slime and bugs. I'm a surveyor, not an ecologist, but even I know this is a delicate ecosphere. I don't think people should be making a real effort to find out what there is to eat here."

"There're already things here eating each other and the plants."

"Take it from a guy who's seen bulldozers mow down forests and mountains in an afternoon. Human beings always end up taking bigger bites than anything else."

"I know. That's why, back in our own time, the world isn't any too homelike any more. People've made it so. The day will come, though, when a few people here decide not to go back. A few determined, resourceful people could live here."

"I don't think anybody could survive here very long. There's no wood for fire or tools. No soil to grow crops in."

"You'd hardly need tools."

"Yeah, not if all you wanted was to eke out an existence as a hunter-gatherer. If you were willing to jettison all the trappings of civilization."

He dared to sneer slightly, and when I didn't immediately assault him, he broadened it. "You mean like computers, television, government?"

"I mean books, music, art, and science and technology."

"Maybe the kind of people I have in mind wouldn't want all those things. Maybe they'd know better this time. They could make this into a very different Earth."

"This is already a very different Earth."

He'd come a good way from mumbling in just a few short minutes; now he spoke with an intensity I had to begun to find creepy. I decided to cut the conversation short and remarked that I really was hopelessly behind in my work and without further adieu stuck in the earbook. It was actually a novel, but he couldn't know. He nodded, backed away, retreated to the stern, where he made a show of admiring the scenery. The Paleozoic landscape is a very nearly bare stage, with a thin fuzz of greenery along its edges. It looks as unpromising as a teenager's first moustache. There's nothing like it to make you mix your metaphors.

But if there hadn't been much to look at while the boat was moving, there was even less now that it had stopped. Ellis must have debated with himself for all of five or six minutes before deciding that I was a lesser evil than boredom. When I saw him start to sidle forward again, I pointedly gazed off into the middle distance and looked rapt. He moved by me and went to the bow, as though that's where he'd been intending to go anyway, and pretended to admire the scenery from that end of the boat.

The sun climbed down the sky. Doug emerged from below decks, with so much machine gunk on him he resembled an old-time minstrel, and told us, "Guess we'll be spending the night here."

I asked, "Can't you call Stinktown for help?"

"I could, but I'm a civilian contractor, and I have my reputation to consider."

"Like your boat breaking down in the middle of nowhere won't affect your reputation."

He smiled tightly. "I can fix the engine, but it's gonna take a while longer." He held up his grimy hands. "Either one of you feel like cooking dinner?"

I looked at Ellis and shrugged and said, "I'll cook." You spend any time in the field, you better know how to fix dinner. But I quickly added, "This once."

Ellis shrugged in turn, trying to look casual. "I'll cook tomorrow."

Doug said, "Okay, good," and went below again.

I went below, too, to the tiny galley. The stores were the usual desiccated stuff, but I flung together this and that and called it an onion soufflé, and Doug, at least, seemed willing to give me the benefit of the doubt once we'd crammed ourselves into the eating area. He'd evidently immersed himself in solvent, because he came to dinner looking spotless and smelling faintly, not unpleasantly, of chemicals.

When he had cleaned his plate, Ellis said Doug, "Are we going to be here very long tomorrow?"

"As long as it takes."

"Then I want to look around. There's an ideal spot at that bend ahead. That bank's bound to have submerged hollows, perfect hideouts."

"Hideouts for what?"

"Fish."

Doug looked just about as incredulous as I felt.

"Be right back," said Ellis, and bolted from the table. He returned dragging, I swear, fishing tackle, which he unloaded untidily in our midst. "First let me show you my rod."

"Not on your life," I said, but he went ahead and showed off his rod, and his net, and the works. "I can't believe you used your personal baggage allowance for this junk."

"I'm one of those rare individuals who's truly able to combine pleasure and research."

"What pleasure?"

"Everyone must have their pastimes."

"I agree. That's why I brought lots of music and long, dense nineteenth-century novels. You can listen to music and read practically anywhere. Fishing, though."

"You don't fish?"

"I was born and raised in a Kansas wheat field."

"So you don't know the first thing about fishing."

That struck me as serious talk from someone I was becoming more and more convinced didn't know the first thing about anything. "The idea's to get the fish on the hook, is it not?"

"Ostensibly," Doug out in. I looked at him in surprise; he lifted a shoulder in a half-shrug. "Definitely, if you're fishing for your supper. I like fishing, too. Or I did, back home. You sometimes fish simply to be at peace with everything."

"Everything except the fish, I guess."

"I bear the fish no malice. Unless I was hungry, I always released the ones I caught. I enjoy fishing for the sake of fishing."

"I see. It's a zen exercise."

We had been ignoring Ellis. "Here and now," he cut in resentfully, "I'm going to catch fish for food and study." He opened a leather case, and its contents lay gleaming in the light from the overhead. "I made all of these lures myself, to experiment with." He pointed to some nasty-looking bare barbs. "Those're just for raw bait, of course, for fish that hunt by smell or taste. But these—" he indicated several colorful tied flies "—are designed to attract those that hunt by sight. And this—" a bullet-like thing "—is for fish that hunt by sound."

"Fish don't have ears."

"They have vibration sensor organs." He motioned for me to hold out my hand, then picked up the bullet-like thing, gave it a twist, and dropped it into my palm, where it lay humming and tickling insistently.

"My ex traded me in for one of these," I said, "only larger."

Doug had been regarding Ellis's battery of lures with undisguised skepticism. Now he said, "I hate to be the one to have to tell you, but there isn't a fish on Earth now with the physical or mental equipment to snap at one of your lures."

"I guess we'll find out if that's true."

I said, "I've heard reports—no, maybe they're only rumors—something, anyhow, about freshwater sharks."

"Pseudosharklets," Doug said, "little things, about as long as your hand. They have jaws, and they eat invertebrates."

"Wouldn't be much sport in catching a fish that tiny."

"The sport," Doug said, "is in standing hip-deep in muddy water for hours."

"Very relaxing, I'm sure."

Once again we were ignoring Ellis. "Well," he announced, "I have a more serious purpose than sport. I am, as the saying goes, after bigger fish."

"Read my lips," Doug said. "There are no big fish here. If you pull anything bigger than my hand out of this creek or any other body of water here in the Paleozoic, I'll eat it."

"Good!"

I didn't like the way he said that. Not at all.

"I've been thinking a lot lately," he went on, "that everybody could use a change from the same old foodstuffs."

Doug looked at him suspiciously. "What's wrong with the same old foodstuffs? We've got all my favorites."

Ellis wrinkled his nose. "Dried vegetables, rice, oatmeal, and the ever-popular meat bar. While, mathematically speaking, the number of possible combinations is astronomical, the practical combinations are limited. I've been experimenting."

Doug shook his head. "Don't like the sound of that word, experiment. Don't like it at all."

I nodded agreement. "Not where food's concerned."

"Hear me out. I volunteer to do lunch if you'll give me a free hand."

"Hell, no," Doug said.

"What he said," I said.

Ellis was clearly disappointed. "I don't get it. I bet, ordinarily, back home, you guys'd eat almost anything. Stale pizza, undermicrowaved frozen food."

"We knew what that stuff was," said Doug.

"You're as bad as little kids."

"There's also the matter of nutrition," I said. "What about vitamins and minerals? Protein?"

"Well, that's part of my project, too. I'm on the lookout for esculent Paleozoic organisms."

"What kind?" Doug asked.

"Suitable for use as human food. This is not off-the-wall stuff. It isn't just paleobiological research I'm interested in. I've always been fascinated by the history of food. I've always wondered who figured out things like how to make bread or what you had to do to an olive to make it edible."

"How about who figured out how to turn a cow into meat bar?"

Ellis pretended I hadn't spoken. "And fugu! What about fugu? Who figured out which part of the blowfish is edible and which part'll kill you dead?"

"Maybe people in some Japanese fishing village," Doug said. "Blowfish was all they could catch that week, and they were starving."

"Well, even if they were, you'd think as soon as the first couple of people keeled over dead—"

"Well, maybe it was some Japanese nobleman who just rounded up a bunch of peasants and told 'em, Each of you eat part of this blowfish, I want to see what happens. What're they gonna do? The choice's between maybe being poisoned if they comply or definitely getting their heads lopped off if they don't."

"Well, be that as it may," Ellis said, "I propose to see what I can do with the materials available locally. Back at Stinktown, I sampled the fish, shellfish, seaweeds. Here—"

"Yuck," said Doug, "seaweed!"

"It's the same stuff you find wrapped around sushi—"

"Yuck," said Doug, "sushi," but Ellis kept right on talking.

"—or it's its ancestor, anyway."

"How can you be sure," I asked, "those things aren't all loaded with defensive toxins? Or that one of those ugly little fish isn't the Paleozoic equivalent of fugu. You want to poison yourself, don't let anybody stop you. But don't be wanting to poison everyone else with you."

"I've devised a few simple tests to determine the presence of toxins. However, this is not a sophisticated biota, relative to what we know back in our own time. In four hundred million years, land plants will have evolved all sorts of chemical defenses against parasites and things. The little stems we see here, though, they're just barely plants as it is. They don't even have roots. They haven't evolved the complex range of chemical defenses their descendants need because there isn't the horde of parasites here."

"Doesn't mean that some preadapted sprig couldn't put us all in our graves," Doug said. "It doesn't even have to kill us, it might just give us the runs."

"I want to give it a try, all the same. I promise you that I shall never set anything before you that I haven't subjected to rigorous chemical analysis." Ellis looked from Doug to me and back. "Come on. In the spirit of scientific inquiry. Look, don't say yes or no now, sleep on it." He gathered up his junk, somehow without putting out anyone's eye, and left us sitting

"Don't know about you," Doug said, "but I'm not inclined to be one of his guinea pigs."

"Think I'll pass, too." I put my tongue between my molars for a second. "Still, he's got a point, hasn't he? The knowledge of what's edible and what's not might come in handy. Survival in the wilderness and all that. What if our boat were to break down in the middle of nowhere?"

"Oh," said Doug, "that's funny. Ha, ha." His pocket beeper went off. "That's for the radio. Must be a weather report." He worked himself free and rose from the table. Over his shoulder, he let me have it between the eyes with one last Ha.

The night was no cooler than the day. The three of us spread pallets on deck, and Ellis tried to launch us into conversation again, but Doug told him to shut up and go to sleep. Their voices were the only sounds under the black starshot Paleozoic sky; the exchange was jarring. I tossed and writhed and don't remember sleeping at all, though at one point I noticed that the moon had suddenly changed position. Then—again, suddenly—I heard the engine turning over. I opened my eyes and saw the sun hovering its own diameter above the eastern horizon. The engine stopped. I sat up and looked around. I was alone on deck.

Doug was in the galley, brewing coffee and mixing oatmeal and dried fruit. "Engine's fixed," he said as he handed me a cup.

"Then we can be on our merry way."

"Not just yet."

"Christ. What's the problem now?"

"There's still something I've got to take care of."

I looked around. "Where's Ellis?"

"Said he was going grocery shopping."

"Uh oh."

"Do me a favor, help me keep an eye on Nature Boy this morning, will you?"

I sat down heavily. "He's really a flake, isn't he?"

"You—we probably don't know the half of it."

"Did he take all that ridiculous fishing gear with him?"

"Nope. Just a net and a couple of plastic buckets. Anyway, we don't want him wandering off or getting hurt."

"We don't?"

"Have some oatmeal."

After breakfast, I went up on deck. At first there was no sign of Ellis, but then I saw him wading well upstream; every now and then he'd bend down, reach into the water, and put something into one of the buckets. My first impulse was to yell at him to get out of the goddamn water. Then I thought. So what if a eurypterid does get him? Eurypterid is Greek, or maybe it's Latin, for "big ugly water bug with an attitude."

No such luck, though. I tired of waiting to see him pulled under and plugged in my earbook and went back to *The Way of All Flesh*. Thus far, it had gone kind of like an Anthony Trollope novel with bamboo splints shoved under its fingernails—Samuel Butler suffered from no deficiency of bile—but now it had a somehow soothing effect. I found myself enjoying it even more, Ellis having provided me with a face for Butler's unlovable main character.

Doug came on deck after a while and busied himself checking the crates lashed amidships, then went into the wheelhouse, came back out, went below, came back up, went back into his wheelhouse, fiddled with the radio, came back out, etc. I hadn't figured him for the anxious type, but you just never know; if anyone had a right to be antsy, it was me. He kept looking downriver, in the direction of Stinktown, and checking his wristwatch, too. Finally I called to him, "Don't worry, I've had my eye on him the whole time, he's right over yonder," and pointed to Ellis. Doug glanced in that direction and nodded to me, but he made no attempt to summon Ellis, just went into a new cycle of repetitions, wheelhouse, deck, look around, check the time.

The morning wore on. Ellis returned lugging his now-filled buckets and went straight down into the galley. A little before noon, he re-emerged and proudly announced that luncheon was served.

I took my time getting up, and Doug, whom I could see in the wheelhouse, hesitated as well before bestirring himself. Down in the galley, Ellis set steaming plates before us.

"What is it," I asked, "creamed spinach?"

"Of course not. The green stuff's a water plant."

"I'm not eating pond scum," Doug said.

"It's not pond scum. The pink strips're fish." Ellis looked at me smugly. "Protein, you know."

Doug said, "I'm not eating this stuff, whatever it is." He pushed the plate away, reached around to grab things out of the food locker, and stuck a slice of meat bar between two crackers.

"Come on," Ellis implored me, "just taste it. Look," and he conveyed some green slime from his own plate to his mouth. I watched carefully to see that he swallowed. "Quite tasty, really."

"That trick didn't work for my mom, it sure's hell won't work for you."

"Do it for science."

I muttered a curse under my breath and picked up my fork. Doug smirked at me around his mouthful of meat bar sandwich. The green stuff tasted a little like turnip greens; Ellis had used a lot of vinegar and tossed in dried shallots, too, which I thought was cheating. I resisted the impulse to ask if Ivan Kelly had just happened to have condiments on him that time he'd got lost in the wilderness.

Instead, I gingerly sampled the fish, and after chewing and swallowing, I said, "Tastes like anchovies, only saltier, oilier. Fishier."

"Nonsense," Ellis said happily. "It's an estuarine fish—the Paleozoic equivalent of catfish."

Picking at my food, I inexorably reduced the volume on my plate. Ellis ate with unabashed gusto. He had finished two big helpings by the time I was down to my last couple of bites. Doug washed down his repast with a beer and left after favoring me with another smirk; to Ellis he said only, "Cook cleans up."

Ellis gave me a big smile, revealing a bit of green stuff stuck on an eyetooth. "Finish up," he said, "there's dessert!"

I draw a merciful veil of silence over what followed.

Afterward, I left him in the galley and went on deck. Doug was leaning against the wheelhouse, looking off downriver. "You waiting for a tow?" I said, but he only shook his head. I tried to take up my novel where I'd left off. Ellis appeared after a time and approached me smiling. The bit of green stuff was still stuck to his smile.

"Well," he said, "was Kelly onto something, or wasn't he?"

I cut off Samuel Butler in mid-tirade and said, "Yes, Kelly was a genius. And you are truly worthy to take up his mantle. Forgive me for having ever doubted it."

"I just meant—since you obviously weren't completely revolted—"

His face had fallen slightly, and in spite of myself I felt I owed him something. "No, I wasn't revolted. In fact, I did manage to clean my plate, so I guess compliments are due to the chef. My compliments, chef. A word of friendly advice, though. Don't go into the catering business when you get back home."

"Okay, so I admit it isn't fun food. The point is, you now know you could survive here if you had to—live off the land."

I thought that was still pretty arguable, but all I said was, "Well, let's hope I never have to."

"What's that?"

I became aware, all at once, of a faint drumming sound. It quickly grew louder and resolved itself into the beating of helicopter blades, and I turned to see a Navy machine approaching us—low and fast, purposefully, like a barracuda—from the direction of Stinktown. Ellis saw it at the same moment. He looked stunned. Then he screamed, "Goddammit!" and leaped over the side of the boat. He flailed through the shallow water and scrambled, muddy and trailing algal filaments, onto the bank. He ran a short distance in one direction, then in another, paused to look up at the helicopter, ran several more yards in several more different directions. The helicopter settled to within a foot of the ground, and three bluejackets jumped out and quickly closed on him. Ellis ran in a circle, then stopped suddenly and plopped down on the ground. Even at that distance I could see that he was crying like a baby. The bluejackets scooped him up, not ungently, and half-led, half-dragged him toward the helicopter. Crouching in the door of the helicopter was a young Navy officer and another man, a civilian I vaguely recalled from Stinktown. The bluejackets loaded Ellis into the helicopter, the civilian patted him reassuringly on the arm, then looked our way, smiled, gave us the thumbs-up. I looked around to see Doug acknowledge with a wave, though he wasn't returning the smile. The helicopter rose, turned, pointed itself, and flew away, back toward Stinktown.

I watched until the machine had dwindled to a dot, then went over to Doug and demanded, "Now what the hell was that all about?"

"Ellis was supposed to go home with the rest of his group day before yesterday. He told me he was going upriver to do field work. I thought he was traveling sort of light, but he'd done a good job of faking his authorizations. Anyway, they turned the camp inside out looking for him, climbed all over the headlands. They were about to start dragging the marsh when somebody thought to send out an A.P.B. I got it after dinner last night and radioed back I'd wait here until they came to collect him."

"So he was really going to go off into the wilderness and try to live on slime and bugs." I spread my hands in a gesture of disbelief. "Isn't screening supposed to keep lunatics out of Paleozoic time?"

"Just the obvious ones."

"How obvious do they have to be?" He had no answer for that, so I said, "Well, you might at least've told them to come get him before I had to eat goddamn pond scum for lunch."

"'S what you get," he said as he turned to go into the wheelhouse, "for making fun of my boatmanship."

Far inland, the river separates into its tributaries. Bands of color mark some of the confluences; the waters rushing down from ancient highlands are relatively clear, those meandering across the peneplain are turbid and brown.

And wouldn't you know it, we ran aground on a sand bar Doug swore hadn't been there the trip before. He said he could rock us off, but it would take a little while.

Strangely calm, I nodded and glanced up at the sky. It was almost noon. "While you're rocking," I said, "why don't I whip us up some lunch."

He nodded absently. "Good idea. You know where everything is."

"Yep, pretty much."

I went to the galley and tossed all of Doug's meat bars through a porthole. Then I went looking for Ellis's net and buckets.

CHAIN OF LIFE

The helicopter flew low over a moon-gray landscape. The island was a succession of barren knife-edge promontories rising steeply from the blue-black waters of the Iaepetus Ocean to converge on a point inland. Streams flowed swiftly between the ridges, emptying into marshy borders. Seated precariously behind Dixon and the pilot, L.V.—not so much in the machine as upon it—French let his gaze travel along the curve of a black ridge toward the volcano's summit. The volcano itself looked like a high rugged hill with a crown of thin gray cloud.

He saw Dixon give L.V. a gentle nudge and point down at a flat spur of rock at the rim of the crater. Shouting to make himself heard above the whir of the blades, Dixon said, "Set her down there, I want to take a look."

French glanced downward between the landing skids and felt a sharp pang of uneasiness. The spur formed a platform no wider, it seemed to him, than a sidewalk. Dixon was a solid barrel-chested man who looked as though he should weigh more than the skeletal helicopter could lift, as though, in fact, he might weigh more than the helicopter itself; French and L.V. were only relatively more compactly built, and the pilot constantly had to compensate.

Moreover, though the two volcanologists had approached the crater's rim before to collect ash samples and French knew the composition of its crusted surface—pulverized mountain, mostly, leavened with new, glassy ash—in spite of himself, he imagined the skids breaking through, sinking, the lip of the crater crumbling beneath the combined weight of men and machine, tipping sundry and all into the volcano. L.V. positioned the helicopter over the spur and descended to within a hand's span of the surface. Dixon unstrapped himself, stepped off, and looked expectantly at French, who thought, Dammit, goddammit, and unbuckled his own seat belt. His uneasiness flared almost into fright as his feet crunched through the surface. He sank, however, only to his ankles in the gritty stuff and easily pulled free. It was no worse than walking in coarse sand.

Dixon leaned toward L.V. and shouted, "Come on, put her down, take a look with us."

L.V. shook his head and shouted back at him, "I better wait here for you."

"Chance of a lifetime."

L.V. shook his head again, more emphatically. "Against the rules."

"Don't be a pussy."

The pilot's face hardened into an unhappy mask. Dixon shrugged and grinned, but there was a sneer tucked into the corner of the grin. Then he gave French a hearty slap on the shoulder and motioned for him to follow.

They crept to the brink of a chasm at least thirty meters wide. French heard the hiss of escaping gas and a cacophony of grinding and popping as rocks cracked and split apart in the intense heat. His skin prickled, and he blinked constantly to keep his eyeballs moist, but through a bright vaporous shimmer he made out a huge jumble of volcanic debris which he at first took to be the opposite wall of the crater, then recognized as the bulge of the lava dome. He cautiously leaned forward to peer over the edge, into the abyss, down a rough wall that looked perfectly perpendicular. He could see down about forty meters, but the bottom was obscured. Okay, he thought, looking at Dixon, we've stuck our heads into the lion's mouth, let's get out of here. Dixon seemed to have noticed French's discomfiture, though, and made a point of taking his time.

Finally, they did fly back down the mountain, back to the camp. As they made their approach for landing, French saw the other member of the geology team waiting below. Toombs ran forward, ducking under the whirling blades, and shouted to Dixon, "Another tremor just now, while you were airborne." He did not wait for Dixon to unbuckle his seat belt but unfolded a long sheet of computer printout across his lap and ran a finger down a column of data. While L.V. worked around them to secure the helicopter, Dixon and French studied the print for some minutes.

Dixon pursed his lips thoughtfully and looked at Toombs. "Didn't knock any of our laser targets out of alignment, I hope."

Toombs' face split in a toothy grin. "Naw. But the pulse is picking up."

French said, "I think the suspense is pretty much over."

Dixon nodded. "We've done all we can do here. I think it's time to get everybody the hell out. I'm giving the order. Let's get 'em all together."

As they walked toward the small camp, de Souza emerged from her tent. Dixon called to her to assemble the other three members of the biology team, Bearden, Gentry, and Pope. French exchanged smiles with Carol Bearden as she strolled up. They had met at the main camp two months earlier, when the Caledonian Land Survey Group was being organized; they now shared a tent, an arrangement that raised eyebrows among neither the biologists nor the geologists. She said, "We had another quake just now."

"So I understand."

Dixon said, "Well, friends and neighbors," and pointed, and every face turned toward the mountain, which at the moment sported a wispy plume, "the big firework show's about due to begin."

"How soon, you think?" said de Souza.

"Damn soon. First rule of the profession is, never bet the farm on predictions of exactly what a volcano's going to do or when it's going to do it. But we knew from seismic data three months ago there was going to be an eruption here. Now we've got two months' worth of data collected on-site that tells us it's definitely coming within the month, maybe within the next week or two."

"Cutting it kind of fine, aren't you?"

Toombs nodded, "It could even happen within the next couple or three days."

"How definite is that *probably*, Dix?"

Dixon scratched his grizzled jaw and said, "It's a pretty damn foregone definite probably."

"Ah, hell," said Gentry. "Are you sure?"

Dixon gave him a good-natured sort of exasperated look and said, "Do we ask you if you're sure about your bugs? You know we've worked our butts off installing instruments all around the crater." He began to count off on his fingers as he talked. "We got geodimeters and stream gauges. We got seismometers to measure movement under the volcano. We got gravity meters to measure vertical swellings. We got tiltmeters and laser targets to detect bulging in the mountainside—and every damn toy we got is linked by remote-controlled telemetry units to computer, so we can process the data quickly. The face of the mountain's swelling laterally at the rate of two meters a day. The instruments we took to analyze escaping gases show a big increase in sulfur dioxide content. High sulfur dioxide content tells us there's juvenile magma rising toward the surface. Infrared aerial photos show hot spots in the crater and on the flanks. We're getting those small-magnitude quakes at the rate of more than a dozen per hour." He put his fists on his hips and surveyed his colleagues with a mock-belligerent expression on his face. "And if you won't take our gizmos' word for it, just now, we just now landed on the rim of the crater to see for ourselves. The kettle's definitely on the boil."

French saw the expression on Carol Bearden's face when Dixon mentioned the excursion on the crater's rim, and he thought, Uh oh. Dixon saw it, too, and just grinned at her, and French thought, again, Uh oh. He knew that it only infuriated her more when Dixon just grinned at her. Dixon looked around at the group. "So. The bang's going to happen, and soon, and it's time for you folks to get the hell out of here."

"But," said Gentry, "I'm just not *finished* here." He appealed to de Souza. The sympathetic expression on her broad face became more so as he said, "Every day, I discover a new arachnid species."

De Souza unfolded her arms and extended a brown hand to touch Gentry's sleeve. "John," she said, "we knew from the first we'd end up clearing off this island in a hurry."

"But yesterday I identified a new species of spider. It's the size of a flea."

She started to speak again, but Dixon beat her to it. "John," he said, "we're all proud for you. But the bulging's on the flank facing us, and the next big seismic shock ought to make it go. When all that fractured rock does go, the blast'll almost certainly be nozzled horizontally, in our direction. Even if it's nozzled vertically, we're expecting a dirty blast. Our surveys of the thick pyroclastic deposits here tell us past eruptions've been extremely violent. Even if it's only a moderately dirty blast, with the prevailing winds, the ash cloud'll smother this whole end of the island. And there go your spiders the size of fleas. And everything else, too. We're talking about a blast that probably kills everything on and around this island. We have a plan for evacuation, and I say it's in effect as of this moment. The Navy's been standing by, and they'll be here tomorrow expecting you to be ready to be flown out. So you need to get everything packed and stacked."

Gentry and Pope turned to de Souza as though she alone could rescind Dixon's order and make the volcano behave. She smiled at them and shook her head, "Dix has the say-so when it comes to the volcano. The word is, packed and stacked." She flashed a look at Dixon. To Gentry and Pope she said, "Sorry, boys. Even if I knew enough to disagree with Dix, I know better than to argue with him."

She walked away trailing two distinctly unhappy-looking biologists. The third unhappy-looking biologist started to follow, then turned suddenly, folded her arms, and glared at French and Dixon. "Landed on the rim of the crater?" she said. "Whose brilliant idea was that? As if I really needed to ask."

French was sheepish, but Dixon put a huge happy expression on his face. "Carol honey," he said, "the only place to land near the crater was practically right in the crater."

"Don't you ever call me that again. And you don't have to look as though you live for landings on active volcanoes."

Dixon seemed to reflect for a moment. Then he said, "Perhaps I do live for it," and his happy expression became more so. "Volcanology is all about fire-spitting mountains. This is what a volcanologist lives for. To peek down Vulcan's chimney. I tell you, some people think the Silurian's dull, but that's just because it's not all full of obvious melodrama."

"Dix," Carol said, "some of us prefer it not to be all full of obvious melodrama."

"Ah, but sometimes you can't avoid melodrama."

"Do you even try to avoid it?"

"Why would I do that? Laurentia and Eurasia are colliding. This end of the Iaepetus is closing, mountains're getting built. But it's all in fits and starts and in slow motion. It takes millions of years. The Silurian ends, the Devonian begins. Or maybe the Silurian's already ended, and the Devonian's begun. The segue's so gradual nobody can agree exactly where the boundary is. But one thing I do know, on this island, we're standing right at the point of contact—right on the leading edge of Laurentia as it slams into Eurasia."

She looked expectantly at French.

Say something, idiot, he told himself, *anything*—

She made a disgusted sound, wheeled, and stalked away.

"I'm sure going to be catching hell for this for a while," French said ruefully. "Maybe for quite a while."

"Female disapproval," said Dixon, "is one of the things I came to the Paleozoic to avoid. If I can't avoid it, I try to ignore it."

"There are compensations."

"Woman like that," Dixon said, "wants it all. Career, marriage, family, your balls."

French exhaled sharply. "Look," he said, "I'll be back directly and give you a hand, okay?"

Dixon waved him away. "Go on. Rush to your doom."

French found Carol sitting on a camp stool in their tent, sorting through a miscellany of papers. She barely glanced at him.

He said, "Well, it doesn't take a genius to tell you're pissed off. I'm sorry."

"I noticed you let Dix do all the talking back there."

"Dix is—"

She threw up her hands and stood. "Christ, Mike! Dix is just not the person I'm really mad at here. Are you trying to get yourself killed?"

"No." He could feel heat starting to creep up his neck. "Of course not."

"Then it must just've been a testosterone surge. I don't like this macho crap. I'm not going to tell you how to do your job, but please answer me one question absolutely truthfully. Does actually sticking your head into a live volcano tell you anything you couldn't learn from checking your instruments?"

He thought, If both of us lose our tempers here—He took a slow breath and said, "No. Not really."

Carol rolled her eyes, closed them, shook her head. "What if the volcano had all of a sudden erupted? No, wait, what'm I saying? The volcano wouldn't *dare* erupt while you were clomping around on it under the personal protection of the great man."

"We had the chopper."

"Can it outrun a pyroclastic blast?"

"Nope, and neither could you," and French pointed through the open end of the tent, toward the distant volcano, "not even with this much of a head start. We're all taking a chance being here."

"That is not the point."

"Carol, I said I was sorry. I mean that. It was a stupid thing to do, and I knew at the time it was stupid. I don't want to fight with you." He sat down on his cot, knitted his fingers, clutched his hands between his knees. "Not when you're right."

She sat down on the camp stool and regarded him. "I know there're hazards in your work. If you got killed in the line of duty, I'd grieve; I'd be heartbroken, but I'd tell myself you got killed doing your job. But if you got killed trying to prove you're as much of a man as Dix is—I already *know* how much of a man you are."

"Look. You're going all the way back to the base camp, and I'm going to be out here at least until the volcano does decide to erupt. I don't want you to be mad at me the whole time we're separated. I want you to—"

"Want me to what?"

"I want you to miss me as much as I'm going to miss you."

"I am going to miss you—terribly. You've just got to promise me you won't let Dix shame you into joining him in any more stupid stunts."

He felt his neck grow warm again, felt his face redden. "He didn't shame me."

"Of course he did. Dix is the person your mother was warning you about when she asked you if everybody jumped off a cliff, would you do it too. I know how Dix operates because my dad was exactly like him. Be a man, he was always telling my brother. Don't be a spineless little faggot. Live dangerously, impress the girls. That advice put my brother in a wheelchair for keeps."

"Dix's just excited about his work."

"Dix is demented about his work."

He moved closer to her, extended a hand to stroke her hair and cup her cheek; after a moment, she moved her head slightly and kissed the heel of his hand. "He's *excited*," he said. "And I'm excited. As excited as you are about finding out if your, your whatsits, your wiggly things—"

"Cosmopolitan Silurian faunas."

"—are already turning into crawly things."

"Giving way to slightly more isolated and parochial Devonian faunas." She smiled, finally. "I'm excited. I'm not out of my mind. I'm not taking needless risks to prove I'm a man."

He ran a hand down her back, slipped it around her side, touched the side of her breast. "Not even needless risks could prove that. So, okay, Dix is overexcited about his work."

"Dix is your id, Mike." She made a moue. He moved his hand slightly. "But to hell with him. Close that tent flap. Let's get excited about something else."

Later, as they lay fitted together like spoons on the cot, she murmured, "I can't say I won't always have wonderful memories of this island."

"If it doesn't blow itself to atoms, maybe it eventually piles up against Scotland or Ireland. We could come back and visit it sometime. Back in the twenty-first century. You know. A vacation. Or a honeymoon."

She did not reply until several seconds had passed, during which his fingers, tucked lightly into her armpit, felt the beating of her heart and he heard to the throb of blood in his own ears. Then: "Why would I ever marry a man who'd fly into a volcano?"

He nuzzled the back of her neck. "Maybe to keep him from hurting himself?"

French spent the afternoon running a detailed instrument check with Dixon and Toombs while L.V. serviced his helicopter and everyone else pulled up stakes, pulled down tents, and packed gear. It was almost dark when they had finished.

That night, French awoke suddenly to the smell of partially digested food. He sat up on his cot and looked around. The tent flap was open, and somebody was standing just outside, making retching noises. He got his flashlight and played the beam over the cot opposite his. It was empty. He called softly, "Carol?"

He found his entrenching tool and leaned out of the tent. She stood illumined by moonlight, with the back of her hand pressed against her mouth.

"I woke up nauseous," she said. "I barely made it out of the tent in time."

"Where is it?"

She took the entrenching tool from him. "It's my mess, I'll clean it up. Go back to sleep."

"Are you okay? Do you feel—"

"Camp cooking always upsets my stomach."

"We eat camp cooking two, three times a day."

"And it always upsets my stomach. Go back to bed. I'll be back as soon—soon."

"Anything I can do in the meantime?"

"You can stop fretting over me."

"Sorry."

The first thing he did when he awoke the following morning was shake out his boots. Thus far during his sojourn in the Paleozoic, however, no venomous invertebrates, nor even any nonvenomous ones, had ever tumbled out. That was fine by him. He thrust his legs into canvas shorts and his sock-clad feet into the boots. Carol lay on the other cot in skivvies with an arm thrown over her face; he bent over her and gently stroked her forearm with a fingertip. She groaned suddenly, opened her eyes, reclosed them, groaned again. She said, "I feel awful. Airsick."

"You haven't left the ground yet."

"It's the thought I'm going to." She sat up and swung her feet to the ground and put her head in her hands. She said, "Christ." She reached out and took his hand and gave him a wan smile. "Go on and get yourself some breakfast. You know where to look for me."

After he had eaten, he found her squatting on the rocky verge of the marsh. It had been part of her morning ritual, every day at sunrise, to reconnoiter the border of what she called The Plant Kingdom. There was nothing very imposing about its inhabitants. There were creeping green tendrils, some with forked aerial stems, some topped with round sporangia. Some of the tendrils were as thick as pencils, others seemed little more substantial than spider web. None had leaves. None had roots; their purchase on the ground was tenuous. All reached more or less upward, but none possessed the vascular rigidity to stand very tall; none came as high as his knee. There was nothing very orderly about them, either: they lay inextricably entwined with one another upon the mushy ground. At first, they had looked to him not so much like plants as a matted litter of twigs and small round unidentifiable bits of plant debris. He had known nothing of botany, but she had taught him the names of the various genera. He knew *Psilophyton, Protolepidodendron, Sciadophyton, Drepanophycus.*

He stood a short distance from her now, and after a minute or so he said, "Hi. Feeling better?"

She had glanced back over her shoulder at him when she heard him coming, then down again at The Plant Kingdom. The marsh, which was cut into a monotonous quilt of greens, grays, and browns by narrow alga-choked waterways, seemed motionless. A patient observer, however, would have eventually noticed small crawling arthropods close by. Occasionally, a scorpion crawled through the miniature forest. There was a smell of decomposition; lying in a muddy puddle amid the plants was a fish part—an eyeless bony head about the size of a silver dollar. Insects and other arthropods swarmed over it. Finally, she said, "They're trying to make soil."

French stepped closer to her, thrust his hands into his pockets, rocked gently on his heels, said nothing.

She looked out over the marsh. "Well," she went on, "if it wasn't the volcano, the next flood would've washed most of it away, and flattened most of the plants as well. And even that little river flows into an ocean that's being squeezed out of existence. Life's coming ashore, against terrific odds. I know that in the long run, soil will cling to the earth. But I grieve for my miniature forest anyway. The organisms on this island are going to die without issue and won't even get to turn into fossils. Except for the anomaly that let us come here, nobody'd know they ever existed. These rhyniophytes are brave little things. I love them for their simplicity and ambition, their fragility and determination. There's this long unbroken chain of life stretching from each and every one of us—from every living thing on earth—all the way back to our most distant Precambrian ancestor. Every link in that chain's an organism that struggled to get us where we are. Here on this island, all that effort's meant nothing."

"Maybe not. Otherwise, why would de Souza want to come back here right after the eruption to check for signs of regeneration?"

"Rene's more optimistic than I am."

"But it is just barely possible some small animals might survive if they were in mud or underwater when the blast reaches here. And there's a plant that can start growing like a week or two after an eruption. Fireweed."

"We're a long, long time from fireweed. None of these plants is nearly that tough. It's all they can do to keep from drying out in air."

"Honey," French said, touching her shoulder, "I'm sorry."

It was mid-morning when the big Navy cargo helicopter came in low over the sea. It circled the camp once and positioned itself above a relatively level patch of rock on which the scientists had marked a long white stripe intersected at a right angle by a shorter white stripe. The helicopter settled to earth, the engine noise died in a whine, and two bluejackets got out and immediately began helping the scientists load equipment. It was a well-organized evacuation and did not take long. The plan was for L.V. to fly Dixon and French in his small helicopter to a rocky islet located at a theoretically safe distance from the volcano, where a field station had already been established. Toombs and other geologists would observe the eruption from positions along the loaf-shaped mainland of Caledonian Land. After they had observed the eruption, the Navy would collect them and return them to the main base, far to the southwest.

As Toombs and the biology team prepared to board the big helicopter, Dixon said, "Well, folks, we'll see you back in Stinktown."

Carol Bearden approached and handed French a book. "In case you get bored on your little desert island," she said.

French turned it over in his hands, read the spine, made a quizzical face. "Jane Austen?"

"It's a comedy of manners. It may have a morally uplifting effect on Dix if you read it to him."

"Carol honey," said Dixon, as French stuffed the book into a pocket, "I appreciate the thought. But—bored? Here? Now?" He grinned and made an expansive gesture. "We're in the last moments, geologically speaking, of pre-Pangaean time! Continents are plunging recklessly at one another at the breakneck speed of a few centimeters per year!"

"Geology is not a contact sport." She gave French a quick kiss. "Take care of yourself. Don't do anything stupid. I mean it." She gave Dixon a warning look. "Dix, if you get him hurt or killed, you'd damn well better die with him."

Dixon flashed her a big grin. "You know, you're beautiful when you're making death-threats."

French did not like flying over open water, but L.V. got him and Dixon to the islet without incident. The islet was a barren, sheer-sided, flat-topped volcanic plug pounded by plunging breakers. L.V. covered the helicopter with a tarpaulin while the two volcanologists unpacked instruments and made a radio check. Then they settled down to wait for the volcano to erupt.

"We may be back home in another month," Dixon said over their simple evening meal.

L.V. smiled; it was almost a dreamy smile. "I can't wait to see my wife and kids again."

"You know," Dixon said, "the more I think about going back and arguing about the data and writing the papers—and fighting for more damn funding—" He snorted contemptuously. "This is supposed to be my last visit to the Paleozoic. They tell me I'm too old and fragile to do any more time-traveling."

"What about you?" French asked L.V. "Think you'll come back?"

The pilot shrugged. "If I can."

"Whaddya mean, if?" said Dixon. "You could almost start your own charter service here."

"Okay, make that, as soon as I can."

Dixon speculatively eyed the tarpaulin-draped form of the helicopter. "When it's time to go," he said to L.V., "I hate the thought of you having to disassemble that thing. I'm glad you showed me how to handle it. I wonder if Captain Kelly'd change his mind about letting me try a deck landing."

"Navy's real particular," L.V. said deliberately, "about who crashes on its ships."

"How much damage could a bicycle with a fan on it do?"

French folded his arms across his chest. "Well, I won't be in any hurry, but I would like to come back some day. Organize a trip out that way," and he nodded toward the unbroken horizon. "Maybe, if I play up the regional angle."

"What do you mean?"

"Out on Laurentia's trailing edge, California, the mountain ranges, they don't exist yet. My home state, Nevada, right now it's all oceanfront property. Back home, we puzzle over a few areas that have folding and warping. We know, because there're no pre-Silurian arc-derived volcanic components in western assemblage oceanic rocks, that there just isn't any major tectonicism in the Great Basin during the time span from the erosion of the Prepaleozoic highlands until the Late Devonian. There're just those few intriguing wrinkles in Siluro-Devonian deep-water rocks in Nevada. So what produced the wrinkles? It's mysterious, tantalizing. The answer's out there—" again he nodded toward the horizon "—somewhere far off."

"Probably," Dixon said, "it's sea-floor plate sliding under the edge of the continental plate. Sea-floor plate melts, light-weight molten components're forced upward through the overlying oceanic plate, back to the surface—maybe creating an offshore arc of volcanic islands."

"There wouldn't necessarily have to be active volcanism," French said. "There doesn't have to be an arc. It could be a continental fragment, drifting toward North America. Those deepwater western assemblage clastics may just've been eroded off the fragment, into the oceanic basin between it and Laurentia."

"Mm. Could be. The siliceous sediments would have—"

"The point I'm trying to make is, I wish we had the resources to find out if there is a landmass out that way. If they'd spend a little extra money on the next photo-satellite they send up, maybe it'll stay in orbit long enough for us to get some good of it."

Dixon grunted assent. "Me, I'd like to go take a look around in the southern hemisphere. Have to bring my own ship, though. Navy's already pitching fits about running back and forth between Stinktown and here. I'll get to visit Gondwanaland the day after you get your satellite. That'll be the day after the astronomers get that big multi-billion-dollar radio telescope array they're always going on about." They laughed.

L.V. said, "Can't you guys ever talk about anything except geology? Here we got a swell moon lighting up a great unknown sea, *and*—" He produced a silver flask from his pocket and unscrewed the cap.

"Speaks to the romantic in me," Dixon said, holding out his tin cup.

L.V. poured everyone a drink, then a second one for Dixon and himself. French declined. "Think I'll be turning in." He stood up and stretched. "'S been a long day."

The flask made a liquid sound as L.V. shook it. "Sure you don't want a nightcap?"

"Leave him alone," Dixon said. "Only one thing speaks to the romantic in him. He's crazy about a cute biologist. Right, Mike?"

"Cut it out," French said, frowning. He was looking down at Dixon, who was grinning up at him; tucked into the corner of the grin was the sneer.

"I guess I see why," Dixon went on, "though that de Souza's more to my taste. A healthy strapping handsome woman, and a model of forbearance."

"A what?" said L.V.

"The sort of woman who'd let a man have his own way for twenty, even thirty years before she up and stuck a knife in him."

"Oh," said L.V. "That sounds like my old lady."

French crawled into his sleeping bag but did not fall asleep immediately. Lying alone after having been with Carol for so long felt strange.

He had first seen her collecting soil specimens at the base camp, colloquially known as Stinktown. He had come up behind her unexpectedly, she had seen him a second or two after he had seen her; her face seemed to lengthen as her eyes widened and her mouth opened; she gave a soft yelp and made a little sideward hop.

"I'm sorry," he said, "I didn't mean to startle you," at the same moment she said, "*Don't* be sneaking up on people like that!"

"I'm really sorry," he told her. "I wasn't trying to sneak up on you. I was looking around up there—" he pointed up the slope, toward a clutter of crumbling boulders "—and when I came out from behind that big rock, here you were."

She studied him suspiciously. "Gabbert's in charge up there, and he doesn't like anyone nosing around." She gestured at the marsh. "And please don't be tromping around out here."

"No one told me so much of the Paleozoic's off limits."

"The astronomers've claimed the ridgetop for themselves, and they're very particular about their equipment. And this marsh is a fragile ecosystem. We don't want people trampling it underfoot." She evidently did not like the sound of that even as she said it, for she softened her tone of voice. "We ask everyone to please stay on the rocks."

"No one asked or told me anything. I just made the jump two days ago. My name's Mike French. I'm a volcanologist."

"Carol Bearden. Biologist. I'm pleased to meet you."

He indicated the specimen case and then a line of small, regularly spaced excavations along the edge of the marsh. "May I ask what you're collecting?"

"Soil samples for the tullgren funnel."

"The what?"

"It's a device for extracting small invertebrate animals from dry soil samples. Then I collect 'em and count 'em and try to figure out what they are."

With the toe of his boot, he nudged the rim of the closest excavation. "Why, it's hardly soil at all."

She picked up a pinch of humus. "It's the primordial humus. The prototype of soil."

"Everything here's a prototype of something. Everything's so primitive."

"I prefer to accept everything here for its own self. I seldom use the word 'primitive.' This pinch of dirt is as exciting to me as trilobites and bony fish and plate tectonics. Humus. Magical, amazing stuff. Every molecule in this little bit I'm holding is subtly different from every other molecule. It's molecular chaos."

"I'm sure it's important work, but it seems so—I'm not sure what to call it."

"Trivial? Here we are, at the dawn of time, and I'm counting bugs in clods of dirt?"

"I don't mean to sound disparaging. It just seems like such an everyday line of research."

"Uh huh. Let me tell you about my everyday line of research back home. I did some disinterments. To study the organisms that set up shop in buried bodies. Including human bodies. Bodies become teeming nests. Larvae of beetles and flies, worms, mites, thysanura, fungi. Result—rich soil and free air."

If she had expected him to blanch, he disappointed her.

"I want to die here," she went on. "At least, when I'm dead, I want to be buried here in this marsh, in Silurian soil. Then, after a while, I want my colleagues to disinter me and see what kinds of organisms've taken up lodging in my corpse."

Oh-kay, he thought. "You'd probably have to take a research proposal like that all the way to the National Science Foundation. So—" he spoke pleasantly but without tremendous obvious conviction "—it isn't just about counting bugs in dirt clods."

"Of course it's not. I—" She looked at him sharply. "Am I'm boring you, or are you just making fun of me. Or both?"

"Neither."

"You're sure?"

"Positive."

"Walk with me back to camp."

They walked together, but neither of them spoke again until they had reached the edge of the camp; then she pointed and said, "I go this way."

"It's been nice talking with you. I hope we can do it again sometime."

"Sometime soon."

"Yes. Well. Be seeing you."

They shook hands, and she turned and went her way. He wondered if she was not at least slightly miffed because he had not been that impressed with her line of research; he truly had not meant to insult her.

That afternoon, she had knocked on his tentpole and said, "Hi, remember me? Venus rising from the mud?"

He looked up the papers before him, blinked, smiled at her. "Why, hello. To what do I owe the honor?"

"Would you like to go on a cheap date with me?"

He blinked at her again.

"Not a romantic date," she said. "Just a companionable, friendly kind of thing. Would you like to come stargazing with me this evening? On the heights above the camp? You've heard about that satellite they just sent up?"

"Yes, of course."

"It passes over every night. My tentmate went out to look at it a couple of nights ago. She says it's really bright up on the hill, away from the camp lights."

"I'd love to see it. What time?"

"After sunset, before midnight. Don't ask me to tell you when it is on the military clock."

He asked, "Shall I call for you at your tent?"

"Why not meet me right after sunset in front of the mess tent?"

"I look forward to it."

"Me, too. Well. Till then."

"Till then."

She backed out of the tent and hurried away. French's head was fairly spinning. Aiee, he thought.

That evening, however, he had felt calm and collected. He and Carol Bearden simply met as they had agreed to do and struck out for the stony slope behind the camp. Gabbert the astronomer, who was notorious, she explained, for his brittle humor, glared at them when they showed up; later, however, he pointed out the moving point of silvery light, and planets, too, and they were properly impressed. Then, after a while, they wandered back down to the camp, and one thing had led to another.

Now she came to him in a dream, came gliding toward him across the rocky moonlit terrain as smoothly as though she were walking on a polished ballroom floor. She wore an evening gown that somehow did not seem out of place, and her close-cropped hair had unaccountably become a corn silk-colored cascade about her shoulders. She said his name, softly, a faraway sound.

"Mike!" The sound was neither soft nor far away. It was loud and right in his ear. French found himself looking at Dixon. "Wake up!"

Dixon drew back as French sat up. The sun barely showed above the horizon. "Sorry—overslept—"

"No, Mike!"

"What? What is it?"

"A five-oh quake! If that doesn't touch off the powder keg—get up! Get up!"

Dixon jumped away. French kicked his sleeping bag off his feet and began scurrying from instrument to instrument. He heard Dixon babbling into the radiophone, "It's going! God *damn!* It's going! This is it!" Then a sound like an artillery barrage came across the sea, drowned out the roar of the breakers below, drowned out Dixon, froze French in place, one hand eternally reaching for but never touching a dial. After what felt to French like an immensely long time, he managed to turn his face toward the source of the sound. Far out on the sea, a vast purple cloud rose into the sky, rose and kept rising—so vast a cloud that, even at that distance, it seemed alive with static electricity. The cloud spread across the sky, eating the light. Within an hour, ash began to fall lightly upon the islet.

"I'd better go check the tarp on the 'copter," L.V. said. Just then, lightning illuminated the overcast from end to end. Visibly awed, he said, "It brought its own weather."

"Yeah," said Dixon happily.

"Straight from hell, from the looks of it," said the pilot.

The following day, the air was clearer, and L.V. flew Dixon and French back over the island. Prior to the eruption French had not been particularly impressed by the volcano; now it was just an ugly gray hole in a landscape devastated beyond recognition. Framed by high ridges, a uniformly gray field of volcanic debris fanned out from the shattered side of the crater and down the slope to the edge of the sea. The edge of the triangle of destruction was as clearly defined as though it had been surveyed beforehand. There was no river any more. Large floating rafts of pumice choked the sea around the island.

After a week, the Navy helicopter arrived to take them away. By then, L.V.'s machine had been disassembled; the scientists and two bluejackets loaded it onto the big helicopter. Then everyone climbed aboard, the bluejackets closed the door after themselves, the helicopter rose. The cabin was too full of noise for conversation. French sat between Dixon and L.V., and the bluejackets sat opposite French, one with folded arms and closed eyes and the look of somebody determined to catch a nap, the other with his full attention apparently riveted to the section of deck bracketed by his boot shod feet. L.V. stared out the small window. Dixon looked tired but immensely satisfied. The cabin was too full of noise for conversation. Adventure's end, French thought, and lapsed into an unfruitful half-sleep.

When he got to Stinktown, he took his photographs of the blasted island and sought out Carol's tent. It was empty when he found it. He sat down on the cot to wait, and presently fatigue sucked him under as though into quicksand and he napped. He awoke to see her standing with crossed arms in the doorway of the tent; her expression was one of exquisite tenderness. He sat up and swung his feet off the cot, and she bent down and embraced and kissed him, then sat down beside him. She said, "God, I've missed you."

"Missed you, too," and after they had continued to embrace and kiss for a while he gently pulled away and handed her the photographs of the island. She studied them for more than a minute.

"Mother Earth," she said in a quiet voice, "has such a split personality. She provides for her children, then she murders them. There are so many potential mechanisms for death. Sea levels rise and fall. Climates change. Ocean chemistry changes. Volcanoes erupt. It's as though the Earth were trying to cleanse itself. As though life were an itch, and the planet has to scratch. Well." She handed the photographs back to him and compressed her mouth into a mirthless kind of smile. "Now that we're both thoroughly depressed, it's time for an abrupt change of subject."

"Uh oh."

"Uh oh is right. Mike, I'm pregnant."

"What?" Carol did not respond to that. The only thing he could think to say was, "But we use contraceptives."

"Accidents happen."

"I don't know if I'm ready for this."

"You think *I'm* ready for it?"

"What do you intend to do about it?"

She regarded him levelly. "I don't know. The question isn't what I'm going to do about this but what we're going to do about it. You and I. I love you, I want to marry you, and I want us to have a child—but under the circumstances—"

"Isn't there some regulation—"

"That's the Navy. I'm a civilian."

"But—"

"Navy policy is, no pregnant personnel can make the jump into the Silurian. Any officer or enlisted woman who becomes pregnant while in the Silurian is immediately sent home. I understand the reasoning. The jump's traumatic, it might induce miscarriages. But there's no policy for civilians."

"Well, what about abortion drugs?"

"If it was just a matter of taking a drug, I'd've done it already, but I've never had a fetus to abort before now, and I don't think it'd be the same as just blowing my nose. Mike, this is *our baby*. And don't tell me we can make more babies. This is ours."

"Carol," he said unhesitatingly, "you know I love you with all my heart. We belong together. So let's just go ahead and get married. We'll have a Paleozoic wedding, invite all our unsocialized colleagues. Maybe the Navy'll even let us walk under crossed swords. Then you can go back, and I'll come back as soon as I can."

Two great tears were suddenly rolling down her cheeks. "So I've just got the two choices, don't I? Abort and stay, go back and have the baby." She shook her head angrily. "I *can't* just pack up and go home. I've only been here a few months. It'd look bad on my résumé. I like my work here and I'm good at it."

Neither of them spoke for almost a minute. Then she said, "Well, look, I've had a little more time to think about this than you, and you can see how much progress I've made. It's not fair to ask you to make any decisions right away. But promise me you will think about it. Men don't get awards for bravery in intimacy—I can't remember who said that—but I now need you to be brave and intimate with me, Mike."

"I promise, Carol. We'll work something out."

She sniffed gratefully. "Now I have got to get some work done, and I bet you do, too."

"Nothing I can't put off for an hour."

"Well, I'm afraid I don't have that luxury. Meet me back here at dinnertime."

"It's a date, mate."

His mood plummeted almost as soon as he had exited the tent, plummeted with such speed and to such depths that he stood for a long moment marveling in a purely miserable way over the suddenness and thoroughness of it. I am not afraid of committing to a relationship, he thought, I'm already committed, heart and soul. It's just, it's just—

He was not sure what it was just. He began to walk in the hope that it would help him get his thoughts in order. He found Dixon at the pier, standing before a cabinless daysailer with a blue hull.

The crimson sail was furled. Dixon grinned at said, "I called in some favors with the head of the oceanographic group. I've the use of this sweetheart for the day."

French regarded the boat without understanding. Gradually, though, he managed to focus on it. Finally, he said, "They must've used up their team's whole weight allowance to get this through the hole."

"They took the same approach we did with the baby chopper. Got it classified as essential equipment. Hey, they say, we can't always be begging the Navy for one of its boats. Besides, it's non-polluting and low-maintenance." Dixon stepped down into the boat and motioned French to come aboard. "Nothing like a sail around the bay, and you have the look of someone who could stand to have a little fun right now."

"You do know how to work one of these things?"

"O'Neal took me out before we went off to Caledonian Land. Showed me how to tack and batten down the bo'sun and everything. It's not as hard to handle as L.V.'s baby chopper."

"Well—"

"Come *on*, Mike. Get your feet wet. Nobody's out on the water today, we got the sea to ourselves."

French stepped into the boat and sat down. Dixon tossed him a life jacket, then had him cast off a line and took the boat out onto the vast prehistoric sea. The wind was good, and the prow sliced the water cleanly, with a continuous hiss.

After a time, Dixon said, "You still look like you've got something on your mind."

French shrugged elaborately. He said, "Do you have any kids?"

"Not hardly. Too many people in the world already. Our world, I mean. I blame, in no particular order, the pope and the rest of humanity."

"Carol's—I think Carol wants to have one."

Dixon fixed him with a solemn brown eye for a moment, then looked away. "So give her one. You're already stuck fast in the tar pit of love, so you might as well—"

"I don't think I'm ready for fatherhood."

"Who the hell ever is? Nobody I've ever talked to. Probably every living creature in Earth's history's felt the same way. What if I louse things up, so my spawn has to be an invertebrate all its life?

What if it never learns to crawl out on land and can't find a decent ecological niche?"

They did not speak again but only sailed for several minutes. Then Dixon nodded toward the sea, the horizon. "Out that way there's probably nothing but an island arc or two until you get most of the way around the planet and start finding pieces of China."

French smiled fleetingly. "Maybe I'll find out some day."

"Some day! You aren't an ambitious enough thinker. I'm talking about us taking a little sailboat like this one out across that sea."

"You're nuts. It's a lot of sea for such a little boat."

"How hard could it be? The trade winds always blow from the east. All I'd have to do is steer into the setting sun."

"For thousands and thousands of miles."

"All, but we'd do it for science." Dixon laughed. "Okay, now, when I say *hike*, we're going to lean backward over the windward rail to keep the boat from heeling."

The boat canted to leeward under the force of the wind in the sails. They hiked. The turn was sloppily executed, but it was executed. In spite of himself, French was exhilarated. Dixon asked "Want to do that again?" and French nodded, and they repeated the maneuver. They sailed thus for some time, cutting back and forth across the water.

Maybe this is the thing, French thought.

Then a sheet of spray drenched him, and he realized suddenly that the boat was bucking through the water. The wind had turned shifty, constantly changing in direction, and the waves, small and close together as they had sailed across the bay, were steep and choppy. He looked around at Dixon, whose mouth was set in a straight humorless line. He looked gray, seasick. French said, "Dix, aren't we out rather far?"

After a long moment, Dixon nodded vaguely and said, "Let's take her back in," and began the turn. The boat tipped to leeward, and the men hiked. The boat wallowed through a turn that still left the bow pointing at open sea. "Let's try it again."

The boat started to come around again.

French heard Dixon curse and looked around at him. He was clutching the line, but his expression was one of pure astonishment. He suddenly let go of the line, seemed to crumple, then toppled sideways into the water.

The boat wallowed, and the sail swung across, striking French on the chest. The life jacket cushioned the blow, but it nonetheless knocked the wind out of him and sent him tumbling backward over the side.

He found himself trying to fill his lungs with air and keep his head above the chop at the same time. His life jacket was gone; he had neglected to secure it when he put it on.

When he could breathe again, he called Dixon's name. There was no answer. He could not see the boat. His clothing began to weigh him down; he kicked off his shoes and slithered out of his shirt and trousers.

As he rose on a wave, he glimpsed land. He struck out toward it, side-stroking, conserving his strength, and as he swam he began to ransack his memory for everything he had ever observed or heard about the bay that would help him in the present situation. He knew that longshore currents must have sculpted the headlands that bracketed the bay, and that he would have to swim across the flow of water, which might carry him some distance down the coast before he reached the shore.

As he swam, he began to fantasize about strange monsters of the deep made all the stranger for being prehistoric. He did not panic—the biggest of the Silurian protosharks was still pretty small, and the real nightmares, the sea scorpions, mostly lived in brackish estuaries and ate worms—yet he felt or thought that he felt a long writhing body brush against his bare leg, and his imagination immediately populated itself with monsters as big as automobiles, with eyes on stalks and teeth like spikes, drawn by the novelty of a strange large warm creature splashing in the water, obviously in distress, obviously vulnerable.

He kept swimming, kept realigning himself with the glimmer of land. When he tired, he floated in the chop until his arms and legs ceased to ache; then he would begin pulling for the shore again.

A volcano couldn't blow me up, he thought. I'm not going to die just because I fell out of a goddamn boat

He was angry now. Angry at Fate, angry at Dixon, angriest of all at himself. Stupid, he thought. Stupid. Carol'll kill me.

His arms weighed tons, then hundreds of tons.

I can't make it, he thought. A roaring filled his head. I'm going to drown. I'm going to die and never see Carol again. The chain of life breaks here. Three billion years of evolution and it all stops here. Don't deserve to live. Stupid. Natural selection.

Unexpectedly, a wave rolled him over in the surf, pounded him against the sand. He dug his fingers in, but wave action sucked the earth out of his grip. Get up, he thought. Didn't come this far to drown in the surf.

He pulled himself forward, pushed himself up. The next wave tried to smash him down again. He crawled out of the sea as painfully as though he were the first creature in Earth's history to essay the trick, and then he lay gasping for a long time with foam swirling about his legs and his fingers clawing at the hard wet sand. When, finally, he could get to his feet, he staggered to the edge of the shingle, sat down, and faced the balked sea. A few arthropods worked the splash zone. Beat you again, he thought. We escaped you before. Escaped you again.

He must have lost consciousness then; he awoke to find himself in sick bay. A Navy doctor gave him a quick but thorough examination, and French asked about Dixon and was told that the man's body had been retrieved from the bay. Dixon had suffered a stroke, but that had not killed him; he had drowned after going into the water.

When he had finished examining French, the doctor let Carol come in and left the two of them alone. She kissed him gently on the mouth and asked, "How do you feel?"

"Like someone who's survived two unsympathetic natural phenomena."

"Sorry about Dix. I know I didn't approve of him. I'm sure he didn't approve of me. But I'm sorry."

"How about you and, you know?" He could tell nothing from her expression.

"Maybe—"

She hesitated long enough for him to have to ask, "What?"

"Maybe neither of us should go back."

He had to say it again: "What?"

"I have this crazy fantasy. About hiding the fact I'm pregnant until I'm so far along they don't dare send me through the hole. Then I'd have to have the baby here."

He stared at her with his mouth open. Then he nodded. "It's crazy, all right. The jump'd kill an infant."

"I know. So the baby and I *couldn't* go back. They'd *have* to let us stay. And you'd have to stay anyway. With Dix gone, someone's got to take over the survey—"

"This is no place for a baby!"

"Why not make it a place for one? It might even do the expedition some good—all the expeditions. Generate usefully sympathetic publicity whenever funding's threatened."

"What you're proposing's *impossible.*"

"I told you I want to die here and be buried here, and I meant it. And you told me I'd have to go all the way to the National Science Foundation with such a crazy idea. Well, okay, I'm *ready* to go all the way if I have to."

"Carol—"

"So far, humans've just been visitors here. But if I had the baby here, we'd be colonists. The first real colonists."

She was serious, he could tell, absolutely serious and absolutely crazy, but he knew that he loved her absolutely as well, loved her with all his being and could not imagine life without her. Yet, though he was conscious of becoming resigned, he felt he must make one final protest. "You know," he told her, "this is going to make just a whole lot of trouble for everybody. Especially us. Whatever you've got in mind to try, they're just going to call you a trouble-maker and a lunatic, and the hell of it is, I'll be right there at your side the whole time. Me, they're just going to laugh at."

"But what've we really got to lose by trying? Maybe we can't pull it off. But let's try. You never know—if nothing else, doesn't it at least appeal to your sense of the absurd?"

"Appeal is not the word for what it does to my sense of the absurd. You'd better tell me what you mean."

She laughed and held him to herself. "Imagine our baby's birth certificate!"

EXILE

I.

Mornings are not good. Anxious? Hell yes I'm anxious. I always am anxious at the start of the day. Matutinal anxiety is par for the course, dependable as sunrise. Out in the world, even in the little I see of the world nowadays, there are usually distractions. When there aren't I can always mask anxiety with attitude, if nothing else hide it behind the new beard. But it shares my bed faithfully. I can't say with complete accuracy that I have nightmares because any more I never remember my dreams, good or bad, which is just as well because every morning I feel unmistakably that they must have been very bad ones indeed, full of dread, menace. Anyway: morning. The clock has told me to rise and shine. I hate cute clocks and curse the day man became the ape that keeps track of time. All the same, have to get up, get to work, achieve those goals, meet those schedules, so I greet the new day, latest in a series, going to collect the whole set eventually. Look like a total jerk in the bathroom mirror, feel like one in person, wonder as I shave shit shower how the other total jerk of my acquaintance sleeps these days. Good morning, Wortham, wherever the hell you are. Another day another doughnut.

The anxiety generally has begun to recede into the background by the time I arrive at work, and even on mornings when it doesn't do so of its own accord there's the jump station's ozone tang to take a body's mind off its troubles. Goes up the nose like an icepick. Talk about bracing, and the joke is that it protects the sinuses against deadly ultraviolet radiation. The old hands say you get used to it in time. Certainly, if you work at the jump station you have the time, your pick (in theory) of one of three shifts, each as grueling as the other two. The station operates around the clock and somebody's making a killing. Takes a lot of food, fuel and sundries to keep the expedition going. And water, tons of it. Potable water is at a premium in Paleozoic time. Even allowing for the truckloads of purification tablets that go in, and those disposable straws that filter and purify water as you drink through them, the arithmetic of H_2o comes down to the indefeasible minimal requirement of six gallons per person per day times the number of persons requiring those six gallons per day. That number has fluctuated over time but it's never dropped below a thousand since the eoan phase of the expedition. And though the U.S. Navy provides the expedition's official support force, the U.S. Army is sending in a welldrilling unit. Must be getting crowded back in Paleozoic time.

Jump station techs work like dogs. Everybody else works like a pit pony. The pace never lets up, mustn't disrupt the holy schedule. If it's not X volume of supplies going in, it's Y number of containerized specimens coming out. Of course, people go in and come out, too, VIPs, SIPs, and even NIPs, Very, Self-, or Not Important Persons as the case may be. If I could go in I'd be a NIP, but even if I had to be a NIP I'd go in. Not that I am not already a NIP. Not that I ever will go in.

First thing this morning a SIP wants to cut in line, his time being more valuable than anybody else's. The boss tech goes into patented It Simply Can't Be Done mode while the subsidiary techs make bets among themselves, will the jerk whine or cajole, threaten or pout? For my own part, watching such exchanges makes me embarrassed ever to have been a member of the fraternity and glad for the moment that I am a member no longer. With a helpless shrug and a regretful tone the boss tech explains, "Folks on the other end have schedules and quotas, too, you see, and everything on both sides is so carefully synchronized that any deviation will throw the whole operation out of whack." This particular Particularly SIP is not one to be so easily dissuaded. "I'm just asking for a *little* flexibility." A little or a lot, flexibility is out of the question. The boss tech ceases to be at all regretful and falls back on the fact that in the jump station itself he outranks everybody, even the prep team, and is more important than any other species of IP. He is TIP, *The* IP.

I am not a tech myself but a peripheral sort of jump station regular, employed by one of the contractors who handle incoming and outgoing cargo. I've had better jobs, better bosses, but worse ones, too. Not naming any names.

II.

By midshift I'm tired but wired and knock off for lunch. On my way out I tell Doris, the youngest tech and the only one I talk to regularly, "I sure am glad I don't have to do this for a living." She grins and nods sympathetically. "Sometimes I wish," she says, "I got paid for subjective time." I bring my lunch from home every day and eat it out of its tube as I walk over to the marine museum, where I can digest in peace while admiring the featured permanent exhibit, The PaleoAquarium.

In my teens the prospects arising from the discovery of the so called anomaly set my imagination afire; I knew then that there was simply no other point in spacetime I'd rather occupy than the midPaleozoic SiluroDevonian boundary, 408 M.Y.B.P., give or take a leap year. Later, as a dweeby twentysomething college graduate aspiring to become a fullfledged scientist and equipped with what I imagined to be useful skills, I tried to convince the right people (though ultimately it came down to trying to convince the right person) that I would be an invaluable addition to the expedition. For "an invaluable addition" read "willing and able to do any amount of dirty work."

Dreams don't come with guarantees. My current job is the best I could get that has any connection whatever with the expedition, the only way I now have of participating in it, but the connection is barely firm enough to support the last shreds of a fellow's pride. I'll never get to go into the anomaly; I'll never get any closer to any part of the Paleozoic world than I am at the PaleoAquarium.

If I am ever actually happy any more it's in the company of trilobites, cephalopods, eurypterids, and armored fish sent back by members of the expedition. First thing, I pass by all the tanks, check to see, among other things, almost as if it were any of my business, if the eurypterid has devoured her offspring again. I've spent so much time with these creatures that I can pick out individuals though I'm not so far gone that I've given them pet names. When I am that far gone I'll stick to the classics. Spot, Stripe, Fluffy. I think Toughy would be a good name for a sea scorpion. I like to watch people at The PaleoAquarium, too, though sometimes it's just gradeschoolkids running around screaming and paying as little attention as possible to the adults in attendance or to anything else beyond their monkey need to run around screaming. Makes you wonder why it never occurred to their mothers to devour them. But one time a loonie dropped by to expose himself to sundry and all, vertebrates and invertebrates alike. Another time a different loonie tried to heave a brick through the glass front of the trilobite tank.

First up today is a small pack of boys in their midteens. Because they communicate among themselves by means of piercing wordless vocalizations I can only speculate that the local VR arcade has burned down and they have repaired to the museum for the purpose of mourning their terrible loss. At least they arrive all broken out in frowns and scowls as well as pimples but soon they buck up and begin showing off for each other and the adoring public, which is to say, me. One kid with luteous hair, disregarding a printed notice that specifically enjoins visitors not to do so, leans far over the rail, raps his knuckles against the eurypterid tank, grins over his shoulder at his chums. They note his daring with approval. The eurypterid (*E. remipes*) pays no attention whatever. I often wonder if anything goes on in its dim arthropod brain, is it remotely aware of the strange creatures inhabiting the strange world on the other side of the glass. Probably if it thinks at all it thinks along the lines of *Hungry, better spawn again soon.* I watch hoping against hope to see the rail give under the kid's weight and him precipitate face first against and perhaps through the tank's glass front. Having a relatively large chordate crash headlong into its tank would undoubtedly enliven *E. remipe*'s day, perhaps even generate a philosophical spark, a notion it could pass on to the next generation of little sea scorpions before it gobbled them down: *Beyond the walls of our world, my children, are other realms, other planes of being.*

As the boys move off mouthing shrilly amongst themselves two of their postadolescent selves, Lem and Clem or maybe it's Fred and Red or Lonnie and Donnie, cut through to the snack bar from the construction site on the other side of the museum. Working outside as they do in an ozonefree environment they're the color of bricks wherever sunlight has touched skin. Some lucky fellow, I think, has melanoma in his future. Passing the eurypterid tank Leroy nudges Elroy and says, "God*damn*, that is the ugliest lobster I ever saw," and Elroy says, "How'd ya like to go giggin' for something like that?" and both laugh. That thing could gig right back, I think as I watch their retreating beefy backsides, that spike on its tail isn't a decoration.

Mommy and Daddy arrive with Child in tow. My daily visit to The PaleoAquarium wouldn't be complete if I did not get to observe these common and yet fascinating creatures. Today's specimens are large florid lostlooking ovoids. Clearly this is not the place where the cute dolphins leap through hoops. As they wobble to a stop in front of a tankful of mudsucking armored fish about as long as your hand I note that Child is pouting and Mommy is patently exasperated with the fruit of her lardy loins. Daddy alone takes notice of the diminutive sea monsters of the Upper Silurian and being momentarily distracted from the business of getting his bearings touches the button. TellAll gives him a carefully modulated earful about his finny forebears that causes him to talk back and tell it a thing or two, from which I am able to infer that he most emphatically does not believe human beings are descended from fish and are themselves in fact rather highly specialized fish. Mommy clearly shares his disbelief because she hugs both Child and handbag to her midriff in the sudden conviction that this wicked place into which she and hers have innocently wandered must harbor not only evolutionists but pederasts and cutpurses as well. The nuclear family of rather highly specialized fish beats a waddling retreat. The sole remaining rather highly specialized fish checks his watch and departs in pursuit of his separate destiny.

III.

Back on the job I get an unpleasant but not an altogether unexpected jolt. I understood the risk I was taking when I applied to work here. Yet a tickly chill runs down my back like a drop of ice water when I realize that someone has noticed and almost but not quite recognized me, a woman waiting with her party to be taken in hand by the prep team.

Not that I let on. I've learned how not to let on about anything to anybody. As far as she can tell I'm unaware of her existence or else regard her as but one more object waiting its turn to go in. And she's just not *sure*. I shave my head nowadays and have grown a beard by way of compensation and, too, I never got nearly as many media minutes as Wortham. It had been *his* project. When, so to speak, the villagers had caught on to strange doings up at Castle Frankenstein and stormed the place they were much more interested in the mad scientist than in his feeble-minded assistant. Not that they didn't bring enough rope to hang both. (No. No, it wasn't noisy and melodramatic, no lynch mob broke down the door, we didn't even get tarred and feathered. But in the scientific community an *exposé* in *Nature* is next best to a noose around the neck.)

Nevertheless this person, thinking she knows me from somewhere, flat out stares. Typical semisocialized paleo geek(ette) going for her doctorate, badskinned, not too cleanlooking, clad in multipocketed workshirt over teeshirt and jeans tucked into desert boots, the number five or *maybe* number four person on a team comprising six people. It'll probably come to her, I think, while she's doing whatever she's going to be doing in Paleozoic time. She'll stop sorting her trilobites and look thoughtfully at her colleagues and say, "You know who I think that guy at the jump station was, the bald one with the beard?" And probably one of her colleagues will reply, "He's got some goddamn nerve. You'd think he'd be too ashamed to show his face anywhere near *scientists*." And maybe another will say, "Naw, couldn't have been him, he'd have to have some goddamn nerve. It'd be like Public Enemy Number Two standing around in front of the police station hoping nobody noticed him."

Wortham, of course, being Public Enemy Number One. With all his media minutes she would have recognized him instantly.

The prep team comes out of the jump station, tells the paleo team it's time, and everyone troops by me. The paleo girl shoots me a last look and her lips part slightly and I know she's dying to ask. I glare back in pure childish defiant hatred.

Well, so it's childish. I'd had my heart set on joining the expedition ever since my early teens. If at the time I had instead been a twentysomething college graduate with useful skills I just might've convinced the right people that I'd be an invaluable addition the expedition. Would've been fairly easy in the early days when research grants practically fell off trees and the NSF had all it could do to keep the various research teams from trampling one another in their haste to get into Paleozoic time. At the peak of activity two or maybe three thousand people must've been in Paleozoic time, every type of scientist plus a sizable support force of Navy personnel, also curious wellheeled wellconnected civilian laypersons. They established permanent camps, built power stations and radio telescopes, launched satellites, all the comforts of home, didn't matter who you were or where, off in darkest coldest Gondwana you could still get your microwave infodump every hour on the hour. There'd have been a place for me. I might never have met Wortham, let alone hooked up with him.

It cost money, of course, and as often happens money became increasingly hard to get as the public grew bored and mostly forgot that there was an expedition. I had my dreams but dreams don't come with guarantees. I cast about for other suitable work and found it. Or it found me. The Devil came in the guise of Wortham and spake unto me, saying, "The line of people waiting to go to the Paleozoic era is very long and moves very slowly, and very obscure researchers such as we are at the very back of it. Shall we wait patiently and work and hope throughout the years or perhaps even decades to come, all the while watching and eating our hearts out as others advance and get the glory and the grants, or *shall we cut in line?*"

And I should have rebuked him, saying, "Get thee behind me, Satan," but I didn't because even the Devil can tell the truth when it suits his purposes. The line ahead of us was very long and—

There I go, dramatizing again. Wortham never misled me, cast no spell over me; I did myself in. It was his idea and his project but I helped. I always knew what we were doing and why: *advancement.*

I just don't know, I can't imagine any more, what I thought I was doing, what the hell I thought I was thinking.

Now Wortham's, I don't know, a cab driver somewhere, a clerk in a pet store or a night watchman, or he's gone and got himself lost in the dozen or so acres that remain of the Amazon rainforest. And I, now I am the stock boy at the jump station.

IV.

Shift ends and it's home again home again. Pop the plastic off an EatMe™. Pay just enough attention to the usual top stories in the evening news, wars whores scores bores, so I can sound informed on current affairs at work tomorrow. Everything revolves around work. Peel off clothes, wash face, stretch out on the bed, dead tired but dreading sleep, because every morning I awaken with a full sense of my sins having been found out. As is in fact the case: found out, duly noted and filed for future reference. A scientist who fudges his results sooner or later but inevitably gets found out, exposed, and once that's happened he's finished in the scientific community, kaput. Say goodbye to titles, so long to the international conferences, oh, and tenure? Forget tenure. Worse, any good work an errant scientist ever has ever done is suddenly under suspicion. Oh, and this goes for aspiring scientists, too.

Thus I am not consorting with my peers in Paleozoic time and not doing brilliant work in my chosen field or in anyone else's for that matter. Instead I'm working at the only job I could get, After The Fall, that pertains in any way to the one great thing that gave my life meaning. I fill out invoices for food toothpaste toilet paper pencils sunscreen salt tablets rubber bands a thousand and one other items. I move cartloads of supplies into the jump station and see them off to the busy folks in Paleozoic time. I have some goddamn nerve alright.

It's like the old joke about the man who cleans up after the elephants in a circus. Somebody asks him how he likes his job, he says the hours are awful, the working conditions are terrible, the pay is lousy. All he does the livelong day is shovel elephant shit. The other person asks him why he doesn't get a better job someplace else. "What," he exclaims, "and give up show business?"

THE END IN EDEN

Phil Morrow looked up from his game of solitaire and said, "Come in," and the door swung inward to reveal a wizened dungaree-clad woman with close-cropped white hair. She made no move to enter; even by shipboard standards, the compartment was quite small.

"Sal," said Morrow.

"Phil," said Sal Shelton, "we're wanted."

"Where?"

"Captain's quarters."

"Excuse me while I fall over in a dead faint, but how do we suddenly rate? Not just the invitation to the captain's, but personally delivered. P.A. system on the fritz?"

"They don't want this broadcast all over." Sal peered at the array of cards before Morrow. "Are you cheating? Even from here, it looks like you're cheating."

Morrow sighed, stood, stretched. "A person never knows what he's capable of until he becomes desperate—and if I'm not desperate, nobody is."

"Well, dear, you don't look desperate."

"Ah, but I am. Desperate as in bored, Sal."

Sal gestured at the cards. "I see. A person gets desperately bored, next thing you know, he's cheating at solitaire."

"In a nutshell."

Sal stood back from the doorway to let Morrow step out of the tiny compartment and close the door behind himself. All around them, the ship throbbed with a dull mechanical persistence. "So," he said, "what's up?"

"Beats me. Brinkman just told me to get you. But he did say it's urgent."

"What could possibly be remotely urgent around here? Somebody misplace a trilobite?"

"Something like that." Sal made a moue. "From what little I gathered from Brinkman, it's the biggest crime in four hundred million years."

They met the grim-faced executive officer coming from the captain's quarters and found the captain already conferring with two other officers, one each from the Naval Criminal Investigative Service and the Judge Advocate General's Corps. The captain barely acknowledged the two civilians with a slight movement of his head, neither a nod nor definitely anything else; he sat at his desk looking perplexed as he turned a clear plastic bag over and over in his hands. Sealed within the bag was a black vial no longer or thicker than his thumb.

"They'd've missed it," said the NCIS officer, "if the carrier hadn't collapsed in the jump station. He seems to have botched the insertion."

"Insertion?" said the captain.

"Had it hidden up his, um, you know."

The captain quickly set the bag down and regarded it with considered distaste.

"He's in sick bay now," said the NCIS officer.

"Has he said anything?"

"Not yet. They're fixing him up. But he knows he's in a lot of trouble," and the NCIS officer sent a purposely significant look at the JAG officer. "We're making formal charges, of course. Starting with smuggling."

"Yes," said the captain, "but smuggling what? What's in that vial? Trilobite larvae, eggs? Seeds?"

"Spores," said Sal. "Seeds don't exist here."

The three Navy officers seemed at last to take notice of the two civilians; the NCIS officer gave Sal an irritated look—by association, Morrow also fell under its baleful beam—and said, "Seeds, spores. It's something, anyway, and contraband no matter what it is."

The captain looked expectantly at Sal, who spread her hands in a gesture of helplessness and said, "Obviously you're waiting for the biologists' report on the contents of that vial. They *are* working on it, right?"

The NCIS officer blinked at her. "Who are you people?"

The captain made an apologetic noise and started to introduce everybody, but Sal cut him short. "Mister Morrow here," she said, "is a United States Customs agent, and I am the chief civilian liaison—"

The NCIS snickered. "Already everybody and his dog are trying to get in on it. I never imagined we had so many special agents lurking in our midst."

Sal smiled her blandest smile. "Whom do you suppose makes sure subversives don't get loose here in the Silurian period?"

"Really?" The NCIS officer concentrated his disregard on Morrow. "What do all you people do?"

"Not a whole lot," said Morrow. "We've been pretty underemployed till now. I want to be present when you interrogate your man."

The NCIS officer and the JAG officer exchanged looks, and the former said, "This is a Navy matter."

Sal cleared her throat softly and said, "More accurately, it's a *federal* matter. It *is* of course a Navy matter, but, just off the top of my head, it's also a Customs and Border Protection matter, and also a Disease Control matter, and conceivably also a matter for the NSF, the FBI, and maybe even the BSA."

"Who? BSA?"

"Boy Scouts of America. Okay, not *them*, but I hyperbolize to make the point that if this truly is a matter of smuggling Paleozoic biological specimens, you suddenly have a lot of federal agencies involved. This is probably where I come in, because no two of those agencies are really on good speaking terms with one another."

"Miz Shelby, this is hardly an occasion for—"

"Shelton," said Sal.

"Doctor," Morrow put in. "Doctor Shelton."

"The point is," Sal said, "there is no shortage of interested parties, and unless some real effort at coordination is made at the outset, they *and* you going to be tromping all over each other. Obviously NCIS and JAG are involved because the individual actually caught with biological specimens in his intimate possession is a member of the Navy."

"Thank you for that concession," the NCIS officer said in a dry tone.

"But that's just for openers. Are these living specimens?"

The NCIS officer nodded warily. "It's tissue of some sort. We *have* been able to figure that out on our own."

"Living specimens mean Fish and Wildlife gets involved."

The captain, the NCIS officer, and the JAG officer each looked more or less astonished, and one of them said, "*What?*"

Sal ignored the eruption. "Specimens smuggled across a border?"

The three Navy officers hesitated, so Morrow said, "The spacetime anomaly does qualify as a sort of a border, does it not?"

Sal beamed at him. "Perfect. I always knew you were clever. Endangered or threatened marine organisms?"

Again the Navy officers hesitated, so again Morrow spoke up. "Well, they are extinct species, back home. Endangered status would seem to be a prerequisite for extinction."

"Excellent. National Marine Fisheries Service will be interested, then. Just for fun, why don't we call these specimens pre-endangered species? A classification that can only exist in time travel. Now, Marine Fisheries only becomes involved here if the species is on a marine organisms protected list of some kind. We'll let that go for the time being, because there are other issues to consider. Such as, whether or not these are specimens of potentially injurious wildlife."

The captain spread both hands palms down on his blotter and lowered his head as though tensing for a spring over the desk. "Christ, who knows?"

"USDA Animal Health Inspection Service would certainly have to know."

"This is ridiculous," said the NCIS officer.

"Not in the least," Sal assured him. "Let's take a listed living trilobite, genus Phacops. Now, all along, ever since the expedition first established itself in Paleozoic time, we've had our proper scientific authorities making recommendations on how to study organisms like Phacops without extending species accidentally into our own dear Holocene epoch. So for legal transport of specimens, you'd have to have permits from the Fish and Wildlife Service. Our smugglers', plural, first mistake has been to ignore and thus defy the authority vested in our dedicated wildlife agents."

"Smugglers *plural?*" echoed the JAG officer.

"Yes, of course. Which means you can add conspiracy to your list of charges. Now, it's easy to skip Fish and Wildlife's authorization—whether our smugglers did it knowingly or unknowingly—because nobody, not even wildlife agents, likes to admit that invertebrates are wildlife in the first place. Now let's assume further that our Phacops can wreak havoc when accidentally released into strange waters. Sort of like snakeheads or zebra mussels. Those were probably before your time." Sal's blue eyes twinkled in her seamed face. "Take my word for it. Awful little buggers."

"Nasty," Morrow said to the glowering NCIS officer.

"Anyhow," Sal went on, "your Animal Health Inspection Service must also issue permission for Phacops to be brought in, based on your bona fides and proof that you house and transport them securely. So, our smugglers' second mistake has been to skip Animal Health. Here is where Mister Morrow comes in, because either violation gets our smugglers into trouble with Customs. So, to make a long story short—"

"And about goddamn time," muttered the NCIS officer.

"—our smugglers have ignored the necessity for permits from Fish and Wildlife to take, transport, and possess specimens. Plus they have ticked off Animal Health if the specimens are injurious to native wildlife. Plus Marine Fisheries if there are special concerns re their wild population. Plus Customs if there are any other problems."

"Other," said the captain, ponderously, "problems?"

Sal shrugged. "Let's say, for example, Phacops smells like drugs. Customs can impound specimens for anything along these lines even if everything else is in order. If wild Phacops carry, say, Ebola, you have to have clearance—not exactly the same thing as a permit—from the Center for Disease Control attesting that *your* specimens do not carry it. In these matters you are guilty until proven innocent. There is a long list of Select Agents of High Consequence Pathogens and Toxins that we have to fill out every year if we have brought in anything identified as a bioterrorism threat."

One or more Navy officers yelped, *"Bioterrorism?"*

"Oh, I almost forgot to mention. Customs and USDA Animal and Plant Health are part of Homeland Security."

"Sleep well," said Morrow.

"It isn't just that we want to discourage a trade in some extremely exotic species," Sal said. "If this sort of traffic has been going on for any length of time, there's no telling what may be in private hands back home. And, eventually, perhaps inevitably, either through somebody's carelessness or even out of maliciousness, Paleozoic organisms will be introduced into Holocene environments."

"But these Paleozoic organisms wouldn't pose much of a threat, would they? I mean, they became extinct in the first place because they couldn't keep up in the race for survival, right?"

"They may just have been unlucky, like the dinosaurs. I don't know if sea scorpions or trilobites could establish a colony in our own time. I don't want to find out. No, what disturbs me is the idea that these creatures must come complete with their own complements of viral and bacterial diseases. Organisms in our own time might not have defenses. Better to err on the side of caution."

"Wouldn't advanced organisms in our own time have immunological defenses more than adequate to combat primitive diseases?"

"Primitive and advanced have different meanings."

"If there's anything here that's deadly to humans, wouldn't we have learned about it long before this?"

"It might be something biomed, biowar researchers have to come up with, but the *potential* for trouble is there. So. To return to our problem. Somebody wants to sneak out stuff they wouldn't have to account for. You don't just get your hands on specimens by simply asking. So people have to smuggle them out." Sal shrugged. "You know, it could just be that the ultimate receiver just has a jones for Paleozoic stuff. Whatever the reason, he, she, or they have broken laws and got a bunch of other people to break them, too."

The captain made a weary sound. "What do you suggest we do, Doctor Shelton?"

"Put Mister Morrow in charge of the investigation."

The captain, the NCIS officer, and the JAG officer peered at Morrow as though actually seeing him for the first time. The JAG officer muttered, "Impossible," and the NCIS officer growled, "Who was it said that for every problem there's a solution that's simple, easy, and wrong?"

"Mencken," Sal said, without missing a beat. "Look, Customs is the big enforcement gorilla if the specimens are being transported across a border, which they arguably are, without the required permits from all or some of those other agencies, which is certainly the case. Mister Morrow is a sworn law enforcement officer with full powers to arrest, search, and seize. And I should have hardly need to remind you that your own Uniform Code of Military Justice states clearly that upon arrival in United States territory a naval unit is subject to customs inspection by federal authorities. The naval unit in this instance is this ship and its personnel. For all practical purposes our patch of Paleozoic real estate is United States territory. And federal authority is vested in Mister Morrow here. A customs declaration is distributed to all personnel returning from this expedition, and it is the duty of all personnel to complete such declarations prior truthfully and accurately, to the effect that, without permission of the commanding officer—" Sal nodded pleasantly to the stunned-looking captain "—they have not brought on board any article, animal or any other thing, the introduction of which into United States territory is forbidden or restricted under current regulations."

"What has that got to do with this?" demanded the NCIS officer.

"Just as you gentlemen are responsible for Navy personnel attached to this expedition," Sal said, "Mister Morrow and I are responsible for its civilian contingent, and Mister Morrow has jurisdiction over it. And it's obvious that civilians are involved, both here and back home."

"We don't know yet that civilians are involved."

"We can infer it until we learn differently. The person who gave it to this poor dumb rating of yours is probably the same person who collected the material and put it into the vial. It was someone who knows his stuff. A civilian scientist."

The captain groaned. "Everybody here knows his stuff."

"Yep. Whether it's sexual dimorphism in eurypterids or plant-cell cutinization."

"And *every*body uses these vials."

"No, actually. The earth-science folks—geologists, fossil collectors—send specimens home in crates. The astronomers just send back data."

"I stand corrected," the captain said. "That reduces the number of suspects to only about five or six hundred people."

"Plus there's that person at the other end. The receiver of smuggled goods. Your sailor was supposed to deliver the vial and its contents to somebody back in Holocene time. Also certainly another scientist. Somebody who knows how to unload the vial without damaging its contents. Find out what was in the vial, and you pare down the number of suspects. If that vial contained plant tissue, it's a fair bet we're looking for a botanist. If it's something else, then it's somebody else. A botanist isn't likely to be trafficking in trilobite eggs."

"But what's the point of trafficking in anything?" the captain asked. "Your scientists can already take out anything they want."

"Not true," Sal said. "As I explained, we have to abide by very stringent guidelines. For all the reasons I've just enumerated, strict tabs are kept on everything that goes back."

"Evidently not strict enough. I have got to find out how long this has been going on."

"I'm not going to interfere," said Morrow, "with your interrogation of this sailor—" the NCIS officer appeared to catch himself just short of blurting out, *Damn straight you're not!* "—but I want to talk to him. I need to know everything *you* find out, because—as Doctor Shelton has explained—this is a little more serious than some civilian scientist selling his liquor ration to enlisted personnel."

The captain gave the NCIS and JAG officers a searching look. "I want this matter taken care of. This has happened on our watch, and how we deal with it goes on the record. Do what you have to do, but do it quickly and as carefully as possible."

"Just don't get under our feet," the NCIS officer warned Morrow.

Sal laughed. "So! Let the turf wars begin!" She glanced at her watch and exclaimed, "Whoops! Gotta run. Phil, you be nice." She dashed out.

The NCIS officer glared after her, and the JAG officer said to Morrow, "Your Doctor Shelton seems to think this whole business is rather funny."

"Sal? Oh, she's just that way. A bit bipolar."

"Well," said the JAG officer, "let's go see what our man in sick bay's got to say."

"Let's stop by the lab on the way," Morrow said. "I want that report on the specimen." He indicated the vial in the clear plastic bag on the captain's desk. "Who has custody of that?"

The captain gingerly pinched one corner of the bag between thumb and forefinger and held it out to Morrow.

The NCIS officer led the way. Bringing up the rear, Morrow asked the JAG officer, "What interrogation technique does the Navy prefer these days? Waterboarding still in favor?"

The JAG officer shot him an uneasy glance over his shoulder. "Is Customs full of comedians like you, Mister Morrow?"

"All the dead-serious Customs agents are back home."

"Imagine that," said the NCIS officer. "We have ourselves Customs' problem child."

"How do you propose to make this poor rating of yours spill his guts?"

"Navy personnel," said the JAG officer, somewhat frostily, "enjoy the same constitutionally guaranteed right against self-incrimination that civilians enjoy," and up ahead the NCIS officer added, even more frostily, "But at the same time the Code of Conduct requires them to truthfully answer any questions put to them by a superior officer."

Morrow clucked his tongue appreciatively. "Quite a bind for accused."

"They also have a right to defense counsel."

They came to a door marked BIO LAB. Morrow led the officers inside and said, "Hi, Sam," to the technician there, who nodded and replied, "Got a prelim report on the stuff in the vial. Spores from some fungus."

"Can you be a little more specific?"

"Dex is still trying to get a precise match." Sam indicated an intense-looking person huddled over a clutter of equipment. "Dex is our mycologist." For the benefit of the two Navy officers, he added, "Fungi specialist. As a psilophyte man myself, I can't imagine why anyone wants to look at prehistoric fungi here in their natural setting. Fungi back home are creepy and weird enough. Beats me why anybody'd want to smuggle some through the hole."

The NCIS officer started. "Just how much have you heard about—what's going on?"

"Good God. You really do think you clamped down on this business as soon as that sailor man passed out in the jump station. Or at least when you got him to sick bay and found out what the problem is. But it's already all over the ship. By now it's probably all over the camp, too. Assume the worst. Whoever prepared the vial knows by now that his courier's been nabbed. He'll hide or destroy anything that can connect him."

"Except the one thing he can't hide."

"Which is?"

"His specialty."

Sam shook his head. "If you're expecting those spores to lead you right to your culprit, you're probably going to be disappointed. You don't necessarily have to be a mycologist to stuff some spores into a vial and seal it."

"You think other stuff has been smuggled through?"

"I'd bet on it."

Morrow flashed the NCIS officer a smile and said, "Consensus is building." The NCIS officer cursed softly, and Morrow went on. "I think Sam's right. I seriously doubt this is the first time it's happened. Maybe it is for the sailor under arrest, but I think it unlikely this is the first time specimens have been taken out illicitly. And as Doctor Shelton pointed out, civilians are involved. One back home is waiting for this." He held up the bag containing the vial.

Sam said, "Have you examined that yet? It's pretty interesting in its own right."

"How so?"

"I looked it over when I removed the specimen. It's identical in every respect except one to the vials in common use here. What it doesn't have is anything to tell us who manufactured it. There are only a few outfits back home that make these things, and they all put code numbers or other marks on them to tell us who made it.

There's nothing on this one to suggest that there ever was such a mark or number."

"Could our prisoner have got hold of it himself?" the JAG officer asked.

"Not unless he's holding down a second job that pays really, really well. Besides smuggling, I mean. Vials like this cost more money than honest bluejackets make."

"Really? Well, then, could he have, I don't know, made it himself?"

"This vial isn't just any old all-purpose container. It's not the kind of thing you just go buy at the exchange here or the shopping emporium back home. It's really sophisticated hardware. A little self-contained machine, specifically designed to keep biological material viable—dormant but alive—for an indeterminate period of time. Long enough after somebody sealed the vial for the person carrying it to go through the anomaly. Long enough for the carrier to get through debriefing back home, have a cold beer, cuddle with the wife or girlfriend, and finally get around to delivering the goods to somebody else."

"So," Morrow said slowly, "it was specially and purposely made by or for somebody who knew it was going to be used for an illegal purpose. Who knew also that there was a chance it might be discovered and didn't want it traced if it was discovered."

"You got it."

Sam turned back to his work bench. The NCIS officer stared after him for a moment, then walked over to Dex and said, "I need to know as soon—"

"Please," said Dex, without looking up from his work. "Even with our database it's going to take a while to get an exact match. The Silurian period holds an embarrassment of fungi species. Enough for every mycologist here to have their own specialty."

"We'll come back."

"Do."

Outside, the JAG officer asked Morrow, "Why not just round all the fungus specialists, put them in a line-up?"

"Because—and I hate to have to tell you this—the scientists here are anti-authoritarian to the bone. They regard the Navy presence as a necessary evil. Tear 'em away from their work, you'll never hear the end of it."

"Then why not show our prisoner's picture around in camp and ask people if they remember seeing him, who he was with?"

"Start by asking his buddies who had liberty with him if they saw him talking with any civilians."

"Christ, how hard can this be?"

"One distinct advantage we have is that this is a small community. Anonymity is hard to maintain for long."

"By the same token, won't our civilian know we're after him?"

"So what if he does? Where's he going to run to? Home is four hundred million years away."

"Let's see if the prisoner can help us narrow the field of suspects."

A perfectly rigid master-at-arms guarded the only prisoner in sick bay, a pale, nervous sailor who appeared to Morrow to be in his mid-twenties; another Navy officer standing at his bedside identified himself as the counsel to the accused. A corpsman hovered unobtrusively in the background.

Introductions were made all around, and then, as though on cue, the prisoner said, in a hopeful tone, "Look, I want to make a deal."

The defense counsel started to speak, but Morrow held up a hand and grinned at the young sailor and said, "This is the Navy. I'm not sure you can cop a plea."

"He's willing to cooperate," said the counsel.

"Then let him prove it. Who gave you the vial?"

"A civilian."

"Who?"

"I don't know."

"You let a perfect stranger talk you into sticking something up your behind?"

"He said it would be better all around if nobody knew anybody's name."

"Better for him, obviously. Describe him."

"He was ordinary-looking. Ordinary height, ordinary looks."

"I thought you wanted to cooperate."

"I do!"

"How old was he?"

"Late forties, maybe early fifties."

"Jesus," said Morrow, "that sounds like half the geeks in Paleozoic time. What color was his hair?"

"Brown. Gray at the temples."

"Eyes?"

"Brown, I think. Dark, anyway."

"Wasn't there something distinctive about him? Anything at all?"

"He had a tattoo. On his neck."

"What of?"

"Hell, I don't know. Just some wavy design."

"How did you meet this ordinary-looking civilian with the tattoo on his neck?"

"One time when I had liberty."

"Which time?"

"About ten days ago, two weeks ago. I went ashore, and the first evening this guy just comes up to me and says, You'll be going home soon, won't you? and would I like to make some extra money."

"Just like that."

"Well, not just like that. There was, I dunno, we talked about other stuff for a while. He just struck up a conversation, you know? He got me a real beer. Not that three-two crap. And I guess I told him I'd be heading home soon, I'm not sure."

"How did the subject of the vial come up?"

"He was going on about the wonders of the primitive world, how amazing it is, how lucky we are. And he said something like how there were people back home who'd pay small fortunes for some of the specimens that were just disappearing into labs and museums. That's how he put it. Disappearing."

"What did you say?"

"I said I could use a small fortune."

The door to sick bay opened, and Sal Shelton stood framed by it. "May I come in?"

"Sal," Morrow said, "who do we know with a tattoo on his neck?"

Phil Morrow, Sal Shelton, and a Marine staff sergeant waited with Rob Brinkman on the helicopter deck, watching as the pilot did his walkaround. Brinkman swore softly and said, "I can't believe it."

"Payne's the only guy we've got here," Morrow said, "with a tattooed neck. And he's a mycologist."

"Well, Phil, you've got to bring him in. We want to keep this affair as quiet as possible, of course. But I'm afraid no matter how things turn out, there're going to be serious repercussions. Up till now, our scientists've been able to work without anybody looking over their shoulders. Now, because some dumb rating thought he'd make a little extra money on the side—"

"It doesn't mean cracking down on everyone who has a legitimate interest—"

Brinkman heaved a great unhappy sigh. "Obviously, it's possible to have a legitimate interest and an illegitimate angle at the same time. Payne's a fine paleomycologist. He wouldn't be here if he wasn't."

"You know," said Sal, "I've always been amused—if only rather bitterly amused—by the popular notion that scientists are somehow insusceptible to the seven deadly sins. Some of the best people I know are my fellow scientists. A few of the worst people I know are also my fellow scientists—fakers, plagiarists, outright thieves, at least one wife-beater, and those are just the *best* among the worst. The crème de la slime, if you will. I know, or know of, scientists who were just out and out lawbreakers, who should have gone to prison. But somehow didn't, because the scientific community closed ranks. Oh, they didn't get off scot-free. They stopped being invited to conferences, couldn't get their papers published because nobody could be sure they weren't plagiarists or hadn't faked their findings. But they were never publicly shamed. Nobody stepped up to them and said, 'Thank you for making us all look like total shits.'"

The pilot waved to them. Morrow said to Sal, "Are you sure you want to come along?" and she answered, "I've got something to say to Doctor Payne, and I may not get another chance." Brinkman nodded a goodbye, and the two scientists and the Marine staff sergeant boarded the helicopter. The beat of the rotor increased, the machine tugged itself away from the deck, and the ship fell away below. It was late afternoon, and the Paleozoic sea stretched to the horizon in three directions, the Paleozoic landscape to a line of low, eroded mountains in the fourth. Nobody spoke. The Marine staff sergeant watched curiously as the helicopter swung high above neat rows of tents and Quonset huts, lifted over the bare stony ridge overlooking the base camp, and pointed its nose purposefully toward the west. Morrow, studying the staff sergeant, was fascinated by the holstered gun at the man's side. He knew the Navy, being the Navy, must have weapons even here, but he could not recall having noticed them before this. He stole a glance at Sal Shelton, seated next to him. She had her arms crossed, her chin sunk upon her chest, and glared out the open hatch at the Paleozoic world as though she hated it.

After about twenty minutes in the air, the helicopter descended toward a small camp pitched beside the turbid river that drained the region. The pilot set the helicopter down carefully upon a level patch of shingle about fifty yards from the camp, and Sal Shelton, Phil Morrow, and the Marine staff sergeant climbed out. A man came out of the tent and stood watching them as they crunched toward him across the shingle.

There was a sign in front of the tent that said KEEP OFF THE GRASS. Cute, Morrow thought, botanist humor. There was no grass in this world, no flowering plants at all. There were barely any plants, period.

"Doctor Payne, I presume," Morrow said to the man.

"Yes." Payne looked puzzled. He matched the description the prisoner on the ship had given: a tattoo of interlocked crescent-shaped designs adorned the left side of his neck, creeping into the hairline behind his ear.

"Doctor Payne," Morrow said, "I am placing you under arrest for smuggling and related charges. You have the right to remain silent. If you do not choose to remain silent—"

"What? What's this all about? This must be some kind of mistake."

Morrow ignored the objection and finished reciting the list of the accused's rights. Payne seemed too surprised to resist as the Marine staff sergeant pulled his arms behind his back and snapped handcuffs around his wrists. Finally he managed to say, "There must be some mistake."

Morrow gave him a tight smile. "Remember that big Navy boat anchored in the bay at Stinktown? There's a scared swabbie on board there who's in the brig. He knows he's in deep ca-ca and thinks somebody else ought to be there to keep him company."

"I don't know what you're talking about."

"Smuggling biological specimens."

"What do *I* know about smuggling?"

"They didn't even have to use the rubber hose on him. They looked real mean at him, and he split wide open and out came his guts. Also a description of yourself. He's facing dishonorable discharge and serious prison time. You're looking at no more lecture and conference circuit, no more awards—and serious prison time. Even without the prison time, you'll never be able to get so much as a job teaching General Science One-oh-one in Podunk."

"Are you feeling well? You talk like a lunatic."

"Yes, I am feeling well," Morrow said, "and probably I am a lunatic. But that's beside the point. The point is, your sponsor, whoever he may be, can't or doesn't want to come to the Paleozoic himself, so he's having the Paleozoic brought to him, a tiny little bit at a time. Spores, DNA, air samples, soil samples. A little contraband specimen each time one of his people comes through the hole. He has to rely on human accomplices to actually go into Paleozoic time, though. No robot, however perfectly fashioned, is going to pass the physical. So he has to hire people to bribe other people who probably bribed someone else."

The Marine staff sergeant began to push Payne, not roughly but firmly, toward the waiting helicopter. Morrow and Shelton fell in behind, and Sal said, with such bitterness in her voice that Morrow was startled, "Thank you so much, Doctor Payne."

After a moment, Payne said, sullenly, "What for?"

"I started out in vertebrate paleontology. Absolutely loved dinosaurs, ever since I knew what a dinosaur was. Back then, in graduate school, I drew a lot of comments from invertebrate paleontologists. There's no money in dinosaurs, they said. Study invertebrates, get a job in oil geology, make big money. Money didn't tempt me, though. What finally tempted me was the spacetime anomaly. As soon as I heard there was this hole into Paleozoic time, I decided, I'm going. This was such a great thing, such a wonderful thing—if I believed in supernatural stuff I'd call this a miracle. And I wanted to be part of it. I figured, There may not be dinosaurs, but there're plenty of other fascinating critters. I was in my fifties by then, but I did the necessary retooling, and here I am. And now—" she flung out a hand, taking in land and

sky with the gesture "—it's spoiled. Thanks to you and the people working with you and whoever all of you were working for. This is the end in Eden. Sin has entered the garden."

LOST PLACES OF THE EARTH

"Of *course* I noticed you right off," he tells her, "how could I not? I noticed you the first time you walked into my class. It was obvious to me right away how little you have in common with the others. The rest of them are there because they have to be somewhere. They sit taking in oxygen and giving off carbon dioxide, and into their heads goes the refined gold of knowledge and out of those same heads comes dross. 'But that one in the second row,' I told myself, 'the pretty one—' Yes! That's exactly what I thought. The pretty one. Why would I lie about something like that? 'That pretty one,' I told myself, 'She's not just pretty, she seems pretty sharp. She bears keeping an eye on.' And you didn't disappoint me. You always listened so attentively the whole time I was lecturing. You listened *raptly*. Um, it means the same thing as *attentively*, but more so. I cannot tell you with what pleasure I saw the look of concentration and purpose on your face as you applied yourself to a test paper. It's the rare ones like you, you know, who make the profession of teaching *worthwhile*. So often we teachers are left feeling that our efforts are for naught. That we might as profitably try to instruct baboons in table etiquette. Every good teacher lives for that magical moment, which may come only once or twice in a career, when he knows he has connected solidly with a student. And any good teacher will step outside confining routine for a good student. A good teacher and a good student can only encourage each other. I told myself, 'I think you should go to a little extra trouble for her. Because she's *worth it*. Because she's obviously special.'"

Well, for now, anyway, he thinks, even as he gives her a very solemn look, by way of preparing the ground—if and when the necessity for it should arise—for him to deploy just that hint of a throb in his voice which he has perfected and used to often devastating effect in connection with variations on this theme. This far in advance, you never can tell; this is a live one—she's already practically salivating at one end and lubricating at the other, but only time will tell.

"Now, to show you how much I think of you, I tell myself, 'I know she's carrying a full course load, she has a lot of work to do, but if she can just fit it into her schedule, why don't you give her an advance peek at the new maparama? Ask her to meet you here after class—yes, after hours would be fine, that way you won't be under the technicians' feet.' Just not after curfew, ha ha, mustn't upset the dean of women, not even in the interests of science, ha ha. You must promise never to tell a soul that I took you into the maparama before the official unveiling. We certainly don't want to get ourselves into trouble with anybody, do we? Of course we don't. Anyway, as I was telling myself, 'Who knows, one day she'—that is, you, not the dean of women, ha ha—'may be in my position, and some promising young student will be in hers, and so the torch will be passed.'"

Yeah, he thinks, like she really is going to leapfrog out of graduate studies over a bunch of tenured professors who are just waiting for me to step down as head of the department. And like I'd carry along some infatuated young thing even if I did step down.

"Oh, well, of course I'm in pretty good shape for somebody my age, active, alert, sharp as the proverbial tack. But I am getting on, you know, so it's natural for me to be thinking about retiring and what comes after retirement. But I'm also keen to ensure that my legacy endures, and can you blame me?"

He knows how this must make her feel because he remembers how he felt, decades before. Then, of course, he hardly cared that the assistantship paid next to nothing, that he was practically indenturing himself to a mentor who required a great deal of picking up after, that his own ambition and energy were to be tapped and made to serve merely as propellant supplements to somebody else's. This is not the first or second or fiftieth time he has had such thoughts, and even as he thinks them he realizes, again, that they are not altogether worthy ones, that his own conduct does not stand comparison. His mentor, at least, did not make the job out to be more than it is, did not have ulterior motives, did not try to seduce him. Proximity to such a distinguished personage and visible association with the paleogeography project, even if in an often demeaning role, were vastly preferable to isolation and obscurity. You haven't done too shabbily, he chides himself, especially not in the area of extracurricular activities. Even the old maparama powerfully stimulated a certain species of science-geekette, and what would you do for fun on your budget, with your work load, if not for science-geekettes? Chat up art or, ew, *drama* majors?

In the event, he has finally got her to step into the maparama. "There's the light, and here's the lock—this is our very own private visit, we don't want anybody barging in on us, now, do we? Of course it's all right, I say so myself. Now, watch!" and he picks up the remote control, the room's bare metallic surfaces somehow brighten, illumined from within, even as the lights dim, and high up on the steep side of the amphitheatre the old man and the young woman seem to hang suspended in outer space. Before them, in the well, spins an oblate blue planet.

She says, with the merest hint of disappointment in her voice, "I've *seen* the world before."

"True, true," he answers, "but—seeing it on a little screen is one thing, practically *immersing* yourself in it is something else altogether. This is absolutely the latest generation of Intelligelatin," and suddenly it is as though they stand on a high cliff overlooking the faceted surface of a sea that reaches the horizon in every direction; above this rim of ocean, the walls and ceiling glow creamily; she gasps admiringly, and he savors the effect for a protracted moment before speaking again. "We haven't even done everything we're going to do yet. We're going to be working up paleometeorology and paleoastronomy effects to enhance the illusion, so there'll be something overhead besides just a ceiling."

"Some illusion already!" she burbles.

"When it's finished, it's going to be your total virtual Paleozoic experience. You'll be able to hear and smell and even feel it when the artificial breeze wafts through. You'll be able to imagine you're there, if that's what turns you on, ha ha." I don't know what the Paleozoic sounds like, he thinks, probably like a dripping faucet, and probably it smells like a backed-up sewer, but that does seem to be what turns her on.

"Can we go up again?" she asks. "To the macro view?"

"But of course! Your wish is a command."

They seem to expand, or the world, to shrink.

"We can do topo, relief, color-code everything according to whatever you want to know at a glance. At this particular magnification, it's like we're looking down at the planet from an altitude of about eighty kilometers. Come, give me your hand."

And she does give him her hand, and they step down into the well itself, and the blue sparkling ocean laps dryly at their ankles. The ocean bottom—actually the memory mat covering the floor of the well—is warm and gently yields underfoot.

"Where are we," she asks, "in relation to anywhere else?"

"Laurasia's over the horizon to your left," and he uses the remote control with his free hand, taking care not to relinquish her hand since she has not drawn it away. The image spins under their feet to the right, and an irregular landmass appears.

"Whoa," she says, and her hand slips from his, "give a gal some warning next time. That made me dizzy!"

And he thinks, but does not say, Dizziness becomes you.

What happens next makes both of them jump: she shrieks suddenly as his doppelgänger appears before them—a handsome, rather patrician figure, immaculately groomed and conservatively dressed.

"No, no, it's all right," the original of this copy hastens to assure her even as he tries to repress his own involuntary shudder of excitement, "it's not *me* and it's not my twin brother, either! Say hello to my hologram! See, I can put my hand right through it!" and he does. "Go on, try it yourself."

She raises her hand, lets it fall. "It'd be just too creepy."

"I must have hit the wrong button here. Just one little second, and I'll make it go away."

"No! Don't you dare! This is fascinating. Creepy, but fascinating. Oh, he's even handsomer than you are!"

"Um, well, they deleted some of the slight physical defects to which all of us are heir."

The hologram regards them fondly, and she gasps, "He makes eye contact!"

"It's designed to. It's programmed to interact with audiences, respond to what people say." To the hologram, he says, "Please introduce yourself," and then, to her, because he is miffed by the interruption and stabbed with jealousy of himself in spite of himself, "It *is* an it, not a he."

"I love maps," the holograph says in a well-modulated voice, and gestures negligently. Latitude and longitude lines close in from the walls of the map pit, intersect, and an ornate arrow points northward. "Of course I do. A love of maps is a prerequisite for pursuing a career in cartography. One must love maps, love looking at them and making them and filling in the blank spots. Satellite mapping doesn't leave many blank spots, of course, not even on a map of the world as it was four hundred million years ago. But we're a hands-on species. We have to go to places and touch the things we find there and give them all names. One must love filling in the names, love writing them out—be a compulsive list-maker. It is never enough for us that we should merely know of a place—any place, whether forty million miles away on Mars, or four hundred million years ago, in Siluro-Devonian time. We must regard it proprietarily, with a view to claiming it as our own—as prospective colonists. We must visit and put our mark upon it. We must name it and everything within and around it. Names are words, and words are tools that enable Homo sapiens, the metaphorical animal, to get on with the real work of interpreting the world."

He uses the remote control to demonstrate, he carefully, oh so casually, clasps her upper arm with his free hand to provide support should she, seemingly mesmerized as she is, again lose her balance. Masses of clouds form, red arrows indicate warm ocean currents and blue arrows indicate cold ones. The weather over the South Pole appears violent. She breathes a happy sigh and trails the tip of her slender foot along an island arc.

Place names appear, and the hologram says, "Just as human names flung across space adorn planets, stars, and galaxies, so, too, does the prehistoric world bear names from our own, names drawn from classical literature and nineteenth- and twentieth-century earth science—relatively speaking, names imposed on a world that is no more, by a world that is yet to be. Thus, the supercontinents Pangaea, Pennotia, Rodinia, and so, too, the divisions of geologic time. The Devonian Period, for instance, was so christened because its rocks were first studied in Devonshire, the Jurassic, from the Jura Mountains. The Mississippian and the Pennsylvanian hardly need explanation. Silurian rocks were first studied in Wales, whose people are descended from the Silures, a warlike tribe whom the Romans conquered, circa. A.D. 80, and whom Thomas Bulfinch much later associated with the historical King Arthur."

The hologram is a confident, affable lecturer. Again, the original feels the stab of jealousy, so fierce now that it verges upon hatred of his image. Yet the young woman is entranced; her resistance is visibly collapsing, he reflects, so blow your own horn, Professor, and down tumble the walls, or the pants, anyway. She listens with such concentration, lips slightly parted, pupils dilated, that he eases his arm around her in such a way that she hardly notices and then, when she does notice, accepts it as the most natural thing.

"On our evolving map of the Siluro-Devonian earth," the hologram continues, "the world ocean, Panthalassa, comprises the Iaepetus, the Rheic, the Tethys, and other seas separating the great southern continent, Gondwana, and the northern landmasses, collectively called Laurasia. Gondwana means 'land of the Gonds,' from a locality in India—Gondwanaland is redundant—and Laurasia is a contraction of Laurentia, the name given proto-North America, and Eurasia. These names are necessarily general because they predate our being able actually to explore the Paleozoic world. Owing to the advances made by quantum physicists, we are now able study the Siluro-Devonian world of four hundred million years ago—study it and label its most minute features. It has been my honor and my pleasure to serve as chairman of the nomenclature committee. Most of the names proposed by the committee are not controversial, but it must be borne in mind that many of the honorees were quite controversial figures in their time, and even now there are sometimes differences of opinion. Field geologists on the committee revere Alfred Wegener as a martyr—not only in the figurative sense of a theorist who attracted more ridicule than support during his lifetime, but as a scientist who perished in the line of duty. Wegener froze to death in Greenland while attempting to prove his theory of continental drift. The committee also includes so-called black-box geologists, however, who accord Wegener his due, of course, but regard him as somewhat of an inspired madman. They find the thought of leaving the laboratory to go out onto ice caps, well, chilling, and they protested that while it was only right to name a cape after Wegener, naming a deep, an archipelago, and a river system after him as well was excessive."

He kisses her and feels her respond, dreamily, and the hologram breaks into a kindly smile as though approving, and she responds to that as well.

"The committee has also named geographical features in honor of the gentleman geologist, Sir Roderick Impey Murchison, who defined the Silurian Period, and his rival, The Reverend Adam Sedgwick, who had the temerity, as Murchison saw it, to challenge that definition. Like the later dispute between Marsh and Cope, which had as its backdrop the, then, still wild American west, this argument over turf between two nineteenth-century English gentleman geologists seems to us rather puerile. Yet it became so heated that it could not be entirely resolved during the lifetimes of its principles. The highlands separating the great Murchison and Sedgwick river valleys bear the surname of William Lonsdale, who spent two years arbitrating a dispute—not even the main dispute, but only *a* dispute—between Murchison and Sedgwick. Other honorees include pioneers and popularizers such as Hutton, Strata Smith, Lyell, Erasmus and Charles Darwin, Thomas Huxley, Lapworth, Jaeger, Schuchert, Wells—John W., not H. G.—Suess, who named Gondwana, Banks, Eiseley, Fortey, Gould, McPhee, McPhetridge, and the improbably trilobitophilic cinema sexbomb Sherita Cheshire. *Her* evocative name graces a particular geologically distinguishable locality that evidently evoked thoughts of certain anatomical features of Ms. Cheshire's. We committee members joked among ourselves that a certain Gondwanan peninsula is shorter than the name it bears — that of the late Vinodh Srinivasasainagendra. Yet Doctor Srinivasasainagendra's contributions are unassailable, and the joke was intended good-naturedly, even affectionately, by those fortunate of us enough to have known the great biologist."

Like some impossible supercontinent, grossly out of scale with other topographical features in the well, she now lies disheveled and disarrayed and half-submerged in illusion, lapped all around by the primeval world-ocean. One outstretched arm lies athwart the island arc of Avalonia, the fingers of her other hand apparently root among the basement rocks of Laurasia, and her feet are sunk almost to the ankles in the shallows of the constricted Iaepetus seaway. Her body heaves like a surrealistic simulation of plate tectonics.

He risks a glance over his shoulder at the hologram, and the hologram gives him a wink and a thumb's up but never misses a beat.

"Scientists, of course, are only flesh-and-blood human beings with all the failings that real people are heir to. It is quite deplorable that Murchison and Sedgwick, and Cope and Marsh after them, should have wasted so much time and energy on personal feuds. It is with no pleasure that we note that Isaac Newton was a vindictive prig. Yet we forgive the great scientists their idiosyncrasies and shortcomings and honor them for their lasting contributions to the body of scientific knowledge—for isn't *that* what's really important?"

The remote control has long since slipped from his hand, but he did not notice at the time, being otherwise occupied. It slipped between and then beneath them, and as they bump and roll against it and mash it unto the memory mat, the lecture continues, and, all around them, the earth moves, oh yes the earth moves.

A SILURIAN TALE

I'm driving with the top down, minding my own business, when a young woman appears overhead, in the sky. She's enough to make any man's heart forget to beat—girl-next-door lovely, long-legged, boyishly slim save for large, succulent breasts. From end to end, she's approximately the size of a Zeppelin. And she wants to have sex with me.

No, actually, she wants to sell me a new soft drink, but I'm too quick for her. I thumb up the power on my sunglasses. Her dulcet voice goes *skeeek*, she shimmers and breaks up into scintillae of light (all primary colors) and vanishes. I say, "Good riddance," and I think, Flogging's the least of what's coming to the man who invented airvertising.

Returning to the modern world—becoming part of it again—has entailed some readjustment on my part, of course, but it's not as if I'm suddenly seeing, hearing, and smelling a 21st-century city for the first time. Sure, I'm still getting used to the way the air tastes (worse), and there're more damn airverts than there were just a year ago, but it's hardly as if I'd never noticed that oily yellow-brown smudge hanging over the skyline until now, or wished I could avoid commercials without having to buy special equipment. And not all of the comparisons are unfavorable to the present. The world today is green, and there's nothing like greenery for softening the contours of a landscape. There were hardly any land plants where I was. It rained every day, too, and without rooted plants to hold soil in place, the cut-up terrain was almost lunar in its barrenness and angularity. Although I was never indifferent to the plant kingdom before, now I'm awed by trees, awed by flowers. I've seen their distant ancestors struggling for purchase on the inhospitable land.

I turn onto Ramrod Drive, which is in a subdivision given over to street names like Gunsight, Hollow Point, Exit Wound. The theory seems to be that members of the criminal class will be warned off. My sister Dala, her husband Tim, and their two children live in an artfully rustic stone house on a full-acre lot at the end of Ramrod. Dala appears at the front door as I pull into the driveway; I see her turn her head and call over her shoulder. I've barely had time to shut off the motor before my ten-year-old nephew Ethan and seven-year-old niece Alesha push past their mom. They come at a dead run, arrive before I can unbuckle my seat belt, dart back and forth like excited puppies, squealing, "Uncle Roge! Uncle Roge! Uncle Roge!" One Uncle Roge fewer than I got last time. Nevertheless, they practically fly into my arms as I emerge from the car, and I have to tell them not to be so shy. Alesha tries to climb onto my shoulder. Ethan accepts a hug, gives one in return, then pulls back in my embrace and tries to regain his dignity. The neighbor kids are watching, and he's just old enough for dignity to have become important to him, sometimes. Alesha wraps her arms around my neck and asks, "What did you bring us from way back when?"

"Show you later, Little Bit."

During the year I was away, I may have missed children more than anything else. Certainly, I've missed these children.

On the patio, Tim turns his attention to building a charcoal fire, Dala's indoors, building a salad. The back yard boasts big old oaks and a fine willow. The kids and I stroll about, Alesha holding me by the index and middle fingers of my right hand, Ethan walking on my left, not touching, in case somebody is still spying on him. I hear birds singing, a dog barking, cars passing on the next street over, a squirrel telling everyone to shut up. The world of long ago was too quiet.

Alesha says, "Did you see dinosaurs?"

Before I can answer, Ethan gives her a superior look. "There weren't any dinosaurs then," he says, in a tone of voice that matches the look. To me he says, "I told her that already, but—" and shrugs, one-guy-to-another eloquent.

Alesha has to hear it from me, though, so I tell her, gently, "Your brother's right. It was before there were any dinosaurs. Before there was much of anything."

"Oh," she says, then adds, very solemnly, "that's too bad."

"Well, at least I didn't have to worry all the time about getting eaten by a dinosaur," and I pull my hand free of hers and assume the theropod position, torso more or less parallel to the ground, arms drawn against my chest, fingers curled into talons. A ferocious expression and a cry of "Roww-ar!" complete my transformation from uncle to giant carnivorous dinosaur. She shrieks delightedly and runs for cover among the drooping limbs of the willow. I start to charge after her but notice Ethan hanging back. "Come on," I growl, "let's go get that little mammal!"

He's visibly pained—embarrassed, I'm startled to realize. "I'm too old to play dinosaur any more."

"That's funny, I'm not," and I go roaring off in pursuit of his sister, in the expectation, the hope, at least, that he will follow.

Still, I'm thinking, Ouch. I taught him and Alesha how to play dinosaur (or, rather, we worked it out among ourselves) one afternoon when I was babysitting for Dala and Tim. I stole liberally from *The Lost World* for the scenario: they were the intrepid explorers who entered my, the Tyrant Lizard King's, jungle fastness and had to be chased out. Next, they wanted to be dinosaurs themselves—predatory ones, of course. Who would ever want to be a plant-eater? Yet, where there are predators, there must be prey, so, by virtue of my relative bulk and pea-sized brain, I was elected to the role of sauropod. In this capacity, I had to go on all fours and browse off the willow while the tyrannosaurlets set up their attack; then I got to lurch about some with them hanging off me before I fell into a twitching heap. Thereafter, I varied the theropod diet, at times impersonating a stegosaur (indicated by an arm held behind, with the fingers sticking stiffly upward to represent the spiky tail) or a ceratopsian (with arms extended forward to form the horns). At the swimming pool, we experimented with plesiosaurs, icthyosaurs, mosasaurs; once, I rose Kraken-like between them, all entangling tentacles, and Ethan broke character to protest. For openers, as far as he was concerned, if it wasn't Mesozoic, it wasn't squat—but if it wasn't even a real monster, as opposed to a mythical one, he simply wanted no part of it. He is truly Tim's son, as Alesha is Dala's daughter. I like Tim, understand, and think he and Dala complement each other very nicely, but he's an analyzer, a stockpiler of facts and solver of puzzles, while we Ovingtons have always been dreamers. Just before my departure a year ago, I made up a little song for the kids:

> *I have a pet, a dip-loh-doh-kus;*
> *both his eyes are out of focus.*
> *When I took him to the park,*
> *he wandered off into the dark*
> *and, being a myopic dragon,*
> *fell upon a station wagon.*
> *So I took him home to mend;*
> *I'll never take him out again.*

Alesha wanted to know what "myopic" meant; Ethan said, "It's pronounced dih-*plod*-ih-kus."

My niece screams in ecstatic terror when I catch her on the far side of the willow. Rather than eat her, I swing her onto my shoulders. Ethan has unhappily waited for us to rejoin him. He rolls his eyes when Alesha asks me, "Why didn't you go where they have dinosaurs?"

I set her on her feet next to him. "Because I couldn't."

"Nobody can," Ethan tells her. "They can only go back to the Sillian—Sil—"

"Silurian," I say, gently.

"The Silurian Period," he says, enunciating as if his life depended on it. Sih Loo Rih An.

"Sillian." Alesha giggles, says it again, giggles some more. Ethan rolls his eyes again. "Ethan read about it. He said it was boring."

He shoots her a look that somehow fails to incinerate her on the spot. I think, Well, spending a year in the Silurian is a lot like pulling a tour of duty in Greenland, only not as dangerous. The vistas are utterly different but about equally stark. The sense of isolation and the tedium are the same. I sat out my Silurian sojourn at a weather station, contributing my vital bit to paleoclimatology. I had wanted to do it and am not sorry I did it, but, frankly, tropical depressions haven't changed in 400 million years.

I say, "Bor-ring is what I thought until the night of the giant sea scorpions."

Their eyes widen, then Ethan's skepticism kicks in, and the question in his mind is plain on his face: *How* giant . . .?

"Would you like to hear the story?"

He nods. She considers for a moment. "Is it scary?"

"Maybe as scary as *Wizard of Oz.* Remember how scary the witch was? Think you can handle anything that scary?"

"Is there a witch in this story?"

"No, but there're big monsters," and I lead them under the willow to a bare patch of earth, and with a stick I draw an elongate teardrop in the dirt, add lines dividing the teardrop into segments, add a pair of sweptback, oar-like appendages and then (having saved the best for last) two arms ending in pincers. "That's what these monsters look like. They live in—lived in the water, and some of them grew as big as me." I can tell from Ethan's expression that he's disappointed. "Or even *bigger.*" How big does a critter have to be to be impressive?

Alesha says, "Do they eat people?"

"They eat anything they can get into their mouths. Tell you what, why don't I show you what I brought you instead, and you can go show Mommy and Daddy, okay?"

"Okay! Show me!"

We sit, me with my back against the willow, each of them by one of my outstretched feet. I put my hand into the left pocket of my jacket and say, "Once upon a time, long before there were people or dinosaurs, most of what is now land was at the bottom of the sea. A few rocky islands poked up out of the water, that was all. Hardly anything lived on land except right at the water's edge. Ah, but in the water—that was different. There were strange-looking fish that wore bony armor, and tiny, tiny sea creatures that formed reefs as big as mountains. There was a tribe of animals called trilobites. Can you say that?"

"Trilobites," Alesha says, perfectly.

"That's very good. I'm glad you can say it, so you can tell everybody what this is," and from my pocket I draw a disk of clear plastic. It just about fills the palm of my hand. Embedded in it are three dainty glistening blue-gray trilobites, trilobite exoskeletons, anyway, cast off during molt. They really are quite lovely. I wasn't authorized to collect any specimens for transport to the 21st century, but a marine biologist I knew was good enough to pick these out of the seabed litter for me. It's extremely gratifying to see Alice's eyes and mouth imitate the letter O as I let the disk slide out of my hand, into hers.

Ethan cranes forward to see. "Are those fossils?"

"Nope. They were fresh when they went into the plastic. Little Bit, don't I get a thank-you hug?" I do, and a thank-you kiss on the cheek as well. "Now why don't you go show Mommy and Daddy?"

"Okay," and off she rockets, clutching her piece of the Paleozoic Era.

I settle back against the tree. Ethan squirms impatiently. The sooner I get on with my story, he knows, the sooner I'll be reaching into the right pocket of my jacket.

I begin.

"When I first got to the Silurian Period, I met a couple of scientists named Doctor Russell and Doctor Vrastil, who were planning a little weekend boating expedition along the coast. Doctor Russell studied fish, and Doctor Vrastil studied plants. They asked me if I'd care to go along for the ride and a change of scenery, which is a laugh, since every place in the Silurian Period looks pretty much like every other place. But I said yes, because right then we were in a place called Stinktown. It's called that because when the tide goes out, all this slimy mud and seaweed lies around in the hot sun and starts stinking to high heaven. I had a few days to kill before I could catch a ride to my weather station, but I thought the smell was likely to kill me if I stayed in Stinktown.

"So, early one morning, the three of us took a boat and headed out along the coast, which was all cut up into inlets. Some had never been explored. Around midday, we put into one that Russell and Vrastil found particularly interesting for some reason. I thought it was creepy, even for the Silurian Period, but I didn't want to say anything. It wasn't my party. We went in past thick floating mats of seaweed and then turned off the motor and drifted for a while. It was so quiet all you could hear was the water slapping against the hull of the boat. High rocky cliffs rose on both sides of us, and nothing grew on the shore except moss. There was a glass observation pane in the bottom of the boat, so Russell could point out all the trilobites and funny-looking fish and things, but as we went in further, the water got murky from a muddy little river that emptied into the inlet.

"After we'd set up camp, they went their separate ways to look at fish or moss. I decided to climb the cliffs enclosing the inlet and see what I could see from the top, only to find that they were too steep to climb. The only way out of the inlet was the way we'd come in.

"At sundown, we met back at camp. We were hungry and very tired, and as soon as we'd eaten supper we turned in for the night. But something awakened me after a while, a strange sound, perhaps, or something else I'd sensed in my sleep. I lay there for a minute or two, trying to figure it out, then sat up and looked around. There was enough moonlight for me to see that the others were sound asleep—and that our boat was missing!

"I gave a yell to wake them up, and we all scrambled down in a panic to the water. There we realized that our boat wasn't actually missing, it just wasn't where we'd left it, tied up to a metal stake driven into the ground. We could just barely see the boat about a hundred feet out and figured it must've pulled loose when the tide went out. Doctor Russell said, I tied the line, I'll go get the boat, and walked right into the water. Doctor Vrastil and I could see the silvery splashes he made as he waded out and started swimming. Then, suddenly, there was a big noisy splash and a sound like he was trying to shout with his mouth full of water.

"We called out, but he didn't answer. I started to run into the water, but Doctor Vrastil stopped me. Let me go, I said, something's happened to Russell! But he said, Wait, there's a flashlight in my pack, and ran to get it.

"I didn't wait but plunged in. I'd waded out up to my knees when the beam from the flashlight stabbed through the darkness and played over the water. What I saw before me froze my blood—a moving mass of sea scorpions, all writhing bodies and snapping pincers. The creatures fed at night, and poor Doctor Russell had blundered right into their feeding ground. Now they were coming after me!

"I backed onto the shore, fast, and thought that would be enough. Doctor Vrastil kept the light on the creatures as they advanced to the water's edge. They hesitated there. And then, to my horror, they began to crawl ashore, alternating dragging and pushing themselves forward. They were gill-breathers, of course, but they could trap water in their gills.

"I dashed back to where Vrastil crouched with the flashlight. Everywhere he trained the beam, we saw dozens of the hideous monsters, converging on us. The only sounds were the clicking of their terrible claws and the scrape and crunch they made as they dragged their bellies over the ground. We could've outrun them easily if there'd been any place to run to, but the cliffs trapped us, and we had no weapons. I don't mind telling you I was scared, and Vrastil was making little whimpering cries.

"But millions of years of evolution have given us brains, and at last I used mine. I had an inspired thought and suddenly dashed the flashlight from Vrastil's hand. It struck the ground I heard glass break, and the light went out. Vrastil screamed and clutched at me in terror. It was all I could do to make him be quiet and listen to me. The light, I told him, it's the light! The light attracts them! Sure enough, the monsters began to mill around uncertainly in the moonlight.

"But if they no longer had the beam of light to guide them to us, they still had the idea of prey fixed in their primitive little minds, and with so many of the creatures blindly groping about, the chance still existed that they'd overrun us. It seemed like hours before their gills began to dry out and, one or two at a time, they slipped back into the water. Even then, I didn't dare relax my vigilance, knowing that they could come ashore at will. Nights are short in the Silurian Period, because the Earth rotates faster, but that night was the longest of my life."

The curtain of willow branches parts, and Dala joins us. "Oh, don't stop," she says, crossing her arms, "go on. There *is* more, isn't there?"

"You bet, absolutely." I'm unabashed. "Well, there's a little more."

"Well, tell," she says, "tell."

"Ahem. When the sun finally rose, we saw no sign of the monsters or Doctor Russell. They must've torn him completely to pieces. Our boat, however, had come to rest against the shore during the night. I told Doctor Vrastil that we were going to be okay, but I don't think he heard me. The experience had been too much for him. He could only gibber and drool—his mind had snapped. But I managed to get him into the boat. I was about to start the motor when something hit the side of the boat. Bump, bump-bump, bump, like that. Behind me, Vrastil suddenly screamed. I whirled about, and there, pulling itself up over the side of the boat, was a sea scorpion as big as a bear! It grabbed at me—" I dart my hand at Ethan and make a clutching gesture, and he recoils sharply "—but I dodged, picked up the boat hook, and knocked the claw aside. I tried to stab the creature, but the point of the boat hook only glanced off its armored skin. As the monster reared back from the blow, however, I saw that it was off balance, so I drove the boat hook hard against its underside. It clutched frantically at the air as it started to topple, and then, with a roar of frustration, it fell back into the water. I didn't wait to see if it would try again but gunned the motor and got us out of there as fast as the boat would take us. A few hours later, poor mad Doctor Vrastil and I were safely back in Stinktown, but nobody there believed my story—"

"Imagine that," Dala says. I recognize the look on her face, the tone of her voice.

"Mah-um," says Ethan, "shh."

"Nobody believed my story until I showed them what I'd found in the bottom of the boat." I put my hand into the right pocket of my jacket and pull out an object encased in clear polyurethane. It looks somewhat like a crab claw but isn't. It's slightly longer than my hand, whitish with blue mottling, and impressively spiky. "The boat hook caught it at just the right angle," I say as I present it to Ethan, who makes a soft vowel sound as he accepts it.

While he sits turning it over and over in his fingers, Dala says, "I came to tell you it's eats in just five short minutes."

"Where's Little Bit?"

"I've got to go round her up, too. She ran next door to show her friend Amy the trilobites you gave her. Ethan, go wash."

Still unable to see anything but the claw, he gets to his feet and disappears through the willow branches.

I stand and dust off my butt. Dala says, dryly, "Thank you for not telling Alesha that story."

"Well, I'd've toned it down considerably for her. She'd've gotten the Disney version. Ethan got the classic pulp version. Three men go out. One gets eaten by things. One goes mad. And I only am escaped alone to tell thee."

She glances down, notices my drawing in the dirt.

"That's what the monsters looked like," I say.

She laughs softly and shakes her head. "Tell the truth now, did you actually see anything remotely resembling this the whole time you were back there?"

"Sure. Saw one from a glass-bottomed boat."

"Only one?"

"They're solitary creatures. According to my friend Russell, they mostly root around in the mud for worms and stuff."

"Ah! So there is a Doctor Russell. And did things eat him?"

"Yes, there is, and no, they didn't." We move out from under the willow and walk slowly toward the house. Ethan is showing the claw to Tim, who's trying to look at it and take chicken off the grill at the same time. "There's a Doctor Vrastil, too, who hasn't been driven mad by terror."

"And that evil-looking animal part you gave Ethan?"

"Part of an exoskeleton shed by a large, indeed evil-looking animal whose path never crossed mine, I'm happy to say. Russell found it and Alesha's trilobites for me."

"Let's hope Ethan never finds out his favorite uncle's thrilling prehistoric adventure is just a tissue of lies."

I stop walking, and she has to wait as I recite:

"Here about the beach I wander,
Nourishing a youth sublime
With the fairy tales of science,
And the long results of time."

"Is that one of yours?"

"Alfred Tennyson. Oh, Dala, Ethan doesn't really believe my story any more than Little Bit believes I'm going to gobble her up when I turn into a dinosaur and chase her. She screams when I catch her, but she knows it's make-believe. And it's not like I ever had to *explain* make-believe to these kids. So give Ethan some credit. He's already smarter than you and me put together."

"Ha," Dala says. "You wreck the bell curve."

"Ha yourself."

"Still, aren't you worried he's going to resent you for telling him a string of whoppers?"

"Not if they're entertaining whoppers. He'll save his resentment for the kind of lies that're meant to cheat him. Politicians' lies, used-car salesmen's lies. The kind of lie that says drinking such and such a brand of soft drink will not only get you laid, but by the kind of slim, leggy, busty gal who doesn't occur in nature. Look. He knows you can't leap out a window and fly away, but he still likes Peter Pan and Superman. He knows outer space is a vacuum, and sound doesn't travel in a vacuum—he figured this out over a year ago—but he didn't stop watching those sci-fi shows where you can hear explosions in space. An hour from now, he'll turn to me all of a sudden and say, Hey, wait a minute, how can an animal that breathes through gills *roar?*"

"And your answer will be—?"

"My answer will be, Like this—*roww-ar!*"

The five of us seat ourselves at the table and hold hands as Tim says grace. I look up from my barbecued chicken and across the table at Alesha. "I'm not sure which I'd rather have for dinner, chicken or—" I draw my arms against my chest, curl my fingers into claws, growl "—Little Bit!"

Over the rim of her glass, Alesha says, "Not at the table, Uncle Roge," and Dala laughs.

THE 400-MILLION-YEAR ITCH

"One gets a bad habit of being unhappy."

—GEORGE ELIOT

She had told the earnest young man repeatedly, "I have no interesting stories to tell." He was determined to interview her, however, and now they sat on opposite sides of the small glass-topped table in the garden room of her home in Riverside. The robutler had brought tea and tea things and retired discreetly. "I can't tell you anything that isn't already in the books. I can't tell you who said what to whom. I have a terrible memory for dates. I can't even remember most of the names."

The young man indicated the perfectly set table and smiled disarmingly and said, "Perhaps one of those might help."

"I beg your pardon?"

"I read somewhere that a crumb of madeleine soaked in tea can be a wonderful memory aid."

"I'm afraid I don't understand."

He seemed nonplussed by the utter collapse of his *bon mot*. He recovered quickly, though, and said, "What's missing from the books is you and your view of things. You were there through the early days. The exciting part."

"The exciting part. Well." She laughed a shivery, silvery laugh. "It recedes in the memory even when I want to think about it. It's become as distant and unreal to me as the Paleozoic itself. There was hardly anything to the Paleozoic, nothing vivid or extreme, unless you count the monotony. It was just like any lonely and desolate place in the world today, without any particular—peculiar element of danger of its own."

"How do you mean?"

"Oh, you don't have to go through a spacetime anomaly to Laurentia to drown or die of dehydration. Any modern desert will do, or any hot day in a major city, for that matter. And you can drown in your own bath tub. And Gondwana, I understand, all Gondwana was, was just Antarctica on a much bigger scale. Four whole continents, including Antarctica itself, plus India, jammed together and sitting right on the South Pole. You can go freeze your tail off in Antarctica. That's if you want to go all the way to Antarctica to do what you could do in Wisconsin in the wintertime."

He smiled, all calculated winsomeness. "I'm sorry, but I just find that very hard to believe. Spacetime anomalies, the primeval earth, prehistoric animals—"

"Small prehistoric animals."

"What about sea scorpions?"

"I think their reputation for ferocity must have been grossly inflated. I never heard of anybody being hurt by one."

"Then what about the so-called jump?"

"The jump doesn't count. That was just how you got there. It rattled my teeth some. It was extremely rough on a few people. Chalk that up to the vagaries of spacetime anomalies. But once you got there, the only extreme thing about it was the monotony. Unless you're the kind who oohed and aahed over trilobites, and even then I'm not sure you'd be distracted for very long. Alcoholism was rampant. So were—you see, when you jump, you go through with all your human baggage. You still have to face the day every morning and deal with other people and get things done. You still have to be who you are. Sometimes who you are isn't enough. Sometimes it's too much."

"Still—hardly humdrum stuff. Plus, you knew and worked intimately with one of the true titans of science."

She fixed a glittering eye upon him. "Yes."

"It must have been great, working with him."

"It," she said, and considered her next words very carefully.

"Amy, if I have to go," Cutsinger had told her, "you have to go, too."

They were lingering over dinner, mildly drunk on wine, Cutsinger humorously self-mocking, but, still, serious in what he proposed they do.

"Well," she said, "You know you don't have to go. Frankly, I'm surprised you'd consider it. We can work on the new book here. You wouldn't have to leave the house."

He nodded. "And yet I feel I do have to go. Much as the Wright brothers had to go up in their aeroplane, or Bell had to speak into his telephone."

"It's not like you invented the spacetime anomaly."

He laughed softly. "Despite my protests, less rigorously accurate practitioners of the journalistic trade have created that impression in the public mind. I am the wizard of time."

He was, she knew, not being falsely modest. He had only understood what the anomaly was, how it could be exploited, and had been able to describe lucidly its least arcane aspects, so that a difficult concept could be comprehended, with a modicum of mental effort, by untrained minds—those of the general public and, more particularly, of people charged with overseeing allocation of funds. In short, he had fired everyone's imagination. Not that he possessed an especially winning manner or that, as the saying went, the television camera loved him. Time Travel Into The Past, inaccurate though the phrase was, had virtually sold itself.

"I am," Cutsinger said, "popularly and inextricably associated with the phenomenon of the anomaly and the Paleozoic expedition. So of course I must go through the anomaly myself. The public, damn them, expect it."

"Didn't you always use to tell your classes that quantum physics isn't a hands-on science? Anyway, it wouldn't be a pleasure trip. That first man who went through the anomaly said it's about as pleasurable as getting hit by lightning can be."

"Not to go," he explained in a heavy self-mocking tone, "will demote The Wizard of Time from the magnitude of a Columbus, a Magellan, to that of a mere Henry the Navigator."

"Prince Henry did vital work without ever putting to sea."

"Yes. But everyone remembers Columbus."

So that had been that.

Yet from their first day after they had gone through the anomaly, there were signs of trouble. Having recovered from the effects of the transfer, she had acted upon a natural impulse to see the strange prehistoric world they now inhabited, Cutsinger had looked irritated and told her, "We have an awful lot of work to do, and we should get to it." She could not always be put off, however, but asked directions and immediately headed topside. At the bottom of a ladder she looked up and saw blue sky and serene clouds. When she emerged onto a catwalk just under the overhang of the helicopter deck there was the calm black sea, and covering it like gelatin as far as she could see were the iridescent float-sacs of thousands upon thousands of graptolite colonies. She turned and saw two bluejackets nearby, laughed and pointed, and they laughed, too, waved, exchanged inaudible comments between themselves, then laughed even harder. Suddenly abashed, she returned below, to Cutsinger, nervous and sweating at the bottom of the ladder. Now that he had indulged her on this occasion, he testily declared that it was time to buckle down and get to work.

The work in question consisted in unpacking and pawing through and generally disarranging notes for Cutsinger's next book. After two hours, Cutsinger abruptly said something about wanting to look in on the jump station.

Amy sat on the edge of her bunk and looked deep into the future and recalled a line from H. G. Wells, to the effect that people were always amazed by the obvious results of their actions. She knew she could have predicted this. The great man suffered from agoraphobia. He could function perfectly well in a large room full of people—the consensus was that he had acquitted himself brilliantly in the early press conferences—for he said that he was fine as long as he had walls around him and a ceiling above. Enclosement equaled security. The big outdoors, however, the open sky, land, and sea, filled him with dread. Now he might risk nausea and glance through a porthole, to calculate the time of day—the familiar twenty-four-hour clock was useless here, maddeningly out of synch with the speeded-up days and nights—but remove him from the protection of a room, and he began to fidget and sweat, to tremble and stammer. And there were no skies, no lands, and no seas more open, more terrifying in the emptiness of the vistas they presented, than those of the Paleozoic.

I knew this, she thought, I knew this I knew this I knew this. He will never leave the ship. He will never go topside. Here we'll remain for month upon month, officially on an expenses-paid sabbatical but actually entombed in this ship. I knew this. She knew he was a theoretician who would have nothing to do with the running of the jump station installed aboard, though he might spend inordinate amounts of time within its ozone-scented confines. The technicians there knew their jobs and would have little interest in the theoretical end of things, and in due course they would regard Cutsinger as a pain in the butt. I knew all this, she said, and still I let it happen.

That evening, their first in Paleozoic time, they were to dine at the captain's table. The captain, they had been reliably informed, was Navy to the marrow, always dressed for dinner, and every civilian invited to dine with him—even paleontologists, a notoriously slovenly lot—was expected or in any event felt obliged to follow suit, to the exhaustion of sartorial resources. Amy had come prepared: she laid out the dinner gown. Cutsinger looked at it dubiously.

"That gown," he said, "defies every physical law. What keeps it from falling off you?"

"Surface tension."

"Are you really intending to wear that thing?"

"You didn't complain at the Nobels. Anyway, the captain's a stickler for form. Besides, at the Nobels I was just another dame in a gown. Here, I expect to be the only dame in a gown."

She did not regret her choice. The table was immaculately set, the stewards seemed to gleam almost as brightly as the polished service. She found herself seated next to the captain himself and across from a newcomer, introduced as "the famous author" So And So, next to whom sat a volcanologist, also a newcomer. The volcanologist beamed at her and said, "I do Empedocles one better. I go down into the volcano like him, but then I come back out again."

"I'm sorry—who was Empedocles?"

"Ancient Greek fellow who jumped into the crater of Mount Etna to prove whether or not he was immortal. Turned out he wasn't."

"Ah. He must have been very disappointed."

"Well, briefly, yes, I'm sure."

The round of introductions continued. There was a Navy chaplain and, at the far end of the table from the captain, a marine biologist, and another man the captain said had been head of the sleep-disorder center at Cornell University's New York Hospital in Westchester County. "I'm not sure," the captain admitted, "how to describe what you're doing in Paleozoic time, Doctor."

"Observing all the observers," said the sleep-disorder expert with a quick smile.

"As you can see," the captain said to Amy, "there is a good deal more to this expedition than simply a bunch of paleontologists collecting trilobites and primitive plants. There are soil scientists here, and an astronomy team."

Probably inevitably, the first question directed to the author was, "What have you written?" and clearly he had been expecting it, or at least hoping for it. He was a large man whose heavy egg-shaped head surmounted a heavy egg-shaped body, patted his red lips with his napkin and favored his questioner, the chaplain, with a warm smile. "Fiction, for the most part," he said. "Perhaps you've read something of mine."

Everyone else at the table appeared more or less to doubt it, but the chaplain, being the sort of man he was, asked, "Please, what are some titles?"

"*Anomalous Al* had just been published and *Planet Janet* was still on the best-seller list back home when I left to come here."

"Ah," said the chaplain. "Science fiction."

The author grinned. "What other kind is there?"

"Space travel," the captain put in helpfully, "alien life-forms," and Amy herself contributed, "Spacetime anomalies," drawing a darting look from Cutsinger.

"My light reading matter of choice," the chaplain said apologetically, "is mythology."

"All I read," said the volcanologist, not in the least apologetically, "are murder mysteries."

"I'm afraid," Amy said, "about all I read are the scientific journals."

The captain offered the crestfallen author a regretful look, and the volcanologist asked, "Do you use Ediot to write your stories?"

The author fixed him with a suddenly cold eye and answered frostily, "I do all my own writing. All my own."

"No offense. I just—you know what they say. 'Ediot, the salvation of many a writing-challenged author.' Not to imply that you're writing-challenged. But I do a fair amount of writing myself. Technical stuff, reports, still, I find it's hard work. I use any help I can get."

"A creative, idiosyncratic writer is on his own. Ediot is for formal memoranda and other business correspondence. It was conceived with those ends in mind. It's purposely devoid of personality. So it doesn't do idiosyncrasy well."

The volcanologist grinned. "Still, I understand it's been used by some uncreative, unidiosyncratic writers to turn out a commercially viable work or two."

The author said, "I don't deny that," but looked as though he wished that he could.

"Still—"

To avert an outbreak of hostilities, the chaplain said, "Are you here to research a new time-travel story?"

"Time travel is part of my stock in trade, of course. But I have to confess I much prefer space-travel stories. Some people go somewhere in a starship and find something peculiar. This junket is something my agent sold my publisher on. If memory serves, their exact words were, 'The Paleozoic expedition has produced a lot of scientific papers, but it hasn't inspired a thing in the way of literature or art.'"

"Oh, I dunno," said the volcanologist. "I read a mystery once about this detective who investigates a—something to do with smuggling trilobite larvae, exotic pets, exotic plants, back to the twenty-first century. Was that something of yours?"

"No, but in *Anomalous Al* there's—"

"The smuggling," the unheeding volcanologist went on, "was just to set everything else in motion, of course, and get you to all the good stuff you expect to find in a detective story. Dead bodies turning up everywhere, beatings, a beautiful nymphomaniac volcanologist! The main bad guy—"

"Please," said the chaplain, "don't tell us. We might find ourselves reading that book one of these days. At least up to the point where the beautiful nymphomaniac comes into the plot."

"You might not last that long, Chaplain. I didn't say it was any good."

The author avoided looking at the volcanologist and said evenly, "As my agent and publisher were saying, about literature. 'The old whaling industry begot *Moby-Dick*, the Civil War begot *The Red Badge of Courage*, World War One begot—"

"World War Two!" The volcanologist laughed. "And then World War Two begat rockets and atomic bombs, which misbegat a lot of wretched pulp fiction!"

The author leaned away from the volcanologist, for whom his dislike was becoming palpable, and the latter, who patently did not care, said to the chaplain, "So, you came all this way to tend the local flock?"

The chaplain was a wiry fortyish man with alert eyes and laugh lines around his mouth, and Amy had already decided that she liked his looks. To his further credit, she thought, he received the question as though it were not entirely inane. "Part of it," he said. "The Protestant portion of it." He smiled at the author, turned his head to flash it at Amy as well. "We have a priest and a rabbi on board, too."

"Ah, of course," said the volcanologist. "Even Navy men of the cloth are specialists. And I imagine there'd be a mullah, too, if there were any Muslims attached to the expedition."

"There are some Muslims. Some Buddhists and Hindus, too."

"Do they just fend for themselves?"

"The Navy," the captain put in from his end of the table, "is only as good as its efforts to maintain its personnel at a peak of physical, mental, and spiritual health."

"How good of the Navy," the volcanologist said, "to see to everyone's needs! And lead them not into temptation, either. The Navy doesn't provide grog and brothels for its people, does it, Captain?"

The captain looked as though he had bitten into something rancid on the end of his fork. "Certainly not!"

"But," the chaplain said, as easily as before, "there are still plenty of temptations, even here. Most of the enlisted personnel are men and women in their twenties. All volunteers, of course, and many of them with families back home. They're young, nevertheless, and a long way from home."

"Then I'm sure it's a good thing that experience has taught the Navy to prefer liberal men of the cloth to reactionary ones."

"Well—"

"After all, what could be more hellish than to be trapped with some raging Calvinist on a ship on the open sea, and a prehistoric sea at that? Seasick, four hundred million years from home, and predestined to eternal damnation! Under such conditions, anyone's morale would collapse! To say nothing of his morals." The volcanologist winked at Amy. "Or hers."

In spite of herself, or in spite of Cutsinger, she smiled.

"It sounds pretty hellish, all right," the chaplain agreed. "The great radicalizing experience of my life—apart from when I felt the call to God's service, that's as radicalizing as it gets—I felt pure revulsion at the ideas embodied in Jonathan Edwards' famous sermon, 'Sinners in the Hands of an Angry God.' I find the doctrine of predestination irreconcilable with the concept of a just and loving deity."

"Well," said the volcanologist, "even a depraved old secular humanist like me knows that."

Amy saw Cutsinger glance from the author to the chaplain. "It seems," he rumbled, "that I'm the raging Calvinist present." Every face turned toward him, except Amy's. She busied herself with her water glass. "Or," Cutsinger went on after a second, "the steel-trap determinist, anyhow. You're talking about free will."

The volcanologist was not easily cowed. He grinned at Cutsinger and said, "Or the next best thing to it."

"For free will to exist means that in a universe that works on the principle of cause and effect, human beings would have to be exempt from rules that apply to energy and matter in all their other forms."

"Doctor Cutsinger," the chaplain said, "that's the basic tenet of Christianity, of the Judeo-Christian tradition, of all religion. An omniscient, omnipotent deity makes the rules but, being also just, merciful, and loving, makes exceptions as well."

"I don't believe in deities, either. I stopped believing in invisible friends when I was still a child."

"Perhaps," the chaplain said good-naturedly, "if you had sought an invisible friend who offered salvation—"

"I believe in the either-or of quantum physics. Down at the micro level, everything's either-or. Either a particle does this or it does that. The universe replicates itself, each replica accommodates one of the possible outcomes. And every either-or begets still more either-or. Whence, endlessly geometrically multiplying universes. On the macro level, each of us makes choices all the time. Sometimes, afterward, we decide they were the wrong choices. We think, If only I'd done that instead of this, or, If only the other thing had happened and not this thing that has in fact happened. In other universes, we did do the other the other thing, and something else did happen. In one universe, I do the things that get me into Heaven. In another, I do the things that send me straight to Hell."

Amy sipped her water and found herself thinking an astonishing thought: Would that it were so.

The author's grin broadened. "You physicists make me fidget. Always arguing over the significance of fractions of a second."

"In terms of practical significance," Cutsinger said, "the argument pertains to nothing less important than fixing this expedition in spacetime."

"Exactly," said the chaplain. "Are we in Silurian time, or Devonian?"

"That," the volcanologist answered, "is the question most often asked by people who least understand that geologic time operates on quite an inhuman scale. It rarely coincides with human time, and then only catastrophically. The Silurian does not end at midnight on a Wednesday and the Devonian begin at twelve-oh-one on Thursday. There's no catastrophic event such as marks the K-T boundary. The significant revolution that does mark the S-D boundary occurs over a period of millions of years as Laurentia, Baltica, and Avalonia close on one another like scissor blades. They swing together as if on hinges, incidentally consuming the Iapetus seaway and raising mountain chains we can trace from Spitzbergen to Venezuela. But slowly. Very, very slowly."

"Yes, of course," the author said, "I understand. Slowly."

"Well," said the chaplain, "I don't mind saying I'm proud to be a member of this expedition. I find it all tremendously exciting. You scientists go forth and come back with the most wonderful lots of specimens, plant, animal, mineral."

"Don't forget indeterminate." The marine biologist at the far end of the table had surprised everybody by speaking up. He looked surprised by his own temerity. Then he said, in a slightly nasal tone, "I like things to be organized, yet I know that taxonomy at some level breaks down as surely as quantum mechanics. At whatever points organisms begin to differentiate into the proto-animal, the proto-fungi, and so forth, gross taxonomy becomes subject to its own uncertainty principle."

She went to her bunk and lay listening to the ship's sounds. She tried lying on her side. She tried lying on her other side, her stomach, her back. She lay with her fists clenched and stared into the darkness, and then she squeezed her eyes shut until her nose stopped up and she had to relax to breathe. What's in the medicine kit for sleepy-time tonight? she wondered. She did not really want to drug herself to sleep, however; she had a hard enough time during the day without a hangover.

Maybe, she thought, I should just reach through the hatch and grab the first Navy boy who comes by and screw his brains out. Screw myself into a coma. I dimly recall that one often falls asleep after sex.

Well, she decided, it just might have to be rape or the next-worst thing. To the best of her knowledge the Navy men aboard, officers and ratings alike, simply did not look upon her as anything more than an appendage of Cutsinger's—though the dirtier-minded ones might, perhaps, imagine she was his lover. In truth, while she had suffered a protracted infatuation with the great man, he had not reciprocated, and their relationship had never moved any further beyond the platonic than occasional mild flirting.

Yes, of course, Amy had told people on occasions beyond counting, it is indeed a privilege and an honor to work with Cutsinger. At one time she had truly believed it, too. Even now, when she had long since decided otherwise, she comported herself as though she still believed it. She never qualified her statement within anyone's hearing by adding "even in the limited and limiting capacity he permits," let alone hinted that it was not that great a pleasure to work with him. The phrase "work with" was beginning to catch in her throat like a sob; she worked *for* Cutsinger, always had. At most, at best, she functioned as a glorified technical assistant, amanuensis, spokesperson—she bit hard on the word: flunky—to A Great Man, without the energy any more to counter, reflexively, this humiliating realization with the argument that the menial services she performed were necessitated by the nature of Cutsinger's affliction.

He and she still dined at the captain's table, he still held forth at every opportunity on multiple universes, infinitely replicated Earths, and continually diverging timelines, and there was no chance of their being banished from officer's country, because, while he might be a bore, he was also a celebrity, and she, well, whoever she was, whatever she was, she was with him. Most of his listeners, however, had signally failed to understand why the paradoxes implied by wave-function collapse could be avoided only by postulating geometrically multiplying universes, had given up trying to figure it out, and frankly admitted that they found it easier, somehow more comforting, simply to imagine that they had indeed traveled into the prehistoric past rather than to some parallel Earth where Paleozoic conditions still obtained. As far as they were concerned, Cutsinger's work was done: he had got them here and convinced them, finally, that they could dispose of those despised spacesuits, by which the integrity of Paleozoic ecosystems was to have been preserved. Cutsinger was gloweringly insistent upon the point or on any of a great many others, and Amy could only sit beside him, embarrassed, trapped by loyalty, until somebody found a way to change the subject. Then he sat mute but still glowering while the captain's other table guests held forth on a variety of less convoluted, certainly less controversial, topics. For her part, Amy had exhausted all conversational gambits and all plausible excuses to quit the table early and would now have foregone dinner altogether but for Cutsinger's insistence upon providing her with detailed summaries of conversation which he had found especially annoying and felt she ought not to have missed. Aboard the ship, there was no escape. Cutsinger had done no important work since his arrival, unless one counted as important his desultory progress on a book for general readers, a follow-up to his unexpectedly and immensely successful *Events Leading to the Infinite Regress*. Amy knew—because she was the person actually performing the work of editing his notebooks and lectures into approximate book form—that he had nothing new to say about the truly important work he had done early on. Cutsinger had no interest in the Paleozoic *per se*, only in the connection between the prehistoric and the modern worlds. He viewed the great majority of the scientists whom he had ushered into and out of the anomaly—a hundred different varieties of geo- and bio-specialist—as a bus driver might view bus passengers, caring neither whence they had come nor what they might do once delivered to their destinations; nor did he want to be bothered with what they might have to say while in his charge, either. They repaid his disinterest with passive contempt, regarding him as the doorman, the gatekeeper: The Wizard of Time had become a professional greeter. The only scientists with whom he felt an affinity and acknowledged kinship were the astronomers, but they were few in number compared with the earth scientists; the turnover among them was generally quite rapid—they tended to stay only a few weeks, if that long, to make their observations, then returned home to spend months, perhaps years, analyzing the data they had collected.

And Cutsinger was impatient with the Navy officers, found them intellectually unstimulating, their personalities rather drearily similar, their routines, regulations, and rituals, petty and childish.

Yet, as he had got into the habit of remarking, most human interaction is talk, all the rest incidentals, and thus he depended on Amy for a great deal in the way not only of the definite services she performed for him, but also in the indefinite purpose she served by being almost constantly at his side, attending his every word. "You are my sounding board for ideas," he sometimes reminded her, "my confidante," but, any more, she could not help thinking, I am only your audience, as anonymous as any other audience. And he had no ideas any more, only beliefs.

Amy had been with him since just before the series of events leading to the purely serendipitous discovery of the anomaly. Once—she recalled this rather vaguely now, like an old dream or something which she had read in an unmemorable book—she had been pursuing her own course, a career in physics quite independent of Cutsinger's; she had had friends, lovers, a sense of humor, all the accoutrements of A Life. Now she had a career in Cutsinger, and increasingly, especially whenever she had retired to her cabin, she found herself wondering what it might be like to have anything in addition to him, anything at all that had nothing at all to do with him.

Maybe, she thought, I should just throw myself overboard. Or throw Cutsinger overboard. Oh, the questions that would be asked then. "How could you drown the great Cutsinger? What drove you to do such a terrible thing?" I was fed up, I'd say. Fed up to here with the great Cutsinger.

On her bunk, she finally slipped into unconsciousness, and the ship's mechanical pulse became Cutsinger's voice. The walls of his world surrounded her, closed in on her, crushed her flat. She slept, but not well, through that night and the many that followed.

Then, one evening, alone in her gray impersonal cabin deep within the ship, as she began to prepare herself for yet another evening's ordeal, she considered her reflection in the inadequate mirror over the tiny metal sink. She had always freckled excessively at the touch of sunlight, but sunlight had scarcely touched her fair skin in—how long had it been? Long enough, she thought, for her flesh to have become greenish white like a frog's belly. Charming, she thought. Good thing the batrachian complexion's in this year. There were lines at the corners of her eyes and mouth which she was certain she had never seen before. Undressed, she thought, I look fat and rumpled. She regarded her small wardrobe; its contents seemed as colorless as the cabin. Almost at random, she picked something and put it on, then tried to gauge the effect in the mirror. Dressed, she thought, smoothing the dress across her belly, in this ridiculous dress, I look rumpled and fat.

Still, there was nothing to be done for it. She resigned herself to that absurd table, on this ugly ship, in this godawful time and place. Oh, the incongruity, and she repressed either a smile or a groan—she could not decide which. And the decisions. Fish or meat? White wine or red? Kill myself, or somebody else?

Some time must necessarily pass between the perception of unhappiness and its being given utterance. Certain individuals seem scarcely to hesitate between the two; others, however long they may live, do not live long enough to find their voices.

Amy, like most people, occupied a position between these poles of almost reflexive complaint and mute abiding wretchedness; but she tended toward the latter extreme. It had taken her many days, or several weeks, or a few months—she considered each unit of time measurement to see which cast her situation in the light least unflattering to herself—to determine that she was more miserably unhappy than she had ever imagined possible. She had always accepted, at least in theory, that people were responsible for their own happiness; she had set aside that responsibility because other possibilities seemed more pressing, seemed worthier; early on, it had seemed to her that her own best prospect for happiness inarguably lay in her being somehow indispensable to Cutsinger. There was The Work to consider, The Great Adventure, the bold new chapter to be written in the annals of science, in which she did not wish to appear as an unsympathetic character.

But no more. If it had taken her a long time, "four hundred million years and some months," as she bitterly put it to herself, to acknowledge her own intense dissatisfaction, she was ready to express it and to want to alleviate it. On their way from the mess, she told Cutsinger without preamble that she was taking some time off, at least a day, maybe two days, maybe more, she didn't know but she was definitely going ashore, she needed time to herself, she was going crazy—she had thought it out during the night, composed what she had to say, mentally rehearsed it, but all her preparation came to nothing, or, rather, she achieved her end but at the cost of further damage to her self-esteem. Like an avalanche, unstoppable, relentless, it impelled her forward and almost immediately downward into trembling and tears. He only looked at her in astonishment tinged with horror, his expression eloquent with the unspoken question: Where did this come from? Crying and shaking, she saw him glance toward the porthole. Beyond lay the limitless sky, the unpredictable sea, the septic, treacherous world. She heard him say, "Yes, yes, of course, by all means, go," granting her leave not because he suddenly understood how she felt but because he wanted to avoid a scene.

She saw him shiver there, and again, later, in the boat bay. The boat bay was a large steel grotto, and Cutsinger was visibly uncomfortable there: any moment, the great gate might swing open, exposing him to the external world. Her composure somewhat restored by his swift acquiescence—though she knew that it had been given not out of understanding and compassion, but to avoid being embarrassed by a public display he patently considered to be out of character for her—Amy nodded to him, then stepped down into the boat and found a place for her sea bag and herself among the carefully stowed crates and equipment.

In the instant that the boat moved out of the boat bay, into the sunlight, she felt as though the weight of the ship had been lifted from her shoulders. Light reflected from the surface of the water dazzled her. The bluejackets themselves were much improved in this natural illumination: pallid drones no more, they appeared fresh, vital, even beautiful.

On impulse she spoke to the nearest of them. "The water looks very inviting." The young man seemed almost startled. She ventured a smile.

"Uh, I don't think so, ma'am. It's not safe."

"Why not?"

"Sea scorpions," he said, "and other things, ma'am. Well, so I hear."

The boat touched the crude jetty, and after a moment's hesitation the bluejacket to whom she had spoken offered a hand to help her out. Here she looked back once at the gray ship sitting in the bay and realized with a start that this was her first sight of it as an entire object, rather than as an environment, since before the transfer. The sight of it called up a memory which she could not quite give form in her mind; she knew only that it was unpleasant, whatever it was, and shrugged it away. She wanted to bring no unhappiness ashore with her.

A work detail fell to unloading the crates and equipment from the boat and moving them along the jetty to add them to a small mountain range of crates and equipment along the shore. Other work details, moving with all the purposefulness of social insects, were engaged in carrying away the substance of this mountain range and assembling it into Quonset huts, vehicles, machinery. There were many more people in uniform than not, she noticed, and she wondered where most of the civilian scientists had got to. Then she glimpsed, on the rocky heights behind the camp, tiny human figures making their ways, singly or in small groups, across the steep rock face, and she thought, Of course. They were getting on with what they had come here to do, while the Navy, acting in its support capacity, built a base for them.

She realized with dismay that she did not know what to do next. She had come ashore uncommitted to any particular course of action but conscious of the need for a change of scenery, perhaps even for catharsis, and half-determined on some arduous physical recreation. She wore hiking shoes and carried in her bag, along with essential toiletries, a modest and now useless one-piece swimsuit. Aimlessly, she walked about the camp. The few civilians whom she encountered acknowledged her presence with nods and smiles but clearly had no idea who she might be; just as clearly, they were too busy to be very curious about her. The bluejackets were intent on their assigned duties; as a work detail assembled pipes into showers and erected walls around the showers, she watched, wholly fascinated, and when they stopped and stepped back to take stock of their handiwork, she looked at her watch and was astonished to see how much time had elapsed. She could almost hear Cutsinger asking her how she had spent her day ashore and almost see the contempt on his face as she fumbled for a meaningful answer. Then she told herself angrily, I'm not here for his sake.

Still, feeling it a point of honor to prevent her excursion's reneging on its initial promise, she resumed her aimless and now slightly desperate wandering. At length she found herself picking her way up the rough slope behind the camp. She did not climb very far before settling onto a shelflike limestone projection. Despite or perhaps because of the human figures she had seen on it, the dark landscape before her looked even more forbidding close up than it had from the ship. She realized, too, how out of condition she was. Could've been using the ship's gym all this time, she thought. Nevertheless, she felt—she had to think about it for a second— good. For ever so long she had been aware of an iron-hard knot of tension at the base of her skull; now, as she began to relax, the tension yielded to a burning soreness in the muscle. It hurt, yet it made her feel better. She gazed down on the camp and its scurrying inhabitants and then out to sea. Again, the sight of the ship filled her with dread; she instantly looked away. Somewhere far out to sea, farther than she could see, the surface would be matted with graptolites drifting through planktonic soup. No scurrying there, she thought, dinner just floats by one's door.

She felt distinctly at a loss. The idea of returning to the ship was repugnant, but not only had her plans for recreation amounted only to vague and now unrealizable notions of hiking and swimming, she had made no arrangements for accommodations. She began to realize that she was famished; she had been too upset to eat breakfast on the ship, had given no thought to eating when she escaped—and the perplexing half-memory returned for a moment, but she still could not grasp it, frowned it away, concentrated on her hunger. It was a good hunger. Eating had been a mechanical exercise for so long that she had forgotten what it was to have a real appetite. She could, she decided, probably eat at the mess tent in the camp, and she imagined other necessary facilities would be available as well. She would need a place to sleep, but finding a bunk on short notice might be an insurmountable matter. The idea of sleeping beneath the stars briefly attracted her. Then she thought of the sea scorpions "and other things" inhabiting the area. She had seen specimens of grotesque arthropods brought aboard the ship, and it now required no great effort of imagination to conjure chitinous night-feeding predators swarming ashore—she quickly shoved the image from her mind and told herself that the creatures could not pose too much of a threat to human beings ashore. She could recall hearing no horror stories along such lines, anyway; perhaps there was nothing in camp to interest sea scorpions— not even cockroaches to eat. Yet, she concluded, discretion was undoubtedly the better part of valor.

The camp appeared to have increased in size in the short time she had been away from it. She judged from the aroma that Navy cooks were preparing to serve the evening meal. The mess tent was full of tired, hungry bluejackets and civilians ready to call it a day. She fell into the mess line. The food was standard fare, slightly tough chicken fresh from the freezer, with side orders of reconstituted vegetables, but Amy was ravenously hungry and ate every bite. She wished for a glass of white wine, or even, she thought with a smile, grog, whatever that might be.

"Why, hello!"

She looked up and saw the man who had been head of the sleep-disorder center at Cornell University's New York Hospital in Westchester County.

"Do you mind if I join you?"

"Please do."

He sat opposite her and began to saw at his chicken.

"Do you mind my asking," Amy said, "what you are doing here? The night I met you, on the ship, you said something about observing the observers."

"Actually, I am building the case that the clocks and calendars and other time-keeping devices on which we depend, back in the twenty-first century, and which we have imported into this Paleozoic environment, aren't just useless here, but injurious."

"How so?"

"The Siluro-Devonian year is about four hundred days long. The Siluro-Devonian day is about twenty-two and one half hours long. It's all wrong for our human bodies, which evolved during Quaternary time. The dominant time cycle of our bodies is the circadian rhythm. From the Latin words circa, approximately, and dies, day. For most of us the circadian cycle is twenty-five hours long, plus or minus a quarter of an hour. This body clock is located in the brain's hypothalamus, lying above the roof of the mouth. But we also have a weekly cycle of internal rhythms regulating rise and fall of heartbeat and blood circulation, our immune system's response patterns, changes in body chemicals. When we ignore or abuse these rhythms in the course of twenty-first-century life—and we do it all the time, obeying the clock on the wall instead of the clocks in our bodies—we feel the effects of sleep deprivation. We have the Monday morning blues and get drowsy in the afternoon. We suffer from sleep disorders and depression. We become irritable and clumsy and, well, stupid. Then we compound our problems by trying to offset our fatigue by using drugs and alcohol. We take stimulants to keep ourselves awake during the workday, and drink or take sleeping pills to knock us out at night so we can get up the next morning and take more stimulants. It's very unhealthful."

He looked at her as he chewed. Then: "May I ask what you are doing here?"

"Everybody here knows what he's doing here," Amy said, "except me."

After dinner, she said goodnight to the sleep-disorder specialist and returned to the communal tent where she had managed to secure a place to pass the night ashore. She sat outside on a campstool and admired the emerging stars for a time. The whole camp seemed to droop in the still, humid twilight. Without warning, a large, somehow familiar shape emerged from the gathering shadows. At first it struck Amy that one of the smaller tents had decided to go for a walk. Then the apparition resolved itself into the author. He drew up before her and favored her with a clearly tipsy grin.

"I think," she told him, "you had better sit down. You're leaning well out of plumb, you know. Another few degrees of tilt out of true, and you're going to roll down into the bay."

"Drink?" he said, holding up a bottle of Scotch.

Amy thought it over for two seconds before answering, "Don't mind if I do." She fetched plastic cups and another camp stool from within the tent; the author sat down like an elephant taking a load off all four feet and poured Scotch into the cups.

"Here's to Robert Heinlein," he said as they clicked cups.

"Who?"

"Twentieth-century science-fiction author."

"Ah."

"Yep." He popped the syllable from his mouth and raised his cup again. "And all the rest of them, too. Clarke, Asimov, Bradbury. Here's to the by God living literature."

"So," Amy said after half a minute had passed, "do you, as a sci-fi writer, find it hard to come up with story ideas?"

"Probably no more than anyone did back in the space age. When events catch up with fiction, you just have to push on a little farther out in front."

"And do you write happy endings?"

"When I can. All stories, all kinds of stories, are about people trying to be happy. A few of them manage to pull it off. But you know what's disheartening about science fiction?"

"What?"

"What's disheartening is when events don't bother to catch up. I expected us to have colonies on the moons of Jupiter and Saturn by now. Research stations. I mean, things like that were supposed to happen in my lifetime. And we'd go on from there. Ever onward and outward. Eventually, somehow or other, Einstein be damned, we'd whip together some warp-drive thingumatron and leave the solar system behind, spread throughout the galaxy. Manifest destiny."

"Not so manifest if you're a physicist."

He looked at her curiously. "Ever visit one of the space stations, back, you know, home?"

"No."

"Well, I did. There're rides at Disney World that're more exciting. Same here."

"Even so. There can't be too many sci-fi writers who can say they've actually done any of the things they like to write about. Space travel, now time travel. Time travel in heavy quotes. You're like a hero in one of your own stories, almost."

"I hope not!" He scowled. "Willingly or otherwise, writers tend to buy into myths about writers. Fitzgerald bought into the myth of writer as drunkard and drank himself to death. Hemingway bought into the myth of writer as man's man. He hunted and fished and boxed and finally blew his own head off. And here I'm a space-traveler and a time-traveler. Space travel's always held much greater fascination for me than time travel. In or out of heavy quotes. Because space travel was possible. Time travel was impossible. All you physicists said so yourself. And, you know, I think—and there're folks I know at NASA and the Jet Propulsion Lab and places who think so, too—the discovery of the spacetime anomaly's the worst thing that ever happened. Just an absolute goddamn disaster."

"You're trampling on my field now," she warned, but gently.

"No offense. But the human race was meant to go to the stars. Not sideways in time."

"Meant to? Manifest destiny again?"

"Priorities. We've got our priorities all wrong. There must be some happy balance between the hopes of the future and the realities of the present. We just don't seem to be able to achieve it. And another thing. Time travel's too private. Everybody and his dog could watch those rockets take off. People come from all over. It was for everybody. But time travel? Feh! It's like when they stopped public executions and did it behind prison walls, in seclusion. Like they were ashamed of it."

The author looked uncomfortable with his own analogy but was slightly too inebriated to figure out why. He pressed on.

"The combined pressure of expanding population, diminishing resources, and simple human curiosity—aspiration, whatever you want to call it—was supposed to launch us at the stars and the future. Instead, we're mucking around here in the so-called prehistoric past and haven't even started planning habitats for ourselves at El-Four and El-Five. Most people just can't see the point any more. There's a push on for a land rush into Paleozoic time. Never mind the lack of soil, plant cover, animals. Even some of my colleagues think it's an excellent idea. Hell, one of them told me, this world is practically terraformed already—we can import the plants and animals we need. Oh, the geoscience types would still be able to study their creatures in special preserves. But they can't, they mustn't be greedy. The Paleozoic's a distraction from our true destiny. One giant step sideways."

"There's another way of looking at it," said Amy. "From the very first, we physicists explained over and over again that we're not talking about time travel, but about traveling from one universe to another."

"It's hard to give up the stars. It isn't just the funding, though it is the funding, of course. It's the public imagination. Such as it is. People can't seem to hold more'n one great big idea in their minds at a time. Space travel or time travel. Well, we already have time travel, or the closest thing to it. And the idea's also started to penetrate that we'll never get to even the nearest star fast enough, soon enough, to suit anybody. Stars are unreachable unless we're willing to spend thousands and even tens of thousands of years traveling interstellar distances at a crawl."

"Don't use that accusing tone with me," Amy said. "It's not physics' fault there's no way to exceed light speed."

"You people could at least have the decency to find some kind of short-cut in spacetime. A gateway through hyperspace via black holes."

"We certainly know now that spacetime anomalies exist, but whether we'll ever find one that can take us to the stars—it may be a chimera. Like El Dorado. Or, more aptly, like the Northwest Passage. Not to belittle the effort behind this expedition, particularly since some of it was my own effort, but it's nothing compared to getting people to Mars and back. This world for all practical purposes is the earth, complete to potable water, breathable atmosphere, UV-screening ozone layer, and fifteen p.s.i. at sea level. You can go into the jump station in Houston at nine o'clock in the morning and eat lunch at noon in Gondwana and be back home in time for dinner at six."

"If," the author said glumly, "you don't get concussed coming or going."

"Practically speaking, though, getting here's a snap compared to getting to Mars and back."

"Pity nobody ever figured out how John Carter wished himself to Mars."

"Who?"

"Never mind."

Later, more than a little drunk, as she composed herself for sleep, she thought, In the morning I'll be back in the real world. Eventually, I have to return to the ship, there'll be work for me to do, another few pages of the book to thrash out at the very least. And she was curious to see how Cutsinger had managed without her. Perhaps it would lead to his appreciating her more. Probably not. However her absence might discommode him, she could not conceive of his venturing ashore to reclaim his errant flunky, or for any other reason; she could scarcely imagine that he would obey the captain's order to abandon ship if it were foundering. Her relationship with the great man, she reflected, was less a relationship between two people than a sort of barycenter, the center of mass in the Cutsinger-Stevenson system. And I can't escape from the system. I not only have to orbit Cutsinger, I have to keep my face turned toward him at all times . . . .

I can see it all. Standing on the jetty, with the boat waiting to take people back to the ship. The boatman says to me, Ma'am, it's time to shove off, please come aboard, and the ship waits like a great iron prison out on the water to receive me—

The hulks, she thought with a start, that's what I've been trying to remember. The derelict ships once used as floating prisons. Already she could feel the weight of the ship settling upon her; she could feel muscles in her face and shoulders contract with tension. No, she thought. No. No. Here is where the universe splits and I split with it. I do one thing in one universe and a different thing in the other. I don't know about that other self, I can't speak for her, but in this universe—

But in this universe it's too late. Time to go back to the ship. Cinderella's got to be in by a certain time or turn into a pumpkin.

Cutsinger, she thought, just might be waiting for her in the boat bay. She would ascend to him, and he would give her an ironic smile and say something like, "Did we have a good time?" but before she could frame a reply he would already be talking about something that really interested him. The walls of his world would first enclose her and then close in on her. She would look down, out the gate of the boat bay, to the black sea, the starshot sky, and the illuminated section of land wedged between them. Then the gates would slam shut, like the jaws of an immense monster.

I know it will happen that way, she thought. I can see exactly how it will happen, and I'll let it happen.

If I let it happen.

Right on schedule, because the Navy adhered rigorously to schedules in defiance of any slovenly Paleozoic notions about day and night, the boat pulled softly away from the jetty, moved out of the circle of illumination cast on the water, and vanished into an oily darkness.

"It," she said, and paused to consider her next words very carefully, and then shook her head and told the young man, "I'm sorry, I just don't have anything interesting to tell you. It wasn't my story."

"But you," the young man said, "he mentioned you in his autobiography just three times."

"I never read it. I knew how it was all going to end. He would live happily ever after, as he understood the word happily. He'd die full of years and full of honors. And by the time he died, everything that should be told about him would have been told." She shook her head. "I really, truly do not have anything to add."

"But don't you feel slighted?"

"I made my choices. Don't you worry about me. I, too, lived happily ever after."

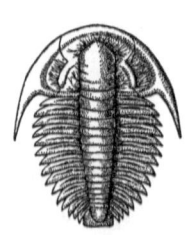

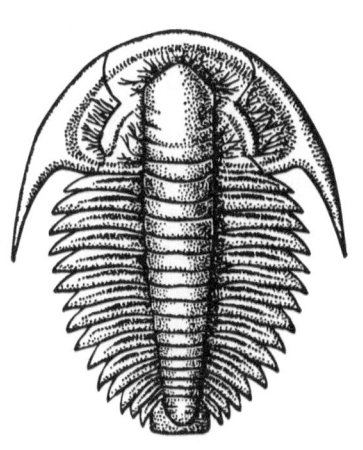

STEVEN UTLEY: MY WHOLE LIFE STORY (COMPLETE IN ONE VOLUME)

I was born the week after Harry Truman had pulled the rug out from under Thomas Dewey, in the year of the Berlin Airlift and network television's first full-blown commercial broadcasts. (Okay, for the history-challenged: 1948.) Over the next couple of decades, my father being a noncommissioned officer in the Air Force, my three siblings and I were herded from place to exotic place (England, Okinawa, Kansas) as part of the Pentagon's master plan to defeat communism.

As a child I enjoyed books and old movies and imitatively worked up my own stories in both prose and comic-book form, but it wasn't until my freshman year of high school, when I discovered Mars—the Mars of science fiction's two great romantics, Edgar Rice Burroughs and Ray Bradbury—that I understood that I, too, must grow up to be A Writer, or at least a rich and famous person.

And ten years later I was one! A Writer, I mean.

By then (we're up to the early 1970s, in case you've lost track), my family had settled in Tennessee, but momentum carried me clear into Texas, where I fell in with a bunch of other young writers and had many adventures. After many years, I returned to the bosom of my family in Tennessee and nowadays lead a quiet life, surrounded as I am by my books, my cats, and my dangerously inbred neighbors.

COVER

Ordovician Sea Life, 460 million years ago years ago.
Shows beached seaweeds, trilobites and cephalopods from
the ocean. Cenozoic era.

Charles R. Knight (1874–1953) is internationally recognized
as the preeminent artist of both prehistoric animals and
contemporary wildlife, through his paintings, drawings
and sculpture. Annually, millions of people are exposed
to Knight's work in major museums and institutional
collections.

ACKNOWLEDGEMENTS

Copyright © 1996, 2000, 2001, 2002, 2003, 2005, 2008, 2010, 2012 by Steven Utley

"The Age of Mud and Slime," "Chain of Life," "Exile," "Half a Loaf," "A Silurian Tale," "Walking in Circles," "The Wind Over the World," and "The Woman Under the World" appeared in *Asimov's Science Fiction*.

"All of Creation" appeared online in *Cosmos* Magazine.

"Beyond the Sea" and "Chaos and the Gods" appeared online in *Revolution Science Fiction*.

"Cloud by van Gogh," "Foodstuff," "The 400-Million-Year Itch," "Promised Land," and "The Tortoise Grows Elate" appeared in *The Magazine of Fantasy and Science Fiction*.

"The End in Eden" appeared in *Analog Science Fiction and Fact*.

"The Gift Horse" is previously unpublished.

"Lost Places of the Earth" appeared in *We Think, Therefore We Are*, edited by Peter Crowther (DAW Books, Inc.).

AVAILABLE FROM TICONDEROGA PUBLICATIONS

978-0-9586856-6-5   Troy by Simon Brown (tpb)
978-0-9586856-7-2   The Workers' Paradise eds Farr & Evans (tpb)
978-0-9586856-8-9   Fantastic Wonder Stories ed Russell B. Farr (tpb)
978-0-9803531-0-5   Love in Vain by Lewis Shiner (tpb)
978-0-9803531-2-9   Belong ed Russell B. Farr (tpb)
978-0-9803531-3-6   Ghost Seas by Steven Utley (hc)
978-0-9803531-4-3   Ghost Seas by Steven Utley (tpb)
978-0-9803531-6-7   Magic Dirt: the best of Sean Williams (tpb)
978-0-9803531-7-4   The Lady of Situations by Stephen Dedman (hc)
978-0-9803531-8-1   The Lady of Situations by Stephen Dedman (tpb)
978-0-9806288-2-1   Basic Black by Terry Dowling (tpb)
978-0-9806288-3-8   Make Believe by Terry Dowling (tpb)
978-0-9806288-4-5   Scary Kisses ed Liz Grzyb (tpb)
978-0-9806288-6-9   Dead Sea Fruit by Kaaron Warren (tpb)
978-0-9806288-8-3   The Girl With No Hands by Angela Slatter (tpb)
978-0-9807813-1-1   Dead Red Heart ed Russell B. Farr (tpb)
978-0-9807813-2-8   More Scary Kisses ed Liz Grzyb (tpb)
978-0-9807813-4-2   Heliotrope by Justina Robson (tpb)
978-0-9807813-7-3   Matilda Told Such Dreadful Lies by Lucy Sussex (tpb)
978-1-921857-01-0   Bluegrass Symphony by Lisa L. Hannett (tpb)
978-1-921857-05-8   The Hall of Lost Footsteps by Sara Douglass (hc)
978-1-921857-06-5   The Hall of Lost Footsteps by Sara Douglass (tpb)
978-1-921857-03-4   Damnation and Dames ed Liz Grzyb & Amanda Pillar (tpb)
978-1-921857-08-9   Bread and Circuses by Felicity Dowker (tpb)
978-1-921857-17-1   The 400-Million-Year Itch by Steven Utley (tpb)
978-1-921857-24-9   Wild Chrome by Greg Mellor (tpb)
978-1-921857-30-0   Midnight and Moonshine by Lisa L. Hannett & Angela Slatter (tpb)
978-1-921857-10-2   Mage Heart by Jane Routley (hc)
978-1-921857-65-2   Mage Heart by Jane Routley (tpb)
978-1-921857-11-9   Fire Angels by Jane Routley (hc)
978-1-921857-66-9   Fire Angels by Jane Routley (tpb)
978-1-921857-12-6   Aramaya by Jane Routley (hc)
978-1-921857-67-6   Aramaya by Jane Routley (tpb)

TICONDEROGA PUBLICATIONS LIMITED HARDCOVER EDITIONS

TICONDEROGA PUBLICATIONS EBOOKS

THE YEAR'S BEST AUSTRALIAN FANTASY & HORROR SERIES
EDITED BY LIZ GRZYB & TALIE HELENE

WWW.TICONDEROGAPUBLICATIONS.COM

THANK YOU

The publisher would sincerely like to thank:

Elizabeth Grzyb, Steven Utley, Gardner Dozois, Barry N. Malzberg, Cat Sparks, Jonathan Strahan, Peter McNamara, Ellen Datlow, Grant Stone, Jeremy G. Byrne, Sean Williams, Garth Nix, David Cake, Simon Oxwell, Grant Watson, Sue Manning, Steven Utley, Bill Congreve, Jack Dann, Jenny Blackford, Simon Brown, Stephen Dedman, Sara Douglass, Felicity Dowker, Terry Dowling, Jason Fischer, Pete Kempshall, Ian McHugh, Angela Rega, Lucy Sussex, Kaaron Warren, the Mt Lawley Mafia, the Nedlands Yakuza, Amanda Pillar, Shane Jiraiya Cummings, Angela Challis, Talie Helene, Donna Maree Hanson, Brian Clarke, Kate Williams, Kathryn Linge, Andrew Williams, Al Chan, Alisa and Tehani, Mel & Phil, Jennifer Sudbury, Paul Przytula, Kelly Parker, Hayley Lane, Georgina Walpole, everyone we've missed . . .

. . . and you.

IN MEMORY OF
EVE JOHNSON (1945–2011)